Suffragette Girl

Born in Gainsborough, Lincolnshire, Margaret Dickinson moved to the coast at the age of seven and so began her love for the sea and the Lincolnshire landscape.

Her ambition to be a writer began early and she had her first novel published at the age of twenty-five. This was followed by twenty-two further titles, including *Plough the Furrow*, *Sow the Seed* and *Reap the Harvest*, which make up her Lincolnshire Fleethaven trilogy. Many of her novels are set in the heart of her home county, but in *Tangled Threads* and *Twisted Strands* the stories include not only Lincolnshire but also the framework knitting and lace industries of Nottingham. The Workhouse Museum at Southwell in Nottinghamshire inspired *Without Sin* and the beautiful countryside of Derbyshire and the fascinating town of Macclesfield in Cheshire form the backdrop for the story of *Pauper's Gold*. *Wish Me Luck* returns to Lincolnshire once more and the county is also the setting for *Sing as We Go*. *Suffragette Girl* is founded in Lincolnshire, but the story takes the central character to London and even to France and Belgium in the First World War.

www.margaret-dickinson.co.uk

Margaret Dickinson

Suffragette Girl

PAN BOOKS

First published 2009 by Pan Books
an imprint of Pan Macmillan, a division of Macmillan Publishers Limited
Pan Macmillan, 20 New Wharf Road, London N1 9RR
Basingstoke and Oxford
Associated companies throughout the world
www.panmacmillan.com

ISBN 978-0-330-53315-7

1 3 5 7 9 8 6 4 2

A CIP catalogue record for this book is available from
the British Library.

Typeset by SetSystems Ltd, Saffron Walden, Essex
Printed and bound in the UK by CPI Mackays, Chatham ME5 8TD

Visit www.panmacmillan.com to read more about all our books
and to buy them. You will also find features, author interviews and
news of any author events, and you can sign up for e-newsletters
so that you're always first to hear about our new releases.

For my grandson, Zachary John,
whose smile lights up my life

One

'How much further is it, Mother?'

Florrie glanced at Jacques. He was sitting in the corner of the compartment, huddled into his thick overcoat, white-faced and shivering. His dark-blue eyes were pools of weariness in his gaunt face. His black hair was dull and lifeless. When he'd coughed the only other occupant of the carriage had risen and left, fearful of the deep, hacking sound and suspicious of the way the boy held his handkerchief to his mouth.

'Not long now, darling.' Florrie put her hand on his arm. 'We're just drawing into Landquart, where we have to change trains and then we'll soon be in Davos Platz.'

Jacques closed his eyes. 'Not another change!' he whispered.

'We have to. It's a different-gauge rail track and these trains . . .' Her explanation faded away. She'd sought to interest the boy, but she could see that he couldn't summon up even the pretence of curiosity.

Florrie bit her lip. The journey had been a long one, even though they'd broken it into four days by staying overnight in London, Paris and Zurich. But today – the last leg from Zurich to Davos – seemed to be taking its toll on the sick boy.

Had she been right to bring him? With customary candour, Florrie questioned her own motives. Had her overwhelming desire to have an excuse to see Ernst Hartmann again made her risk the boy's health – perhaps even his life? But no. The Harley Street physician had suggested Switzerland without any prompting from her.

'Davos,' he'd said, making his swivel chair creak as he'd leaned back in it, rocking it gently. He'd steepled his fingers, regarding her over the top of his spectacles. 'That's the place. They're doing wonderful things there. It's become a centre for the treatment of tuberculosis. There are some very clever doctors at the sanatoriums there—'

She hadn't been able to prevent a gasp of surprise. Of all the places in the world, he'd chosen Davos.

'Jacques may be there for weeks, even months,' Dr Harris had warned. 'You do realize that, don't you? Your family can afford it, I presume?'

He knew the family lived at Candlethorpe Hall surrounded by its vast Lincolnshire estate of hundreds of acres farmed by tenants, whilst Edgar Maltby and his family lived in idle splendour on the rents, untouched as yet by the unstable economy and its hardships.

No, Florrie thought as the train rattled nearer and nearer their destination, she should not feel guilty that their privileged position enabled her to bring Jacques here. But perhaps what she should be feeling guilty about was the excitement that surged through her with every mile that brought her nearer to Ernst Hartmann.

As the train drew out of Landquart, Florrie settled Jacques in a corner seat near the window and tucked the travelling rug around his knees. Then she sat down in the opposite seat and looked out of the window, soaking up the sight of the snow-capped mountains with their sharp, pointed peaks. This was Ernst's beloved homeland.

The train rattled past steep-sided cliffs, the trees clinging to the bare rock. For a few seconds, she glimpsed a stream and then the train plunged into a tunnel. As they emerged into the light once more, she saw the river again, its water a strange opaque bluey-grey.

'Why's that river such a funny colour, Mother?'

Florrie turned towards him and smiled, relieved to see that he still had the energy to take a little interest in the scenery. 'I'm not sure, I—'

The only other traveller in the compartment – an elderly bearded gentleman dressed entirely in black and sitting in the corner near the corridor – emerged from behind his newspaper and glanced towards them. He was thin, hunched over in the seat, his overcoat seeming to swamp him, but his pale eyes behind his spectacles were friendly.

'It's a glacial river, my boy.' His English was perfectly pronounced, but spoken with a strong German accent. Hearing it – even after all these years – still gave Florrie a shiver and brought back memories of those terrible days . . .

Her thoughts were dragged back to the present.

'We are climbing gradually and when we reach Davos—' the stranger was explaining. His glance turned away from the boy to Florrie for a moment. 'You are going to Davos?'

She nodded. Was Jacques's condition so obvious – even to a complete stranger? She sighed inwardly. Maybe so. Perhaps the local people who travelled on

3

this train regularly were used to seeing the sick and could recognize the outward signs of the illness at once.

The man was leaning towards her, holding out his hand. 'My name is Hans Meyer.' He smiled wryly as if anticipating a reaction. 'From Germany.'

The outstretched hand wavered slightly, but Florrie didn't hesitate. She put her hand into his and shook it warmly. 'Florence and Jacques Maltby. Pleased to meet you,' she said and her tone was genuine. Time to put aside the dreadful memories and the bitterness. She'd never forget – that was impossible – but she could move on. 'You live here?' she asked. 'In Switzerland?'

Hans Meyer shook his head. 'I am coming to see my wife. She is in the Schatzalp Sanatorium.'

'Why – that's where we're going.'

He glanced again at Jacques. The boy was huddled down into his seat, his head lolling to one side as he fell asleep. The man nodded sympathetically. 'It is a good place. Your son – he has every chance. Every chance. But for my wife . . .' He shook his head sadly. 'They say I must take her home. They can do no more for her.' There were tears in his eyes and, impulsively, Florrie leaned forward and touched his hand. 'I'm so sorry,' she whispered. Silently she shuddered, realizing afresh just how dangerous this dreadful disease was.

Hans Meyer blew his nose noisily. 'Ah well,' he said bravely. 'It will be good to have her back with me, even if – even if – I am taking her home to die.'

Now Florrie could think of nothing to say.

For a while they were silent. Hans observed the young woman covertly, forgetting his own sorrow for a brief moment. He guessed her to be in her late thirties, for her son looked fifteen or sixteen years old. He smiled a little to himself. To him, she was still a young woman. She was certainly a beautiful one, with flawless skin and only the hint of discreetly applied cosmetics. She was wearing a dark-purple crossover coat with a fur collar that gave her both warmth and comfort. He imagined she was slender. Her stockinged legs were definitely shapely, her ankles slim. She wore a close-fitting cloche hat that covered most of her hair, but a few wayward strands of brown curls touched her cheeks. But it was her eyes that drew him back, time and again, to her face. Dark-brown pools of dread as she watched over her boy, and yet . . . ? And yet, he mused, there was a hint of excitement in their depths.

He leaned towards her again and, whilst Jacques slept, they talked in low voices. He pointed out all the places they passed through, marvelled with her at the wonderful scenery that for both of them was so poignantly beautiful.

'I love the wooden houses perched high up on the mountainsides,' Florrie said. 'With their balconies and shutters on the windows.'

Herr Meyer nodded wisely. 'They're useful when the snow comes and it's very cold.'

Now, though, the shutters were wide open, and window boxes still overflowed with the last summer flowers.

'How pretty they are,' Florrie murmured. 'And look,' she pointed, 'some have the dates on when they were built. That's nice. I like that.'

'This is Grüsch,' Meyer said. As they gathered speed, Florrie saw men and women and even a young boy working in the fields, turning the cut grass that she imagined would be fodder for their cattle through the winter.

The train began to climb again.

'We're still going up.' For a brief moment, Florrie

was able to laugh, even though the terrible anxiety never left her completely.

'Davos Platz lies at the same height as the top of your Ben Nevis, and then the mountains are higher still.'

'Really?'

'That is why the air is so good for—' He tapped his chest, but said no more.

The train paused briefly at Schiers and then rattled on beside the glacial river once more. From Küblis it travelled on a twisting track with a steep drop on the right-hand side. Florrie glanced across at Jacques, wondering if he would be alarmed if he looked out of the window.

'He's not used to hills and mountains,' she explained.

'Where is it you live? You are English?'

Florrie nodded. 'In Lincolnshire. It's very flat. There are gentle hills in the Lincolnshire Wolds and where the county town of Lincoln lies, but near the coast where we live it's flat as far as you can see.' She smiled. 'So Jacques has never seen a proper mountain.'

'Ah,' Hans nodded. 'Your Lincolnshire is like Holland, yes? I know Holland, but I've never been to England.'

Florrie's eyes widened in surprise. 'Never? Then – then how do you speak such wonderful English?'

'My brothers – I have two – and I had an English tutor.' Hans smiled wistfully. 'A long time before our two countries were so foolishly at war with one another.'

They sat in companionable silence whilst the train rattled on through tunnels, past more houses dotted on the slopes, past square-towered, white-painted churches with spires. Through Klosters-Dorf and Klosters.

'I'm sure I've just seen that church a minute ago.' Florrie laughed. 'But it was on the other side of the train.'

'Of course it was,' Hans smiled. 'We're going zigzag up the steep mountainside.' He traced the path of the train on his knee, looping backwards and forwards. 'So – that is the same village we keep seeing, but sometimes it is on the left and then sometimes on the right.'

'Oh.' Florrie was thoughtful for a moment and then she nodded. 'Yes – yes – I see what you mean.' She glanced towards the sleeping figure in the corner. 'I wish Jacques could see it all.'

'Leave him to rest,' Hans said gently. There was a pause before he asked, 'Whom are you going to see? The doctor, I mean?'

'Dr Hartmann. Dr Ernst Hartmann.'

Even to speak his name aloud made her heart beat a little faster.

'He is very good. He will help your son, I'm sure.' Tears welled again in his eyes. 'But for my Eva—' He lifted his thin shoulders in a helpless shrug and left the end of the sentence unspoken.

He asked no more for they were drawing near their destination. Florrie was thankful. She didn't want to have to explain that, yes, she knew Dr Hartmann. Knew him very well. She turned her head away and looked out of the window as the train passed by a lake surrounded by dark pine trees. Higher up the mountainside, snow still nestled in crevices in the bare rock and mist shrouded the topmost peaks. Then they were pulling into Davos Dorf and finally into Davos Platz.

*

A horse-drawn carriage took them from the station to the funicular that hauled the single cabin up the steep mountain. Alighting, they walked the short distance to the sanatorium and Florrie found that her knees were trembling. In a few moments she would see Ernst. After sixteen long years she would be with him again.

'It's such a beautiful place,' Hans remarked. 'And such a magnificent building, don't you think?'

Florrie looked up at the four-storey building towering above her.

'The best rooms are here on the front,' Hans explained. 'And, as you see, each room has its own balcony for taking the air.'

Indeed, the rows of balconies stretched the whole length of each of the upper three floors, and even on the ground floor, a covered veranda was crowded with cane day-beds for the patients.

'They lie outside all day – even in the winter.' He glanced up and to the left. 'That is my Eva's room. I wonder . . .'

Florrie wasn't really listening now. Despite the dreadful reason that had brought them to this place, she couldn't help gasping with sheer delight as she stood in front of the imposing building and looked out over the valley to the magical mountains beyond. Below where she was standing, a forest covered the steep slope down to the town where the houses, and even the white church with its square tower, looked like tiny little boxes far below. On the opposite side, grass swathes rose gently up the lower slopes of the mountains, where isolated homes were dotted here and there. Cattle roamed the hillsides, the bells around their necks clanging as they moved. It was so peaceful and the air so clean and fresh. Surely, in a place like this, Jacques would be cured.

As they went up the steps into the entrance hall, Florrie held out her hand. 'Herr Meyer, it has been a pleasure to meet you, though I wish we could have met in happier circumstances.'

He took her hand and raised it to his lips. 'So do I, dear lady. And I wish you and your son good health and all the happiness in the world.'

Florrie nodded, tears springing to her eyes at his thoughtfulness when he was bearing such grief himself. Good health for Jacques? Yes, oh yes, but dare she even hope for happiness for herself?

Her voice was husky as she said, 'And I wish you well. I – I hope things are not as bad as you fear.'

He patted her hand, gave a sad little smile and turned away.

As she watched him go, a nurse came bustling towards them, carrying a sheaf of papers. She paused briefly as she passed Hans Meyer to greet him and then approached Florrie and Jacques. She was small and slim and quick in her movements. Her shining black hair was tucked neatly beneath her white cap. Her blue eyes twinkled and when she smiled her cheeks dimpled prettily.

'Ah, you must be Frau Maltby.' The nurse spoke in German, but both Florrie and Jacques could understand her. Thank goodness, Florrie thought, that Jacques's school taught both French and German, despite the latter language still not being a popular choice, even after fourteen years of peace. 'And this is Jacques?'

The nurse turned to the boy with a smile, but Florrie could see that her professional eye was already appraising him. The young woman held out her arm, ushering them forward. 'I am Sister Emmi Bergamin. I work with Dr Hartmann and he asked me to watch out for your arrival. When Jacques has settled in, Dr Hartmann would like to see you both.'

Florrie nodded, unable to speak for the mixture of fear and excitement that rose in her throat.

'I'll take you to Jacques's room, Mrs Maltby, but then that is the last time you will be allowed there. You can visit your son, of course, but always it must be out in the fresh air. Visitors are not allowed to mix with the patients indoors – only in exceptional circumstances.' For a moment her eyes clouded, then briskly she changed the subject, but Florrie had understood the sister's meaning. Only when a patient was seriously ill – perhaps dying – would relatives be allowed to visit them in their rooms. Like poor Hans Meyer. The sister had made no attempt to stop him going up the stairs.

Her voice interrupted Florrie's unhappy thoughts. 'You have accommodation in Davos?'

'Yes. In a pension. I – I'll see it later. I want to see Dr Hartmann first.'

The sister nodded understandingly. 'I'll show you around down here first and then I'll take you up to the bedroom.' She glanced at the white-faced boy. 'Perhaps you should rest before you see the doctor.' She turned to Florrie. 'You could sit on the balcony of his room with him – just this once.' Her manner was brisk and authoritative, yet kindly. Florrie had no qualms about leaving Jacques in this capable young woman's care.

Sister Bergamin led the way to the right of the entrance hall into a magnificent dining room, where long tables were set with white cloths and napkins in front of each place setting. Florrie glanced around the light, airy room. On the right-hand side long windows, looking out onto the covered veranda, stood open to the warm day. Panels, painted with tranquil scenes of lakes and lilies and gliding swans, decorated the room and huge mirrors dominated one wall.

Seeing Florrie gazing at them, the sister laughed. 'It's not a matter of vanity, Frau Maltby. Well, not really.' She moved closer and lowered her voice so that Jacques, who'd wandered a little away from them, wouldn't hear. 'One of the symptoms of this disease – as you will know – is severe loss of weight, so our patients must eat huge meals. A big breakfast with a five-course midday meal, bread and milk in the afternoon and then a seven-course meal in the evening.' She chuckled. 'The mirrors are for them to check if they are putting on weight. If they think they can see an improvement, it gives them hope. And here, determination to get well is half the battle.'

Florrie nodded.

Back across the entrance hall, Emmi Bergamin showed them the lounge area, furnished with deep leather sofas and chesterfields. Oil paintings hung on the walls and there was a large bookcase crammed with books. An ornate fireplace and stained-glass windows brought colour and light and harmony to the room. A few patients were seated in the room reading. In the far corner a section of the room had been set aside as a games area, where three or four men were playing cards and dominoes. But the majority of the patients were out on the veranda or the grass terraces or lying on their bed chairs on their private balconies.

'Dr Hartmann's room, the X-ray room and treatment rooms are through there—' Sister Bergamin waved her hand towards the end of the long room. 'But come now, I will show you your bedroom.' She led the way up the stairs, which wound around a huge wooden lift.

'That's a big lift,' Jacques remarked, using his school-boy German as he panted his way up the stairs. All the time, Florrie noticed that the sister was assessing the boy. It was the first time he'd spoken since their arrival.

'It's so we can take patients up and down in their beds if we have to. For X-rays, treatment and so on.' Her smile broadened. 'But you, young man, don't look as if you need a lift.'

Jacques paused a moment, clinging to the banister rail. He grinned weakly at her. 'Not if I can help it, Sister.'

They came to the first floor and stepped into a corridor running the full length of the building, with doors on either side. They turned left to the room at the very end. Opening the door, Emmi Bergamin said, 'All the rooms on this side are at the front of the building and each room has its own balcony. The rooms on the other side do not. They are usually for staff or for visitors, though we discourage family or friends staying here. The disease is infectious, you know. Here we are. This is one of our very best rooms.'

As they entered the room, Florrie looked about her. This was where Jacques would get well. She had to believe that.

The bedroom at the very end of the corridor was furnished for single occupancy. The walls were panelled in white, with pictures dotted here and there. Pristine white sheets covered the hospital-type bed. There was a wardrobe, a chest of drawers, a bedside cabinet, a table, and two chairs and a daybed. The floor was covered with linoleum. More hygienic, Florrie supposed. Sunlight streamed in through the window and the door leading onto the balcony, making the room light and airy and cheerful.

The sister opened a door to the left. 'This is your bathroom.'

Jacques stepped inside, turning slowly to look around him, whilst Florrie peered in from the doorway.

'It's very – luxurious,' the boy murmured. Indeed it was. The walls and floor were of pale-grey marble. Even the side of the huge white bath was panelled with marble. A white-painted chair stood at the end of the bath with a towel rail above it. Fresh white towels were folded neatly on it and to the right of the chair was a radiator. In the opposite corner was a square washbasin with a glass shelf and a mirror above it.

'The lavatory is through there.' Emmi pointed to another door leading off the bathroom. As they all moved back into the bedroom, the sister put down her papers on the small table and opened the door leading onto the balcony. 'Come, Jacques, you can begin your treatment right away. Sit out here whilst your mother and I unpack your things. Then, when you've rested, I'll take you both down to see Dr Hartmann. He is expecting you.'

The boy sat on one of the cane bed chairs and stretched out. From one of the cupboards, the nurse pulled a thick blanket and tucked it around him, saying, 'You're lucky it's such a nice day.'

Florrie was unpacking his clothes as Emmi Bergamin picked up the sheaf of papers again and flicked through them. 'I need to take down a few details . . .' She began to move towards the balcony to speak to Jacques.

Florrie's head snapped up. 'What sort of details?'

Emmi half-turned towards her. 'Oh, just full name, date and place of birth, parents' names. That sort of thing. Just for our records. And, of course, most importantly, if there is any history of tuberculosis in the family.'

'History?' Florrie's voice rose a little. 'Why – why do you need to know about his family?'

The nurse turned back and sat down on one of the two chairs. 'Come, sit down. I will explain.'

Florrie sank onto the chaise longue and clasped her hands together to stop them trembling. Wide-eyed, she stared at the nurse, her heart thumping and fear rising in her throat.

'Dr Hartmann believes that although this disease is not hereditary as such, there may be a weakness within a family that makes them susceptible to contracting it. He would be the first to say that it is only a theory at present, but he is making a study of family histories and hopes to write a paper for the medical journals one day.' Emmi Bergamin smiled and her eyes were afire with something akin to adoration. 'Dr Hartmann is making it his life's work.'

Florrie continued to stare at her in silence.

'So, you see,' Emmi went on. 'All the details we collect from families will form part of his study.'

Florrie turned pale. 'And – and must you have everyone's?'

'Oh yes,' Emmi was firm. 'It is a condition of your son being here.'

'I – I didn't know.'

'You should have been told. I am sorry if it was not made clear to you.' Her pen was already poised over a blank sheet of paper. 'Now, shall we begin?'

Florrie's mind was in turmoil. What could she do? How could she possibly tell this girl everything when Jacques himself didn't even know the truth? She should have told him, Florrie castigated herself. She should have told him as soon as he'd been old enough to understand. And now she was caught in a trap. She couldn't get up, repack his things and whisk him away. He needed to stay here. He needed treatment. And she? Well, she had to see Ernst Hartmann again.

Begin? Where should she begin? The war? No, no, before that. When had it all started? And then she remembered.

It had all started the day she'd refused to marry Gervase.

Two

Edgar Maltby thumped the desk with his fist. He rose slowly and menacingly to his feet.

'If I say you will marry Gervase Richards, girl, then marry him you will.'

Florrie faced him squarely. Her knees were trembling and, behind her back, her fingers were twisting nervously. Even at eighteen it was bold, perhaps even rash, to go against her father's wishes. But outwardly she was calm.

'I don't love him, Father, and I won't marry someone I don't love.'

'Love! Don't be so foolish, girl. He's the sole owner of the whole of the Bixley Estate since his father died. How can you possibly refuse him?' Edgar shook his head. 'I don't understand you sometimes, Florence, really I don't. You've been friends for years. You and Gervase. You've been inseparable. And even your brother, young though he is, has idolized the man. So, why—?'

'Perhaps that's why, Father. He feels like another brother to me. Not – not a husband.'

'Well, you'd better start thinking of him as just that. He's asked my permission to propose to you and I don't want to hear that you've refused him. Or else—'

16

Now Florrie's brown eyes blazed with anger. She stood tall and straight-backed, holding her head proudly and defiantly, but without arrogance. 'Or what, Father? You'll cast me out? Send me to the workhouse?'

'Don't be ridiculous, girl,' Edgar growled. He sat down in his chair again and leaned back, regarding her through half-closed eyes. He was a big man – tall and broad – and now, in middle age, he was acquiring the rotund shape that came with good living. He was a serious man, smiling rarely and laughing even less. Even as a child Florrie had wondered what it was in his life that made him seem so cross most of the time. And at this moment the frown lines on his forehead were even deeper than normal. His mouth tight beneath the dark moustache, he said slowly, 'If you refuse Richards you will seriously displease me.'

Florrie softened a little. Despite his dictatorial manner, she respected her father and disliked making him angry. Yet there was a streak of stubbornness in her that wouldn't allow her to let him ride roughshod over her and direct the rest of her life. She believed she'd the right to decide her own future. Fond though she was of Gervase – he was a good, kind man and she knew he'd be her lifelong friend – she couldn't imagine herself married to him.

'Florence, listen to me—' Edgar spread his hands, palms upwards. In anyone else the gesture might have been seen as a sign of weakness or submission – but not in her father. 'Richards loves you very much. He'll give you everything. You'll want for nothing. Can't you see that?'

'Of course I can, Father. But I'm not in love with him.'

'But you like him, don't you?'

'Of course I do. There's nothing anyone could *dis*like about him.' She smiled at the thought of the young man who'd been her friend for as long as she could remember.

'And you get along with his sister, don't you?'

There were only the two of them left now, living between Bixley Manor and the Richards' London town house. Isobel Richards seemed to spend most of her time there, leaving her brother to live at the Manor and run the family estate.

'Of course.'

'Then for Heaven's sake, girl . . . ?'

'Because I care enough about him *not* to marry him. He deserves better than me.'

'What on earth do you mean by that? Our family is of equal—'

'No – I don't mean that.' She gestured impatiently. Why, with her father, did everything have to revolve around their position in society? 'He deserves a wife who loves him in return.'

'But then,' Edgar said quietly, for once with an insight that was anathema to his nature, '*he* won't love *her*, now will he?'

For once, Florrie couldn't think of a reply.

Dismissed from her father's study in what amounted to disgrace, Florrie flew up the stairs, two steps at a time, and ran along the landing to the south wing of the house where Augusta Maltby had her rooms.

'Gran!' Florrie burst into the elderly lady's bedroom without so much as a knock on the door.

'Goodness me, child, whatever brings you flying into my room shrieking like a banshee and without even the courtesy of announcing your impending arrival?'

Florrie was halted in her tracks, but she grinned. 'Sorry, Gran.' She loved the way Augusta pretended grandness when in truth she could have held her own amongst the rough and tumble of the stable-yard lads.

'And don't call me "Gran". It's "Grandmama" or "Grandmother" to you, my girl.'

Florrie took a flying leap and landed on the end of the bed. 'On our high horse today, are we, *Grandmama*?'

The twinkle in the old lady's eyes belied her words. 'Not for long with you around,' she muttered, pretending to be offended. She gazed at the lovely face of her granddaughter. Such clear skin – and without the aid of any cosmetics, she was sure; such mischievous eyes that gave warning of a steely resolve. And that beautiful long hair – a rich, dark brown – curling and waving around her head. So like Augusta's own 'crowning glory' had once been.

Florence Maltby was what many would call 'a little madam', but to her grandmother she represented all that was good in the youth of the Edwardian era. Though, Augusta reminded herself, even those days were gone with the death of the old king two years earlier. Now his son, George V, ruled an unsettled world – a world where a young woman would need spirit and determination to survive.

Augusta smiled fondly, her brief irritation forgotten. 'So, what is it this time? You're going to London to join Mrs Pankhurst and her followers?'

Florrie's eyes widened. 'How – how did you know?'

Augusta's eyes sparkled with mischief and the indomitable spirit that even age could not quench. 'Because if I was your age right now, that's exactly what I would

19

do. But I'm a little old to be chaining myself to the railings outside Number Ten or Buckingham Palace.'

'Fiddlesticks!' Florrie laughed. At sixty-eight, her grandmother was still slim and energetic and Florrie could easily visualize her marching at the head of a protest waving a banner.

'Besides, I'm needed here.' Her eyes twinkled wickedly. 'Who would keep your father in check if I disappeared off to London?'

They exchanged a smile, then Augusta said, 'Brush my hair, dear girl, will you?'

As Florrie scrambled off the bed, her grandmother raised her eyes to the ceiling. 'Tut-tut, whenever are we going to get you to behave in a more ladylike manner, child?'

'Never, I should think,' Florrie said cheerfully as she picked up the silver-backed hairbrush from the dressing table and returned to the bedside. Gently, she brushed her grandmother's grey hair. It was thinning now, but once it had been as luxurious and vibrant as Florrie's own locks. There was silence in the room for a moment. Augusta shut her eyes and submitted to the pleasure of the brush strokes and the feel of the girl's tender fingers.

Florrie glanced around her. She never tired of coming to her grandmother's rooms. Augusta's belongings, cluttered around her, had fascinated Florrie for as long as she could remember. The furniture was heavy, Victorian mahogany that was polished lovingly every week. Every surface was covered with lace runners, photographs and ornaments – mementoes of a happy life. Even the walls were almost covered with paintings and pictures, hung haphazardly, and every one of them held a special meaning for the old lady. Especially the huge portrait of her late husband, Nathaniel Maltby, that hung opposite the end of her bed.

'Actually, it wasn't about that,' Florrie confided, bringing her attention back to her grandmother's question. 'He – he doesn't know about that yet.'

'By *he* I presume you mean your father.'

'Mm.'

'So – what is it that my son won't let you do now?'

'Well, this time, it's what he wants me to do that I won't.'

'Ah, that makes a change,' Augusta remarked drily.

There was a pause whilst Florrie continued to brush.

'So, out with it, girl.'

'He – he wants me to marry Gervase.'

Augusta twisted round to look up at her grand-daughter, so quickly that Florrie almost caught her face with the brush. But she managed to snatch it away just before the bristles touched the soft, wrinkled skin.

'You don't want to?' Even Augusta was surprised at this. 'But – but you're always together. He's your best friend. Yours and James's too.'

Florrie dropped the brush and sat down on the bed again. 'I know,' she said and now there were tears in her eyes. Gervase was the last person in the world – outside her own family – whom she wanted to hurt. 'I do love him, Gran—' This time Augusta didn't complain at the shortened name. 'But not like that. I – I love him like a brother, not – not—' A faint blush tinged her cheeks. 'Like a husband.'

'Ah.' Augusta gave a deep sigh. 'I see.' She lay back against the plump pillows and regarded her grand-daughter thoughtfully.

21

'Are – are you angry with me too?' Florrie asked. She could stand up to her father, but her grandmother was a different matter.

'I should be.'

Florrie clasped the thin, purple-veined hand. 'But you're not! Oh, Gran, please say you understand.'

'My dearest girl, of course I do.'

'I – I thought this time you might agree with Father.'

Augusta snorted. 'That'd be a first.' Florrie giggled, but now her grandmother was thoughtful. 'I had a similar problem with my own father. Only he *dis*approved of the man I wanted to marry.'

Florrie gasped. This was something she hadn't known. 'You – you mean, you were in love with someone before Grandpops?'

Augusta laughed. 'Good Heavens, no! Your grandfather was the only man in my life. No, it was him my father disapproved of.'

'Disapproved of Grandpops?' Florrie's voice squeaked in surprise. She couldn't believe it. 'But how could anyone have disliked him?'

'Exactly!' Augusta's mouth twitched with amusement, then more seriously she added, 'Actually, he quite liked him, but he thought he wasn't suitable.'

'Ah – he thought he wasn't good enough for you? Not your class?'

Augusta chuckled. 'Well, he certainly wasn't my class, but it was the other way about, my dear. *I* wasn't good enough for *him*.'

'What! I don't understand.'

The elderly lady regarded the guileless young face in front of her. 'I think perhaps I should explain,' she said slowly. 'Though you must promise me not to speak of this in front of your father – or your mother for that matter.' Her mouth moved with wry amusement. 'Your dear papa doesn't like to be reminded of the lowly stock he comes from.'

'Lowly stock? Father?' Florrie began to laugh.

'Oh, you can laugh, child, but your father takes it all very seriously and has been at pains to hide his true ancestry.'

'But – but we've a family tree in copperplate hand-writing hanging in the hall for all to see. It even has a coat of arms somewhere way back in great-great-great somebody or other's time.'

Augusta chuckled. 'I know, but have you ever noticed that it just follows the *male* line of the Maltbys – never the distaff side?' She paused and then added pointedly, 'There are none of *my* family shown on the tree, are there?'

Florrie stared at her. 'No – there aren't. But I never realized.'

'Well, you go and take a good look.'

'I will – but first tell me about you. Why weren't you good enough to marry Grandpops?'

Augusta's eyes glazed over for a moment. She began slowly at first, but then the past came flooding back. 'My father worked on this estate, but he wasn't even a tenant farmer. He was even lowlier than that. He was a good man – a God-fearing man, hard-working and as honest as the day is long – but he was a waggoner for one of the tenants. We lived in a tied cottage and at twelve years old I was sent to work in the big house.'

'Here?'

'Yes.' Augusta nodded. 'Here in Candlethorpe Hall as a scullery maid.'

Astonished, Florrie said, 'Like little Beth was when she first came here?'

'Yes – just like Beth, though I hope we've always been kinder to the little lass than they were in my day. After a year or so, your great-grandmother took a liking to me and made me her personal maid. The other servants didn't like it when a lowly scullery maid became a lady's maid in one jump. But I was determined to go up in the world, though I never imagined . . .' Her voice faded away for a moment as she became lost in her own memories.

Florrie was thoughtful. It hadn't escaped her notice that her grandmother always treated the household staff with great respect. 'Little Beth' as they called her was just such a case. She'd come to Candlethorpe Hall as the lowliest of all servants – a scullery maid. But she was quick and eager, and Augusta soon made sure she was promoted to second housemaid and, before long, to her own lady's maid. Florrie smiled as she remembered the consternation her grandmother's action had caused both above and below stairs. The first housemaid was aggrieved that she'd been passed over and Mrs Dewey, the housekeeper, who had charge over all the female staff, had been none too pleased either. But it had all settled down, most probably because it was *Augusta* who'd wanted Beth. Florrie had seen for herself how everyone from the lowliest kitchen maid to the superior butler adored her grandmother. They'd even been known to go against the master's wishes if Augusta decreed differently. Edgar Maltby might think himself the head of the household, but it was his mother who still ruled. Now, it seemed, Augusta had been helping a young girl who deserved a better place in life, just as she'd once been helped.

Florrie's thoughts came back to her grandmother and a dreadful image entered her head. She'd heard tales of how the sons of the well-to-do took their pleasure with the servant girls. She bit her lip to stop the question escaping, but it seemed her shrewd grandmother had already guessed what was running through the young girl's mind. 'No,' she said, answering the unspoken question that must have shown itself in Florrie's expression. 'Nathaniel didn't seduce me, if that's what you're thinking.'

'Oh, Grandmother, you know me too well.'

'So I should. I've looked after you since you were born. Your poor mother – well, we won't go into that just now. Let me carry on with my story, else I'll lose my thread. That's the trouble with being old. One gets so forgetful.'

Florrie chuckled. Anyone with a sharper mind than Augusta Maltby she'd yet to meet.

'We fell in love. It was as simple and – in the circumstances – as complicated as that. Nathaniel's family disapproved, of course. That was to be expected, but I was surprised that my own father did too. He took me away from my position in the big house and sent me to work miles away for a crotchety old lady who used to lash out at me with her stick if I didn't suit.'

'But – but Nathaniel followed you?'

'Oh yes. He found out where I'd gone from one of my brothers and he came one night and took me away with him.'

'How old were you?'

'Seventeen by then.'

'Did you get married? I mean, right away, because you'd have been underage, wouldn't you? Oh, Grandmother—' Florrie laughed delightedly. 'You eloped. Do tell me you eloped.'

Augusta laughed. 'Yes, we did. We went all the way to Scotland to be married.'

'To Gretna Green? Oh, how romantic!'

'Your father doesn't think so.' Mention of Edgar's name sobered them both. 'So – stick to your guns, child,' Augusta said firmly. 'You'll never know a moment's happiness unless you do.'

'And you were happy? You and Grandpops?'

Nathaniel Maltby had died when Florrie had been nine, but she still remembered the rotund, bewhiskered, kindly old gentleman who'd always smelt of tobacco smoke when she climbed onto his knee.

Augusta returned her gaze steadily, but her voice trembled a little as she said, 'More than I can ever put into words, my dear.'

There was a knock on the bedroom door and Beth's heart-shaped little face peered around it. ''Scuse me, madam, but Mrs Maltby says would Miss Florrie come down to the morning room. Mr Richards is here to see her.'

'Thank you, Beth.' As the door closed behind the maid, Augusta touched her granddaughter's hand. 'Off you go then, my dear, and get the dirty deed done.'

Three

'Oh, Florrie dear, there you are.'

'Yes, here I am, Mother,' Florrie said gaily, closing the door behind her and walking towards the fireplace where her mother and Gervase sat, one on either side.

The young man had risen at her entry and was now smiling at her, looking, Florrie thought, unusually nervous. Now Clara rose and there was no mistaking her agitation, but then her mother was always anxious about something or other and was often confined to her room, quite unable to face the rigours of running the household in the way that Edgar demanded. That was left to Augusta.

'I'll – er – go to my room,' Clara murmured, scuttling out as if desperate to escape from a scene that she feared was going to erupt into angry words and cause a tense atmosphere throughout the house that would linger for weeks, if her wayward daughter refused Gervase's proposal.

'Gervase – how lovely to see you,' Florrie said brightly. 'Can I offer you a drink? Tea? Coffee? Or maybe something stronger?' she added mischievously.

'No – thank you. Florrie – I—'

'My word, Gervase, you look very smart today.'

He was wearing a dark, pinstriped three-piece suit instead of his usual country tweeds. He was tall and broad-shouldered, happiest when he was striding about the fields of his estate, but not out of place or awkward in an elegant drawing room. He was at ease in any surroundings – but not today.

'Florrie – darling,' he held out his hands. 'Please, come and sit down.'

She allowed him to lead her to the sofa. They sat side by side.

'You know why I'm here, don't you?'

She looked up into his gentle blue eyes that usually twinkled with merriment but at this moment were unusually serious and intense. She felt an urge to smooth the wiry fair hair that curled so vigorously that no amount of plastering it down would make it lie flat.

'Please, Gervase, don't say it. Please don't. I – I don't want to hurt you. You mean the world to me as my dearest friend, but I really can't marry you.'

His handsome, craggy face fell into lines of disappointment. 'Why not, Florrie? Just tell me why not?'

The young girl sighed. This was so difficult. How much easier it would be just to give in and say 'yes'. All her family would be pleased with her, and she'd no doubt – and it was not conceit – that her acceptance would make Gervase 'the happiest man on earth'. She could almost hear him saying it. But what none of them could understand was that it would be a fleeting happiness. It wouldn't last forever. And she couldn't bear to think that they might come to hate each other. She couldn't do that. Not to Gervase – or to herself.

'I love you dearly,' she began badly. That was quite the wrong thing to say.

Hope sprang into his eyes. 'Then—'

'As I love James,' she added firmly, trying to make him understand. 'And you know how much that is.'

Her brother, younger than her by four years, was the

darling of the family. Their mother doted on him, their father had high hopes for him, and even Augusta – though she'd never admit to having favourites – melted like butter at the sight of him. Florrie had never felt jealous of James; she adored him just as much as everyone else. He'd been a handsome little chap and at fourteen showed all the promise of breaking girls' hearts throughout the county. Florrie just prayed that when his turn came he would fall in love with someone whom Father would think 'suitable'. She believed that she could get away with disappointing him, but if James were to go against Edgar's wishes, then ... Well, it didn't bear thinking about.

'You mean you love me as a brother and not as a husband,' Gervase said flatly.

'That's it exactly.'

'I won't stop trying, Florrie. Every New Year's Eve, I shall propose again.'

'Please don't,' Florrie pulled a face. 'I shall dread every year end if you say that.'

Gervase laughed and some of the hurt left his eyes for a moment. 'Well, I'm sorry, but you're just going to have to put up with it. Maybe you'll get so fed up of saying "no", one year you'll say "yes".' He raised her hand to his lips and kissed her fingers one by one and, quite serious now, added, 'Just remember, Florrie, that if ever you change your mind, I'll be waiting.'

'Oh no, you'll meet a lovely girl, get married and have a huge family. And I'll be the best adopted auntie in the whole world.'

He regarded her steadily. 'That's not going to happen, Florrie. You're the only girl I'll ever love.'

His words and his tone were so sincere, so heartfelt, that for once Florrie could not make light of them. 'I'm sorry, truly I am,' she whispered, tears spilling down her cheeks.

With tender fingers Gervase wiped them away. 'Please don't cry, Florrie.' He smiled. 'You always tell me you never cry.'

'I don't,' she said fiercely. 'At least – not often.'

'So – let's just go on being the good friends we are, eh? But I meant what I said.'

'I know.'

'I suppose I forget how young you are. Only eighteen. You need a little fun before you settle down, don't you? You haven't even "come out" yet, but you see I'm so afraid if you go to London for the Season, one of those very eligible young men will snap you up. I wanted us to be engaged so that couldn't happen. But I know it's your mother's dearest wish that you should be presented at court. Just as she was.'

Now Florrie laughed aloud, her tears brushed away. 'Well, it's not going to happen – I promise you. If I go to London it will be for quite a different reason than doing the round of balls and parties to meet eligible bachelors.'

'What do you mean?'

She tapped him playfully on the nose. 'Now *that* is my secret.'

'Oh, you girls and your secrets. Well, I must be off. Still a lot to get ready for tonight. You're all coming, aren't you?'

It had long been the tradition that the two families spent New Year's Eve together, alternating between the two homes. One year the Maltbys would play host at Candlethorpe Hall, the next year it would be the turn of the Richards at Bixley Manor. It had been their great-grandfathers who'd begun it. The two men had been brought together by business, their estates on the edge of the Lincolnshire Wolds stretching to join each other. The natural progression had been that their families became friends. They dined together often, held shooting parties, picnics, balls and bonfire nights. Together they'd seen the dawn of a new century, the passing of the old queen and her strict morality into an age of change. Over the years, the New Year's Eve celebrations had come to include not only the household staff of both grand country houses, but also all the estate workers and their families. Most of the inhabitants of the local villages worked on one estate or the other, but even those who didn't joined the merry parties that set off in farm carts and traps – the youths and young girls on bicycles – from Candlethorpe to Bixley or vice versa. Laughter filled the frosty air as they travelled the six miles. Old and young alike were entertained to music and dancing in one of the huge barns, where trestle tables were laid out laden with beer and enough food to feed an army. This year it was the Candlethorpe folk who were to travel to Bixley Manor.

'Wouldn't miss it for the world.' Florrie smiled.

'And tell your grandmother,' Gervase said, 'she can sit in the bay window overlooking the field where the bonfire's been built.'

Florrie hooted with laughter. 'Gran? Sit indoors whilst we're all outside? I think not. Mother might – but not Gran.'

Gervase smiled fondly. 'What a character she is. She's a remarkable old lady.'

'Old? Gran? Don't let her hear you say that. She doesn't think sixty-eight is old.'

Gervase laughed. 'Well, on her it certainly isn't.'

As Florrie led the way to the front door to see him

out, the butler hovered in the hall. 'It's all right, Bowler, I'll see Mr Richards out.'

'Very good, Miss Florrie.' He gave a small bow and turned away.

As they crossed the hall, Florrie asked casually, 'Is Isobel still at home?'

'Oh yes. She's not going back to London until next Monday.'

Florrie held open the heavy front door and, as he passed by her, she reached up impulsively and kissed his cheek. 'Dear Gervase,' she whispered softly.

He paused a moment, looking down into her upturned face. The face he knew so well and loved so dearly. But the look in her eyes was that of a very dear and devoted friend, not of a girl madly in love with him. He gave a little sigh as he put on his trilby. 'Until tonight, my dear.'

'Hey, Florrie!' James was leaning over the banister at the top of the stairs looking down at her in the hallway below. 'Have you quite broken poor old Gervase's heart then?'

She closed the front door and turned to look up at him. She grimaced and then grinned. 'So you've heard. I expect everyone knows by now then.'

'Cheek!'

She climbed the stairs towards him. 'You're not renowned for keeping secrets, my dear little brother.'

James threw back his head and laughed. 'You can't keep any secrets in this place. The servants have their own grapevine and the tiniest whisper goes round them all in a flash.'

She reached the top. 'You know I've refused him then?'

'Not exactly, but I guessed you would.' James

chuckled as he added, 'I've always wondered why he cultivates my friendship. After all, he's so much older than me. I must seem only a boy to him. Now I know. It isn't me at all he wants to be with, it's you.'

Florrie was thoughtful for a moment before saying, quite seriously, 'I think he likes being here with all our family. He's no brother, and his only sister is six years older than him. And she has her own circle of friends—'

'Oh, the Votes for Women brigade.'

Florrie ignored his remark. 'His mother died when he was a baby and his father five years ago. And Isobel spends a lot of time in London.'

'Rumour has it,' James said in a loud whisper, 'that his sister has a lover in the city.'

'James! What do you know about such things!'

He guffawed. 'A chap can't be at a boys' boarding school for the last four years without learning all that sort of stuff. Want to know what else I know?'

'No, thank you!' She held up her hand, palm outwards, as if fending him off. 'I don't want to hear your smutty schoolboy talk, thank you very much.'

'It isn't smutty,' he began indignantly and then grinned. 'Well, not all of it.'

'Oh – you!' She linked her arm through his and they walked together along the landing towards the room that had once been the nursery and which they still used for their own private space. Nannies and tutors within the household were a thing of the past. James had attended a boys' boarding school since the age of ten and there was talk of Florrie being sent to a finishing school before being presented at court. But she had no intention of going, not since Gervase's sister had told her all about the wonderful things the suffragettes were doing. Florrie knew exactly why Isobel Richards spent a lot of time in London. That was where all the action was to be found. And soon – very soon – Florrie hoped to be a part of it. How on earth her grandmother had guessed her plans, she couldn't imagine. Sometimes she wondered if the old lady had second sight!

Once they were safely in the nursery, James said, 'So, what *are* you going to do, old girl?'

Florrie looked at him sharply. Surely, he hadn't heard too? 'Do? What do you mean?'

'Well, won't Father banish you from the old homestead and tell you you're never to darken his door again?'

Florrie breathed a sigh of relief and laughed. 'James, I've just refused a proposal of marriage. I'm not pregnant.'

'That might be as bad in his eyes.'

'Oh no, nothing could be as bad as that. Not in Father's eyes. I certainly would be cast out if that happened.'

James flung himself down on the battered old sofa and put his feet up on the arm. Crossing his ankles and putting his hands behind his head, he said languidly, 'Then perhaps I should tell you the facts of life, old thing.'

Florrie picked up a cushion and began to beat him about the head with it until they fell to the floor together, laughing and rolling over and over, their arms around each other. At last they lay still, panting from the exertion of their mock fight. James's arms tightened around her. 'Oh, Sis, just so long as you know you're doing the right thing. Gervase is an awfully decent chap, you know.'

Florrie rested her head against James's chest. She could hear the pounding of his heart and her voice was muffled as she murmured, 'Yes, I do know. That's just why I have to be honest with him.'

James stroked her thick mane of glossy hair. 'Poor old Gervase' was all he said now. There was a long silence before he went on, 'But we're still going to the bonfire and fireworks tonight at Bixley Manor, aren't we?'

'Of course.' Florrie's heart quickened with excitement. She would see Isobel tonight and their plans would be finalized. And next Monday – as soon as that – they would both be on their way to London. And there was something else she hadn't told any of her family. James was quite right. Isobel had a lover in London, but there was nothing furtive about it. Tonight, at the New Year's Eve party, she was to announce her engagement to the Honourable Timothy Smythe, son of Lady Leonora Smythe – a well-known figure in London society and an ardent supporter of Mrs Pankhurst and her followers. Lord Smythe, it seemed, indulged his wife and was happy to stay on his Dorset estate.

Florrie got up from the floor and pulled her brother to his feet. Impulsively, she flung her arms about him and gave him a bear hug.

'Hey, what's that for?'

'Oh, just – you know,' she said and her voice was a little unsteady. No one – not even James or her grandmother – knew of her plans. And she couldn't tell them, not yet. 'Just because I love my little brother.'

'Hey, not so little now, old thing. I'm taller than you.'

'So you are.' She gazed at him fondly, as if committing every line of his face to her mind.

For after Monday, she realized, it might be a very long time before she saw him again.

Four

'You haven't told anyone,' Isobel Richards whispered as she drew Florrie into her bedroom at Bixley Manor and closed the door firmly behind her.

'Of course not.'

'Right. Now – I need to speak with your grandmother tonight and ask her if you can come with me to London on Monday. You're sure they don't know about my – um – activities?'

Pushing aside her grandmother's remark, Florrie answered, 'No one's said anything and I'm sure they would've done if they'd known.'

'Mm. I've been lucky nothing's got into the local papers. Not even Gervase knows.'

'What about your fiancé? He's here tonight, isn't he? Does he know?'

'The Hon. Tim? Of course he does, but he'll not say anything. He's a darling about it all. His mother ropes him in to help out all the time. He's always waiting at the prison gates for her.'

Florrie's eyes widened. 'Prison? Lady Smythe has been to – to prison?'

'Oh yes. Twice,' Isobel said airily. 'I think Tim's very proud of her, though he worries, of course.'

'I can't wait to meet him. He sounds wonderful.'

'He is.' In the flickering candlelight, Isobel's eyes

shone with happiness. 'I can't believe he's actually fallen in love with *me*.'

Isobel Richards could be described as a handsome woman, but never beautiful. She had thick, curly fair hair like her brother. Her eyes were a startling blue, but her nose was a little too long and her chin too square and strong on a woman. But she was nevertheless striking and utterly feminine. She wore the latest fashions and used cosmetics skilfully. That she'd never been engaged or married before the age of thirty-one was her own fault rather than because she'd lacked suitors. She knew her own mind and what she wanted from life, and nothing and no one were going to get in her way. It was her good fortune that she'd found the Honourable Timothy Smythe, who was willing to indulge her eccentricities. They'd met through his mother's suffragette activities and it was possibly because he was used to – and secretly admired – strong, determined women that he fell in love with Isobel. With her – just as with his mother – he knew there'd never be a dull moment.

'Actually, I don't think my father will object,' Florrie mused. 'I'm not in his best books at the moment.'

Isobel laughed. 'Because of my little brother, you mean?'

Florrie nodded. '*You're* not angry with me, Iso, are you?'

'Heavens, no! I'd only be angry if you married him when you didn't love him. That'd be far worse, in my book. No, I admire you for sticking to your guns, though I have to say, I'm sorry not to have you as my sister-in-law. Goodness knows what sort of dithery creature I might get now. Ah well . . . Now, let's get back to making plans. Are you all ready? Your clothes and everything? Have you any money of your own?'

Florrie shook her head. 'Not much, though I think Gran might help out there.' She bit her lip, not wanting to confide in Isobel that she believed Augusta had partially guessed she was up to something. She was glad that Isobel planned to speak to her tonight. If there was one person she hated deceiving other than perhaps James, it was her grandmother. 'Do you want me to come with you to talk to her?'

'Best not, I think. Tim and I will look after her at the bonfire and you make yourself scarce. I think – once she's met Tim – she'll be happy that you're going to be well looked after.' Isobel pulled a face and muttered, 'Little does she know what I'm getting you into.'

But Isobel didn't know Augusta Maltby quite as well as she thought she did.

'I'm delighted to meet you, Timothy.' The old lady's eyes twinkled mischievously when Isobel introduced her fiancé after the two families had drunk the health of the newly engaged couple. 'You wouldn't by any strange coincidence be Leonora Smythe's son, would you?'

The young man stared at her. The flickering light from the bonfire shone with a gentle light on the elderly lady's face, smoothing away the wrinkles and pushing back the years. In the kindly glow she looked – for a moment – like a young woman again. A very beautiful young woman.

'Well, yes – actually – I am.' The surprise was evident in his tone. 'How – how did you know?'

Augusta chuckled. 'Oh, it's all right, young man, I haven't got second sight.' She leaned forward, confiding a secret. 'Your name was in the paper when she was last released from prison, and so – was Isobel's.'

Isobel gave a startled gasp and her eyes widened. 'Oh no,' she breathed. 'I didn't think it'd reached the papers here. Oh botheration!'

Augusta flapped her hand. 'Don't worry, my dear. It didn't. I order a London newspaper to be delivered to me.' She sniffed. 'I like to know what's going on in the outside world and our provincial newspapers are full of local tittle-tattle that's of no interest to me.'

Isobel was suddenly nervous. 'So – does Mr Maltby know about – about—?'

'Good gracious me, no. No one in our household sees the newspaper except me—' Her eyes sparkled with intrigue. 'And possibly Bowler,' Augusta referred to the Maltbys' butler, 'who smuggles the paper up to my room and out again to the rubbish.' She laughed deliciously. 'No doubt he reads it, but he's far too discreet ever to admit it. He followed his own father into the position, you know. I don't know where I'd be without him. Oh dear, I'm in danger of starting to ramble.' She shook her shoulders and, turning to Isobel, said briskly, 'Now, my dear, I understand you're returning to the city on Monday and I suppose what this is all leading up to is that my wayward granddaughter wishes to go with you.'

For a moment Isobel stared at her and then threw back her head and laughed aloud. Those nearby looked around curiously. Seeing that she was attracting unwelcome attention, Isobel stifled her laughter. 'How did you know?'

'I didn't, but let's go indoors. Warm though the bonfire is, my old bones are starting to feel the cold. I think I may have to succumb to your brother's kind invitation to watch the rest of the proceedings from his study window. Timothy, you may take me in. It's not often nowadays that I get the chance to take the arm of a handsome young man.'

Gallantly he held out his arm to her and the three of them made their way steadily over the rough ground of the field behind Bixley Manor towards the warmth of Gervase's study.

Settled in front of the window, with only the firelight from the grate to illuminate the room, they could see the bonfire and the fireworks very well.

'Ah,' Augusta sighed, sinking into Gervase's deep leather chair. 'That's better. I don't like to give in to old age, but there are times when one has to be sensible.' She glanced at the other two. 'But you two go back now. Don't miss the fun because of me.'

'No, it's fine,' Isobel said, pulling up another chair and sitting down beside her. 'I'd rather like this opportunity of a chat with you.'

Timothy, too, sat down. Having asked the ladies if they minded him smoking and received their permission, he lit up a cigar and puffed happily whilst Isobel explained their plans.

'Florrie is desperate to come back with me. She wants to be involved in the suffrage movement, but—' Isobel sighed. 'But our families have always been so close and I wouldn't want to do anything to upset our friendship.'

Augusta was thoughtful for a moment. 'Well, you won't upset me, but I can't speak for Edgar or Clara. He'll no doubt rant and rave for a while and Clara will shed copious tears and take to her bed for a day or two. But I fully expect that'll all happen anyway following Florrie's refusal of Gervase's proposal.'

Timothy sat up suddenly. 'Has she refused him?'

Isobel nodded. 'Yes – and rightly so, if she doesn't love him.'

The young couple exchanged a fond glance, which Augusta pretended not to notice. 'Let's get down to practicalities. Is she to live with you in London, Isobel?'

'Oh yes. I'll certainly do my best to look after her, but I have to be honest with you. If she becomes really involved in the movement, I can't guarantee that she won't be caught up in a demonstration or even arrested.'

Augusta's eyes shone with excitement. 'If only I was your age again.' She patted Isobel's hand. 'I won't try to stop her, but you must promise me one thing.'

'Of course – if I can.'

'You must keep me fully informed of what's happening. And I mean *everything*. I don't want to read in the papers about her being force-fed in prison.'

Isobel shuddered. 'I hope it won't come to that, Mrs Maltby, but yes, I promise. Florrie or I will write to you at least once a week.'

A deep chuckle came from the other chair. 'And if they're *both* in prison, ma'am, I'll let you know.'

They laughed together and Augusta said, 'Then she can go with my blessing, though what her father will say when he finds out, I dread to think.'

Edgar Maltby had plenty to say.

He thumped his desk and sprang to his feet with the agility of a man half his age. Then he marched up and down his study with swift, angry strides, whilst Florrie stood in front of him dressed in her travelling hat and coat. Whilst Isobel and Timothy waited in the hall, Florrie had come to say 'goodbye' to her father. Her trunk was already packed and on the back of the carriage waiting on the front driveway. Augusta had wished her well, but her mother had dissolved into tears and begged her not to leave.

'Mother darling, you still have James.'

'But he'll be going back to school next week. I'll have no one to talk to.'

'There's Gran and Father, surely—'

Clara covered her face, muffling her voice as she said, 'Your grandmother doesn't like me. She never has.'

'Oh, Mother, that's not true. She's very fond of you. I know she perhaps gets impatient with you sometimes, but – but – well, you could try to be a little more cheerful. Not so – not so *downtrodden*.'

'But I am,' Clara wailed. 'That's the whole trouble. They're so strong. You're all so strong. But at least when you're here, you stand up to them. I – I don't feel so alone.'

Florrie had kissed her mother's forehead and murmured, 'Gran will look after you and I'll write every week. I promise.'

'But you'll need a maid. And you really can't expect your grandmother and me to spare Beth.'

'Isobel's maid will look after us both, I'm sure. Please, Mother, don't worry so.' Giving her mother's cold hands a final squeeze, she said, 'Now – I have to go and see Father.'

Clara broke into fresh sobs. She hated family rows and there was going to be one now. She knew there was. Florrie was so rebellious and Edgar would be so angry. She held her breath and, as she feared, only a moment later heard his loud voice from the study.

'I will not have a daughter of mine disgracing herself

in such a way. I'm fully aware of what Isobel Richards has got herself into. All this suffragette nonsense.' He raised his voice to an even louder pitch. 'And yes, I do know you're standing in the hallway, Miss Richards, and can hear every word I say.' He turned to his daughter once more. 'You're a sad disappointment to me, Florence. What if your name should appear in the papers? We shall be the laughing stock of the county.'

So, Florrie thought mutinously, he's not concerned about my safety, only the precious reputation of the Maltby name.

The door was flung open and Augusta stood there. 'What on earth is all the shouting about?'

Edgar rounded on her, stretching out his arm and pointing at her. 'This is your fault. I blame you, Mother, entirely. Encouraging Florence's disobedience. No doubt you were behind her refusing Richards's proposal. I suppose you want her to marry a stable lad,' he sneered. 'To keep up the family tradition.'

There was a moment's shocked silence, but Augusta merely smiled and said mildly, 'If a stable boy was the man she loved, then, yes, I would encourage her. But you're wrong about Gervase. I would've been delighted for her to marry him. He's a fine young man, but I do agree with her decision, if she's not in love with him.'

'Love! Bah!'

'Nor have I encouraged her to go to London with Isobel, though I have given her my permission.'

'*Your* permission?' Edgar was incensed. 'What about *my* permission? Her *father*'s?'

'Don't be such an old fuddy-duddy, boy.'

Florrie almost laughed aloud at hearing her father called 'boy'. But, she supposed, to his mother he would always be just that. He was certainly acting like a schoolboy in a tantrum now. He stood very still for a moment and his angry gaze rested on Florrie. Then he turned his back on her deliberately and stood looking out of the window. Without turning round again, he said, 'Go, then. I wash my hands of you. I just hope your brother never disappoints me in this way.'

For a brief moment, Florrie hesitated, but then her chin rose higher. She turned, kissed her grandmother's cheek, squeezed the old lady's hand and left the house without another word being spoken.

Five

Aboard the train, the three of them had the carriage to themselves. The two young women sat opposite each other near the window, whilst Timothy, sitting next to Isobel, stretched his legs and disappeared behind his newspaper.

'I've sent word that you're coming and a room will be ready for you.' Isobel spoke of the Richards' town house in London. 'Lady Leonora lives just around the corner so it's very handy.' Isobel's blue eyes sparkled with intrigue.

Florrie leaned forward, asking softly, 'What is she like?'

Isobel put her head on one side as she considered the question. 'Rather like me, I suppose. Not beautiful and rather manly.'

'Oh, Iso, you're not manly,' Florrie said swiftly.

Isobel laughed merrily. 'Kind of you to say so, Florrie, but I have been described as "handsome" and that's usually a word applied to a man, don't you think?'

Florrie shook her head. 'Not always. People talk about a handsome woman quite often.'

Isobel nodded her head towards her fiancé, engrossed in his paper. 'Tim is very like her, but, of course, on him the family resemblance is perfect.' She chuckled, quite secure in her own view of herself and not a bit envious of the lovely girl sitting before her. No wonder poor Gervase was besotted with Florrie. 'Are you coming out this year?'

'It's what Mother wants – and Father too, I suppose – but it's not the sort of thing that I'm interested in.' Changing the subject from debutantes, Florrie said, 'I'm more interested in what the suffragettes are doing.'

Isobel was thoughtful for a moment. 'How much do you know about the background to the movement?'

'I've read about it in Gran's newspapers. I don't think she ever guessed that I knew exactly where Bowler put them in the barn to be burned after she'd thrown them out. I used to sit in the hayloft and devour every word. I know that Millicent Fawcett formed the National Union of Women's Suffrage in the 1890s, but she only believed in peaceful protest and, whilst she did get a few Members of Parliament to support them, most MPs believed that women wouldn't understand the workings of Parliament sufficiently well to be able to vote.'

'That's right.' Isobel's tone became scathing at the insult. 'And Parliament stubbornly refused to debate the subject of women's emancipation.'

'So,' Florrie went on, anxious to prove to Isobel that she knew exactly what she was getting herself into, 'Mrs Emmeline Pankhurst, who wasn't prepared to wait years and years, formed the Women's Social and Political Union in 1903. Her followers were – and are – prepared to resort to violence to get themselves noticed to further the Cause.' Now she frowned. 'But couldn't violence have the opposite effect? I mean, chaining themselves to railings and smashing windows: doesn't that tarnish their credibility as serious-minded women?'

Isobel stared at her for a moment, a flicker of doubt in her expression.

Hastily, Florrie sought to reassure her. 'Oh, don't get

me wrong. I'm all for anything that will work – believe me.' She shrugged. 'I'm just trying to work out why it's become necessary to resort to such tactics. I want to understand, that's all.'

'Talking hasn't done much good. So our motto is "Deeds, not Words". Membership is only for women.' Isobel chuckled. 'So even the Hon. Tim here can't be a member.'

He peered round the edge of his newspaper. 'Ah, but I am an *"honorary"* member.'

The two girls groaned at his pun.

'Did you know that Emmeline and her daughter, Christabel Pankhurst, were imprisoned in 1908 for inciting a rush on the House of Commons?' Isobel went on. 'One woman actually reached the Chamber and declared that she'd made her first speech on the floor of the House.' Her eyes shone. 'I'd love to do that. To stand up in front of all those old fuddy-duddies and tell them what's what.'

'No, that was before I started taking a real interest.'

'Of course, it's not just in Britain that the cause for women's suffrage is being fought. There was an international convention held in London in 1909 and an American woman chaired it. I wasn't there, but Lady Leonora has told me all about it. Then two months later she was involved in demonstrations outside Parliament and Number Ten. There were over a hundred women arrested that day and Lady Leonora was one of them.'

'Arrested? Lady Leonora?' Florrie was appalled and yet fascinated at what she was hearing. Then she remembered what Isobel had told her previously. 'Was that one of the occasions she went to prison?'

'Yes,' Isobel waved her hand nonchalantly. 'And we've got to be prepared for that, too, Florrie dear.'

'I never realized it would involve – well – someone of Lady Leonora's position actually going to prison.'

Isobel laughed. 'It's a great leveller, this suffrage business. All classes of women are involved.'

'So what's been happening recently?'

Isobel's face sobered quickly. 'We've been burning pillar-boxes, setting off false fire alarms, breaking windows in city-centre stores. There've been more arrests. Nowadays, those arrested normally go on hunger strike in prison. Marion Dunlop started it first, I think, and because the authorities were afraid she'd die in custody, they released her. So, after that, all the suffragettes who were imprisoned tried it.'

'As a way of getting out of prison, you mean?'

Isobel laughed wryly. 'If only! No, the authorities brought in force-feeding.'

Florrie nodded and said soberly, 'Yes, I've read about that too. It sounds ghastly.'

'It is, and quite dangerous. We all think that Mrs Pankhurst's own sister died as a result of being force-fed in Holloway. She didn't die *in* prison,' Isobel added hastily. 'Oh no, they minded that didn't happen, but she died soon after her release and we all think that was what caused it.'

'I see,' Florrie said thoughtfully. This was no longer a 'lark'. This was serious stuff – deadly serious. Violence that resulted in imprisonment, and the dire treatment she might receive there.

'And I think I should warn you I have the feeling that activities are going to escalate. We've tried peaceful demonstrations.' She smiled. 'And not so peaceful ones. We've lobbied the House of Commons, written to MPs and refused to be counted in the Census of 1911. The government dangled the carrot of the Conciliation Bill that would give the vote to property-owning women, but then kept putting it back. Promises – that's all we ever get. But you know all this, Florrie, I'm sure, if you've read your grandmother's newspapers.'

'Some of it,' Florrie murmured.

'So,' Isobel ended, 'are you willing to do whatever it takes?'

Her fine eyes alight with the fire of battle, Florrie whispered, 'Yes – oh yes, I am.'

Tim lowered his newspaper. 'You do realize, don't you, that involvement with us will more than likely wreck your chances of being presented at court? I mean, are you *really* sure that's not what you want?'

Florrie laughed. 'It's little more than a marriage market. Oh great fun, I'm sure, but no – it's not for me.' She sighed. 'Mother and Father will mind dreadfully, but I don't think Gran will.' She chuckled. 'I doubt she was ever a debutante.' But she said no more about that. She didn't want to divulge her grandmother's secret to anyone, not even to Isobel and Tim, though she had a feeling that the Richards knew all about Augusta's lowly beginnings. The scandal of Nathaniel Maltby marrying his mother's lady's maid must have been talked about at Bixley Manor. 'So, no, it doesn't worry me if "high society" doesn't want to know me.'

'Funnily enough,' Isobel remarked, 'Lady Lee hasn't been ostracized by her aristocratic friends.'

'Not yet,' Timothy murmured and turned a page of his newspaper noisily.

The two young women glanced at each other. He'd not been as deaf to their chatter as they'd thought!

*

'Here we are,' Timothy said, as the train slowed and drew into the London station. 'Get your things together, girls. Now, where's your man, Isobel? He should be here to meet you. Ah, I see him. He'll sort out the luggage from the guard's van. Come along.'

They were caught up in the flurry of travellers alighting from the train and carried along the platform towards the waiting manservant.

'Miss Richards – how nice to see you again.'

'And you, Lambert,' Isobel said. 'Is all well?'

'Yes, miss. I've got a hansom waiting just around the corner for you, miss. The boy's holding the horse. Him an' me'll see to all the luggage an' bring it along later.' His glance went to Florrie.

'Ah yes,' Isobel said. 'Miss Maltby will be staying with me for a while. Her trunk is labelled. And could you take the Hon. Tim's to Lady Smythe's?'

Florrie chuckled inwardly. It seemed that Timothy was known to one and all as 'the Hon. Tim'.

'Very good, miss.'

As Lambert moved away to summon a porter to help him retrieve the luggage from the guard's van, Isobel led Florrie out of the station and round the corner, Timothy following in their wake.

'Good afternoon, Joe,' Isobel greeted the young boy holding the horse's head.

''Af'noon, miss,' he grinned. 'Can I 'elp yer?'

'We're fine. You're doing a grand job there.' She paused and stroked the nose of the patient horse. 'Now, old fellow.'

Then Timothy handed the two young women into the vehicle and squeezed in beside them. They travelled through the busy city streets and came to an elegant terrace of Georgian town houses. The cab halted in front of the tall, narrow house three doors from the end of the street.

'Welcome to number six Chalfont Place,' Isobel cried, climbing down. Lifting her skirt, she went up the steep steps leading to the white-painted front door with its gleaming brass knocker. The door opened and the Richards' town-house butler gave a little bow.

'Welcome home, Miss Isobel,' he murmured.

'Thank you, Meredith.' Isobel stepped into the hall-way and explained at once about her guest.

'Lucy has prepared a guest room, Miss Isobel, and Cook has dinner ready for seven thirty.'

Isobel glanced back at her fiancé standing on the top step. 'Will you join us, Tim?'

'Not tonight. I'll go to my club. Mother is holding a meeting later.' He smiled. 'I'd better make myself scarce.'

Isobel nodded and her eyes sparkled. 'I hadn't for-gotten. I'll see you tomorrow, then.'

Tim nodded, raised his hat in farewell and ran lightly back down the steps.

As Meredith closed the front door, Isobel began to show her guest around. She waved her hand towards two doors directly in front of them. 'That's the morning room, Florrie, and that's the library.' She laughed. 'A grand name for a rather small room that we use as a study, but the walls *are* lined with shelves of books. The drawing room and dining room are on the first floor and the main bedrooms on the second floor. The servants' quarters and kitchens are in the basement through that door.' She indicated a door at the side of the staircase. 'The upper servants' bedrooms are on the third floor and the rest sleep in the attic bedrooms.' She smiled. 'We only keep a skeleton staff here. Just enough to look after me – and any guests, of course. Gervase rarely stays long in town. He's happiest at home. Now, come along upstairs. I'm sure you'll want to freshen up after that train journey . . .'

A few moments later Isobel was flinging open the door to a luxurious bedroom. 'This will be your room. And Lucy – my maid – will look after you too. Now, is there anything you need, my dear?'

'I don't think so, Isobel. It all looks perfect.'

'You'll hear a bit of noise from the street below – even through the night. You'll not be used to that at home.'

Florrie smiled. Far from being disappointed, she felt excited to be here in the hustle and bustle of the city.

'I'll see you at dinner then.'

As the door closed behind Isobel, Florrie looked about her. The bedroom was furnished in the Regency style. In fact, from what she had seen so far, the whole house appeared to be. The bed, perhaps once a four-poster, now merely had a headboard with drapes above it on a pole attached to the wall. The dressing table was satinwood inlaid with ebony and the chest of drawers and wardrobe matched it, as did the cheval mirror standing in the corner.

There was a tap at the door and a young maid peered around it nervously. 'Miss Isobel said I was to ask you if you would like me to unpack for you, Miss Maltby?'

'You must be Lucy?' Florrie smiled at the girl, who nodded. 'No – I'll see to that myself, thank you. But I would like a bath about six, if it's no trouble.'

The young girl smiled and stepped further into the

room. She crossed to a door near the bed. Florrie had presumed it led to a cupboard, but as Lucy opened it, she saw that it was a marble bathroom.

'My very own bathroom,' Florrie exclaimed. 'I hadn't expected that. Thank you, Lucy.'

'I'll come back just before six and run it for you, miss, if . . .'

But Florrie put up her hand. 'Oh, no need. You must have plenty to do.'

'Well, if you're sure, miss. But if you want anything, just press the bell at the side of the bed.'

As she descended the stairs just before seven thirty, Isobel was waiting for her in the hall. Her eyes were sparkling with excitement. 'There's a meeting at Lady Leonora's at nine. Maybe you heard Tim mention it. Would you like to come?'

'Oh yes, please.' Florrie hadn't expected things to start happening so quickly.

Six

At five minutes to nine, after they had dined together seated at one end of the elegant mahogany table, Isobel and Florrie set off with Lucy accompanying them, to walk to the next street running parallel to their own. A maid, who greeted Lucy affectionately and bobbed a curtsy to Isobel, opened the door of Lady Leonora's house.

'None of that tonight, Betsy,' Isobel wagged her forefinger playfully at the young girl. 'We're equals – remember.'

The girl laughed and blushed a little. 'I'll try, Miss Richards.'

They were ushered into a large room.

'This was once used for balls and parties and soirées, but now it's used for our meetings,' Isobel whispered. 'Come, let's find Lady Leonora. She's dying to meet you. I've told her all about you.'

They threaded their way through the room, crowded with chattering women. Florrie looked about her. There were grandly dressed women in silks and satins, sporting huge hats with purple, white and green ostrich feathers. Then there were smartly dressed women who, Florrie guessed, would be the wives or daughters of professional men. Their dress was not so elaborate but nonetheless elegant. And then, just as Isobel had hinted, there were young women dressed in drab garments as if they'd come from the city back streets. All, it seemed, were welcome in Lady Leonora's grand home. Florrie glanced over her shoulder and saw that Lucy was following closely and behind her came Betsy, still in her maid's uniform but quite at home amongst the gathering. Here she was no longer a maid, but a suffragette.

Briefly, Florrie wondered what 'little Beth', as Augusta called her, would make of all this. But her thoughts were interrupted by their arrival in front of Lady Leonora, who stretched out both her hands to Florrie as Isobel made the introduction.

'My dear, I am so very pleased to meet you. And how is your grandmother? I had a letter from her only the other day.'

Florrie's eyes widened. 'From Gran – I mean – Grandmother, Lady Smythe?'

Lady Leonora laughed. She was, just as Isobel had said, a very handsome woman and her son was indeed like her. Her black hair was piled high on her head in the style of a fashionable Edwardian lady and her use of cosmetics was skilful and discreet, yet to her definite advantage. Her exquisite silk gown proclaimed her position in society – a position that she was determined to use to further the cause of her own sex. She leaned towards Florrie and grasped her hands. 'Your grandmother and I are old friends and we write to each other regularly. She knows exactly what you're getting yourself into, my dear. Have no fear on that score. And please – call me Lady Lee. Everyone does.'

If Florrie still had any misgivings about being here, any lingering doubt now fell away. Augusta had given her granddaughter her blessing, knowing, it seemed, far more about the suffragette movement than even Florrie herself knew yet. As she took her seat amongst the other women, she felt the thrill of excitement well up inside her and knew that, despite the unpleasantness with her father and her mother's tears, there was no place she would rather be.

Lady Lee stood on a small dais at one end of the room, waiting until everyone was seated and the gathering fell silent.

'Exciting times are ahead of us,' she began. 'Support for our cause is spreading through the country. Women from the northern towns and cities are conducting their own fight there, but plan to join us on a deputation to the Prime Minister or the Chancellor . . .'

Enthralled, Florrie found herself swept along on a tide of enthusiasm. These women were determined – no matter what – to succeed in their aim. They wouldn't rest until all adult women, whatever their station in life, were granted the right to vote.

'The Reform Bill,' Lady Lee was saying, 'is supposedly making its way – *slowly*,' there was a ripple of laughter, 'through Parliament. It will shortly reach the committee stage, where we understand our supporters among the MPs will press to include the right of the *wives* of voters to vote themselves.' There was a pause and a murmuring.

'This,' Lady Lee declared, 'is not enough. We want the vote for *all* women. It's long been suggested that they might grant the vote to women of standing. For example, women landowners in their own right, who – let us not forget – are obliged to pay taxes.' The murmuring grew. 'Oh yes—' A note of sarcasm laced her tone. 'When it comes to paying taxes into the coffers of the Treasury, there is no problem with being a woman then.' The laughter was louder now. Lady Lee paused until it died down. Now she was utterly serious once more.

'Mrs Pankhurst has written to us all.' She waved a piece of paper in the air. 'I have it here. She asks us to step up our militant activities if, as we fear, we are unsuccessful in adding an amendment on women's suffrage to the Reform Bill. We should know the outcome by the end of January – but we need to be ready. We need to be prepared and we need to be willing to take action.'

Cries of 'We are, we will' resounded through the room and even Florrie found herself raising her fist and joining in.

Lady Leonora glanced around the room and smiled.

'So, what did you think to it?'

They were in the street once more, walking the short distance to the Richards' town house. Lucy, readily resuming her role as maid, walked a deferential few paces behind them. Although it was late by country standards – at home Florrie would have been in bed by this time – the streets seemed as if they never slept. Horses' hooves rang through the night air and even the chug of a motor car sounded in the distance. Hearing it, Isobel murmured, 'Tim plans to get a motor car.'

'Really! Oh, I do hope he'll take me for a ride in it. Father won't entertain the idea of such a noisy mode of transport. He says it'll never replace the horse.' She forbore to add that her father believed the motor car was merely a plaything for the idle rich.

Isobel linked her arm through Florrie's. 'I think he's wrong. Tim says the motor car is the future.'

They walked a few more paces until Isobel prompted, 'So . . . ?'

'It was wonderful,' Florrie breathed. 'I've never felt so – so *alive*!'

'And you're willing to take part in the demonstrations and acts of violence Lady Leonora spoke about?'

'Yes, oh yes. I can't wait to *do* something. Instead of just reading about it, I'm really here and part of it all.'

In the darkness, Isobel smiled, but her joy in the girl's enthusiasm was tinged with anxiety. She wondered if Florrie really understood what it meant to be a suffragette.

No doubt she'd find out soon enough.

Over the next few weeks the two young women attended rallies, marched down Whitehall waving banners, joined a deputation to the Treasury and waited outside the gates of Holloway to greet the release of one of their number.

It was Florrie's first sight of a young woman who'd been imprisoned, had gone on hunger strike and been force-fed. The sight appalled her, yet perversely she found it exhilarating too. These women were so determined to achieve their goal that they'd stop at nothing. They'd suffer the cruellest humiliations to gain their right to vote and she was more determined than ever to be one of them.

Lady Leonora came in a hansom and, as the huge doors opened, the gathering of five or six women – Isobel and Florrie amongst them – hurried towards the young woman emerging into the bright winter's day. They helped her into Lady Leonora's cab and then stepped back as she was borne away to the Smythes' residence to recuperate.

'Will she be all right?' Florrie asked. 'She looked dreadful.'

'I hope so,' Isobel replied grimly. 'But she'll be back as soon as she's fit enough. In the meantime,' her eyes sparkled with excitement, 'we must carry on where she left off.'

Florrie felt a thrill run through her. 'What? What are we going to do?'

'You'll see,' Isobel said mysteriously.

When the debate on the Reform Bill began towards the end of January, there was much heated legal wrangling. The Speaker of the House announced that no amendment on women's suffrage could be added and, only a few days later, the Bill was withdrawn – just as Lady Lee had feared.

'Everything we've worked for,' Lady Lee raged, pacing up and down her drawing room. 'Well, they've asked for it now.'

Florrie and Isobel glanced at each other. Until this moment, they'd only joined in relatively peaceful demonstrations and marches. Now, they must do more. Florrie felt a shiver of fear, and yet excitement too.

'So, what's been planned?'

Lady Lee paused a moment, looking at the eager faces of the two girls before her. They were so young and Florrie was so lovely. She couldn't bear to think of that clear skin and those innocent eyes being ravaged by prison life. She sighed inwardly, telling herself that she couldn't shoulder the responsibility for others, and yet she did feel an obligation to look after the welfare of the members of her 'little band of sisters', as she referred to the group of women who met regularly under her roof.

She sat down, clasping her hands in her lap. 'How are you at breaking windows?'

Isobel laughed. 'With a toffee hammer?' She glanced at Florrie. 'I think we could manage that, don't you?'

Florrie nodded. 'Is that all you want us to do? Nothing – nothing more?'

'Not at the moment. I suggest you try some of the shops in Knightsbridge. Night-time would be best – when the stores are closed. But there are a couple of things you should remember. Firstly, no one, no one at all, must be hurt by your actions. We aim only to damage property, not to injure anyone. And secondly,' she ran her tongue nervously round her lips, 'you will run a greater risk of arrest and – and imprisonment than hitherto.'

The two young women regarded her solemnly. 'We're ready for that,' Florrie said, speaking for them both.

Seven

Late that night, dressed in dark clothing and with a black veil to cover their faces, the two young women set off. Quietly, they opened the front door and crept out.

'We mustn't wake Meredith whatever we do,' Isobel whispered as they closed the door behind them. 'He'd try to stop us. He thinks it his duty to look after me – and you too now. Especially as he knows how much Gervase thinks of you.'

Florrie stopped suddenly halfway down the steps and stared at Isobel through the gloom. '*Meredith* knows?'

Isobel paused and looked up at her from two steps below. 'My dear girl, servants know everything about us. Especially someone like Meredith, who's been with our family for *centuries*!'

Florrie giggled. 'He's not *that* old!'

Isobel tried to stifle her laughter. 'Don't start me off. Someone will hear.'

Nervousness made them want to laugh all the more so that they hurried down the steps and along the street, stuffing their black gloved hands into their mouths. At the corner, they paused and pulled in deep breaths.

'We'll get ourselves arrested for being drunk and disorderly in the street if we're not careful. Now, a little decorum wouldn't come amiss, Miss Maltby, if you please,' Isobel tried to say sternly. 'After all, we're supposed to be in mourning.'

Florrie pulled her face straight and walked with her head bowed dutifully, but every so often a stifled giggle welled up inside her and forced its way out.

'Stop it, Florrie. You'll set me off again. Just concentrate on what we've got to do.'

The thought sobered the girl at once.

It was the first time Florrie had seen the busy streets in the hours of darkness.

'It's deserted,' she said in surprise.

'Not quite. There's always someone about – even if it's only a policeman,' Isobel added, glancing nervously around her. 'Come on, we'd better get on with it or we'll get ourselves arrested for something quite different.'

'What do you mean?'

'Oh nothing, dear.' Isobel hid her smile. 'Right – now this looks a good window to start with. Nice and big. It'll make a lovely mess. Glass all over the clothes displayed in the window. You keep a watch out up and down the street while I . . .'

Isobel stepped towards the huge window, took the little hammer out of her reticule and hit the window. It cracked, but didn't break. She hit it again and this time the whole pane shattered, glass flying everywhere. The sound echoed through the still night.

'Are you all right?' Florrie asked anxiously, afraid that shards of glass might have caught Isobel.

'Yes – yes, I'm fine.' Isobel stepped back and, arm in arm, they hurried away. 'Walk slowly,' she panted. 'It looks more suspicious if we're hurrying.'

After a short distance, they stopped and listened. All was quiet.

'My turn now,' Florrie said, taking a deep breath as she held out her hand for the hammer. She stepped towards the window of another shop and, raising her arm high above her head, brought the hammer down. The glass shattered at once and a splinter hit her forehead just above her left temple. She turned and once more they hurried on, putting as much distance as they could between themselves and the scene of their crime.

They had just broken the eighth window when they heard the sound of a police whistle in the distance.

'Right, that's it for tonight,' Isobel pronounced. 'Throw the hammer away.'

'Throw it away?' Florrie repeated. 'But—'

'We don't want to be caught with it in our possession. Do as I say, just drop it on the ground. Come on, round this corner and into the next street. Now, if we're stopped, our story is that we've just been visiting our dear sister-in-law. We've just lost our brother. If they want names and addresses, we both become too distressed to talk any more. No policeman will want a couple of wailing women to deal with when he has criminals to chase.'

Florrie giggled. They walked and ran a little until they rounded the corner. In a different street, they felt a little safer, and now they bowed their heads and walked on, arm in arm, as if in deep mourning and comforting each other.

Running footsteps sounded in front of them and they held their breath, but continued on slowly and sorrowfully. The policeman took no notice but ran by them, heading for the next street. They walked on, still afraid that any moment they would feel a hand on their shoulder and a gruff voice ordering them to stop. But at last they reached their own street safely and hurried up the steps. Once inside the front door of number six, their legs gave way beneath them and they sank to the floor in the dimly lit hallway, thankful to be home. They threw back their black veils and stared at each other.

'We did it! And without being caught too—' Florrie began triumphantly, but Isobel's eyes were full of concern.

'Oh, my dear, you're hurt. Your forehead's bleeding.'

'Is it?' Florrie put her fingers up to her temple. When she withdrew them, there was a smear of blood on her fingertips. Isobel pulled herself up and held out her hand towards the girl. 'Come, let's bathe it at once. Perhaps it isn't as serious as it looks.'

The cut was tiny, but quite deep. 'It might leave a scar,' Isobel said worriedly.

But Florrie only murmured, 'My first battle wound. Now I'm truly one of you.'

'We never doubted it for a moment,' Isobel said softly.

Two days later their actions were headlines in the newspapers.

'"*Outrageous attacks were perpetrated on Monday night on Knightsbridge shops,*"' Isobel read out over the breakfast table. '"*Nine front windows...*"' She paused and looked up. 'Nine? We only broke eight, didn't we?'

Florrie, her mouth full of kipper, nodded. 'The papers never get things right,' she murmured as Isobel read on.

'"... *together with merchandise displayed therein, were damaged. The work is thought to have been carried out by suffragettes. No one was caught in the act and therefore, as yet, no one has been apprehended for the offence. The police are still making extensive enquiries.*" We were very lucky, you know, to escape,' Isobel said solemnly. 'We could be waking up in a cell this morning.'

Florrie grinned. 'But instead, here we are, eating kippers and planning what we're going to do next.'

Above the newspaper, Isobel eyed her with amusement. 'Got a taste for it now, have we?' Then her face sobered. 'Quite seriously, I think we should lie low for a day or two.'

As they were finishing breakfast, the telephone in the hall shrilled and they heard Meredith's modulated tones answering. 'The Richards' residence.' A silence and then, 'One moment, if you please, sir.' A pause and the door opened.

'Mr Richards is on the telephone, Miss Isobel.'

Isobel leapt up, casting aside the newspaper. 'Oh dear, I hope nothing's wrong.'

As she hurried from the room, Florrie picked up the discarded paper to read the account of their misdeeds for herself. Vaguely, she heard Isobel's side of the conversation.

'Well, yes, it was, actually ... No, we weren't caught. We're quite safe ... Just a little scratch on her forehead, but—' Then her voice became shriller and Florrie listened more attentively. 'She's fine – it's nothing and, no, there's no need for you to come

66

rushing down.' There was another silence before she heard Isobel replacing the handset and returning. As she came into the room, Florrie looked up and noted Isobel's bright eyes and pink cheeks.

'My dear brother is most seriously displeased with me for leading you into danger.' She threw her hands into the air. 'Not a word about *my* safety, mark you. And I was foolish enough to say you had a little scratch and he wanted to come rushing down here at once.'

'But how did he know about the other night?'

'It's reached our papers and he just "*felt*", he said, that it was us. Oh, bother Gervase, he's taken all the fun out of it now. He's made me feel so guilty about you.'

'Well, don't be,' Florrie declared. 'I know exactly what I'm getting myself into. And he's no right to be so – so heavy-handed. It's not as if we're engaged. Now the Hon. Tim, if it was *him* trying to stop you, that'd be different.'

'He wouldn't dare,' Isobel chuckled, reaching for another piece of toast.

Isobel and Florrie remained indoors for several days, but at last they could stand the inactivity no longer, so they walked round to Lady Lee's house to take afternoon tea with her. As they sat sipping tea and eating home-made biscuits, Lady Lee told them, 'Sylvia Pankhurst's in prison and threatening to go on hunger strike and there's something big being planned. I'm not sure what it is yet and we're not involved, but – but it's big.'

'An act of violence, you mean?'

'I – I'm not sure.' Lady Lee seemed evasive and extremely agitated.

Later, as they walked home again, Florrie remarked, 'Do you think she's involved with whatever's going to happen, but didn't want us to know?'

'I'm not sure,' Isobel was thoughtful. 'I'll have a word with the Hon. Tim tonight.'

But Timothy knew no more than they did. 'Mother can be very uncommunicative when she wants to be,' he smiled, putting his arm around Isobel. 'I do hope my *wife* is not going to keep secrets from me.'

Isobel laughed heartily. 'Only when it's for your own good.'

Tim blinked. 'I'm not sure I like the sound of that.' Then his tone sobered. 'I don't suppose you'll have heard yet – it'll be in the news tomorrow. Poor old Captain Scott and two of his fellow explorers have been found dead in a tent returning from the South Pole. They were only ten miles from safety.'

'Oh, that's terrible.' Tears sprang to Isobel's eyes. 'He was such a courageous man.'

For a while news of the tragedy drove all other thoughts out of their minds. But a week or so later another event occurred that was to have repercussions on all their lives. A bomb, allegedly set by Emily Davison and others, severely damaged the unoccupied new house belonging to Lloyd George in Surrey. The following week Mrs Emmeline Pankhurst accepted responsibility and was arrested and charged with the crime.

'Go home, both of you,' Lady Lee urged them. 'They'll be pouncing on anyone involved with the Cause for the merest trifle. Go to the country out of harm's way. Please!'

'But . . .' Both young women tried to protest, but the acknowledged leader of their group was adamant. 'Just for a week or so.'

Eight

On 25th February, the day that Mrs Pankhurst's trial began, the two young women travelled home to Lincolnshire.

'I was hoping to go home for my birthday on the twenty-eighth anyway,' Florrie said. 'But only for a few days,' she added hurriedly, in case Isobel thought she was beginning to lose her commitment to the Cause.

'I suppose Lady Lee's right.' Isobel sighed. 'They're going to be arresting anyone in sight who's sporting the suffragette colours. Perhaps we're better out of the way until things have calmed down a bit. But then,' her eyes sparkled as she clasped Florrie's hand, 'we'll go back.'

'Oh darling,' her mother enveloped Florrie in welcoming arms. 'How glad I am to see you. I've been so lonely. But everything will be all right now you're back home.'

'Mother dearest, I've only come home for my birthday. I – I'm going back again next week.' Mentally, Florrie crossed her fingers, hoping that it would be safe to do so by then.

Clara's face fell and tears welled in her eyes. 'Oh. I – I thought you'd come home for good. I—' She broke off, startled as the door of the morning room was flung open and Edgar strode in.

'Ah, you're back,' he stated unnecessarily.

'Father.' Florrie moved dutifully towards him to kiss his cheek, but before she reached him he said harshly, 'So, we'll have no more of this suffragette nonsense.' Florrie drew in a breath sharply and her eyes widened in surprise as her father nodded grimly. 'Oh yes, their antics have even reached our local newspaper now. And as Miss Richards's name was mentioned, it doesn't take a great leap of imagination to realize that you too have been involved. Well, my girl, it's at an end now. You'll settle down and marry Gervase and we'll say no more about it.'

Florrie stopped and returned her father's glare steadily. 'I'm sorry, Father, but I will not marry Gervase. Not now or ever. And I intend to return to London as soon as I can. I only came home for my birthday on Friday.'

Edgar's face grew purple and the veins in his forehead stood out. For a moment Florrie's heart skipped a beat, afraid that for once she'd gone too far. Stand up to him she might, disobey him she might, but she'd no wish to cause him harm. If he should have a seizure because of her rebelliousness, she'd carry the guilt for the rest of her life.

When he could bring himself to speak, through gritted teeth he muttered, 'Then you can return this instant. You're no longer welcome in my house.'

'Now, now, what is all the shouting about, Edgar?' Augusta said, coming through the open door behind him. 'Ah, the return of the prodigal, I see.' She came towards Florrie, her arms outstretched. 'This is cause for celebration indeed. How long are you staying?'

Florrie cast an uncertain glance at her father. 'Well—'

Edgar gave an angry 'ha-humph', turned and marched

out of the room. Serenely, Augusta seated herself on the couch and patted the seat beside her. 'Sit down and tell us all about it. We want to hear everything you've been doing, don't we, Clara?'

'Yes . . .' Poor Clara wasn't so sure, but she sank back into her chair and took a deep breath as if steeling herself to listen, even though she might find the conversation worrying.

'I've been staying with Isobel, as you know, but I've met all sorts of interesting people. Lady Leonora Smythe, for one.' She paused, eyeing her grandmother before she said more.

Augusta raised her eyebrows. 'Oh – a member of the aristocracy. How exciting!' It seemed that her grandmother still wished to keep her acquaintance with Lady Lee a secret.

'Oh, darling,' for a brief moment Clara's face was animated. 'Did she take you to balls and soirées?' She clasped her hands together in happy expectation that perhaps her wayward daughter's visit to London had been more fruitful than she'd dared to hope. 'Did she introduce you into Society? Would she arrange for you to be presented at court, d'you think? I'm sure your father would forgive you if . . .' Her voice faded away as she caught Augusta's amused expression and her daughter's anxious one.

'Mother—' Florrie bit her lip. 'Lady Leonora is a stalwart of the WSPU.'

'The – the what?'

'The Women's Social and Political Union. It's the organization Mrs Emmeline Pankhurst founded.'

Clara's face fell and she shuddered. 'The suffragettes. Oh dear! I did so hope you might have forgotten all about that. Once you got to London and went to balls

71

and such, I thought . . .' Her voice trailed away in disappointment. She sighed heavily and then asked, 'So – what have you been doing?'

For the next hour, Florrie recounted some of the activities in which she'd been involved. She described the rousing rallies, the meetings where all classes of women met together as if they were of equal rank. She spoke of the MPs and other gentlemen of standing who were sympathetic to their cause, but she omitted – in front of her mother – to mention the more militant acts in which she'd recently taken part. She'd save that for later when she was alone with Augusta.

'Is James coming home for my birthday?'

The two older women exchanged a glance. Clara's eyes filled with tears, but Augusta's mouth pursed with indignation. 'Your father won't allow him to come home during term time and miss his schooling. And for once, I could not sway him.'

Despite the acute disappointment that her beloved brother would not be home for her birthday, Florrie couldn't help but be amused at her grandmother's reaction. She was sure that Augusta's annoyance was caused as much by the fact that she'd lost a battle with her son as by the fact that her grandson would be missing from the celebrations.

'Never mind,' Florrie said gaily. 'We'll just have to have another party during his holidays. I'll be sure to come home again then.' In her mother's hearing she forbore to add the words, 'As long as I'm not in prison.'

On the evening of Florrie's birthday, Augusta insisted that a special dinner should be held in her honour.

'It's her nineteenth birthday, Edgar, and should be

marked with a special occasion. She is no longer a child now, but a young woman.'

'She's not of age yet,' he growled. 'Though she seems to ignore the fact. And you encourage her.'

'Edgar, my dear boy. I was married and carrying you by my nineteenth birthday—'

Her son held up his hand and said loftily, 'I do not wish to be reminded of the fact, Mama.'

Augusta laughed. 'Still ashamed of me, are you? Well, well. We can't change the past, Edgar dear. But we can change the future. And that's just what your lovely daughter is trying to do. She's trying to make the world a better – a fairer – place for women. You should be proud of her, not condemning her and trying to marry her off to the nearest available eligible bachelor. A dear boy though Gervase is, I wouldn't want to see her married to him if she doesn't love him.'

At this point, Edgar felt himself to be losing this particular battle. He glared at her for a moment, turned on his heel and disappeared into his study, slamming the door behind him.

Augusta chuckled, dusted her hands together and murmured, 'That's one to me, I do believe.'

Nine

A few local people, who were considered suitable, were invited to dine with the Maltbys for Florrie's birthday, most notably the Richards and the Hon. Timothy, who was staying at Bixley Manor for a Friday-to-Monday shooting party that Gervase had arranged. Florrie's birthday, falling on the Friday, fitted in very conveniently. And because James was not present, only eleven sat down to dine. The four members of the Maltby family, Gervase, Isobel and Timothy, the local vicar and his wife, the Reverend and Mrs Ponsonby, and two members of Gervase's party, who were also acquaintances of Edgar.

George Jervis was a portly, bewhiskered and jovial gentleman. In his early sixties, Florrie surmised. He was the local MP. The other guest, Henry Davenport, was a magistrate. Tall and thin – a little younger than Mr Jervis – he was very serious-looking, with a long nose and pale eyes behind the thick lenses of his spectacles.

'Thank goodness he has no jurisdiction in London or we might find ourselves clapped in irons before the evening's out,' Isobel whispered.

Florrie's eyes narrowed thoughtfully. 'Mm. It's not him I'm interested in. Mr Jervis, now – I think a conversation with him might be a good idea. What d'you think, Iso?'

'I wouldn't want to offend your father, not when I'm a guest at his table, Florrie.'

The younger girl's brown eyes were full of mischief. 'Well, I'm not a guest, now am I?'

Isobel chuckled. 'No, you're not, but on your head be it, my girl.'

Florrie bided her time. She was the epitome of politeness and correctness throughout the meal. She knew she'd have to hold her tongue during the stilted conversation around the dinner table, and during the inane gossip when the ladies retired to the drawing room and left the men to their port, as was the custom at Candlethorpe Hall. It was afterwards, when the men rejoined them, that she hoped the evening would become livelier. But, whilst the courses were served by Bowler and the first housemaid, Florrie was pleasantly surprised to find that the vicar's wife was, if not an active member, an ardent supporter in theory of the suffragette movement. The Reverend Horace Ponsonby was new to Candlethorpe village. His formal induction had taken place only the previous month, and Edgar had decreed that this relatively small dinner party would be an ideal opportunity to invite the new incumbent and his wife to the Hall.

'If I was your age, my dear,' Mrs Ponsonby said in a high-pitched tone, addressing Florrie, 'I'd be marching with banners with the rest of them and pounding on the doors of the House of Commons. It's high time we had a woman MP.' She cast a meaningful look down the table. 'What say you, Mr Jervis?'

George Jervis stroked his moustache. He was thoughtful for a moment, considering. He cleared his throat. 'It would rather depend, dear lady, on who was elected. They'd need to be very thick-skinned to withstand the ribaldry of the Commons.' He chuckled. 'We're rather a childish lot at times. The Chamber seems like a public schoolboys' common room on occasions.'

'That's why you have a Speaker, isn't it?' Henry Davenport put in mildly. 'To keep order.' The man had been rather quiet until this moment, only speaking when spoken to, but now he joined in the conversation of his own accord.

'Very true,' George Jervis agreed.

Ignoring a warning glare from her father, Florrie leaned forward. 'Are you in favour of women entering Parliament, Mr Jervis? In principle, at least?'

Again, he was thoughtful. 'In principle, yes, but like I say, it would need a very special character. A woman with enough years of experience.' He glanced at her and smiled. 'It would not, I'm afraid, my dear, be a job for a *young* woman. She would need to be a strong-minded, determined and ambitious woman, who'd probably have to be prepared to sacrifice a great deal in her personal life. And, of course, until you get the vote . . .' He spread his hands helplessly.

Mrs Ponsonby turned her wide, toothy smile upon Augusta. 'I've been hearing a lot about you, Mrs Maltby, since we've been living at the Vicarage. It seems to me that you'd make an excellent MP.'

At the end of the table, Edgar spluttered and for a moment everyone thought he'd choked on a fish bone.

When he'd recovered, Mrs Ponsonby continued as if uninterrupted. Leaning forward she said in a stage whisper, 'And are the tales of your birth and upbringing true, my dear? An elopement with the young master from this very house.' She clapped her hands in delicious delight. 'How romantic!'

At the end of the table Edgar turned purple, whilst Clara gave a little flutter of alarm and looked as if she might faint at any moment.

Catching sight of their hosts' obvious displeasure, the Reverend Ponsonby put his hand on his wife's arm. 'Matilda, my dear, this is neither the time nor the place to bring up such a topic. You are being very indiscreet.'

His wife turned her wide eyes on him, 'But, Horace, dear, it is so intriguing, so utterly enchanting. I—' She turned to look at Augusta. 'I would think your family is so proud to have such a story in their family history. I know *I* would be.'

Stifling her laughter, Florrie looked at her grandmother to see that she was having a similar difficulty. Augusta cleared her throat. 'Thank you for your compliment, Mrs Ponsonby, but I'm afraid my son does not view my lowly beginnings in that same light.'

'Oh, but *why*?' Now the good lady turned her guileless eyes upon Edgar. 'Mr Maltby, how can you not recognize such romance, such – such—' She sought for the word. 'Such *honesty* in a time of "arranged" marriages? I applaud your dear father for being a loyal and upright young man – I really do.'

Edgar flinched visibly. 'You are entitled to your opinion, madam,' he said stiffly. The remainder of the meal continued with stilted conversation until Edgar was able to motion to Clara that she should lead the ladies from the room. She rose swiftly at his bidding and almost scuttled out, relieved to be escaping. Personally, she didn't mind what Mrs Ponsonby – or anyone else for that matter – said about the family, just so long as it wasn't in her husband's hearing.

'Oh dear,' Matilda Ponsonby said as they crossed the hall, 'I seem to have upset Mr Maltby. I *am* so sorry. I didn't mean to offend.' Now she looked genuinely distressed, and Florrie moved to take her arm and say, 'Don't worry, Mrs Ponsonby', whilst Augusta replied mildly, 'Think no more of it, my dear. My background is an irrefutable fact and it's high time my son came to accept it.'

As they seated themselves in the drawing room and Clara began to pour the coffee with a hand that still shook, Matilda asked, 'And did you live "happily ever after"?'

For a moment, Augusta's eyes misted over. Her voice was a little unsteady as she replied, 'Yes, we did.' Florrie glanced at her anxiously. It was quite unlike her spirited grandmother to betray any sign of emotion, especially in front of someone outside the immediate family circle.

'Ah,' Matilda gave a satisfied smile. 'Then that vindicates your – and his – action, does it not?'

'I'd never thought of it quite like that, Mrs Ponsonby,' Augusta said slowly, her head on one side reflectively. 'But you're quite right. We did live happily for almost forty-two years until his death ten years ago.' Augusta bowed her head and gave a small, sad smile.

Realizing that she was indeed now treading on delicate ground – she was not, it seemed, completely devoid of tact – Matilda turned to Florrie and changed the subject. 'As I was saying earlier, my dear, I so admire these women who are seeking emancipation for us all. How I'd love to join them! Horace and I have come from Manchester to this area, you know. He felt his calling late in life and is only recently ordained. This is his first ministry.'

'How did you come to choose this area?' Clara felt sufficiently recovered to join in the conversation.

'It was for my health,' Matilda put her hand on her large bosom. 'I have chest problems and my doctor in Manchester believed the East Coast air would be good for me.' She paused and then added proudly, 'Mrs Pankhurst is from Manchester, you know. She and her two daughters are doing so much to further the cause of women. One sees so much poverty and hardship in the cities and the women—' She threw up her hands in despair. 'They're so *downtrodden*. No – I don't care what anyone says – Mrs Pankhurst is doing her very best to elevate the position of *all* women in society and I, for one, applaud her. I've met her, you know, and her two daughters.' She raised her cup delicately to her lips and took a sip. 'Of course, I'm not sure I agree with their acts of violence. This recent act, bombing Lloyd George's new house.' She shook her head. 'No one got hurt – this time – thankfully, but if they're not careful . . .'

Florrie was about to open her mouth to protest, but she caught her grandmother's eye and the slight shake of her head. Instead Augusta herself said, 'Well, I have to admit I follow the activities of the WSPU very closely.' Clara's eyes widened, but her mother-in-law continued serenely, 'And as I understand it, they're always careful that the properties are unoccupied.'

'Yes,' Mrs Ponsonby nodded. 'That's what I understood too, but on this occasion workmen were due to start work only minutes after the explosion occurred. That was running it a bit fine, don't you think?'

Now Augusta could say nothing.

Florrie and Isobel said little, not wanting to give anything away about their own involvement in militant activities. They merely listened to Matilda's prattle and waited with increasing impatience for the men to join

79

them, but it was a very long time before Edgar led them into the drawing room.

When Bowler had brought fresh coffee, Florrie and Isobel descended upon the MP. Coming straight to the point, as they sat down one on either side of him, Isobel asked candidly, 'So – you do have some sympathy with the emancipation of women, Mr Jervis? Do you intend to support the Cause openly?'

He set his cup down carefully on the nearby sofa table and glanced at each of them in turn. He linked his fingers together across his paunch and smiled. 'I must admit, I was most disappointed when the Reform Bill was thrown out.'

The two young women exchanged a glance. This was more than they'd dared to hope for.

Adopting her friend's directness, Florrie said, 'Is there anything you are willing to do to help us?'

George Jervis stroked his moustache thoughtfully. '*Us*, you say?' He smiled. 'Do I take it that you two young women are – involved?'

Florrie and Isobel looked at each other and then nodded. There was no point now in hiding their allegiance.

'Ah, I thought as much.' He was silent for a moment before he said slowly, 'There's a group of us – small at present, I'm afraid – who support the principle, but it's not easy. There's still a lot of opposition and—' He shrugged with a gesture of helplessness. 'I'm not sure these militant acts are furthering your Cause.' He chuckled and glanced at them again in turn. 'I do read the newspapers and if I'm not mistaken, you, young lady,' his gaze rested on Isobel, 'were "mentioned in dispatches" recently.' Now he looked across at Henry Davenport seated close by. He rumbled with laughter. 'Just be careful you don't get hauled up in front of old Davenport here.'

The other man's serious face lightened a little. 'Actually, Jervis, old fellow, you're wrong. I've a lot of sympathy with the Movement.' He cleared his throat and smiled wryly. 'My own sister in Leeds is actively involved. She was one of the women who travelled to London at the end of January to take part in a deputation to Lloyd George at the Treasury. Perhaps you read about it?'

Now Isobel and Florrie burst into laughter.

'Heard about it?' Isobel spluttered.

'We were there,' Florrie added, wiping tears from her eyes.

'In fact,' Isobel went on, 'two of the women stayed overnight with Lady Lee—' She waved her hand towards her fiancé. 'The Hon. Tim's mother.'

'Ah, yes,' Mr Jervis nodded. 'Lady Leonora. I know of her.'

They talked, quite animatedly at times, for the rest of the evening until the guests – other than the Richards family – departed at eleven.

'Wasn't that wonderful?' Florrie clapped her hands. 'I never dreamed our own MP would be so sympathetic to the Cause.'

'And Mr Davenport too. Did you hear him say he thought the courts were dealing too harshly with us?'

As the front door closed behind the departing guests, Gervase drew Florrie to one side. Clara and Augusta exchanged a glance and returned to the drawing room to sit with Isobel and Timothy until Gervase was ready to leave. With a disgruntled 'ha-humph' at the events of the evening, Edgar retired to his study and slammed the door, but not before he'd cast a meaningful glance at his daughter.

Florrie sighed and linked her arm through Gervase's, leading him into the dimly lit morning room. 'Let's get it over with then,' she murmured.

Gervase chuckled softly. 'If you think I'm going to propose to you again, miss, then you're sadly mistaken.'

Florrie stared at him, wide-eyed, her mouth dropping open. 'Oh!' She let out a sigh of relief and murmured, 'Well, thank goodness for that.'

'I told you – every New Year's Eve.'

Florrie grimaced comically. 'Thanks for the warning. I'll make sure I'm not around.'

'Oh, I'll find you. Wherever you are each New Year's Eve – I'll find you.'

Florrie sighed dramatically. Nothing, it seemed, was ever going to deter Gervase from his annual proposal. Not unless, of course, she were to marry someone else. That might stop him, she thought. But, strangely, the thought of marrying at all was unimaginable.

'No, tonight,' he was saying, 'I just wanted to give you my birthday gift in private. I thought it more – discreet.' He chuckled. 'More than can be said for the redoubtable Mrs Ponsonby.'

Florrie laughed with him. 'She's certainly a character, isn't she? She'll liven up the people of Candlethorpe, I've no doubt.'

Gervase took a small box from his pocket and handed it to her. 'With my love,' he said simply.

Despite his denial, for a moment she thought he was giving her a ring with all its implications, but when she opened the lid she saw a brooch nestling in the black velvet lining of the box. Set in silver, the central stone was purple with alternating green and white gems around it.

'Oh Gervase – it's beautiful. And in the suffragette colours too.' She looked up at him and whispered, 'I'll wear it always.'

'I hope it keeps you safe, my love.' He gazed at her for a long moment before giving a little sigh and rising to his feet. 'It's late. We should go.'

Florrie rose too, then reached up and kissed his cheek. 'Dearest Gervase – thank you.'

Ten

Isobel and Florrie returned to London towards the end of the following week to learn from Lady Lee that, over the weekend, a peaceful meeting of suffragettes in Hyde Park had been disrupted by mobs and mud had been thrown at the speakers.

'Is public opinion turning against us, d'you think?' Isobel asked.

Lady Lee shrugged and sighed. 'It's always been against us. Sadly, I still think our opponents outweigh our supporters. Still.' She brightened. 'It's certainly getting our Cause noticed. There are items in the press about us almost every day. Now, are you both game for something a little more than smashing shop windows?'

The two young women glanced at each other and chorused, 'Of course.'

'There's something else you should know,' Lady Lee said. 'There's talk of a Bill being rushed through Parliament now called the Prisoners' Temporary Discharge for Ill-Health Bill. It's been suggested before, but now it looks as if they're really going to do it.'

'What does it mean?' Isobel frowned.

'Hunger strikers in jail will be released when their health deteriorates. When they're sufficiently recovered, they'll be rearrested. It's being referred to already as the Cat-and-Mouse Act.'

'Very appropriate,' Isobel said wryly.

Over the next few weeks Isobel and Florrie took part in several acts of violence. They smashed windows, dug up four greens on a golf course and set an explosive device in a cricket pavilion.

'There's a job for just one of you,' Lady Lee glanced from Isobel to Florrie and back again. 'We want you to attack paintings in the National Gallery.'

'I'll do it,' Florrie said at once. 'What do I have to do?'

'Take a sharp knife hidden in your reticule and don't draw attention to yourself. Don't wear our colours – not even your brooch on this occasion, my dear – or it's likely you won't get beyond the door.'

Florrie nodded, her eyes afire with excitement. At last, she was being allowed to do something on her own without Isobel to nursemaid her.

She dressed with care in demure white, with a broad-brimmed hat decorated with white ostrich feathers. In her silk reticule she carried a sharp, pointed knife. Her heart was beating fast as she passed through the door of the gallery and wandered through the rooms, looking pure and innocent in her white gown.

She chose the room where there were several large paintings and sat down on a seat in the centre of the room, pretending to rest whilst she admired the works of art. In truth, she was waiting until she was alone.

Her heart beat even faster and bile rose in her throat as, slowly, she withdrew the knife, stood up and strode towards one of the pictures. She raised her knife and slashed at the canvas – once, twice, three times – before a cry behind her made her turn to see one of the gallery's officials running towards her.

'Hey, stop that!'

She turned to face him, the knife pointing threateningly at him. The man stopped a few feet from her and held out his hands. 'Now then, lady, no need for that. I ain't goin' to hurt you.'

'And I'm not going to hurt you. We don't hurt people, just – things.' She lowered the knife.

His face cleared. 'Oh, you're one of them suffragettes, are you?' He paused and looked her up and down, but not in an offensive manner. 'You're far too pretty, love, to be involved with them mad women.'

'We're not mad. We're just determined to get the vote.'

'Women voting? You *are* mad. It'll never happen . . .' At that moment, another official came running into the room followed by a policeman. The first man held out his hand warningly. 'She's got a knife.'

'I told you – I'm not going to hurt anyone.' She held out the knife, turning it in her gloved hand so that she held the blade and the handle was towards her captors. The constable inched forward, his gaze fixed on the knife. Gingerly, he took it from her grasp. 'Now then, miss, you'd best come quietly.'

Florrie bestowed her most winning smile on him. 'Gladly, officer.'

When Florrie didn't return home that afternoon, Isobel, who'd waited nervously all day, hurried round to Lady Lee's. Timothy was at home too.

'She's not come back. Do you think she's been arrested?'

'I'll find out,' Timothy said at once. He kissed his fiancée's cheek hurriedly and squeezed her hands. 'You stay here with Mother. Try not to worry . . .' And he was gone.

The two women sat in silence, but now and then they paced the room agitatedly. 'I should never have let her do it,' Isobel moaned. 'Gervase will kill me.'

'That girl has a mind of her own. She's only young, but she's strong and determined,' Lady Lee declared, confidence and admiration in her tone. 'We'll get the vote – I don't know when – but with her sort on our side, we'll get it one day.'

It was two hours before Timothy returned. Two hours in which Isobel had gone through all sorts of horrors in her mind, imagining what might have happened to her friend.

'She was caught slashing a painting in the National Gallery. I presume you two both knew about this?' He eyed them suspiciously, but then continued without waiting for an answer. 'She's been arrested and will appear in court tomorrow.'

'We'll be there,' both women chorused.

The following morning, the three of them took a hansom cab to the courtroom and were seated in the gallery when Florrie was brought up from the cells. She glanced around and caught sight of them, smiled and waved.

'She – she looks all right,' Isobel murmured.

Lady Lee laughed softly. 'She's positively glowing. I think this is what she's been wanting. To be arrested and have her day in court.'

The court procedure commenced, and at last the moment came when Florrie was asked if she'd anything to say for herself.

She smiled up at the magistrate and said, 'Indeed I do, Your Worship. I'm truly sorry for damaging a valuable painting—'

Shocked, Isobel drew in a breath. Was Florrie so easily cowed? She'd never have believed it. But the girl's next words swept away any doubts.

'But my action was regrettably necessary,' Florrie went on. 'Until the right to vote has been granted to women – *all* women – we shall continue to commit whatever acts we deem appropriate to bring this about.'

The magistrate (for once a benevolent gentleman) looked at her over the top of his spectacles. 'And do you think,' he said in a sonorous tone, 'that such acts as the one perpetrated by you yesterday, and other outrages against property and possessions, are going to get you the vote?'

'We've tried peaceful tactics and they haven't worked. We've been driven to this.'

'Don't you think this sort of militant action will damage your Cause rather than help to further it?'

In the gallery, Lady Lee gripped Isobel's arm and whispered, 'If only it was Mrs Pankhurst standing there. This is the first time I've ever known a magistrate at least show an interest, if not exactly sympathy. If only it wasn't Florrie there. She's far too young to be able to put our case across effectively.'

'Oh, I don't know,' Isobel murmured. 'She's not doing too badly.'

The girl was still speaking, holding the courtroom in thrall. Even the hard-hearted police officers standing around the room were at least listening to her words.

'We're in the twentieth century now. It is a time of change and a time *for* change. All men and women should be allowed to have a say in matters which affect their lives. Women are going to university, gaining degrees, becoming doctors and scientists and teachers. Do you really think they should not be given the vote? And women who are landowners – they pay taxes just like the men, so why shouldn't they have some say in how their money is used by the government?'

'What about the mass of uneducated women who wouldn't know what they were voting for?' the magistrate countered. 'There are still a great many who can neither read nor write.'

'He's really a most unusual man,' Lady Lee murmured.

Florrie was smiling impishly at him, 'Your Worship, they only have to put a cross to vote.'

The court erupted in laughter, and in the gallery Lady Lee, Isobel and Timothy cheered loudly. Even the magistrate covered his mouth with his hand, but his eyes sparkled with amusement. As the noise died down, he said soberly, 'The fact remains that you have committed a wilful act of destruction and I have no choice but to send you to prison for a term of twenty-eight days.'

There was a murmur around the courtroom and a shuffling as the onlookers believed that to be the end of the matter, but the magistrate wasn't finished yet. 'And a fine of fifty pounds towards the cost of the restoration of the painting by an expert.'

Then he rose and left the court, whilst a warder grabbed Florrie by the arm and led her down the steps back to the cells, but not before she'd given a cheery wave to her three friends in the gallery.

'Well, it could have been a lot worse,' Lady Lee said as they arrived back home and she rang the bell in her morning room for tea to be served.

'It's bad enough.' Isobel was still anxious. 'Gervase will get to hear of it for sure. Florrie's "speech" will make headlines.'

'Wasn't it splendid? And from one so young too. Oh, she'll deserve our medal when she comes out, for there's no doubt she'll go on hunger strike.'

'Oh, don't,' Isobel groaned and covered her face.

Eleven

It was dark by the time Florrie was led from the cell and pushed roughly into the prison van, along with three other suffragettes arrested and sentenced on the same day. A small crowd had waited outside the court and pressed forward as the four women appeared.

A voice rang through the night air. 'Take heart, girl. Be strong.'

'Thank you . . .' Florrie tried to shout back, but her voice was only a whisper and, before she could say more, she was in the vehicle and being shoved into a tiny compartment, locked away from the others. The vehicle bumped over the rough road and Florrie was thrown from side to side. By the time it stopped outside the ominous high walls of Holloway women's prison, she felt battered and bruised. The prisoners were led along cold, dimly lit corridors, through heavy doors that clanged shut behind them with a terrifying finality. The four women were shut in a cubicle together. There was nowhere to sit, nowhere to lie down except on the stone floor. They squatted against the wall, huddling together for warmth.

'What will happen to us?' Florrie murmured.

'This your first time, dear?' The woman next to her spoke kindly.

'Yes,' Florrie answered, trying to keep her voice steady.

The woman put her arm about Florrie and drew her close. 'All new to you, ducks, is it? Well, they'll leave us here till morning, by which time they hope the damp and the cold will have broken our spirit and made us see the error of our ways.' She chuckled. 'No chance of that, I'm afraid. We're all old hands at this game. It isn't pleasant, dear. I won't lie to you. But our sufferings won't go unnoticed. You can bank on those outside to see to that.' The woman ran her fingers gently along Florrie's cheek. 'You're very young, my dear, and far too lovely to be in this awful place. Who are you with?'

'How – how do you mean?'

'Who introduced you to the Cause?'

Florrie hesitated. She wasn't sure whether it was wise to give names to strangers. This was such an alien world to her. She was no longer sure what was right or wrong. If anyone had told her only a few months ago that she'd have taken part in an act of violence, she'd have told them they'd lost their senses. Yet now, here she was in prison for having committed a criminal act.

'A friend, I . . .' She hesitated again.

The woman's chuckle came out of the darkness. 'It's all right. You're among friends. They haven't yet thought of planting spies amongst us.' She laughed again and the other women joined in. 'They're very slow – these men.'

'I think I know you.' One of the other women spoke up for the first time. 'You're with Lady Leonora and Isobel Richards, aren't you?'

There was no point in trying to hold back the truth now. 'Yes – yes, I am.'

'I saw you at one of Lady Lee's meetings a few—'

What more she might have said, Florrie didn't know and was never to know, for at that moment the door was opened with a rattle of keys and a wardress shouted for them to come out. They stumbled after her, their limbs cramped and cold, as she led them to a room where a doctor waited to give them a cursory examination and pronounce them fit enough for their sentence to be carried out. Then they were led to a room where they were made to discard all their own clothes and dress in a rough cotton chemise. Their clothing and belongings were handed to an officer and carried away. For the next few hours they were harried and pushed here and there. There was another examination by an officer, this time more of a bodily search than for medical reasons. They were taken to the dingy bathroom and told to step into almost cold water and then dress in some clothing heaped on the floor. Shivering, the four women sorted through the coarse green garments, picking out chemises and drawers, skirts and bodices and thick woollen stockings. Most of the items, drab and shapeless, were marked with arrows. There was no escaping where they were and what they were. Next they scrambled for shoes, but amongst the heap, Florrie couldn't find a matching pair. One shoe pinched her toes; the other – far too big – flapped as she walked.

'Be quick!' the wardress snapped. 'You're not going to a garden party at the Palace.'

Lastly, they were each given a white cap, which tied with strings under the chin, an apron and a handkerchief. Then the four prisoners were marched through the forbidding building, through heavy doors and along dismal corridors to the cells. Provided with a Bible and a hymn book, Florrie was at last alone in her cell. The room, about seven feet by five, had a stone floor and a tiny barred window near the ceiling that would give little light even in the daytime. But there was a gas light, behind a pane of glass in an opening in the wall, which was lit from the corridor.

Resting against the wall was a plank bed, which was lowered to the floor at night. The mattress and blankets were rolled up in one corner, with a pillow and a small, almost threadbare towel on top. There was a small tin washbasin, a slop pail, a dustpan and brush and a stool. On the table beneath the gas light was a well-used wooden spoon, a pint-sized tin vessel, a tin plate, a piece of hard soap and a small scrubbing brush, a comb and some cards listing the prison rules and prayers. Florrie glanced about her, taking in the grim place that was to be her 'home' for the next four weeks. The last thing she noticed was a prisoner's badge: a circle of yellow cloth with the number of the cell – fourteen – printed on it.

'Make your bed quickly,' had been the last words the wardress said to her. 'Lights out in ten minutes.'

Florrie moved stiffly to the plank bed and pulled it down into position, then unrolled the mattress and laid it on top of the rough boards. She was reaching for the blankets when the cell was plunged into darkness.

'Hey,' she shouted. 'I'm not ready. Put that light back on.'

But, of course, there was no response.

Feeling about in the blackness, she managed to make the bed after a fashion and almost laughed aloud to think that the first bed she'd ever made for herself was in Holloway jail! The surge of amusement raised her spirits and she huddled, fully clothed, on the hard mattress, with a lingering smile on her lips. Surprisingly, sleep claimed her at once and she slept soundly through the night until the early-morning banging on the door of her cell woke her.

Florrie refused to eat from the very first day. She left untouched the food that was pushed into her cell, though she drank the water. Days passed – almost two weeks – and then the moment came that she'd been dreading and yet, with some perverse pleasure, welcomed. At last, she would really prove herself to her fellow suffragettes.

She heard the ominous sound of the footsteps of several people coming along the landing. They stopped outside her cell. A key rattled in the lock and the door swung open. She saw the wardresses, four or five of them, and two doctors. One was carrying a long tube with a funnel at one end, the other a jug of liquid. Her heart missed a beat as they all crowded into the cell.

'One moment.' The elder of the two doctors spoke in a booming voice. 'Young woman, you have refused all food and drink, save water, for twelve days now. Do you intend to continue this ridiculous hunger strike?'

Florrie gazed up at him. 'I do,' she said quietly and firmly, though her insides trembled at the thought of what her refusal would bring about.

'Very well then. You leave us no alternative.' The wardresses advanced towards her. Two grasped her arms and two more her legs. They wrapped a towel around her and dragged her to lie flat on the bed, and held her down. One wardress clamped Florrie's mouth shut whilst the doctor inserted the end of the tube into her left nostril. Her eyes began to water. The pain was excruciating as the tube was pushed in further and further. She was aware of a burning sensation and her ears felt as if they were going to burst. Pain welled in her chest. But struggling was futile against the six of them.

One of the doctors stood on the stool above her and the other handed him the jug of liquid. 'It's a mixture of milk and egg, young woman. If you do not value your own life, I am sure there are others who do. We won't let you die in our custody.'

Florrie made a gurgling noise, longing to shout at him, 'You stupid old man. I'm young and fit. I could survive for weeks on water alone.' But she couldn't speak; she couldn't say a word in protest. As the liquid was poured into the funnel and down the tube, her right nostril was pinched so that now she had no way of breathing. She began to struggle, feeling she was going to suffocate, but the four wardresses were too strong for her. As she fought for breath, the liquid was sucked up her nose and down her throat.

At last it was over as the tube was withdrawn. The rough hands that had held her down released their grip. Slowly, Florrie sat up, retching and spitting. She felt dizzy and sick and her chest heaved painfully. One of the doctors checked her pulse. He nodded and they all trooped out of the cell, leaving Florrie to fall back on her bed and shed tears of humiliation and remorse at what she felt to be the failure of her hunger strike.

The dreadful force-feeding went on for several days until Florrie was exhausted and in constant pain. She was lying on her bed, where she now spent most of her time, only dimly aware that someone she thought to be one of the doctors was standing over her. There were other figures behind him. Any moment now, it would begin again. She tried to brace herself for the rough handling once more, but she was too weary and dispirited to care. She closed her eyes as she felt a hand on her forehead. But this man's touch was gentle and the arms that raised her up were strong and caring. And then she heard a voice she knew. No, no, it couldn't be. He couldn't be here.

'How is she?'

'Not good. We must get her out of here as quickly as possible.'

'What must I do? Who do I have to see?'

'Leave it with me. I'll see my colleagues. You stay here with her, if they'll let you.'

'They'll have to drag me out by force,' he said. 'And I might just put up a little more resistance than a defenceless woman.'

The doctor chuckled as he turned away. 'I'll be as quick as I can.'

The heavy door was left swinging open and, though Florrie was dimly aware of a wardress standing at the door and saying loudly, 'This is most irregular', no attempt was made to remove her visitor.

'Gervase,' she croaked. 'Is it really you?'

'Yes, my darling, it is. I've come to take you home.'

Florrie rested her head against his shoulder and wept tears of exhaustion and relief. She'd stood it all, she'd not given in of her own accord, but now she was thankful to let Gervase take control. She couldn't remember ever being so pleased to see anyone in her life as she was at this moment.

Twelve

Florrie drifted in and out of consciousness over the next few hours. She was aware of being lifted and carried, of being in a hansom cab and finally of being put to bed in the Richards' town house.

Isobel sat beside her, spooning nourishing soup into her sore mouth, washing her from head to toe with gentle hands. But she was aware too of angry whispers between the brother and sister.

'As soon as she's strong enough, I'm taking her home.'

'You can't do that, Gervase. What will her father say – and do?'

'I don't care. She can stay at Bixley Manor.'

'He won't like that either, if he gets to hear of it. Unchaperoned, her reputation will be in tatters.'

'I don't give a fig about her reputation. There's not much of it left, after this fiasco you've involved her in.'

'Oh, my fault, is it?'

'Well, isn't it? If you hadn't brought her to London, she'd never have become caught up in all this nonsense.'

'Nonsense now, is it? Just because it's *Florrie*—'

But he cut her short, saying, 'Isobel, you know I've never agreed with the use of violence. I don't think it does your Cause justice. In fact, I think it hinders it.'

Florrie waited for Isobel's heated reply, but none came.

*

After a few days of Isobel's tender care, Florrie was well enough to travel. They were driven to the station and Gervase carried her aboard the train.

'I hardly need to tell you to take care of her, do I?' Isobel tried to be light-hearted, but Gervase was not amused.

'You do not,' he remarked curtly as he set Florrie down gently in a corner seat and turned back to his sister.

'Meredith's organizing her trunk into the guard's van.' Isobel stood on the platform looking up at him. 'I'm sorry, Gervase.'

He softened a little and sighed. 'You do understand, if it's in my power to stop her, she won't be coming back again.'

'She may have to,' Isobel said. 'She hasn't completed her sentence.'

'Bugger her sentence,' he muttered. Slamming the carriage door, he turned his back on his sister. He didn't even wave to her as the train drew out of the station.

Florrie didn't think she'd ever seen Gervase so angry. He sat stiffly beside her in the compartment, his gaze on the countryside passing by the window.

She was thankful not to have to converse. Feeling weak and ill, Florrie huddled into the corner of the seat, wrapping the warm rug around her. She closed her eyes and dozed fitfully. In her exhausted state, even the noise of the train and the arrival and departure of other passengers couldn't keep her fully awake. But her rest was disturbed by dreams – unpleasant dreams that bordered on the nightmarish. They were holding her down, shaking her, and the doctor was advancing menacingly towards her, that awful tube in his hand . . .

She awoke with a little cry of terror to find Gervase's hands on her shoulders, gently shaking her awake.

'We're here. Bates is waiting for us with the carriage,' he said and added harshly, 'You'd better stay at Bixley Manor. I can hardly take you home in this state.'

Florrie blinked up at him. His face was partially in shadow, yet she could see the anger in his eyes. And there was something else too. A dreadful fear. 'My dear sister has a lot to answer for.'

He carried her off the train whilst his coachman, Bates, hovered anxiously.

'Organize the luggage, Bates, if you would.'

Gervase lifted her into the carriage and then climbed in beside her. With a sigh she settled back against the cushions and slept fitfully until she felt herself being lifted out once more and carried up the steps and into the house.

The Richards' housekeeper, Mrs Forrest, took charge at once, and soon Florrie was tucked up in bed in one of the guest rooms, a fire roaring in the grate and a maid tiptoeing in and out and watching over her.

She slept for the next few hours. She was dimly aware of a man leaning over her and touching her with cold fingers. She moved restlessly, trying to push away the hands, fearing their intention. Later, she learned it had been the local doctor summoned by Gervase. When, finally, she opened her eyes and recognized her surroundings, she turned to see Augusta sitting beside the bed.

'Gran . . .' Her voice was a weak croak.

Augusta took her hand. 'Just rest, my dear. Don't try to talk. Not yet.'

But there was one question Florrie had to ask her. 'Are you – very angry with me?'

'Angry?' There was surprise in her grandmother's tone. 'Good Heavens, child, whatever gave you that idea?'

'Gervase is. He's – disgusted.'

Augusta patted her hand. 'Dear girl, Gervase is helplessly in love with you. You know that. He's frightened out of his mind for you, that's all. As we all are. But some of us are proud of you too. Very proud. Well – at least *I* am.'

'Really?' Florrie whispered.

'Of course.' Augusta was adamant.

'And the violence? The – the painting I damaged?'

Augusta sniffed. 'Regrettable, but necessary.'

Florrie relaxed and closed her eyes. Now she slept peacefully, her thin hand resting gratefully in Augusta's comforting grasp. The older woman watched over her, refusing to leave her granddaughter's side until she showed definite signs of recovery. At last, Gervase was able to persuade the older woman to take some rest.

'We'll have you ill next,' he said firmly. 'The maid has prepared the room next to Florrie's, and Beth has brought your things from the Hall.'

Augusta rose stiffly from her vigil at Florrie's bedside and followed Gervase downstairs to the drawing room, where afternoon tea awaited them both. 'She seems a little better. She took some soup earlier, though I fear her throat is still very sore. What barbarians the authorities are! And to think, when she's well enough she will have to endure it all again, until she finishes her sentence. They'll play cat-and-mouse with her, just like the nickname for their wretched Act implies.'

Gervase's face was grim. 'Not if I can help it. I intend to keep her hidden. No one knows she is here, except

Isobel and my staff. And they will say nothing if they value their jobs.'

Augusta glanced up at him. For the first time in days, amusement sparkled in her eyes. 'You'd really defy the law?'

He returned her gaze steadily. 'I'd do anything – *anything* – to keep her safe. You should know that.'

'Oh, I do – I do. But she thinks you're very angry with her. "Disgusted" was the word she used.'

His mouth was a tight line. 'I abhor the use of violence. I think it does the Movement more harm than good. They'll be seen as criminals rather than pioneers.'

Augusta was silent for a moment. 'I take your point, Gervase, and part of me agrees with you. But non-militant ways didn't seem to work, did they?'

Gervase paced the room. Augusta had never seen him so agitated. 'But I can't see violence working either. It will turn people against the women rather than gain their sympathy.'

'Is that what it's done for you?'

He sighed and the stiffness went out of his shoulders. He sagged, suddenly very weary. 'No – no. Not really. It's just that I'm so afraid for her.'

Augusta nodded, satisfied. 'Go up and see her. Reassure her.'

He looked at her, anguish in his eyes. 'Does she really care about my good opinion?'

Augusta returned his gaze steadily as she said softly, 'I think – in time – you'll find that your opinion of her matters more than anyone else's.'

He sighed heavily as he turned to leave, murmuring, 'I wish I could believe you.'

*

The next time Florrie stirred, she found Gervase sitting beside the bed. She rubbed her eyes and stared at him for a long moment before whispering hoarsely, 'You're very angry with me, aren't you?'

'Angry, no. Afraid for you, yes,' he said simply. 'If I'm angry with anyone, it's Isobel for leading you into such danger. She appears to have nine lives the way she always seems to escape getting arrested.'

'She's very clever. Oh, she's in the thick of it—' Florrie winced as she cleared her throat. 'But she keeps her eyes and her ears open all the time and, at the first sign of trouble, she just melts away. It's not that she's a coward or wouldn't face jail bravely, it's just that she believes she can be more useful by staying free. And I think she's right. If we all ended up in jail, the Cause would founder.'

In spite of his grave anxiety, Gervase smiled. 'I doubt they would be able to arrest everyone. The prisons would overflow.' He leaned forward and took her hand. He regarded her steadily, taking in the lank hair, the hollowed cheeks and the prison pallor. The tiny scar on her forehead was a vivid purple. How very altered his beloved Florrie was. 'You must stay here until you're quite well, and even after that. If you go back to London you will be rearrested at once.'

Florrie closed her eyes. 'No doubt they'll find out where I am and come here for me.'

'No one knows you're here except your grandmother. And my staff, of course. But they won't say anything.'

She turned her head on the pillow. Her eyes widened. 'Doesn't Isobel know where I am? Or – or Lady Leonora?' Her memory was so hazy she couldn't piece together the last few days.

'Isobel does, of course, and I expect by now Lady Lee and the Hon. Tim know too. But they're hardly likely to say anything, are they?'

'You – you got me out of prison, didn't you?' She squeezed the hand that was holding hers in a gesture of wordless thanks.

Gervase nodded. 'I persuaded our London doctor to accompany me to Holloway. Luckily for us, he knew one of the prison doctors and was able to persuade him to release you on licence.'

'I wonder how long it'll be before they come looking for me,' she murmured.

'Never, I hope!'

'But, if they really want to find me, they'll surely guess that this is one of the places I might be.'

Gervase even chuckled now. 'Then in that case I shall hide you in the church and claim sanctuary.'

Florrie smiled weakly and closed her eyes. Weariness claimed her once more and she slept again. But Gervase did not move. He continued to sit beside her, her hand safely in his.

Thirteen

It took a month for Florrie to recover her strength and, in all that time, she did not go home to Candlethorpe Hall. There was no need. Her father, now having heard of her escapades, had no wish to see her. James, who was desperate to see her, had returned to school after the Easter holidays on the day before Gervase brought her home. Augusta came to stay for a few days at the Manor at the very beginning, and afterwards visited frequently, even, one day, bringing a greatly daring Clara, though the poor woman was a bundle of nerves that Edgar would find out where she'd been.

'As far as he need be concerned, Clara dear,' Augusta had planned it all, 'we've been for a drive, and on the way back we'll call and see Mrs Ponsonby. She's sure to mention it to Edgar at church on Sunday.'

'But we can't call uninvited or unannounced. It would never do,' Clara worried.

'I've already written a note to the good lady and asked if we may call. Word came back that she'd be delighted to see us.'

And so the subterfuge continued until the beginning of May, when Florrie announced to a startled Gervase that she would be returning to London.

'Will you drive me to the station in your brand-new Morris Oxford?'

Gervase was the first person in the vicinity who'd

bought a motor car and its arrival a few days earlier had caused a great stir of excitement in Bixley. Every time he drove through the village, the children ran after him. 'Gi' us a ride, mister.' If he'd the time to spare, the good-natured man would stop and allow them to scramble aboard, causing the locals to laugh and wave at the motorist with his urchin passengers.

'Oh, Florrie,' Gervase shook his head sadly. 'I beg you, please don't go back.' Although he longed to take her for a drive in the vehicle, this was not what he'd planned for their first trip out. The occasion would be completely spoilt by his anxiety for her. 'I don't want you to go back. None of us do. You've only escaped being rearrested thus far because you've been hidden away in the country. If you set foot in London, word will get out that you're back and they'll slap you in prison again. And because you've been out for longer than you should have been, they might well add to your sentence.'

'Can they do that?'

He shrugged and muttered darkly, 'They can do anything they want to.'

'But since the Cat-and-Mouse Bill had its final reading they've suspended the force-feeding. I'll just get let out again in a few days.'

'Not before you've endangered your health by going on hunger strike again.' He glared at her. 'And you mean to do that, don't you?'

Florrie didn't answer, but her glance fell away from meeting his gaze.

'I thought as much,' Gervase sighed.

'I'm sorry,' she said at last in a small voice. 'But this is just something I have to do.'

He did as she asked and drove her to the railway station, but their farewells were tense and awkward.

'I'm sorry, Gervase, truly I am,' she said again out of the carriage window as the train began to move.

He nodded and raised his hand in farewell. But he could say nothing to her; he could not trust himself to speak, for tears, which he never allowed a soul to see him shed, were all too close.

As Gervase had predicted, Florrie was arrested three days after her arrival back in London. But this time, though the prison regime was hard, there was no force-feeding. Of course, she at once went on hunger strike again, but by the time the doctors and prison officials deemed that she should be released under the new Act, she had in fact completed her full sentence. She was fortunate that no more days had been added on for her being out of prison for longer than she should have been.

Her arrival back at Chalfont Place was greeted with great celebration. Isobel threw a party and Lady Lee and a few others came to congratulate her.

'And we have a little present for you, my dear,' Lady Lee said, opening a small, satin-lined box. 'It gives me great pleasure to award you the hunger striker's medal.'

Pink with pleasure and pride, Florrie stood whilst Lady Lee pinned it to her blouse. The circular medal was inscribed with the words '*Hunger Strike*', hanging from a bar that said '*For Valour*', beneath which was a ribbon of the three colours of the Movement and below that another bar that bore the date of Florrie's final release. 'And Mrs Pankhurst herself has sent a message of congratulation to you. You are one of our youngest members to undergo force-feeding and we're all so very proud of you.'

'I shall wear it with honour,' Florrie said, her voice unsteady with emotion as all her friends around her applauded. As the noise died away, she asked, 'So, what are we doing next?'

And everyone in the room laughed.

'Girls,' Lady Leonora hurried towards them as they were ushered into her morning room one sunny morning in early June. 'Tomorrow, we're going to the races. To the Derby, to be precise. You must wear your finest gowns and sport the colours of the Movement. And you must be sure to wear your lovely brooch, Florrie, my dear.' Her excitement was obvious.

'I'm never without it,' Florrie murmured.

'Is something planned?' Isobel asked. 'Are we to take part in a demonstration?'

'Yes. Emily has suggested it.' Lady Leonora's eyes were afire.

'Emily? Emily Davison?'

'Yes.'

Florrie glanced from one to the other. 'Is that Emily *Wilding* Davison?'

'Yes. You must have heard about her. She's an ardent supporter of the Cause,' Lady Lee smiled. 'And a very clever and well-educated woman. She's asked us to stand at the side of the racetrack and wave the purple-white-and-green.'

'But – but won't that frighten the horses? Someone might get hurt,' Isobel began, but Lady Leonora waved her protests aside.

'Jockeys are used to taking falls. No one will be seriously hurt, I'm sure. We only mean to interrupt the proceedings – to stop one of the races, if we can. Just to bring ourselves to the notice of the crowd.'

Isobel and Florrie exchanged a worried glance, though they said no more. The aristocratic race-goers, they both believed, would not take kindly to their day being disrupted. Florrie bit her lip, wondering for the first time if Gervase did indeed have a point. They were silent as they walked home together, each busy with her own thoughts. Florrie shuddered even though the June day was mild. She had a dreadful premonition that this particular demonstration would do more harm than good to their Cause.

'There will be a great many people at Epsom tomorrow,' Isobel murmured, breaking the silence at last. 'The King's horse is running. He and the Queen will probably be there.'

'Perhaps Lady Lee is right. Perhaps it's a very good occasion to get ourselves noticed.'

Isobel frowned. 'I'm just so afraid the horses will get hurt. I don't give a jot about the people, but the horses – now that's a different matter. We shouldn't be about hurting innocent creatures.'

They had arrived at the steps of number six and Meredith opened the door. As Florrie followed her friend into the house, she couldn't prevent a smile. Isobel had always been a magnificent horsewoman from an early age. In her childhood and awkward youth, it had always been plain to see that she was happier amongst the horses in the stables at Bixley Manor than entertaining in the drawing room. Until the arrival in her life of the Hon. Tim, people – apart from her beloved brother – had certainly taken second place in her affections. It seemed, Florrie thought, there were occasions when this was still the case.

The following morning, Lady Lee, Isobel and Florrie set out for Epsom. They were wearing purple gowns trimmed with green and white, and Lady Lee wore the most elaborate hat with ostrich feathers in the same colours. Florrie, of course, was wearing the brooch Gervase had given her and they each carried a banner declaring, 'Votes for Women'.

'Emily is going to Tattenham Corner,' Lady Lee told them. 'She wants us to choose another spot. If there are too many of us in one place, she thinks we might get moved on by the police. If we spread ourselves amongst the crowd, they'll have a harder job to get to us. I suggest we separate and keep on the move; though, on second thoughts, maybe you should keep Florrie with you, Isobel.'

'Oh, but . . .' Florrie began, then stopped as she felt a warning squeeze from Isobel on her elbow. Charming though Lady Lee was, she did not like to be crossed and, after all, she was the leader of their small group.

'Of course,' Florrie murmured obediently. She'd already proved her commitment and willingness to do whatever was asked of her. There was no need to annoy Lady Lee by going against the plans already in place.

'Come, we'll go this way,' Isobel said. 'Just round the bend of the corner. We'll be able to see Emily from there and, if we can get near the rails, we can wave our banners between the races, but not,' Isobel whispered as they moved away from Lady Lee, 'when the horses are passing close to us. I just don't agree with frightening the poor creatures.'

Florrie hid her smile, but she agreed with Isobel.

They pushed their way to the front of the race-goers lining the white-painted rails.

One or two women drew their skirts away as if they would be contaminated, should they come into contact. The whisper rippled amongst those nearby. 'It's two of those dreadful suffragette women. Look at the colours they are wearing.' But surprisingly, the men raised their hats, bowed politely and stepped aside to let them near the rails. Perhaps they regretted their courteous actions when Isobel and Florrie unfurled their banner, held it aloft and began to chant, 'Votes for Women, Votes for Women.'

The races began and, each time the horses came thundering near them, the two young women lowered their banner and ceased their shouting, only to begin again when the animals and their riders had passed safely by.

'Can you see Miss Davison?' Florrie asked Isobel as they waited in the lull between races. 'Or Lady Lee?'

'I think Lady Lee's gone the other way, but see, over there, close to the rail. That's Emily.' Isobel waved, but the woman didn't appear to notice.

'I've not met her yet,' Florrie murmured, watching the tall, slight figure in the distance.

'Maybe you'll get the chance at the end of the meeting. She's been to prison four or five times and once, when she went on hunger strike and they were going to force-feed her, she barricaded her cell. But they put a hose-pipe through the window and filled her cell up with water. Oh, watch out, the next race is just about to start,' Isobel added, shading her eyes and squinting into the far distance towards the start line. 'The King's horse is running in this one.' They lowered their banner and stood very still and quiet, watching the horses thundering round the curve of the track. Though they doubted that their thoughtful action really mattered, for the noise of the excited crowd around them was far louder than their own 'Votes for Women' chant had ever been.

The horses were coming nearer, rounding the bend at Tattenham Corner. The leaders passed by and then, suddenly, Florrie screamed and clutched Isobel's arm as she saw Emily Davison duck beneath the rails and launch herself into the path of the last few horses. She seemed to be trying to catch hold of the bridle of one of them, and the galloping animal had no chance to swerve to miss her. It hit her full on and she was tossed into the air. Her hat flew off as her body hit the ground and bounced, rolling over and over several times before finally coming to a stop in a broken heap. The horse stumbled and fell and the jockey was thrown over its head to the ground where he, too, lay motionless. The two young women held their breath as the following horses managed to swerve around all three bodies on the ground.

'That's Anmer – the King's horse – I know the jockey's colours,' Isobel cried. 'She was making for it deliberately. I'm sure of it. She's planned this, Florrie. That's why she wanted to be alone – just in case one of us might have tried to stop her.'

'What's happening? I can't see.'

'I think the jockey's moving. They're trained to lie still until all the other horses have gone by,' Isobel said, craning her neck. 'And Anmer is on its feet. It doesn't seem to be hurt. But Emily – oh, Florrie – Emily's not moving . . .'

They stood for a moment, shocked and horrified.

Then they dropped their banner and struggled towards the place where Emily lay. But the crowd, surging onto the track, prevented them from reaching her. Race officials and police reached the injured, but Isobel and Florrie could only watch with terrified eyes as the jockey and Emily were borne away on stretchers.

'Do you think she's badly injured. And the jockey? What about the jockey?' Florrie was frantic for news. She couldn't bear to think that hurt had been caused to any person – something that the suffragettes (even the militant ones) vowed they'd never do.

'I couldn't really see,' Isobel faltered, 'not properly.' But the grim faces of those nearer the injured told them the worst.

A man close by rounded on Isobel and Florrie. 'Now look what your foolishness has done. Likely maimed a good horse and injured a jockey. As for that young woman – whoever she is – well, she's brought it upon herself. I hope you're satisfied to have ruined a good day's racing.' With that he jammed his top hat on his head and pushed his way through the throng.

There were murmurs of agreement all around them as Isobel and Florrie walked away. It took every ounce of their courage to keep their heads held high and the tears from falling. Behind them a man picked up their banner and tore it to shreds.

Fourteen

'She's been taken to Epsom Cottage Hospital,' Lady Lee informed them that evening when Isobel and Florrie hurried to her house for news.

'How is she? Have you heard?'

'She's very seriously injured. They fear a fractured skull and serious internal injuries. They may try to operate, but they – they don't hold out much hope.'

'Why did she do it?' Florrie was appalled.

Lady Lee sighed. 'She's tried to kill herself before. Three times, I believe. None of us condoned it, of course. But she's a strong-willed woman who seems to think that the only way forward for the Movement is for it to have its own martyr.'

For a moment they were silent, each thinking her own thoughts as they sat in Lady Lee's drawing room.

'I can't say I agree with her,' Isobel said at last. 'But one certainly can't deny her courage.'

News came four days later that Emily Davison had died without regaining consciousness.

'A huge funeral procession is being arranged. It's what she'd have wanted and it's the least we can do,' Lady Lee told them.

'Are you ready?'

Isobel and Florrie regarded each other solemnly.

They were both dressed in white gowns with a black sash diagonally across their chests and they were both carrying white lilies. Florrie wore her brooch and Isobel her hat with purple, green and white ostrich feathers. It was Saturday – the day of Emily's funeral.

Florrie nodded, for the moment unable to speak. She was finding it hard to come to terms with Emily's martyrdom and yet part of her was filled with admiration. That someone could be so passionate about the Cause as to give their life for it . . .

'Come, we're to go to Lady Lee's and travel with her.'

A little later when the three women reached the place where the procession was to start, they gazed about them in awe. Thousands of women thronged the street; the younger women in white, the older ones – like Lady Lee – dressed in purple or black. Most carried flowers: purple irises or laurel wreaths. One or two women held banners aloft. One proclaimed *Fight on and God will give the Victory*, another declared *Give me Liberty or give me Death*.

'I didn't realize there'd be so many,' Florrie gasped. 'They must have come for miles. And look, there are men too and – oh, Iso – there are *clergymen* here. At least a dozen.'

'I know and look, Florrie, look at the bandsmen lining up. There must be ten bands here, all going to march with us.'

The crowd formed up behind the coffin drawn on an open carriage by black horses and followed by four more carriages laden with hundreds of wreaths.

'Is Tim here, Lady Lee?' Isobel asked, trying to scan the crowd for sight of her fiancé, but there were just too many people for her to be able to pick him out.

115

'Oh yes – and Gervase is here somewhere, I believe.'

'Gervase!' Isobel and Florrie spoke together.

'Yes, he came up early this morning, so I understand. No doubt you'll see him later. I expect he'll stay overnight at least.'

The cortège moved off slowly and Isobel and Florrie fell into step with all the other young women dressed in white, whilst Lady Lee joined the older women. The procession, accompanied by the bands playing funereal music, wound its way through the streets to St George's Church and the crowd watched whilst the coffin, covered with the colours of the Movement, was carried up the steps and into the church for the service.

'It's no good trying to get inside, there are far too many already. We might as well wait out here.'

'What happens next?'

'The procession will go to King's Cross. She's being taken by train to the family grave in Morpeth.'

'Where's that?'

'Northumberland. I expect there'll be another service there.'

'What a sad day,' Florrie murmured. 'Her poor mother.'

'It is,' Lady Lee agreed. 'But it's also a triumphant one.' She glanced around at the vast crowd. 'Emily's death – and the reason for it – will be remembered for generations.'

'But will it serve any purpose?' Isobel persisted. 'Will it get us the vote?'

It was a question that even Lady Lee could not answer.

*

Gervase believed he did know.

'She's set the Cause back twenty years,' he growled, standing in front of the drawing-room fire after they'd eaten their evening meal.

'Nonsense, Gervase. People will begin to take us seriously if one of our number is prepared to give her life for her beliefs.'

'I'm sorry, Iso, I can't agree with you. A great many will dismiss such an act as that of an hysterical woman, and that can do your Cause no good. No good at all.'

'Did you hear about Mrs Pankhurst on the day of the funeral?' Florrie put in, trying to defuse the argument between brother and sister.

They both looked at her. 'No,' Isobel said. 'What happened?'

'She was determined to attend the funeral, but she was only out of prison on medical grounds and her licence had expired. She was arrested just outside her home.'

Isobel groaned. 'Oh no!' She was silent a moment, then she rose. 'I'm so very tired. It's been an exhausting day. If you'll both excuse me.'

Their 'goodnights' said, Isobel left the room, closing the door quietly behind her. After a moment's pause, Gervase sat down beside Florrie and took her hand in his.

'You won't do anything foolish, will you, my dearest girl?'

Florrie looked into his eyes and saw the anxiety there. 'If you mean will I become a martyr for the Cause, no, I won't. But I can't promise that I won't take part in activities that might get me arrested again.'

'And then you'd go on hunger strike, wouldn't you?'

'I expect so,' Florrie replied cheerfully. 'But at least they've suspended the force-feeding for now.' She shuddered involuntarily. 'I have to admit – though only to you, Gervase – that took every ounce of my willpower. To my chagrin, I almost gave in several times. But next time, it won't be so bad.'

'You could damage your health, nonetheless – perhaps permanently.'

She smiled, leaned forward and kissed his cheek. 'Don't worry about me.'

But Gervase did worry. He was fearful for the safety of this girl he loved so very much.

Through the summer months the suffragettes continued their campaign of militant activity. The country homes of several Members of Parliament were bombed. Sylvia Pankhurst was imprisoned, but escaped. Her mother, Emmeline, visited America, was threatened with deportation, but then allowed to stay. When she returned to England in early December, she was arrested.

And all the while Lady Lee and her little band of women kept up a steady stream of 'nuisance' activities, as she called their demonstrations, petitions, window-breaking, and so on.

On the 19th December, Gervase arrived at the Richards' town house.

'Good Heavens!' he exclaimed, teasing. 'Are you both still here? I expected to have to scale the walls of Holloway at the very least.'

'Whatever are you doing here, brother dear?' Isobel greeted him with a fond kiss.

'I've come to take you both home for Christmas and,' Gervase paused and glanced meaningfully at Florrie, 'New Year.' He laughed as he added mischievously, 'And I won't take "no" for an answer.'

Florrie laughed with him, knowing that only the two of them knew the double meaning behind his words. She turned to Isobel. 'What do you say? Shall we go?'

'James is home and longing to see you,' Gervase put in craftily. 'He says he's hardly seen you all year. He missed your birthday and you only came home for a flying visit during the summer.'

'Well, I'm staying in London with the Hon. Tim and Lady Lee this year, brother dear. You can come here instead, if you wish.'

Gervase's gaze was still on Florrie's face. Softly he said, 'But her family want to see Florrie.'

The girl gave a wry laugh. 'My father won't miss me. I'm sure he'd rather I stayed away. That way he can pretend I'm not disgracing the family name.'

'But there's Augusta and your mother and – like I say – most of all, James.'

At the thought of her little brother, Florrie capitulated. She turned to Isobel. 'I won't be missed here, will I?'

'Of course you'll be missed, my dear, by us all,' Isobel laughed, 'but you should go home for a couple of weeks. There's nothing much planned for over the Christmas period – at least not by Lady Lee's little band. No, Florrie, you go.'

So the next two days passed in a flurry of shopping for presents and packing her trunk. Gervase gallantly accompanied her around the London shops until he was hidden behind a mound of parcels.

'If we're coming again tomorrow,' he gasped. 'I shall bring Meredith. Good Heavens, Florrie, who on earth are all these for?'

'Oh – just everybody,' Florrie waved her hand.

'Well, all I can say, it's a good job your father hasn't stopped your allowance.'

'Oh, he has,' Florrie replied cheerfully. Then she added impishly, 'But Gran hasn't.'

Gervase hooted with laughter and almost dropped the packages he was carrying. 'Do let's find a cab. My arms are breaking.'

'Just one last thing. I must get Grandmother something in the suffragette colours. A hat, I think, for her to wear to church. It'll turn Father puce, but he won't be able to say a word, particularly as the good Mrs Ponsonby is such a supporter.'

She set off at a swift pace through the store in search of the millinery department, Gervase following in her wake with an amused smile on his face. How he did love this girl!

Fifteen

Augusta wore the hat decorated with purple ostrich feathers and ribbons of green and white to church on Christmas morning. Beside her, Florrie wore a green coat and a huge purple hat with white flowers and green ribbons. The brooch Gervase had given her was pinned to her lapel. Augusta and Florrie sat side by side in the front pew alongside Edgar and Clara, gazing up innocently at Mr Ponsonby in the pulpit, but not daring to glance at one another for fear of collapsing into laughter.

'Oh, you're wicked,' Augusta murmured as they left the church, her arm through her granddaughter's.

'I know. But so are you.'

'Isn't it absolutely *delicious*!' Augusta chuckled. 'I can't remember when I last had so much fun. Did you hear the whole congregation whispering behind us? And I thought your father was going to burst a blood vessel.'

They paused as they heard pounding footsteps behind them and turned to see James running to catch them up.

'I do declare you've grown taller since the summer.'

At fifteen, he towered over both his grandmother and his sister. He was no longer a boy, but a young man. 'Here, give me your arm, Grandmother.' He stepped to the other side of Augusta and crooked his arm. The two young people matched their steps to hers.

'And you're growing so like your dear grandfather . . .' Augusta stopped suddenly. 'Take me to his grave. Bowler promised to leave some flowers there today, but I've a mind to go and see him for myself.'

They turned off the pathway and wound their way amongst the gravestones until they came to the one bearing the name of Nathaniel Maltby. They stood for several moments before Augusta stooped and rearranged the fresh flowers in the holder. 'It's so nice our greenhouses produce flowers at this time of the year. We're very lucky.'

'Do you think Grandpops would have approved of – of me? Of what I'm doing?' For the first time, Florrie was unsure.

Augusta put her head on one side and thought for a moment. 'I think so, though I have to say he abhorred violence of any kind. He would have agreed with the principles of the suffragettes, but perhaps not condoned all their actions. He didn't even agree with some of the wars that went on during his lifetime.'

'Didn't he?' James was surprised. 'But – but I thought he fought in the Crimea? Father's always telling me how proud he is of him and how I should follow in his footsteps and join the army.'

'He did,' Augusta said shortly, 'but it didn't mean he agreed with it.' She sighed heavily. 'Of course, I knew nothing about it at the time. I was only – let me see – about ten. Although I lived on the estate and knew the family, Nathaniel was this very handsome son and heir—' She smiled pensively. 'So far above me – and so much older – I never thought for one moment that one day he would marry me. I do remember him going off to war, though. All the estate workers turned out to cheer him on his way, and he looked so smart in his uniform. I think all the girls in the neighbourhood were in love with him. He was away six months and came home wounded. Nothing life-threatening, though his stay in the Scutari hospital could have been the end of him. The conditions were appalling and disease was rife, never mind no proper treatment for wounds.'

'But – but I thought that was where Miss Nightingale was?' Florrie said.

Augusta nodded. 'It was, but he was there in the October just before she arrived in November. Later on it was so much better, but Nathaniel was lucky to survive. He was invalided out of the army because of his wound. He walked with a limp for the rest of his life, but like I say, he was lucky.'

'I can just remember him walking with a stick,' James murmured.

'And we always had to sit on his right knee, never his left,' Florrie smiled, remembering the bewhiskered old gentleman fondly. She always thought of him as a 'Father Christmas' figure. Perhaps, within the family, he had been.

'Why did he join the army then, if he didn't believe in the war?' James asked tentatively.

'To please his father,' Augusta said bluntly as if it answered everything. And it did. Augusta chuckled. 'The only time he defied the old man was to marry me.'

'And did his father ever forgive him?' James asked.

The tone of the young man's voice made Florrie glance at him. There was something troubling him. She knew him so well. It seemed Augusta sensed it too, for she squeezed his arm. 'Oh, Grandfather Maltby huffed and puffed for a while – your father's very like him – but he came around in the end. Parents forgive their children most things, you know. In time.'

The three of them turned away from the grave and walked back to the path and to the carriage waiting at the gate. Augusta and Clara were driven to church, whilst the rest of the family and their servants walked across the fields. Edgar stalked ahead, swinging his cane.

'I think he's angry with Grandmother and – and you,' James whispered.

Florrie chuckled. 'Of course he is. He doesn't agree with all this "suffragette nonsense".'

'You're very brave to flout him, Florrie. I – I don't think I'll ever have the courage to go against what he wants me to do.'

'Oh, you will.' His sister was confident. 'If you believe in something strongly enough, you will.'

James said no more and, for the rest of the way home, seemed lost in his own thoughts.

Florrie was dreading New Year's Eve. This year the celebrations were at Candlethorpe Hall. She loved Gervase dearly, but like another brother. Knowing he was going to propose again, it became a game between them. All through dinner and the family games afterwards, she teased him by sitting close to him one moment when all the family were around them, but when there was the slightest chance of them being alone – even for a few moments – she avoided him.

At last, just before midnight, during a variation of Hide and Seek, Gervase found her hiding in a huge cupboard on the landing. 'Aha, caught you.' He squeezed in beside her and closed the door behind him, plunging them into darkness. 'There's something I want to ask you.'

'Oh, dear Gervase, please don't—'

'Miss Florence Maltby, will you do me the honour of becoming my wife?' Though he was serious, there was nevertheless a bantering tone in his voice.

'Thank you, kind sir, for the great honour you do me,' she said in the same light manner, 'but my answer must be the same as last time.'

He gave an exaggerated sigh of disappointment. 'Oh dear, another year to wait then.' But there was a lightness to his tone and she knew he'd fully expected her answer. They waited in the darkness and the cold for someone else to find them. She shivered and he put his arm around her.

'When are you going back to London?'

'Next Monday.'

'You – you will take care, won't you? I don't want to see you get arrested again.'

'Oh, I won't be,' she said airily. 'I'll stick close to Isobel. She seems to be able to avoid arrest.'

Gervase chuckled. 'She does, doesn't she? And so does Lady Lee. Mind you, she served time a few years ago.'

'She keeps in the background now. She organizes us. Sometimes she marches, but she doesn't do any – um – she doesn't take part in anything more – well . . .' Her voice trailed away.

'In any of the acts of violence, you mean?'

'Mm.' Florrie was reluctant to discuss it with him. Whilst Gervase supported the emancipation of women, they differed on the means by which to achieve it.

'Just so long as you keep yourself out of trouble, darling girl. That's all.' A moment later, the cupboard door opened and James was squeezing in too.

'Ho, ho, ho, you two. Caught you.'

They whispered together in the darkness, stifling their giggles, until Augusta found them. 'If you think I'm squeezing in there,' she chuckled, 'you're quite mistaken.'

They scrambled out, dusting down their clothes. 'So what shall we play next?' James asked.

'Charades,' Augusta replied promptly.

Florrie pretended to groan. 'That's because you always win.'

Laughing, the four of them descended the stairs for another game before it was time to greet the New Year of 1914.

Sixteen

For the first few months of the year, Florrie was taken up with the activities of the Movement. She marched in protest, handed out leaflets and obtained hundreds of signatures on numerous petitions destined for 10 Downing Street. In March they joined a demonstration in Trafalgar Square. Sylvia Pankhurst was arrested on her way there and the following day her mother was arrested in Glasgow. Then Mary Richardson was arrested for slashing a valuable painting in the National Gallery.

'You got off lightly,' Isobel remarked drily. 'Mary's got six months. So, just be warned, they won't go so easy on you next time. Do be careful, Florrie.'

But towards the end of May Florrie was one of a number of women arrested outside Buckingham Palace trying to hand in a petition to the King. And this time Isobel did not escape either. They were both charged with 'causing a disturbance' and sentenced to twenty-eight days. But inside the jail they were kept strictly apart and Florrie had no way of knowing how Isobel was coping with her first time in prison. At once, Florrie went on hunger strike, drinking only water. She saw Isobel fleetingly one day and, by the sight of her friend, knew that she had taken the same action. Florrie lost weight rapidly and was thin and pale by the time she was released after serving only half her sentence. Isobel had been released on licence two days earlier and was waiting for her outside Holloway with Lady Lee.

'We'd better get you both back to Lincolnshire,' Lady Lee said as she helped Florrie into the carriage. 'They'll only arrest you again if you stay in London. Gervase will be here by tonight to take you both home tomorrow.'

This time, Florrie insisted on going to Candlethorpe Hall. 'I'll face the music with my father,' she said. Her voice was husky and weak, but her spirit refused to be broken. 'It's not fair to inflict myself on you and Gervase again.'

Isobel laughed. 'I don't think he'll see it that way.'

'Exactly!' Florrie murmured and Isobel sighed, torn between sisterly loyalty to Gervase and understanding for her young friend.

'Well, I hope you've got this nonsense out of your system. You're a disgrace to the family. If I had my way—' Edgar stopped, as if unwilling to admit that he was not, in practice, the head of the household. 'Oh, get out of my sight,' he growled. Florrie went, glad to escape.

Slowly, she pulled herself up the stairs, one at a time. She'd no strength left. Her hair was lank and dull. Her clothes hung limply on her thin frame and she felt ill and exhausted. But before she went to her own room, she had to see her grandmother.

'My dear child.' Augusta, seated near the window in her first-floor sitting room, held out her arms. 'You look dreadful.'

Florrie smiled wanly and her voice trembled a little as she knelt down beside her grandmother's chair. 'I know I'll always get the truth from you, Gran.'

128

Wearily, she leaned her head against the old lady's knee and closed her eyes. 'I used to sit like this as a little girl. And James would sit on your lap whilst you read to us both.'

Augusta stroked her hair. 'I'm so proud of you, Florrie. Was it very bad?'

'Pretty bad, but not so awful as last time. There's no force-feeding now. They'll just rearrest me in a couple of weeks' time.'

'If they can find you,' Augusta said grimly.

'Oh, they'll find me if they want to.'

'And Isobel?'

'She's come home too. Lady Leonora sent us both home for a couple of weeks to recover.'

'You're going back?' Even Augusta was surprised this time.

Florrie gritted her teeth. 'Oh, yes.' The determination was evident in her tone. 'The fight goes on, Gran. Until we get the vote, the fight goes on.'

Augusta rested her cheek against the girl's hair. 'Oh, my dear girl, how brave you are.' She held her close for a few moments and then she said briskly, 'Now, you must ring for Beth. A nice hot bath and into bed with you. Plenty of rest and good food – that's what you need.'

As always, Augusta was right. Florrie slept for two days, rousing only to eat the food that Beth brought to her on a tray. On the third morning, her grandmother came to her room after breakfast. 'Now, child, up you get. You need some fresh air.'

Florrie snuggled in the soft feather bed and pretended sleep, but Augusta grasped the covers and pulled them back. 'Up you get. Gervase is here. He's going to take you for a drive.'

Florrie groaned.

'Now, I won't hear a word said against the boy. Where you might have ended up without him, I don't know. I know his sister was involved, but he'd no need to bother with you, now had he? He's been very good to you.'

'Yes, he has,' Florrie murmured as she sat up. 'Too good.'

She exchanged a glance with Augusta and the old lady nodded. 'I expect the poor boy's still hoping, but I think he would've done it all anyway. He's a good friend to us all, apart from the fact that he's besotted with you. Now, come along. He's waiting. The least you can do is go for a drive with him.'

A short while later, Florrie descended the stairs towards Gervase, waiting in the hall below.

'So, are you going to let me have a drive, then?' She forced a gaiety she didn't quite yet feel.

Gervase looked up at her and smiled, though the anxiety never quite left his eyes. He held out his hand to her. 'If you promise not to run it into the ditch.'

He didn't say a word about her thin face or the way her clothes hung loosely on her as he helped her into the driving seat of his motor car. But he tucked a warm shawl around her shoulders, making the excuse, 'It can be quite draughty.'

Gervase gave her a few basic instructions and moments later they were bowling down the long drive-way of Candlethorpe Hall and out of the gateway onto the main road. Florrie turned the wheel to the right and headed towards the coast.

'I've a mind to see the sea,' she yelled above the noisy engine. 'It makes me feel I'm really home.'

They parked the car near the pier at Saltershaven,

climbed the steps and passed through the entrance. The tide was in, so they hadn't gone many yards before the waves were splashing beneath the boards on which they walked. The wind whipped in from the sea, catching the plumes on Florrie's hat and trying to tear it from her head. But she'd fastened it firmly with a scarf for her drive in the motor car. She breathed in deeply, closed her eyes and raised her face to the breeze. 'How good it feels. How clean and fresh.'

'It must do – after Holloway.'

'Now, now,' she said, putting her hand through his arm. 'We're not going to talk about any of that today. Tell me what's been happening here.'

They walked and talked until they were about half-way down the long pier. 'I'll have to sit down a moment, Gervase,' Florrie gasped. 'My knees have gone all wobbly.'

'Oh, Florrie, I'm sorry. I should have realized. I was doing my best not to fuss.'

'Quite right too.' She sat on a seat and looked up at him. 'I'd have only got cross if you had. I'm fine. I just need a little rest and then we'll walk back.' She looked down the length of the pier that stretched out into the sea and said regretfully, 'I don't think I'm going to make it to the end. Not today.'

Gervase sat down beside her and stretched out his long legs. 'They do say this pier is a third of a mile long, so you've done very well.'

She wanted to snap, 'Don't patronize me', but for once she bit the end of her tongue – quite literally – to stop the words spilling out. He was being so kind and trying so hard not to irritate her, she knew.

'So,' she asked, 'what do you think to my driving?'

He chuckled. 'You're a natural.' And this time there

was no hint of a patronizing tone in his voice. His compliment was utterly genuine.

She laughed. 'There's no need to sound so surprised.'

'Sorry – but I honestly didn't expect you to get the hang of it so quickly.' He leaned towards her. 'Are you sure you haven't been driving secretly in London and haven't told me?'

She shook her head. 'No – it's a little scary in London. All those people and other vehicles, horse-drawn and motorized. I'm much safer learning in the country.' She touched his hand. 'Thank you for trusting me. It was very generous of you to put your precious motor car in the hands of a complete novice.'

He raised her hand to his lips as he murmured, 'You're far more precious to me than any motor car.' The words, though seriously meant, were said lightly and, before she could make any reply, he got up and hauled her to her feet. 'We should be getting back. I don't want you catching a chill. Even though it's June, it's quite blustery and we are almost out at sea.'

They returned to the car and Florrie drove all the way home.

Her grandmother had been right – as always. Florrie felt so much better for the outing. The bracing sea air had brought colour to her cheeks and given her an appetite.

'You'll stay to dinner, won't you? Perhaps we could send word to the Manor and Isobel might join us too.'

Gervase grimaced. 'I'd love to, Florrie dear, but I must get back to Isobel. She's still rather under the weather. She hasn't quite got your stamina.'

'Well, it was her first time in prison. She did remarkably well.' And then Florrie castigated herself silently. Now who's sounding patronizing?

At the end of June, Florrie and Isobel returned to London, where they were rearrested to serve the remainder of their sentence.

On their release, Lady Lee was waiting for them outside the jail. Her eyes were anxious. 'I don't know how much you've heard whilst you've been in Holloway, but – well – war looks inevitable now.'

The two young women gaped at her with wide, horrified eyes.

'War!' they cried together and Isobel added, 'But – but why? What's been happening? We've heard nothing.'

'Let's get you home, bathed and into bed – both of you – and then I'll explain everything.'

A little while later, the two girls snuggled into Isobel's huge four-poster together and nibbled at the food that Lucy had brought up to them on a tray.

Lady Lee entered the room. 'Are you feeling better, my dears, now that you've got rid of that dreadful prison smell?'

Though she was trying to be cheerful, they could both see that she was agitated. She perched herself comfortably on the end of the bed.

'Did you know about the assassination in Sarajevo of Archduke Ferdinand and his wife? It happened two days after you were rearrested.'

The two young women glanced at each other and then shook their heads.

'Who's he?' Florrie asked.

'The heir to the Austro-Hungarian throne.'

'You don't get to hear much about what's happening in the outside world in there,' Isobel explained. 'They keep all the suffragettes segregated – deliberately, I feel. And we spend most of the time alone in our cells. If we're allowed out for exercise, we're not supposed to talk to anyone else.' She smiled grimly. 'It can mean extra days added onto our sentence, so we tend not to risk it. At least,' she added wryly, 'I didn't. I couldn't wait to get out of that place.' She shuddered dramatically. 'I don't know how Florrie stood that awful force-feeding. I'm sure I wouldn't have been able to.'

Florrie squeezed her arm. 'Of course you'd have coped. It's surprising what you can do if you put your mind to it.' She turned back to Lady Lee. 'So, how has that precipitated Britain getting into a war? And who with?'

'It's all to do with alliances. It's said that the young student who killed them was a Serb, or at least the Serbs were behind the plot. If so, we can expect Austria to retaliate against Serbia.'

'But what's that got to do with Britain?' Florrie frowned.

'Germany has an alliance with Austria. And Russia,' she added ominously, 'is Serbia's ally.'

'I still don't understand how it involves us.'

Lady Lee gave a wry smile. 'Well, I have to admit I had to ask Tim to explain it all to me. He's been down at the House of Commons in the public gallery all week. France has an alliance with Russia and we have an "entente" with France.'

'What's that mean – exactly?'

'A gentleman's agreement.'

'Ah.' Isobel sighed and murmured with a little

sarcasm, 'And of course the British are always "gentle-men".'

'I think there's a treaty – Tim said so anyway – that binds us to protect Belgium's neutrality. So,' Lady Lee said finally, 'if there is a war, this will alter things for us.'

'How – how do you mean?'

'Word has already gone round. Mrs Pankhurst feels that, if war does break out, we should suspend our activities for the duration of the war. England's need is greater than our own. We should devote ourselves to serving our country in a time of crisis. And who knows,' she added with a brief glint of her impish humour, even amidst such trepidation of what was to come, 'if we show our mettle in such difficult times, well, it might do our Cause more good than all the arson and picture-slashing.'

'You could be right,' Florrie murmured and then added, 'I think I ought to go home. James will be coming home from school very soon and . . .' Her voice faded away as a new fear clutched at her heart. If there was a war, what would it mean for young men like her brother? He was only sixteen, but . . .

'Me too,' Isobel said, interrupting Florrie's thoughts. 'Is that all right, Lady Lee?'

Lady Leonora nodded. 'I think you should.'

Seventeen

Once more they returned to Lincolnshire, Isobel to Bixley Manor and Florrie to Candlethorpe Hall. When they'd been at home for almost two weeks, both young women were itching to get back to the city.

'Nothing's going to happen,' Florrie moaned, when Isobel called for afternoon tea and they were sitting with Augusta and Clara in the drawing room. 'I'm sure they've spread all these rumours of war just to put a stop to our activities.'

Augusta burst out laughing. 'I rather think the Prime Minister and his Cabinet have a lot more on their minds just now than a few mad women chaining themselves to the railing outside Number Ten.' She replaced her cup on the tray. 'But do stay until after the weekend. It's the Bank Holiday, and my birthday on Tuesday. We've arranged a special party.' She beamed. 'I am going to be seventy, you know.'

They all laughed. For months, Augusta had allowed no one to forget that she was about to reach such an auspicious age.

'Of course we wouldn't miss your party, Mrs Maltby,' Isobel said. She turned to Florrie. 'We'll go back at the end of next week and see what's happening.'

*

'Gervase is here again with that noisy contraption of his,' Augusta announced at breakfast on the morning of the August Bank Holiday Monday as she glanced out of the long windows overlooking the driveway. 'No doubt he's come to take you for a trip to the seaside. I've a mind to come with you,' she added playfully. 'What about you, James? Shall we both go with Gervase and Florrie? I'm sure there's room in his motor car. And seeing as it's my seventieth birthday tomorrow . . .'

Gervase was good-natured about the suggestion, and not even the slightest flicker of disappointment that he would not be alone with Florrie showed on his face. Gallantly, he said, 'It'll be a pleasure, Mrs Maltby.'

Half an hour later, the party set off to spend the day on Saltershaven sea front five miles from Candlethorpe Hall. Florrie perched on the front seat beside Gervase, whilst Augusta and James sat, a rug over their knees, in the back seat. Augusta was wearing her hat with the purple feathers, held on securely by a white silk scarf, and Florrie, as always, had the brooch that Gervase had given her pinned to the lapel of her jacket.

Leaving the vehicle at a sea-front hotel, where Gervase ordered lunch for the four of them for one o'clock, they walked down the road from the clock tower to the beach. They stood for a moment, watching the holidaymakers.

Little girls, barefoot with their skirts tucked up into baggy bloomers, paddled in the shallows, squealing with delight as the waves caught them unawares and splashed their legs. Then some boys, teasing and irritating, deliberately kicked water at the girls, making them shriek all the more. Women with wide-brimmed hats and parasols to shade their delicate complexions from the sun walked sedately along the beach, the hem of their skirts brushing the sand. Men, dressed uncomfortably in collars and ties and caps or boaters, took off their shoes, rolled up their trousers and paddled too. They stood watching as a bathing machine was manoeuvred into the water and two daring young women emerged from it, dressed in striped one-piece bathing costumes. They plunged into the sea, gasping and laughing at the shock of the cold water.

'Now, off you young ones go,' Augusta said, waving them away. 'I'll be quite happy sitting here on the sand.'

Gervase spread out the rug he'd brought and Augusta sat down, arranging her skirts modestly around her.

'You too, James. I don't need looking after. I'm not quite in my dotage yet.' She chuckled. 'At least, not until tomorrow!'

Arm in arm, Gervase and Florrie walked along the shore, in companionable silence, the only sounds the gentle lapping of the waves, the screeching seagulls and children's merry laughter.

James capered around them like a five-year-old.

Gervase smiled. 'You wouldn't think he was a sedate sixteen-year-old from a private boarding school, would you?'

'Sedate? James doesn't know the meaning of the word. Besides, it's time he had a little fun. He's had a tough year, I think. Father's pushing him to try for university.'

'He's a bright lad – he'll make it. That's if—' Gervase stopped abruptly and changed the subject hurriedly. 'Are you warm enough, Florrie? You're so thin now. I worry about you. You mustn't walk too far today. Just tell me when you've had enough.'

She smiled up at him. 'I'm fine. I'm tougher than I look.'

His expression sobered. 'You must be to go through all that. I'm so proud of both you and Isobel.'

'Are you really?' she said in surprise.

They skirted two children building a sandcastle. Florrie smiled down at them as she murmured, 'I thought you didn't approve of the – the militant acts.'

'I – didn't.'

'Didn't?' she questioned. 'But you do now?'

He sighed. 'I don't really agree with any form of violence, yet we could be on the brink of the very worst sort of fighting. A war. And if we are – well, I'll be fully in favour of defending ourselves.' He smiled wryly. 'Defending our country and our rights. And I have to agree that that's what you've all been fighting for. What you see as *your* rights.'

'But you joined the army when you left school,' Florrie reminded him. 'Why, if you don't really agree with fighting?'

Gervase nodded. 'Family tradition. But Father died just as I finished my training and I came home to manage the estate. I have to admit – though only to you, Florrie – that I was quite relieved. But then I felt guilty for feeling like that because it was my father's death that had – released me, if you like.'

She squeezed his arm understandingly, but steered him away from a subject that was perhaps still painful for him. 'So, you do agree with what we're trying to achieve then? I mean, it's not just because Isobel's your sister and I'm – well . . .'

He put his hand over hers where it lay through his arm. 'Because you're the girl I love? No, not altogether. I believe women should have the vote. At least, educated women. If it were given to women of all classes, some wouldn't even know what they were voting for.

139

Or, worse still perhaps, they'd just vote the way their husbands told them to.'

'But that's not a class thing,' Florrie said thoughtfully. 'Can you imagine my mother voting any other way than my father told her to do?'

'Mm.' Now it was Gervase's turn to ponder. 'I understand what you mean.'

'As for being uneducated, that doesn't hold true either,' she went on. 'I've met women from all levels of society recently. Some of those whom you would see as being uneducated, because they can't speak foreign languages or, in some cases, can't even read and write properly, are actually more intelligent than some of the upper-class society girls. *Their* empty heads are filled only with thoughts of the next party and which handsome suitor is going to propose to them.'

'I expect you're right, Florrie. They're not all like you and Iso. You've both been so lucky to have had a good education. Not many girls – even from families like ours – can speak French and German.'

Florrie laughed. 'Well, that's thanks to Gran in my case. "Just because your first-born is a girl, Edgar,"' Florrie did a passable imitation of her grandmother's clipped, authoritative tones, ' "doesn't mean to say she can't have the same education that you would have given a son." And so, though I didn't go to boarding school, she personally supervised my education with the three governesses I had at home.'

'Well, Father was very keen on Iso being similarly educated. In fact, didn't you take lessons together for a while, even though she was quite a bit older than you?'

'Yes. She'd finished school by then but she'd always wanted to learn German, so she used to cycle over to

Candlethorpe Hall to have German lessons with me. By the way, how is she?'

'Fine. She had a day or so in bed when you first came home again, but now she's eating like a horse and already talking about going back.' He looked down at her and squeezed her hand. 'She's not had it as bad as you, though. She says so herself.'

Florrie grimaced. 'Bad enough, and just you tell her,' she tapped his arm, 'that she's not to go back to London without me.'

Gervase stopped and turned to face her. He put his hands on her shoulders, his expression more serious than ever she could remember. 'My dear, things are getting very serious. I don't think war can be avoided and if it does happen, it's going to be catastrophic.'

She stared up into his anxious eyes. 'You – you really think there's going to be one then?'

He nodded.

'Oh no!' she whispered and leaned her cheek against his broad chest. He put his arms around her and they stood together near the water's edge, listening to the soothing sound of the waves and the distant happy laughter of children playing.

'It's difficult to believe it on a day like this; everyone enjoying their Bank Holiday in blissful ignorance of the storm clouds gathering.'

'And you believe it's going to happen soon?'

Gervase's face was grim. 'I think it's imminent.'

Florrie turned a little in his arms so that they stood looking back the way they had come, back to the children playing and couples walking arm in arm along the shore. They stood for a long time, Gervase's arm about her shoulders, watching the folk enjoying their day's holiday and hearing the screams of laughter and shrieks of delight from the beach fairground, with its swings and helter-skelter. There was even a big wheel.

James came running along the beach, his bare feet sending up a shower of soft sand. He ran to the water's edge and played 'catch me if you can' with the waves.

'Well, at least he's too young to have to fight,' Florrie murmured.

Gervase cleared his throat. 'It depends how long it lasts.'

She twisted to look up at him. 'What are you saying? That it could last for years?'

Soberly, Gervase nodded.

'Oh no! You're wrong – I know you're wrong. If there is a war, it won't last long. It'll all be over by Christmas.'

'Look out, Florrie,' James's warning shout drifted towards them.

Startled, Florrie looked down to see a wave, bigger than the rest, sweeping towards her. Together they both turned and tried to flee, but still with their arms around each other, they stumbled and fell into the sand, laughing together at the ridiculous sight they must make. The wave came on relentlessly and soaked their ankles, then retreated. For a moment they lay on the sand, staring up at the clear blue sky.

'Oh, Florrie, darling Florrie, I wish we could stay here for ever.'

'Well, we can't,' she said scrambling up. 'Because my feet are wet.' Laughing, she held out her hand and hauled him to his feet. They turned and began to walk back the way they had come. Grinning, James ran to meet them.

'He's no doubt going to tell us he saved us from drowning,' Gervase laughed.

Florrie said nothing. She was watching her brother coming towards them. A tall, lanky youth of sixteen, the sun glinting on his hair, his face young and innocent and carefree. A cloud passed across the sun and a dark shadow covered him. He tripped and fell and, for a moment, lay very still.

Florrie shuddered with a sudden coldness that had nothing to do with her wet feet.

'James—' She started towards him, her hand outstretched, a fearful foreboding pounding in her chest.

But the cloud passed away and the beach was bathed in sunlight once more. James scrambled up, grinned and waved and then galloped down to the water's edge for one last paddle before lunch.

Florrie breathed a sigh of relief, yet it was a while before she could fully shake off the feeling of dread that had come over her when she'd seen her brother fall.

Eighteen

'How *dare* they declare war and spoil my party?' Augusta said, sitting at the head of the dinner table the following evening. She glanced around at the solemn faces, trying to raise a smile with her indignant remark. Lady Leonora, Timothy and the Ponsonbys were guests along with Gervase and Isobel, of course. At the opposite end of the table, Edgar bristled. Seated next to Lady Lee, he could think of nothing to say to the woman whom he partially blamed for his daughter's wild behaviour.

But Lady Leonora Smythe could be charm personified when she wanted to be and she exerted all her feminine wiles on the gullible country gentleman, whilst Matilda Ponsonby was beside herself with delight to meet a genuine member of the aristocracy. And such a zealous campaigner too.

'Oh, Lady Leonora, I am so *thrilled* to meet you,' the dear lady chattered, claiming connection with the Pankhursts by the very fact that they were from the same city. 'I did meet Mrs Pankhurst once, you know, but it was at a meeting and she was surrounded by her ardent supporters. But to think – you know her *personally*.'

'Well, a little,' Lady Lee said modestly and smiled kindly.

'And you, dear boy,' Mrs Ponsonby leaned her ample

bosom on the table to speak to James. 'Are you going to enlist?'

There was a stunned silence around the table and Clara gave a little cry of alarm.

'Not on my birthday, I assure you, Mrs Ponsonby,' Augusta said spiritedly. This time her guests laughed dutifully.

'And not at all, I hope,' Florrie muttered, but her remark earned her an angry glare from Edgar.

'Now – no more talk of war or of suffragettes,' Augusta decreed. 'I don't want my son having an apoplectic fit at the table.'

But the conversation was stilted and awkward. The war was on everyone's mind and, with so many supporters of the suffragette movement sitting around the table, the subject was scarcely avoidable.

It was Edgar himself who brought the topic up again, but, for once, he seemed genuinely interested. Florrie glanced at Isobel and raised her eyebrows in surprise. Even they had underestimated Lady Lee's charm offensive.

'So, what will you ladies do now our country's at war?'

Lady Lee glanced down the table towards Augusta. She'd no wish to offend the woman whose birthday they were celebrating. But Augusta smiled and inclined her head graciously. She too wanted to hear the reply.

Lady Leonora cleared her throat. 'There are two schools of thought about what we should do. One section – which has never supported militancy – will no doubt continue the struggle in their own way. As for those of us who agree with Mrs Pankhurst – well, it looks likely that our – our operations will cease at least for the duration of hostilities,' she added, with pointed emphasis. 'Despite what you might think of us, Mr Maltby, we are patriots, and our country's need at this time is greater than our own desires.'

Edgar nodded, 'Well said, my dear. I'm sure – in time – the vote will be given to the likes of you,' he added condescendingly, 'ladies of quality and education, but I shudder to think what would happen if it were extended to the lower classes. Personally, I never entirely agreed with the '85 Act that gave the vote to most men over the age of twenty-one. What do illiterate labourers know about the way the country should be run?'

Lifting his wine glass, he failed to see the spark of anger in Lady Lee's eyes. Florrie saw it and hid her smile. But Lady Lee was a superb actress. Keeping her voice level and with deceptive mildness, she said, 'But men from all classes will be expected to *die* for their country, now won't they, Mr Maltby?' She left the question hanging in the air, and to that even Edgar had no answer.

Once the ladies had withdrawn, leaving the men to their port, the conversation in Clara's drawing room became more personal.

'Our son intends to enlist at once,' Matilda began. 'He's twenty-two and just finished at theological college. He intends to follow his father into the Church.'

'You surprise me,' Augusta said with her customary bluntness. 'I'd have thought he'd have been against war.'

'He is – in principle. We all are.' She stared around her with wide eyes. 'Aren't we? But one must do one's duty. What say you, Lady Leonora?'

Lady Lee smiled pensively. 'It's the same old story, isn't it? It's all very patriotic and glorious until it comes to sending one's own son.'

Isobel let out a startled gasp, the colour drained from her face and the dainty cup she held rattled in its saucer. 'Oh! You don't mean – you don't mean *Tim* will go? I mean, he's not in the army.'

Lady Lee's expression was bleak as she said softly, 'If they call for volunteers, my dear, I'm afraid it's very likely. I come from a military family. I think he will feel it his duty to go.'

Until the gentlemen rejoined the ladies, Isobel was in a state of high agitation and, as soon as the door opened, she leapt up and hurried towards Tim, pulling him into the far corner of the room where their intense whispered conversation could not be overheard. The voluble Mrs Ponsonby gave admirable cover, but Florrie watched them anxiously, a small frown on her forehead.

'What is it, Florrie?' Gervase's soft voice spoke at her side. 'You look troubled. If you're concerned about Mrs Ponsonby's tactless remark about James, I wouldn't worry. They won't be calling for boys of his age.' He forbore to add 'Not yet, anyway', although the thought was in his mind.

'Yes, it was at the back of my mind, I admit, but my more pressing worry is what those two are talking about.' She nodded towards Isobel and Tim.

'Ah!' Gervase sighed softly. 'You know then?'

Florrie looked up at him. 'Know? Know what?'

For a moment Gervase looked flustered. 'Oh dear, obviously you don't. I – I thought by what you said . . .' His voice trailed away.

Now it was Florrie who manoeuvred Gervase towards the French windows and out onto the terrace where they would not be overheard.

'Now, tell me. Has Tim said anything about volunteering?'

Miserable to be betraying what he now thought might have been a confidence amongst the gentlemen, Gervase nodded. Seeing his discomfort, Florrie put her hands flat against his chest. 'Dear Gervase, don't worry. Lady Lee said as much just now. He's from a military family, she said, and he might feel it his duty. I expect that's why Isobel's cornered him.'

Gervase looked relieved and even smiled. 'You're a little minx, Florrie Maltby. I can't keep anything from you, can I?'

'Not a lot, no,' she replied cheerfully, but then the smile faded from her face. 'So, is it definite?'

Gervase nodded soberly. 'He's going tomorrow to apply to go to a military college somewhere for officer training.' He glanced across at Isobel and her fiancé. 'He wants to bring their wedding forward, Florrie. He wants them to be married before he goes.'

At that moment the young couple stood up, glanced around the room and then, seeing Gervase and Florrie standing together outside the long windows, came towards them.

'Has Gervase told you?' Isobel said at once, putting her arms about Florrie.

'Told me what?' Florrie tried to keep up the pretence, but Isobel knew them both too well.

'Don't worry, you'd have been the first to know anyway. Tim is volunteering and he wants us to be married before he goes.' She tried to force a laugh, though there were anxious tears in her eyes. 'Oh, I know it will cause a scandal. The gossips will have a field day, but I don't care. We want a little time together before . . .' Now the tears spilled down her face, but she brushed them away impatiently and added, 'You will be my bridesmaid, won't you?'

'Oh, darling Iso, I'd love to be.'

As the two young women hugged each other, Tim put his hand on Gervase's shoulder, 'And – dear brother-in-law to be – I would ask you to be my best man, but, naturally, Isobel wants you to give her away.'

'It was kind of you to think of it, but yes, I must stand in for our father.' The brother and sister exchanged a brief glance of mutual sadness, as Gervase added softly, 'They would both so loved to have seen you married, my dear.'

Isobel smiled through her tears and said bravely, 'It'll be a difficult day for all sorts of reasons—' She glanced at Tim. 'But we'll make it a happy one for everyone. Will your mother mind us being married in Bixley Manor church? I – I'd like to be married from home.'

'Of course she won't. Let's go and tell them all now. There's no point in keeping it secret because we'll have to move fast.' They made to turn away back into the drawing room, but Gervase cleared his throat and said, 'A moment, if you please. There's – there's something I would like to tell you too.'

Florrie caught her breath and her heart beat rapidly. Oh no, she thought, he's not going to suggest us having a double wedding, is he?

But what Gervase had to say was far more frightening than another proposal of marriage and filled her heart with dread.

'Iso, I don't know if you realize, but – well – I'll probably be going too.'

Isobel gave a little gasp and her hand fluttered to her mouth. Even Florrie's eyes widened.

'As you know, I joined the army on leaving school.' He smiled wryly. 'It was what Father wanted and,

149

before I had to come home because of his death, I'd completed my officer's training.'

Isobel nodded and whispered, 'Yes, I remember.'

'I'm probably on a reserve list somewhere anyway – I seem to remember agreeing to it at the time,' Gervase went on. 'But I don't intend to wait for them to send for me.'

'But – but what about the estate?' Isobel cried.

'I'll get everything sorted out before I go, but I was rather hoping that, with the suspension of your suffragette activities, you'd be willing to move back to Bixley Manor and take care of things while – while I'm gone?'

'Oh no, Gervase dear, you can't possibly go, because I'm going to offer my services as a nurse. Lady Lee says they'll be badly needed.'

Before either of the men could say any more, Florrie linked her arm through Isobel's and declared, 'Then I'm coming with you.'

Gervase and Tim glanced at each other and shook their heads. 'I don't think,' Tim said slowly, 'that arguing will do any good.'

'Not a scrap,' Isobel and Florrie said together.

As the two young women turned away, Tim put his hand on Gervase's shoulder. 'Don't look so worried, old chap. Iso will probably change her mind once we're married. I'll do my best to talk her out of it.'

But Gervase looked none too sure. He knew his sister – and Florrie. Once they'd made up their minds, there was no dissuading them.

So it was all organized very quickly and, contrary to Isobel's prediction, the locals did not nod and wink and nudge each other over the swiftly arranged marriage.

They all understood the desire for it, and applauded the gallant young man and his lovely bride when news circulated that she too was to volunteer her services.

'And you mark my words,' they said to one another. On and on their tongues wagged, but it was not unkind gossip, as the gifts that arrived for the couple and the offers of willing hands to help prepare Bixley Manor for the big day testified. 'Miss Florrie'll be going too. And have you heard? Mr Richards has asked Mr Maltby to oversee the running of the Bixley Estate in his absence. Now if only Miss Florrie would marry him . . .'

Nineteen

'Well, I'm going and there's nothing you can do about it.'

Once more, Florrie stood in her father's study. He was standing before the fireplace, resting his arm on the mantelpiece and gazing into the flickering flames of the log fire. Slowly he raised his head and turned to face her. He watched her for a long moment, his gaze seeming to take in every aspect of her face; a face that was thinner now, but still every bit as beautiful and, if it were possible, even more determined.

'We're going back to London. Isobel and I. But we're going to volunteer to be nurses. At—' She licked her lips nervously. 'At the Front, if necessary.'

Her father's voice was filled with sadness and yet a strange longing as he said heavily, 'I wish James had half your spirit.'

Florrie was startled. 'James? What – what do you mean?'

'James is refusing to go.'

'Go? To war, you mean? But he's not old enough. He's only sixteen and he's still at school. Besides, I thought you wanted him to go on to university?'

'I did.'

'Did? Why "did"? Don't you still?'

Edgar shrugged. 'Things are different now. Our country's at war.'

Florrie moved closer to him. 'You can't – you can't possibly want him to volunteer? Not at *sixteen*?'

Edgar squared his shoulders. 'I most certainly do.'

'Father, for pity's sake, he's a *boy*.'

'Boys as young as sixteen are volunteering. Young Ben Atkinson has enlisted already. He'll be going away any day. And he's only just turned sixteen.'

Florrie gasped. Ben was the son of one of the estate's tenant farmers, Joe Atkinson and his wife, Olive. He was their only boy out of a family of five children. She was appalled. The war was only days old. 'They *let* him go?'

'I don't think there was anything they could do. He went to a recruitment rally in Saltershaven and joined up there and then. Besides, I don't think they'd have wanted to stop him. They must be very proud of him. I just wish I'd sent James to the rally too. It might have put some courage into the boy.'

'You'd encourage him to leave school? To give up all his expensive education?'

'He'd go into the officer-training corps. Like Timothy. He wouldn't be in the ranks.'

'An officer? Leading men more than twice his age? Father, have you taken leave of your senses?'

'Now, look here, my girl, don't you talk to me like that. I'm your father. Have a bit of respect.'

Quietly now, Florrie said, 'I have always had the utmost respect for you, Father. Though you might not believe it, I have. But this! This is preposterous.' She whirled around and ran from the room. 'I'll see what Gran has to say about this.'

'Florence . . .' he bellowed, but she paid no heed.

Augusta was descending the stairs, with a speed and lightness of step that belied her threescore years and ten. Behind her, Beth carried her shawl, her spectacles and her book. It was plain that Augusta was heading for her favourite spot in the corner of the terrace to soak up the summer sunshine.

'Gran—' Florrie began impatiently, mounting two steps to reach her even more quickly.

'Grandmother,' Augusta corrected mildly. 'Now, what is it this time? You're going to become a nurse? I know that.'

. 'Yes, yes. It's not about that this time. It's about James.'

There was a cry from behind them and Florrie turned to see that her mother, probably hearing the commotion in the hall, had emerged from the morning room. Clara had overheard her daughter's words. She moved forward, her hands to her face, her eyes wide. 'What – what about James? He's not ill, is he? He can't be. He was all right at breakfast. What's happened? Where is he? Is he in his room?' She began to mount the stairs. 'Has your father called the doctor?'

'Mother dear,' Florrie began just as her father appeared in the doorway of his study.

'Now look what you've done, girl!' His face was thunderous. 'You shouldn't go upsetting your mother, not when there's nothing to get upset about. At least – not yet.'

Clara gave another cry of alarm. 'Edgar, what do you mean. What is it? What's happened? Oh, he's had a fall from his horse. He was going out riding this morning. That's it, isn't it? How badly is he hurt? Oh, do tell me, please?' Tears flooded down her face.

'Now, now, Clara.' Augusta had reached the bottom of the stairs. Briefly, she paused and took her belongings from the maid. 'Thank you, Beth.'

'Ma'am.' The girl bobbed a curtsy and scuttled away. Augusta took her daughter-in-law's arm and gently urged her towards the morning room. 'Let's sit down and talk about whatever is going on. I'm as much in the dark as you are. Florrie, come along. You too, Edgar.'

Meekly, they all followed her.

Augusta seated herself on the sofa. 'Now – explain yourself, Florrie.'

Florrie and her father exchanged a glance, but it was Edgar who cleared his throat, strode to the fireplace and turned to face them all.

'Florence has decided to volunteer for nursing duties.' He forbore to say that she might end up at the Front. Time enough for that news to be imparted to his sensitive wife when it happened. He glanced at his mother and saw that she already knew as much.

'But what about James?' Clara cried. The news about her daughter scarcely seemed to register. Her mind was still on her son. Florrie smiled wryly. She wasn't hurt by her mother's lack of solicitude for her. Indeed, she was grateful for it. It left her free to follow her heart.

'I – er – rather hoped James would volunteer, like so many of his peers,' Edgar said. 'I understand that more than half his form at school have already done so. And—'

'Volunteer!' Both Clara and Augusta spoke at once. Then Clara collapsed back against the cushions in a faint.

'Ring for Beth to bring the sal volatile,' Augusta instructed Florrie and then turned her attention back to her own son. 'Are you serious, Edgar?'

'Absolutely. Why shouldn't I be?'

She stared at him for a moment, whilst Florrie's anxious glance went from one to the other. Absent-mindedly, she pulled the bell cord to summon the maid. When Beth appeared she was already carrying the little bottle of smelling salts. No doubt, the scene in the hallway had prepared her for this eventuality. Florrie gave the girl a brief smile and then turned her attention back to her father and grandmother.

'Because the boy's only sixteen,' Augusta snapped. 'He should stay where he is, at least until he finishes his schooling. After he's taken his examinations, well, we'll see then.'

Edgar spread his hands. 'But it might all be over by then and he'll have missed his chance.'

'All the better,' Augusta replied promptly.

'I don't want my son to be thought a coward.'

'Don't be ridiculous, Edgar.'

'Ben Atkinson's going and he's only sixteen.'

For a moment, even Augusta seemed shocked. She shook her head and muttered, 'More fool him, then.'

'But they're calling for volunteers. They're holding recruitment rallies the length and breadth of the country.'

'But not for sixteen-year-olds. I do read the papers, Edgar.'

Her son eyed her speculatively. 'And what does your *London* newspaper tell you then, eh?'

Augusta glared at him. 'A lot more common sense than your provincial rag, which seems to be whipping up a fever of patriotism that is sadly misplaced.'

'How can patriotism be misplaced?'

She leaned forward, saying slowly and deliberately, 'If it expects sixteen-year-olds to become cannon fodder, then it's – it's – ' She sought the word to prove her point. '*Immoral!*'

Clara, reviving at that moment, promptly fainted again.

The argument was over. Edgar retired to his study and slammed the door, leaving his mother and daughter to tend his wife. They reassured Clara that James was not volunteering now and they were sure that, by the time he was old enough, it would all be over.

'It'll probably be over before I've even finished training to mop fevered brows and feed the wounded,' Florrie said, making light of her own plans.

'You'll make a very good nurse, dear,' Clara said weakly. 'You're always so kind to me when I have one of my turns.'

Above her head, Augusta and Florrie exchanged a grim look. They both knew that what Florrie would face would be far more than a few fainting fits.

Florrie breathed a sigh of relief when, at the beginning of September, James returned to school for the autumn term. She'd been so worried that their father would shame him into volunteering. Although she was anxious about Gervase and the Hon. Tim going, she accepted their decision as being right and admired their patriotic courage. What she couldn't come to terms with was the thought of boys as young as sixteen being accepted into the services. Determined to find out how such a thing could happen, she walked across the fields to the Atkinsons' farmhouse.

'Oh, Miss Florrie,' Mrs Atkinson, her white apron to her face, greeted the young woman as she opened the door. 'How kind of you to come. You've heard, I suppose, that our Ben's goin' soldierin'?'

Florrie nodded. 'How did it happen, Mrs Atkinson? He's only sixteen.'

Fresh tears welled in the woman's eyes. 'He's nowt more'n a bairn, Miss Florrie.' She poured boiling water into a brown teapot from the kettle over the fire in the range and set two cups and saucers on the table. 'He went to one o' them rallies in Saltershaven and joined up there an' then. His dad went next day to see if he could get 'im out of it, but there were nowt 'ee could do. Ben'd taken the King's shilling and that were it.'

Florrie was appalled. 'And did they know he was sixteen?'

'Huh! I s'pect he lied about his age.'

'And they didn't press him too closely, you mean?'

Mrs Atkinson nodded. 'That's about the size of it, miss.'

'But he doesn't even look eighteen. He's strong and wiry, I grant you, but he's a *boy*. Anyone can see that.'

'I don't think they're bothered, miss. They just want volunteers. As many as they can get, an' they're not that worried how they get 'em.'

They gazed at each other now, lost for words.

As they sat over their tea, Mrs Atkinson said, 'Word's goin' round, miss, that you're going to nurse our lads at the Front.'

'Maybe, Mrs Atkinson. I haven't heard yet if I've been accepted, but if I can get some training and they'll let me go . . .'

The woman nodded and gave a weak smile. 'Oh, they'll take you, miss. I don't doubt that.'

A little later as Florrie got up to leave, she took hold of the woman's careworn hands. 'If there's anything – anything – we can do for you, you let my grandmother know. Promise me!'

Mrs Atkinson nodded and her voice was husky as she said, 'Thank you, Miss Florrie. And – and if you see my boy out there, you'll take care of him, won't you?'

The poor woman had no inkling of how vast the theatre of war would be, but Florrie nodded and said quietly, 'Of course I will. And try not to worry. I don't think they'll send him abroad yet and, if the newspapers are right, it'll all be over by Christmas.'

The woman smiled thinly, but did not answer. Her fear outweighed her hope.

Twenty

Florrie itched to be gone, though Isobel, caught up in the flurry of wedding preparations, was unconcerned.

'Once the Hon. Tim's gone, Florrie dear, I'll be only too delighted to have something to do. It'll take my mind off worrying about him. And Lady Lee has promised to speak to one of her friends in the Red Cross about arranging for us to do some nursing training at one of the London hospitals. She'll let us know as soon as she has something to tell us.'

But no news came from Lady Leonora, and Florrie was still at Candlethorpe Hall when James arrived home unexpectedly one Friday afternoon at the end of September.

Clara cried at the sight of him. 'Oh, my darling boy! You're so thin and pale. Are you ill? Aren't they feeding you properly?' She hugged him to her and sent for Cook at once to discuss the most nourishing meals they could devise to 'build the boy up'.

'But build me up for what?' he muttered when he and Florrie were alone in the former nursery.

'What d'you mean?' she frowned, concerned too by his thin face and anxious eyes.

'For war,' he said flatly.

'What are you talking about?'

'It's as bad at school as it is here – with Father,' he blurted out, tears in his eyes. He brushed them away, embarrassed at such an unmanly display of emotion, even in front of his beloved sister.

Florrie drew him to the sofa and held his hands. 'Tell me,' she said gently.

He leaned his head against her shoulder and sighed. 'More than half the sixth form have volunteered already and with the headmaster's blessing.' James was now in the Lower Sixth. 'Can you believe that? He says it will bring glory and honour to the school. I think he wants a plaque in the school hall bearing all the names of the fallen and everyone paying homage to it,' he added bitterly.

'And you're feeling pressured to go too?' Florrie said softly.

'What with Father and – and all the chaps at school . . .'

'What about the rest of the sixth form? Are they *all* going to volunteer?'

He nodded miserably. 'The talk in the common room was of nothing else. Several said they're going to volunteer at half term. They're – they're not even going to wait until Christmas.'

'And what did the Head say?'

'Patted them on the back and wished them well. Told them that somehow he'd see that there'd always be a place for them back at school when they'd done their duty – "Done the honourable thing," ' he said.'

'But you can't go,' Florrie cried. 'You're much too young. You don't *want* to go.' She paused and twisted round to look directly into his eyes. 'Do you?'

James bit his lip and lowered his gaze. Then, slowly, he shook his head.

'Then why?' She spread her hands in a helpless gesture. 'You're thinking of volunteering just because

Father and the headmaster say it's what you should do? Is that it?'

When he didn't deny it, she said, 'Oh, James, that's ridiculous. Stand up to him – to them both.'

'I – I tried. Before I went back to school. B-but Father said I was being cowardly. And that's the feeling around school too. Even those that haven't actually done it yet – they're all talking about the day they're going to. And if a chap doesn't join in . . .' He faltered and stopped, but Florrie understood. 'And – if I can't stand up to him – to them – then I must be a coward.' He laughed wryly. 'Whatever I do.'

Florrie sighed and squeezed his hand. 'Not really. Grandpops evidently didn't stand up to his father. Gran told us, didn't she? That didn't make him a coward, now did it?'

James shrugged as if he didn't know how to answer. 'But he isn't here any more to understand me – to help me.'

'No.' Florrie smiled suddenly. 'But Gran is. She'll stick up for you and so will I. And I'm sure Mother will too,' she was unable to keep the doubt out of her tone now, 'in her own way.'

'I think Gran's changed her mind,' James's tone was flat.

'What d'you mean?'

'I – I think she agrees with Father now.'

'Agrees with *Father*?' She gaped at him. This was a first. She grabbed her brother's hand and pulled him up. 'We'll see about this. Come on.'

Down the stairs from the old nursery and along the landings until they came to Augusta's sitting room. So angry was she that Florrie forgot to give the usual courteous knock and barged into the room unheralded.

Augusta was sitting in the window seat, looking out over the front garden watching Ben Atkinson rake up the leaves on the lawn. The boy was leaving the following day for training camp. At the sudden unannounced intrusion, she turned. She opened her mouth to admonish her grandchildren, but, seeing at once the look of agitation on Florrie's face and the fear in James's eyes, she bit back the retort.

'Is James right in what he says?' Florrie burst out.

Augusta glanced back out of the window once more as she said quietly, 'That rather depends on what he's been telling you.'

'That you agree with Father? That he should volunteer?'

Her gaze still on the boy on the lawn below her window, Augusta said slowly, 'Young Ben has volunteered. Caught up in the passion of the moment at a recruiting rally on the sea front.' She was pensive for a moment, remembering the day she had spent there with Florrie, James and Gervase. Despite the cloud of war hanging over them, they had managed to make it a happy, carefree day.

'I know all that,' Florrie cried impatiently. 'But there's nothing we can do about it now. It's done. But this is James we're talking about.'

Augusta continued to look out of the window.

'Grandmother – about *James*.' Florrie released her hold on James's hand and moved towards Augusta, leaving her brother standing where he was just inside the doorway.

Florrie, her gaze still on her grandmother's face, sank on to the window seat beside her. 'I don't understand. When all this started, you said – you said James should finish his education before even *thinking* about it.'

Augusta sighed and then held out her hand towards James. 'Close the door, my dear, and come and sit with us. Let's talk this through.'

The young man did as she bade him and then sat on a footstool facing the window, whilst Augusta and Florrie sat on each side of the seat, facing each other.

'Now, what is it that you don't understand?' their grandmother asked.

Florrie glanced at James, but when he made no effort to explain, she spoke for him, telling Augusta all that he had told her about the patriotic fervour at school, egged on by the headmaster. 'Father is calling him cowardly because he won't volunteer. And – and he seems to think you might be agreeing with him now. Gran, James is only sixteen.' She leaned forward earnestly. 'He has his whole life in front of him.' She bit her lip, glanced again at her brother, apology in her eyes, but it had to be said. It had to be voiced aloud. 'You've seen the casualty lists in the paper already. And we're scarcely two months into the war. It's carnage out there. "A Bloodbath at Mons" – that's what the papers called it. Our troops were forced to retreat two hundred miles as far as the River Marne.'

'But they saved Paris,' Augusta murmured.

'So – are you really telling me you want James to go into *that*?'

Augusta was thoughtful for a moment. 'I'm afraid it doesn't look as if this war is going to be "over by Christmas" like they've been saying. I'd hoped they were right, that if we hung on, James wouldn't even be faced with such a dreadful decision.' She reached out and ruffled his hair fondly. 'But, you see, if it goes on for – for a while, they're going to have to bring in conscription.'

Florrie glanced at James, but he was resting his elbows on his knees, his fingers linked, his gaze on the floor.

'Conscription?' she asked. 'What's that?'

'All men between certain ages are called up to go into the armed forces. To – to refuse is classed as an act of cowardice and punishable. Either prison or – or worse.'

'My God! What is this country coming to?'

For once, her grandmother did not check the girl's blasphemy. Instead, she sighed heavily. 'I don't want James to go any more than you do. But if he doesn't volunteer, then it's likely he'll be called up anyway eventually.'

'But it might all be over by then. And surely they won't call anyone up who's still at *school*, for Heaven's sake!'

Augusta looked out of the window once more. 'Your father's view is very simplistic. If Ben Atkinson – the son of one of his tenants – can go, then the son of the biggest landowner and employer in the district should do no less.'

'But James is the only male heir to the Maltby estate.'

Augusta faced her squarely. 'Hence his ambition for you to marry Gervase Richards and provide him with a grandson. He still hasn't given up that hope entirely.'

Florrie gasped. 'How – how,' she searched for the right word, 'calculating of him! Doesn't he care about *either* of us?'

'In his way, I'm sure he does. But pride and tradition and the family's good name are everything in Edgar's eyes.' She sighed as she added in a whisper, 'Everything.'

Florrie couldn't ever remember having felt so

shocked about anything in the whole of her young life. It was not what Augusta had said about their father's attitude – she'd expected as much – but never in a million years would she have anticipated that their grandmother would agree with his sentiments.

As if still needing, yet at the same time fearing, to hear the words from her own lips, Florrie said, 'And – and is James right? *Do* you agree with Father now?'

Augusta was silent for a long moment, still gazing down at Ben. Slowly she turned to look at them both, glancing between them, her fond gaze resting on them in turn. 'I can understand your father's reasoning.' As Florrie opened her mouth to argue hotly, Augusta raised her hand and her face broke into smiles. 'But, no, of course I don't agree with him. I don't think James should volunteer. I think he should wait until he *has* to go, whatever it looks like to other people.' She cocked her head on one side and said impishly, 'Florrie, how could you ever think any differently of me? When have I ever cared for the opinions of others?'

'Oh, Gran, Gran! I knew it!' Florrie flung her arms around the older woman. 'I knew you wouldn't be so – so heartless.'

'Now, now, I can't have you implying such a thing about your father,' her grandmother admonished, but her eyes were twinkling as she added slyly, 'But you seem to be forgetting, Florrie dear, that your idol, Mrs Pankhurst, is in favour of the war. That's why you find yourself at home once more, isn't it? Fidgeting because you've nothing useful to do.'

'Yes,' the girl admitted.

'And Emmeline Pankhurst always advocated any means by which to achieve one's aims? Even violence?'

'Well – in a way.'

'So why are you against our country defending itself?'

Florrie blinked. 'Oh, I'm not against the war,' she said blithely. 'I just don't want James to go, that's all.'

For a moment there was silence between them as Augusta and James glanced at each other. Then they both burst out laughing.

'What? What have I said?' Florrie demanded.

'Oh, my dear girl,' Augusta said, wiping the tears of laughter from her eyes. 'Never mind gaining the *vote* for women – you should be Prime Minister.'

Twenty-One

Florrie hoped the matter of James enlisting would end there and she was thankful to wave him off on the Monday morning to return to school. But the same night, as the family was rising from the dinner table, the ladies to the drawing room and Edgar to his study to smoke a cigar and drink brandy, they heard the noise of a pony and trap drawing up outside the front door.

'Now, who on earth can that be at this hour?' Edgar muttered crossly. He enjoyed his solitary hour in the study after dinner and hated interruptions to the routine of the household.

Bowler opened the door as the family crowded into the hall.

'James!' Clara hurried forward, her arms outstretched. 'What's happened? Has there been an accident? Are you hurt?'

Florrie sought her brother's face as he moved into the light. There was a strange mixture of emotions in his expression: triumph and yet a dreadful fear too and, worse still, a sense of the inevitable.

Clara was still gushing over her son, but Florrie gripped her grandmother's arm and whispered, 'Oh, Gran, he's volunteered. I know he has.'

Florrie was right and, whilst Clara dissolved into floods of tears and Edgar patted him on the back and called for Bowler to open a bottle of champagne, Florrie and Augusta looked on, their hearts clutched with foreboding.

'Well, that's it, then,' Florrie muttered. 'I'm not waiting any longer for Lady Lee to get in touch. Tomorrow, I'm going back to London.'

'You can't. It's Isobel's wedding in two weeks' time. Surely you hadn't forgotten?'

Florrie sighed. 'Yes – for the moment – I had.'

The date had originally been fixed for the beginning of December, but the Hon. Tim had received notice that he was to report to military college at the beginning of that month. The date of their marriage had therefore been brought forward to the second Saturday in October so that they could have a few weeks together as man and wife before he had to leave.

'You can't let her down. She needs you here. There's so much to be done before the big day and, my dear,' Augusta put her hand on Florrie's arm, 'when Timothy goes away, she'll need your support more than ever. How about waiting until he's gone and you can go back to London together?'

'You're right. That's what I'll do. It's not as if we've heard from Lady Lee yet. In the meantime . . .' They exchanged a solemn glance as they watched Beth help a wailing Clara into the drawing room.

'Oh, James, James – how could you?' she cried, with the desolation of a mother believing her boy is going to certain death.

'My dear boy,' Edgar was saying, even putting his arm around James's shoulders in an unusual expression of affection. 'I'm so very proud of you.'

Augusta wriggled her shoulders. 'Well, there's one good thing, Florrie. With him being so young, his training to be an officer might take a long time. Hopefully long enough that he won't need to go to France at all.'

'I hope you're right,' Florrie muttered grimly.

But both Florrie and her grandmother were in for another shock. Too young to enlist for officer training, James had joined the ranks. Once he'd completed his basic training, he might be sent to France at any time.

The weather was kind to Isobel and Tim on their wedding day – cold, but fine and bright. Bixley Manor, nestling in a vale, lay on the edge of the Lincolnshire Wolds, about six miles from Candlethorpe Hall. In front of the large, square Georgian house was a lake with a pair of swans that nested there and reared their young. The ground then rose gently to a small church, built some generations earlier by the Richards family and attended too by all those who lived on the estate, workers and tenant farmers alike. It was a friendly congregation – like one big family – and the vicar from Bixley village who took the services was a benevolent father figure to them all. In turn they adored and revered the merry, white-haired gentleman. On the day of Isobel's wedding, the little church, crammed with family, friends and estate workers, was so crowded that a few had to cluster round the church porch and eavesdrop through the open door.

Everyone was determined to put all thoughts of the war aside. They resolutely ignored the disturbing news that Antwerp was under heavy attack from the enemy as both sides tried to race to the sea and command the Channel ports. Instead, the wedding guests vowed to enjoy the young couple's special day. Everyone except Clara, who found such strength of will quite impossible.

She spent the day with a handkerchief pressed to her lips and tears streaming from her eyes every time she looked at James.

'Iso – you look lovely,' Florrie said as they finished dressing together. She stood back to make sure that Isobel's veil was firmly in place. Despite the anxiety that hung over everyone and the austerity that would surely come, Gervase had insisted the wedding should be traditional. Isobel's oyster satin gown had a fitted bodice embroidered with French knots, a high neckline and long, narrow sleeves. The front panel of the straight-cut skirt was also decorated with French knots, and a narrow train hung from the back of the waist.

Isobel laughed merrily. 'There's no need to sound so surprised.'

Florrie laughed too. 'I wasn't. I've always told you, you're a handsome woman, but today there's something special about you.'

'Aren't all brides supposed to look beautiful on their wedding day? Even the ugly ones?'

'You're far from ugly.'

'I know.' Isobel put her head on one side and regarded her friend. 'But you're the one to whom the word "beautiful" really applies. That blue silk dress really suits you.' She chuckled mischievously. 'I rather think that Gervase will bring forward this year's proposal when he sees you.'

As Florrie groaned, they both burst out laughing.

Then they sobered.

'Your Hon. Tim is such a lovely man, but he's a lucky one too: to be marrying you. You're so strong and – and daring, and he's so proud of you.'

'Thank you, Florrie darling,' Isobel said with a catch in her throat. Then suddenly she chuckled. 'Just look at this.' She raised the hem of her gown. 'How daring is that?'

Florrie laughed as she saw that the garters Isobel was wearing to hold up her white stockings were threaded through with purple, green and white ribbons.

'Now, it's time I was going,' Florrie said. 'I'll tell Gervase you're ready. And, darling Iso, I'll see you at the church porch.' They kissed each other's cheek. 'Be happy, Iso,' Florrie whispered, her voice husky with emotion. Tears glistened in Isobel's eyes and, not trusting herself to speak, she nodded.

As Florrie descended the stairs, Gervase was in the hall. He looked up at her and held out his hand to help her down the last few steps.

'You look wonderful, Florrie darling.'

'Thank you, Gervase. And your sister looks lovely too, so don't you forget to tell her so.'

'I won't.' He led her out of the door and handed her into the carriage, tucking a rug warmly around her knees, though she scarcely needed it.

The route up to the church was difficult, for there was only a mud track up the grassy slope. Today, though, it was fine and dry and so most of the guests walked up. But Gervase had insisted that Florrie and the bride should travel in the carriage. Leaving Florrie at the church gate, the carriage returned to the Manor to bring the bride and her brother.

The service, apart from the solemn moments of the exchange of vows, was a merry one. The vicar kept his address light-hearted – teasing almost – and his words lifted the spirits of everyone there. For, though never mentioned, thoughts of the war were never very far from anyone's mind.

After the service, the bride and groom led the way

back to the Manor, walking down the hill in the late autumn sunshine, followed by all those who loved them.

'Lady Lee – Mrs Maltby,' Gervase addressed Lady Leonora and Augusta in concern. 'Would you like to ride in the carriage? Perhaps Mrs Edgar would care to—'

He got no further, for Augusta said, 'Good Heavens, no, Gervase. I'm happy to walk with you all.'

'Oh, I wouldn't miss this. This is such a beautiful setting for a country wedding. Just perfect.' Lady Leonora's eyes misted as she watched her son and new daughter-in-law setting off down the hill as if stepping out into their new life. 'Though I think Henry,' Lady Smythe referred to her husband, who'd been persuaded to leave the sanctuary of their country home and travel to 'foreign' parts, 'might be very glad to ride back. His gout is bothering him cruelly today.'

They turned to see a portly gentleman hobbling with a walking stick.

'The dear man never complains,' Lady Lee said softly. 'But I fear he's often in great pain.'

Gervase hurried towards Lord Smythe and beckoned for the carriage. When he'd helped him into it, he returned to the ladies.

'Thank you, Gervase, and now, you may escort Augusta and me back to the wedding breakfast.'

He'd hoped to walk with Florrie, but gallantly he smiled at the two older women and held out an arm to each of them.

The rest of the day passed happily and it wasn't until everyone stood on the front terrace of the Manor and waved the couple off on their honeymoon that a feeling of gloom settled on the gathering when Clara dissolved into heartbreaking tears once more. Even Lady

Leonora, watching her only son drive away, had to bite down hard on her lip and hold her head high. Lord Smythe patted his wife's hand comfortingly and murmured, 'There, there, dear heart.'

Florrie clung to Gervase's arm and fought back the tears. 'Oh, Gervase, what's going to happen? Will we ever be all together again?'

'I wish I knew, my dear. I only wish I knew.'

What happened – when the bride and groom returned six weeks later – was that Tim left for military training and a dreadful row broke out between Isobel and Gervase.

'You can't possibly expect me to stay here at Bixley on my own. I'll go mad. I must have something to *do*.'

'You'd have plenty to do,' Gervase growled, uncharacteristically angry. 'Running the estate is a full-time job.'

The argument between brother and sister had been raging since early morning and now, over the dinner table, it seemed to be reaching fever pitch. Isobel was emotional and Gervase's frown deepened.

'You've a perfectly capable estate manager in Mr Tring, Gervase,' Isobel reasoned. 'And I'm sure Florrie's father would be on hand to give him advice if there were any real problems.'

'I'm sure he would, but it's hardly fair on him, Iso. He'll have plenty of his own problems with this war. He's lost several of the young estate workers already. Oh,' he added hastily as he saw Florrie's eyes widen, 'I don't mean literally. I mean they've volunteered.'

Florrie lowered her glance, biting her lip to keep silent and wishing herself anywhere but sitting between them.

But the atmosphere at home since James's departure had been tense. Clara had taken to her bed and scarcely a civil word passed between Augusta and Edgar. But here, listening to the normally loving brother and sister arguing so heatedly, was as bad, if not worse. Now Florrie wished she hadn't accepted their invitation to dine with them. This discussion was none of her business.

'Besides, I don't see why you have to go yet,' Isobel went on. 'At least wait until you're called up.'

Gervase sighed. 'Iso, I *want* to go.'

'So do I,' Isobel said grimly, 'I want to go nursing, but you're expecting *me* to give up *my* plans.' Her mouth pursed as she muttered, 'Just because I'm just a woman, I suppose.'

Now Gervase smiled and his fond glance included Florrie too. He even chuckled as he said, 'I'd put my shirt on either of you against the Kaiser. He'd run a mile.'

Florrie smiled and even Isobel's mouth twitched.

Gervase's expression sobered and he sighed. 'Iso, you're needed here. Really you are. Good though Tring is, he can't handle the financial side of things. And it wouldn't be fair to ask Mr Maltby, now would it? You must see that.'

'Our accountant can handle that side of things, surely?' It seemed she had an answer for everything. 'And besides, rumour around the estate has it that you've already spoken to Florrie's father.'

'Well, yes,' Gervase admitted reluctantly, 'but only to – to be on hand to give advice if – if you needed it.'

'Oh, I see.' Isobel was offended. 'You don't actually trust me to run it on my own then? There has to be a *man* in the background to help the little woman—'

'Iso!'

Florrie spoke up for the first time. 'Sleep on it. Both of you. I don't like to see you quarrelling. It isn't like you. Either of you.'

Brother and sister looked at each other and then smiled.

'No, it isn't,' Isobel said softly. 'I can't remember us ever falling out quite as badly as this. Oh, we bicker a bit – all brothers and sisters do . . .'

We don't, Florrie thought. James and I don't. A fresh wave of fear and sorrow washed over her as she thought of the boy she loved and the untold dangers he would surely have to face. But, for once, she held her wayward tongue.

They went to bed still with nothing resolved, and the following morning Isobel came down looking pale and decidedly queasy. She refused breakfast. 'It must be all this upset with Gervase, Florrie. I've hardly slept. I hate falling out with him, but I must stick to my guns. What on earth would Lady Lee think of me if I chickened out now? Hardly the actions of a suffragette devotee!'

'I don't think Lady Lee would think anything of the sort,' Florrie said, glancing anxiously at Isobel. The young woman looked positively ill this morning. 'And I expect Tim would be relieved.'

Isobel gave an unladylike – but wholly characteristic – snort. 'No doubt,' she said tartly.

Gervase entered the room with two letters in his hand. He went to stand near Isobel's chair and stood looking down at her for a moment. Then, suddenly, he bent and kissed her cheek.

'Dear Iso, I'm sorry. Don't let us part with bad feeling between us.'

Isobel drew in a breath and looked up at him. 'Part?' Then she noticed the letters he carried. He nodded.

'This one addressed to me is telling me I have to report for duty next week. And this one,' he held out the other envelope, 'is – I think – the one both you and Florrie have been waiting for. I recognize Lady Lee's hand.'

Isobel stared at it for a moment and then took it from him with trembling fingers.

'Oh, open it, Iso,' Florrie urged. 'What does she say?'

Isobel scanned the single page of Lady Lee's scrawling handwriting. 'Not very much, really. Just – just that if we can go back to London now she should have definite news for us in a day or so.' Isobel glanced up. 'She must be fairly sure. She wouldn't ask us to go back otherwise.'

Florrie glanced up at Gervase, fearful that the quarrel was going to break out again. But Gervase put his hand on his sister's shoulder and smiled down at her. 'You go, Iso. I know it's what you want. I'll sort something out before I leave.'

The two young women watched as he wrinkled his brow. 'I'm to report next Monday, so that doesn't leave me much time.' He turned away, murmuring, 'I'd better see Tring and then ride over and see your father, Florrie.'

As he strode out of the room, Florrie said, 'Whatever made him change his mind? He seemed so adamant last night that you should stay here.'

Iso was thoughtful. 'Oh, that's Gervase. He's so kind-hearted really and can usually be relied upon to see the other person's point of view.' Softly, she added, 'He's a good sort, Florrie. You could do a lot worse, you know.'

Twenty-Two

Isobel and Florrie boarded the train to London and the Richards' town house. And it wasn't many days before Lady Leonora came with the news.

'You're to go along to the VAD headquarters in Piccadilly and volunteer for hospital work.'

'Where? In France?' Florrie asked eagerly.

Lady Lee shook her head. 'Not immediately, my dear. You must have some training first. I believe you have to have certificates in first aid and home nursing, at the very least, to be accepted as a VAD nurse. Many of the hospitals throughout the country are giving volunteers practical experience, though you should be warned – a lot of the professional nurses don't welcome them.'

'But we want to go to France – or Belgium. To the Front, if necessary,' Florrie persisted.

Lady Lee smiled at the young woman's spirit. It was that same spirit that had equipped her to undertake militant acts for the sake of her beliefs, and to take the consequences so bravely. And now, she was prepared to face unknown horrors for the patriotic defence of her country. 'Well, you can make it clear that you're willing to go to France, if needed.' Then her smile faded. 'Florrie, my dear, there's just one thing you ought to know. The age range for VADs is twenty-one to forty-eight. And – and I think you need to be twenty-three to work in the war zone.'

Florrie stared at her. Then her mouth tightened. 'If my little brother, James, can lie about his age and be accepted, then so can I.'

Now Lady Lee chuckled. 'I thought that would be your answer. And, Isobel, my dear,' she went on, 'I think you should take off your wedding ring and keep the fact that you are married secret. I'm not sure if they welcome married women, and I know how keen you are to go.' She shrugged. 'Personally, I think it's ridiculous, but there you are. You can always put your ring on a tiny chain around your neck. Tim will understand, I know.'

'Well, I shall continue to wear my suffragette brooch whether they like it or not,' Florrie declared.

'So, how do I look?'

The two young women faced each other in Florrie's bedroom. They were both dressed identically in ankle-length cotton dresses, a white apron with a red cross on the bib, a stiff white collar, black woollen stockings and sturdy, sensible shoes.

'You look great,' Isobel said. 'But how do we fasten our caps on?'

'Haven't a clue,' Florrie said cheerfully. 'Let's wear these cloaks and bonnets to travel to the hospital and then get someone there to show us how to put these white caps on when we go on the wards.' She grinned. 'If they let us anywhere near the patients. Come on, we'd better go, else we'll be late, and that would never do on our first day.'

A little while later they were standing meekly in front of Sister Blackstock's desk whilst her steely gaze seemed to be boring right through them. The woman pursed her mouth.

'So, you've come to tend the fevered brows and hold the hands of heroes, have you?' Her sarcasm was evident and her feelings abundantly clear. Florrie guessed the sister to be in her mid-thirties. She was tall and slim. Her large nose dominated her face and consequently her mouth seemed small in comparison, but her bright-blue eyes were sharp and intelligent.

With surprising humility, Florrie said quietly, 'We've come to help wherever we can be useful, Sister. We realize we've a lot of training to do before we could even think of going to France, but—'

The woman's lip curled. 'Oh, I think we can safely say the war will be long over by the time you two could be let loose amongst wounded soldiers. However, if you mean what you say, we can certainly make use of you.' The look in her eyes told them that she didn't expect them to last out the first week. 'Several of our *professional* nurses have been released for work at the Front and so we're short-staffed.' She stood up and moved around the desk, leading the way out of the room. 'Come along, I'll introduce you to the women's medical ward. That's *my* ward and you'll be in my charge.' As she opened the door and walked through it, Florrie was sure she heard the sister mutter under her breath, 'More's the pity.'

At first, they were treated as ward skivvies, cleaning, washing and at the beck and call of everyone. But Sister Blackstock was the one who worked them the hardest.

'She never gives us a moment's peace,' Florrie moaned as they went home in a hansom cab at the end of their first week. 'Thank goodness for a day off tomorrow. I'm sure I could sleep for a fortnight.'

By the middle of the second week, Florrie said, 'I was actually allowed near a patient today. I spoon-fed the poor old dear in the end bed. You know the one?'

Isobel, looking white with fatigue, nodded. 'Count yourself lucky. All I've done is wash floors and carry bedpans backwards and forwards. And the ward we're on is for old women, Florrie. How is that ever going to help us nurse wounded soldiers?'

'I know. I'm going to have a word with Lady Lee tomorrow. You'd think they'd be screaming out for a couple of fit and eager young women to go to the Front, wouldn't you? But no, here we are, willing and able, and all we do is scrub, scrub, scrub.'

But Lady Lee could do no more. 'You'll have to be patient, Florrie, my dear. I'm sure it's a test of stamina.'

'Oh, it's that all right. Though I'm worried about Isobel. She looks awfully tired.'

At the end of their second week, only a few days before Christmas, as they alighted from the hansom carrying them home and staggered up the steps, Meredith opened the front door.

'Good evening, ma'am. Miss Florrie. Lucy has your baths ready and supper will be served in an hour.'

'Oh, Meredith, you're an angel,' Florrie said, pulling herself up the stairs towards her bedroom. She heard a sound behind her and looked back to see that Isobel was sagging against the butler, and poor Meredith was having difficulty in holding her from falling onto the floor. Florrie rushed back down, her tiredness forgotten. They eased Isobel to the floor and Florrie turned her on to her side. She loosened Isobel's collar.

'Shall I send for the doctor, miss?'

'I think it's only because she's so weary, but – yes,

perhaps you'd better. Gervase – and Tim – would never forgive me if it's more serious.'

After only a few seconds, Isobel moaned and started to come round. She tried to sit up, but Florrie said firmly, 'Lie still, Iso.'

'What – am I doing down here?' Isobel murmured and lifted her head again.

'No, Iso, lie there for a moment or two. Meredith is calling the doctor.'

'Oh, there's no need to fuss. I just feel so – so sick all the time. I think it must be the smells in that place . . .' But she did as Florrie asked her and lay still, her eyes closed.

Meredith came hurrying back into the hall. 'I've telephoned for the doctor, miss. He's out on a call, but as soon as he gets home, his wife will give him the message.'

'Do you think you can stand now, Iso, and we'll help you into the morning room?'

'I – think so.'

Between them, Florrie and Meredith helped Isobel onto the sofa, where she lay back against the cushions looking pale and drawn. Lucy was summoned to fetch a drink of water, and Florrie held the glass to Isobel's lips. 'Well, I suppose this is nursing, but it wasn't quite what I expected – or wanted,' Florrie tried to be light-hearted, but in truth she was worried about her friend. She wished the doctor would hurry up.

The Richards' London doctor was a bluff, no-nonsense man, but kindly and would move heaven and earth, as the saying went, to help a patient. As, indeed, he had when he'd helped Gervase get Florrie out of prison. She greeted him in the doorway.

'Well, Miss Maltby,' he said as he shook her hand.

'You look a good deal better than you did the last time I saw you. Hard work must agree with you,' he added, for he knew all about their nursing activities.

As she led him into the morning room, she said in a low voice, 'You're right – I think I thrive on it, but I'm not sure the same can be said of Isobel. Anyway, here we are . . .'

With a light tap on the door, she led the way into the room and stood to the side whilst Dr Tomkinson sat beside Isobel and gently took hold of her wrist to feel her pulse. 'Now, Miss Isobel,' he greeted her with familiarity. He'd known her and the family since childhood.

'Oh Doctor – I feel such a failure – so useless!' Her voice trembled and her eyes filled with tears.

Florrie watched in concern. This was so unlike Isobel. She was always so strong, so resilient, so – so purposeful. But at this moment she reminded the younger girl of her own mother, Clara, who seemed to have spent most of her days lying on a sofa shedding tears about one thing or another. Florrie was suddenly afraid. Was her dear friend really ill?

'I feel so nauseous all the time,' Isobel was saying weakly. 'Especially in a morning . . .'

The doctor leaned closer to her and murmured something so softly that Florrie could not hear what he said. But she saw Isobel's response, saw her raise her head from the cushion and stare, with wide eyes, into the doctor's face. 'No – no,' Isobel whispered. 'I – I haven't. I never realized – never thought for a moment . . .' She gave a sigh, leaned back against the cushions and closed her eyes.

Florrie could contain her fear no longer. 'What is it? Is she ill? Should I send for – for—' She faltered. There

was no one she could send for – not immediately. Both
Tim and now Gervase too were away at training camp.
But if it was really serious, then she must get word to
them somehow. They were both still in this country.
Perhaps they could get compassionate leave, perhaps . . .

Dr Tomkinson was standing up and turning round
towards Florrie. She braced herself to hear the worst.
But the doctor was smiling, beaming in fact. 'Don't
look so worried, Miss Maltby. Miss Isobel – though
I should now start calling her by her married name,
especially in these circumstances—'

'Circumstances? What – circumstances?'

'I believe, though it's early days yet, that she is with
child.'

'With – with— Oh!' Now it was Florrie whose eyes
widened. 'She's going to have a baby. Oh, Iso—' Arms
outstretched, she rushed towards her and dropped to
her knees beside the sofa. 'How wonderful! Tim will be
thrilled and so will Lady Lee.'

Isobel opened her eyes and smiled weakly. 'It – it just
takes a bit of getting used to. I – I never thought that
could be the reason. I just thought it was all the hard
work we've been doing. You seem to cope so well,
Florrie. It's as if you were born to it. But me – I just
thought I was an idle rich girl who'd never had to do a
day's hard work in her life.'

Florrie smiled inwardly at Isobel's words: 'As if you
were born to it.' Well, it was in her genes, after all, for
her grandmother Augusta had indeed been born into
a hard-working life. Aloud, she said, 'Of course, you'd
have coped. You were doing, but this explains it all.'
She glanced up at Dr Tomkinson. 'She should give it
up, shouldn't she? Straight away.'

The doctor nodded. 'I'm afraid so. I know you both

want to do your bit, but you must think of the well-being of your child now.'

'Besides,' Florrie grinned, 'the Hon. Tim – once he hears about this – will put his foot down very firmly. And so will Lady Lee.'

Isobel smiled, looking a little mesmerized, as if she still couldn't take it in.

'Will Tim want you to go to their home in Dorset?'

'Perhaps – I don't know.' Isobel put her hand to her forehead. 'Tim was born there and he might want our child,' Isobel savoured the word for a moment, 'to be born there too, and if that's what he wants, then that's what I'll do. But, for the time being, the least I can do is go home to Bixley and run the estate for Gervase.' She looked straight into Florrie's eyes. 'Don't you think?'

'I think that's the very best thing you could do. My father – and Gran – will be on hand to help. And then, nearer your time, you could travel to Dorset – if you need to.'

They both looked up at the doctor who nodded his approval. 'Capital idea.' Then he smiled again and wagged his finger. 'But no more working at the hospital. You must tell them what's happened, Miss Maltby, and that she'll not be resuming her duties. Doctor's orders.'

As he took his leave and the door closed behind him, Isobel and Florrie clung to each other, overcome by a fit of the giggles. They were laughing with relief and joy and the thought that Florrie would have to explain everything to Sister Blackstock.

'Oh, I can just see her face,' Florrie spluttered, 'when I tell her that *Miss* Richards is having a baby.'

'She'll think I'm a fallen women. I bet she doesn't believe you . . .'

Twenty-Three

Just as Isobel had anticipated, Sister Blackstock took a lot of convincing and even when she began to accept that truth, she still wasn't pleased.

'So – Miss Richards has been married all the time? Even when she first applied to become a nurse?'

'She was married in October and, when she came back from her honeymoon, her husband went away to military college and we came back to London and volunteered our services.'

'So she deceived us. She led us to believe she was single. She's wasted our time *trying* to train her to be useful.' The woman fixed Florrie with a steely gaze. 'And what about you? What lies have you told us?'

Florrie answered quickly. 'I'm single – quite unattached – and willing to do anything you ask of me, but,' she paused before, greatly daring, she added, 'I'd like you to be honest with me. Am I really working towards being accepted as a VAD *nurse* or am I just being used as a skivvy?'

For a moment, Florrie thought she'd gone too far. The sister's eyes widened and a flush of anger spread up her face. She stared at the girl standing in front of her, taking in the lovely, yet strong face, the determined look in those brown eyes, the bold tilt of her head, and knew there was no deceiving her. To Florrie's astonishment, Sister Blackstock's stern expression lightened and she smiled, looking suddenly much younger. She glanced down at her watch, pinned just above her left breast. 'You're not due on duty for another ten minutes. I was just going to make myself a cup of tea. Won't you join me? Sit down a moment.'

Florrie sank down into a chair, her legs giving way beneath her in surprise.

When they were once again facing each other across the desk, but this time both seated with a cup of tea before them, Sister Blackstock said, 'I know I'm an old dragon on the ward – I have to be. We get all sorts coming in here – and I don't mean just the patients.' She smiled with a brief flash of humour. 'And especially since the war started. All the debutantes coming here with the fanciful notion of being a heroine smoothing the fevered brow of the wounded officers, and perhaps finding themselves a husband in the process.'

Florrie grimaced.

'Oh yes,' the sister went on. 'I had you – and your friend – marked down as two of them. At least I did until I saw you working. I have to admit I was mistaken. You've done everything asked of you cheerfully and without a word of complaint. You must have seen for yourself that several young women have come and gone, even during the two weeks you've been here?'

Florrie nodded.

'Well, they couldn't stand the pace and were never going to. They hadn't a clue what they would face out there in the field. They'd never have coped, whereas—' She paused again and held Florrie's gaze. Then she nodded slowly as if her own question had been answered. 'Whereas I think you will.'

Florrie gasped. The sister had said 'will', not 'would'. Did that mean . . . ?

Sister Blackstock was smiling. 'You were a suffragette, weren't you?'

Florrie nodded guardedly. Not everyone had agreed with their beliefs or their actions, but it seemed the sister did. 'I applaud you. I wish I'd had half your courage. I'd have joined you, but—' She spread her hands. 'If I had done, I think I might have lost my job and my career, and I have to admit that nursing is all I've ever wanted to do. And – and now—' She faltered a moment and, deep in her eyes, there was the look of loss. It was the same look that Florrie saw in the eyes of so many women these days. The sister's voice dropped to a whisper. 'It's all I'm ever likely to do.'

Still Florrie made no comment, even though she was now curious about the woman before her. Had she lost someone in the war? But her mind wasn't really on the sister – not totally. She was waiting with bated breath, hoping . . .

Sister Blackstock cleared her throat and martialled her wandering thoughts. 'Miss Maltby, from now on I will see that you're able to do some proper nursing. You do know that you have to obtain certain qualifications, don't you, before you'd be allowed to go overseas? Reach certain standards?'

Florrie nodded. 'How long should that take?'

Sister Blackstock shrugged. 'Not long – with my help.'

'Thank you, Sister.'

'But I do have an ulterior motive. I'm hoping to go to France myself. I've volunteered my services to the Red Cross.' She smiled as she added, 'With Matron's approval of course.' Matron's arrival on the wards had the younger nurses – Sister Blackstock too – scurrying to see that everything was in order. Florrie had even seen one of the probationers become so flustered in the austere presence that she'd actually curtsied. The VADs just merged into the background and tried to make themselves invisible. 'I had word only last week that it's likely I shall be sent out to France about April, and they'd like me to hand-pick the nurses to take with me. And you – if you make the grade – would be one of them.'

Florrie's face was a picture. 'Oh, thank you, Sister.'

Rosemary Blackstock's eyes twinkled suddenly. 'You didn't quite answer my earlier question. I don't think you've been entirely truthful about your age, have you?'

A flush of embarrassment crept up Florrie's face. 'No,' she said candidly. 'I'm not quite the age they say I should be. But,' she added with a trace of bitterness in her tone, 'if my sixteen-year-old brother can be allowed to take the King's shilling, then I don't see why I can't be allowed to go to the Front as a Kitchener nurse.'

'It's a little different.' The sister sighed sadly. 'You will be expected to *save* lives, whereas your brother—'

'Will be expected to *take* lives,' Florrie whispered, facing the awful truth. 'Until he gives his own.'

Now Sister Blackstock was silent.

They drank their tea, lost in their own thoughts until the sister stood up and said briskly, 'Now, work hard for me for the next two days, then home you go for Christmas and when you come back, we'll start you working for your certificates. By the way, please give my good wishes to Miss Richards.' She smiled impishly. 'Obviously that's not her name, but it's the only one I know. I do hope her work here hasn't done her any harm.'

'I'm sure it hasn't. She'll be fine once she's rested. She's planning to travel home to Lincolnshire in time for Christmas. And now I'll be able to go with her. Thank you, Sister.'

'Where will you stay when you come back?'

'Oh, Iso has said I can stay on in their London home.'

So it was that Isobel and Florrie returned home for Christmas and New Year, Isobel to stay, but Florrie meaning to return.

On the train Isobel leaned towards Florrie. 'I know you won't accept Gervase, but Florrie dear, do be nice to my brother this year. I received a letter from him earlier this week. He – he sails for France early in the New Year.'

Horrified, Florrie stared at her. 'I didn't think it would be so soon. I mean, hasn't he got to undergo training?'

'No, don't you remember? He did his basic training for the army just before our father died. He was going to make the army his career, but then he had to come home and manage the estate.'

'Oh yes, now I remember,' Florrie said apologetically.

'Anyway, because of that he's only going on a much shorter retraining course. I'm not quite sure how it works. All I know is, he thinks he'll be posted quite soon.'

Florrie said no more and was silent for the rest of the journey.

Gervase, dear Gervase, was going to France – possibly to the Front and she might never see him again.

The mere thought filled her with dread.

*

'Hey, what's all this?' Gervase laughed as Florrie flung herself into his arms when the Maltby family arrived at Bixley Manor to spend New Year's Eve together. None of them felt they could call it a celebration. Not this year. 'My darling girl, what's the matter?'

'I'm sorry – I'm being silly.'

'Is it James?' Gervase asked gently. James had not been allowed home for Christmas, throwing his mother into another frenzy of weeping and wailing.

'No – no – it's you.'

'Me!' Gervase was startled. 'Why? What have I done?'

'You – you're going abroad – to France, aren't you?'

'Well, yes, but, my dear, so will you.'

'Oh yes, but that's only nursing.'

Gervase laughed wryly. '*Only* nursing. My dear girl, don't underestimate either the value of what you'll be doing or the danger you'll be in.'

'But it won't be like being at the Front, will it?'

'That depends. If you're asked to go to a field ambulance near the fighting you'll go, won't you?'

Florrie stared at him as he nodded slowly. 'Oh, I know you, Florence Maltby, you'll go all right. And if you do—' His face was suddenly grey with anxiety. 'You'll be in almost as much danger as the men in the trenches. And *you're* worried about *me*!'

He held her close and stroked her hair. She heard the laughter in his voice as he tried to lighten the moment by saying, 'I suppose now's the perfect time to ask you to marry me, isn't it? After all, it is New Year's Eve.'

'Oh, Gervase!' Florrie buried her face against his chest and clung to him all the harder.

*

Florrie returned to London on the 2nd January 1915 and reported for duty the following day. For the next three months, Sister Blackstock worked her harder than she'd ever worked any of the other volunteers. She was testing her – and Florrie knew it. With the co-operation of her fellow sisters, Rosemary Blackstock arranged for Florrie to work on each type of ward in turn throughout the huge hospital.

'And now,' she told her in the middle of March, 'you're ready to be let loose on the soldiers. You'll be going to Sister Carey.' It was one of the wards that had been given over to wounded soldiers brought home from France.

'Edith Carey and I did our training at the same time,' Sister Blackstock went on. 'And we've remained friends ever since. In fact,' she smiled, 'we're hoping to go to France together. She has a couple of professional nurses that want to go too, but you're the only volunteer that we feel is reaching the required standard. By the end of this month I hope you'll get the certificates you need and then—' Her smile broadened. 'We'll be ready when the call comes.'

Florrie was pink with pleasure. 'Thank you, Sister.'

The woman shrugged. 'You've done well, Maltby. You've done everything I've asked of you and even more.' She nodded. 'Oh yes, I know you covered for one of the young VADs when she couldn't cope. Don't think I don't know. There's not much I don't see.'

'She suffers terribly each month—' Florrie tried to explain, but the sister shook her head.

'Not good enough. It's not an illness and, if she can't cope, then she shouldn't be here. However, she is good most of the time, and I think Matron feels she could be kept on to work here. But going overseas is out of the question, I'm afraid.'

Florrie was disappointed. She'd become quite friendly with the tiny blonde girl who looked as if a puff of wind would blow her over. But she said nothing. No doubt the sister was right.

The work on Sister Carey's surgical ward was more heartbreaking than arduous. Some of the injuries were hideous. There was one poor boy with half his face blown away. Florrie marvelled that he was still alive and at how cheerful he was. As she'd been warned to do by Sister Blackstock, she looked straight at him and forced herself not to avert her gaze.

'Got to 'ave another op tomorrow, Nurse,' he told Florrie, his speech slurred and scarcely recognizable, as one of the professional nurses – Grace Featherstone – took her round the ward. 'A ya goin' to 'old me 'and?'

Grace looked decidedly miffed. 'She's not a proper nurse. She's a VAD. You call her "Maltby", not "Nurse".'

Florrie smiled at him and followed Grace as she marched to the next bed. 'This patient is nil by mouth. He's due for his operation later today.'

The bedclothes were a mound above the man's legs. Florrie glanced at his face and saw that there were tears in his eyes. 'Got to come off – both of 'em. Gangrene, they reckon.' He paused a moment and glanced at Nurse Featherstone, before turning back to Florrie and saying deliberately, '*Nurse*.'

Grace Featherstone gave a loud sniff of disapproval.

'I'm sorry,' Florrie murmured, then she smiled and nodded at the patient. 'I'll see you later then.'

The man returned her steady gaze. 'I hopes so – Nurse.'

'So?' Grace Featherstone asked. She led Florrie back to the small room at the end of the ward where a window looked out over the beds packed closely together. 'Do you think you can cope? We can't do with any hysterics or fainting at the first sight of blood.'

As they entered, Sister Carey looked up from her desk and smiled. She was an older woman – in her forties, Florrie guessed – with brown hair flecked with grey, a wide smile and gentle brown eyes. 'I don't think Miss Maltby is the fainting type.' Her voice was low and cultured. 'She's a suffragette girl.'

Grace stared at her and – to Florrie's surprise – her mouth actually dropped open. 'Are you really?'

Florrie nodded. 'Was. All our activities are suspended because of the war.'

'Did you ever get arrested? Go to prison?'

''Fraid so.'

Reluctant admiration crept into the other girl's eyes as Sister Carey put in slyly, 'They tell me she went on hunger strike and had to be force-fed.'

Grace gasped. 'No!'

'So, I don't think, Nurse Featherstone, that our new recruit is going to let the sight of a little blood and gore upset her.'

'Maybe not, Sister,' Grace Featherstone was still not quite ready to admit defeat. 'But that doesn't make her a good nurse, does it? A *trained* nurse.'

'True,' the sister acknowledged. They were talking now as if Florrie were not in the room. 'But that's rather up to us, don't you think?'

'And what happens after the war, might I ask? These

VADs will think themselves proper nurses. They'll take our jobs, they'll—'

'Some might,' Florrie interrupted them now. 'But not all of us.' She grinned saucily as she added, 'Most of us will want to slip happily back into our cosseted, privileged lives.'

Sister Carey hid her smile as she added, 'And you should perhaps know now, Nurse Featherstone, that if Maltby *does* cope well on our ward, Sister Blackstock intends her to come with us to France.' Her expression hardened. 'I hope you will help her over the next few weeks. I'm sure she'll be an asset to our little party.' She paused a moment and then added pointedly, 'Professional nurse or not.'

Grace turned a faint shade of embarrassed pink. 'Of course, Sister,' she murmured, taking the rebuke well, for now there was a new-found respect in her eyes.

The following two weeks were gruelling. If Florrie had thought the work exhausting before, nursing on the soldiers' ward reached a new level. It wasn't just the physical weariness; it was the strain on her emotions that was the hardest. To see such brave young men maimed for life, to hear their tales of the hardships they'd suffered and the pals they'd lost tore at her heart strings. And worst of all, the man who'd had his legs removed and who'd been her champion died three days after his operation. His heart just gave out after the trauma his body had suffered.

'If only,' she heard one of the surgeons, Dr Johnson, mutter, 'we could get to them sooner. We could save so many more lives. But by the time they've lain for hours on the battlefield, maybe trapped in No-Man's-Land or in a stinking shell-hole, been carried to the field hospital where they might receive only minimal medical treatment and finally been put aboard trains and boats before they reach us – what hope do we have?'

And all the time Florrie couldn't stop thinking: this could happen to the Hon. Tim, to Gervase or, worst of all, to her little brother.

Twenty-Four

'So,' Augusta regarded her with solemn eyes, 'you're really going?'

'Yes, Gran. I'm going back to London tomorrow.' Florrie could not hide her excitement. She was home for a flying visit over Easter, but couldn't wait to get back. She'd seen Isobel, but both Gervase and the Hon. Tim were away. 'We cross the Channel next Monday.'

'The 12th April,' Augusta murmured. 'Your grandfather's birthday.'

Florrie knelt beside her grandmother's chair. 'I'd forgotten. Sorry.'

Augusta smiled, but deep in her eyes there was still the sorrow of her loss and now there was a new anxiety. For James and for Florrie.

'To the Front?' Augusta asked bluntly. There was no hiding the truth from her.

'More than likely,' Florrie replied cheerfully. 'Sister Blackstock will go where she can be of most use – though we have to go where the Red Cross sends us. And I'm to go with her, another sister and two nurses – *professional* nurses. Sister Blackstock's been a brick. She's helped me get the certificates I need in record time and thrown all the nursing duties she can at me. We've been inoculated, vaccinated – any reason they could think of to stick a needle in us, I think they've done. So, we're ready to go.'

'And you've coped? With everything?'

Florrie was not a conceited girl, so when she nodded and said, 'Well, most of the time', Augusta knew full well that the girl had more than likely tackled every gory task set her – and done it. This Sister Blackstock, whose name littered Florrie's conversation, wouldn't be taking the girl to the battlefields of France with her if she didn't think she could cope. Of that, Augusta was sure. And at this moment, she didn't know whether to be extremely proud of her granddaughter or to wish – secretly – that the girl had failed dismally. That, at least, would have kept her safely at home. But that was not Augusta's way.

As if reading some of her grandmother's thoughts, Florrie said softly, 'But please, Gran, don't tell Mother. Let her think I'm at a hospital miles behind the lines – well away from the danger.'

Augusta smiled wryly. 'My dear girl, convincing your mother you'll not be in any danger would be a miracle.' Her mouth twitched with amusement. 'But I'll do my best.' She paused and then added imperiously, 'Write to me, Florrie dear, just as often as you can. And let me know what you need.'

'I've enough clothes and equipment to survive in the wilderness, let alone in a civilized country. D'you know, besides our uniforms, personal under-garments and possessions, we have to take camping gear.' She ticked off the items on her fingers. 'A folding bed and sleeping bag, a camp chair, washstand – all canvas – to say nothing of knife, fork and spoon, scissors, an enamel mug, towels – oh, all sorts of things. So many I can't remember them all. Much of it packs into a kit bag. And we're allowed a trunk and a holdall. I just don't know how I'm going to carry it all.'

Augusta chuckled. 'I'm sure you'll manage, and it's wise to take as much as you can with you. The poor French folk—' She shook her head sadly. 'They can't have much left to give. And if you need anything else when you get out there, be sure to let me know. And not only that; if there are things your patients need, the good Mrs Ponsonby and I will rally the ladies of the local area. I'm sure you will soon have more socks and balaclavas than you have soldiers to wear them.'

Florrie laughed and then sobered as she added seriously, 'Try to involve Mother. It might help if she were to feel useful.'

Augusta nodded, but shrugged doubtfully.

'And James,' Florrie said softly. It tore at her heart that she hadn't seen him again before leaving the country. 'D'you know where he is now?'

Augusta pursed her lips and shook her head. 'No. We haven't heard from him for two weeks. Your poor mother is demented with worry, whilst your father—' She gave a snort of disgust, but said no more. But she didn't need to. Florrie understood perfectly. Edgar would be strutting about like a proud peacock, broadcasting to anyone who'd listen that his son had volunteered.

'Let me know what's happening, won't you? And Gran—' She fixed the old lady with a stare. 'I want the truth. Always.'

'Of course, my dear. Would you expect anything less of me?'

'No, I wouldn't.'

In a rare moment of pride, Edgar himself drove Florrie to the station. Augusta had said her goodbyes in private and Clara had taken to her bed. So only Edgar stood beside her on the platform, saw that her luggage was loaded into the guard's van and then waved her off as the train pulled out of the station.

'Take care of yourself, my dear. I'm very proud of you. Very proud . . .' His words were lost amidst the noise of the train and the smoke hid him from her view, but as Florrie sat down in the carriage, she had a lump in her throat. It was the closest she'd ever felt to her father and the first time she could ever remember him showing such affection to her. But it still seemed strange to her that the only time Edgar had ever displayed pride in either of his offspring had been when he was waving them off to war.

The Channel crossing was choppy and poor Sister Blackstock was seasick.

'I didn't think my first real nursing duty would be for you,' Florrie teased. 'You look positively green, Sister.'

Rosemary groaned. 'Less of your cheek, if you please, Nurse.'

Florrie smiled. It gave her a thrill to hear herself addressed as such. And by Sister Blackstock too – that was a real achievement.

There were fifty medical staff aboard the ship, made up of members of the St John's Ambulance Brigade and the British Red Cross, to which Sister Blackstock and her nurses were attached. There were six from the London Hospital: Sisters Blackstock and Carey, Nurses Featherstone and Newton and VAD Maltby. To their surprise the sixth member of their small group was Dr Johnson.

'Can't let you ladies go on your own,' the big man

boomed with a hearty laugh. He was tall and broad with a handlebar moustache, and Florrie for one was delighted he was going with them, though whether they would all be working together remained to be seen.

Thankful to step ashore again, the whole group travelled south from Boulogne for about ten miles to Camiers, a village near the coast. Several camp hospitals had recently been erected behind the sand dunes. Nearby were base camps, training camps and a machine-gun school. A railway line served them all.

'Is this it?' Florrie gazed around her at the rows and rows of tents of all sizes, some as big as marquees.

'I think so. We've to report to a Sister Warren, so if we can find her, we'll know we're in the right place,' Sister Blackstock said and added grimly as she glanced about her, 'Though how we're expected to keep our patients warm and dry in *tents* beats me. And no doubt we'll be expected to sleep in a tent too.'

She was right. Florrie found herself sharing a bell tent with Grace Featherstone and Hetty Newton. Grace seemed to have accepted Florrie now, but Hetty looked askance at having to share with a mere VAD. Florrie took no notice and arranged her clothes and few belongings in boxes close to her camp bed. As she unpacked, she realized a little sadly that any friendliness that had existed between herself and Sister Blackstock might be at an end. Here – more than ever – she suspected that despite her hard-won certificates, she'd be relegated once more to the status of a skivvy whilst the 'real' nurses looked after the patients. But she didn't mind. She was here in France and 'doing her bit'.

Sister Mabel Warren, who'd been in France almost from the beginning, greeted their party. Dr Johnson was borne off by another doctor, leaving the sister to show the newcomers round. She was small and wiry – in her fifties, Florrie guessed – but her sharp grey eyes missed nothing. She rarely smiled and then only at the patients, but her manner was quiet and reassuring, bringing calm and order to chaos. Though in fear of her displeasure, it seemed that all those under her revered and worshipped her. As for the patients in her care, Florence Nightingale herself could not have been more loved.

To her delight, Florrie was assigned to the 'wards' under Sister Blackstock's charge along with Grace Featherstone and Hetty Newton. Work for them all began the following day and Florrie eased herself quietly into the background. Every morning she made the beds, dusted the lockers, helped the patients to wash, took temperatures and served lunch. Later in the afternoon, the beds were made again and tea was served at five o'clock. Then she should have been off-duty, but Florrie found herself once again at the beck and call of everyone, just as she had been at the London Hospital at first. The nurses who'd been there a while were quick to put the new VAD very firmly in her place.

'Maltby – get rid of these filthy clothes . . .'

'Maltby – clean up that mess . . .'

'Find a cradle for this lad. He's got trench foot. And if you can't find one here, Maltby, beg, borrow or steal – just get one. But mind you return it when we're done with it. That's the unwritten rule round here.'

'Maltby – Maltby – Maltby . . .'

Then gradually, as more and more wounded arrived and the wards became stretched to bursting point, they began to ask for her help with nursing duties.

'Help me give this man a bed-bath.'

'Maltby, help Nurse Featherstone with that young man's dressing.'

And finally, when Hetty Newton fainted whilst cleaning the septic stump of a man whose arm had been blown off at the elbow, 'Maltby, take over . . .'

Later, Hetty, sitting on her camp bed in the shared tent, wept. 'I feel such a fool. Me – a nurse – passing out at the sight of a wound.'

'Well, it was pretty gruesome,' Florrie said, handing her a strong, hot cup of tea and sitting down beside her. 'Far worse than just an ordinary wound. We're all used to the sight of blood, but that . . .' Florrie shuddered.

'It's all gruesome,' Grace remarked, coming in at that moment and catching Florrie's words. She sat down on her own bed, eased off her shoes and rubbed her feet. She closed her eyes and shook her head. 'I never in my worst nightmares imagined it could be as bad as this.'

Hetty gulped her tea and began to feel a little better. 'You know, Maltby, you're doin' ever so well, ain't she, Grace? You ought to train to be a nurse after this is all over. You're a natural.' She pulled a comical face. 'An' I never thought I'd say that to a debutante VAD.'

Florrie laughed. 'I'll take that as a real compliment. But I'm not a real debutante. I was too wild to be presented at court.'

Grace leaned forward and in an exaggerated whisper said, 'She was one of them suffragettes. Been in prison, she has.' She cast her eyes upwards as if in despair. 'The types we have to put up with.' But it was said in teasing good humour and not without a hint of admiration.

Hetty's eyes widened. 'Were you? My auntie was one of them, but it's all stopped now 'cos of the war, ain't it?'

203

Florrie nodded, 'But once – like you say – this is all over . . .' She said no more, but the two girls were left in no doubt that Florrie Maltby meant to resume her militant activities to win the right for women to vote.

'Well, I reckon you've got a point, girl,' Grace said, easing her shoes back on. 'If we're good enough to do all sorts of jobs to help the war effort, then I reckon we're good enough to vote. Now, you an' me'd best get back. Sister'll be looking for us. You rest a bit, our Het. We'll cover for you, won't we, Florrie?'

'Of course.'

From that day, the two girls called her by her Christian name in private and now they often called upon her for real nursing duties. Even Sister Warren, who visited the wards every day, seemed to recognize Florrie's capabilities, even though she still wore the VAD uniform.

They'd scarcely settled in when rumours of a huge battle near the Belgian border reached their camp. Sister Warren called all her senior nursing staff together, and Rosemary Blackstock related the information to her nurses later.

'We're to expect a great influx of patients and Sister Warren has asked me to take charge of one of the operating theatres.' She glanced at Florrie, Grace and Hetty. 'And you three are to come with me. Are you sure you're up to it, Nurse Newton?'

Hetty nodded, anxious not to be left out. 'It was only that one time, Sister. It won't happen again.'

Satisfied, Sister Blackstock nodded.

'Sister,' Grace asked, 'do we have to move? Our sleeping quarters, I mean?'

Rosemary smiled. No doubt in her mind that the girl was hoping for some improvement in their billet. 'No,

I'm afraid not. You'll just have to walk a little further each day, that's all.'

Behind her back the three girls exchanged a glance and grimaced.

However tired she was by the end of her shift, Florrie had managed to scribble a few lines home each day, to either her mother and father, Augusta or Isobel. Word from home came spasmodically as the arrival of mail was erratic. Her mother's letters were full of tales of woe, her father's full of glee that both his children were doing their bit, but whenever she saw Augusta's scrawling handwriting, Florrie pounced gleefully on the letter.

Well, my dear, the miracle has happened. Your mother is knitting furiously and attends all Mrs Ponsonby's fund-raising activities in the village. We even held a fair here at the Hall last Saturday. Your mother performed the opening ceremony and was made a great fuss of by all the locals. Do try to send her cheerful news, my dear, though you can always tell me the truth. James is still safely on British soil at gunnery school at present, so there's no need to worry about him just yet. I saw Isobel last week. She is well, but anxious about both the Hon. Tim and Gervase. They all send their love to you. We're not sure where they are and they can't say, but Timothy and Isobel devised a kind of code. She believes he is near a place called Ypres . . .

Twenty-Five

Two days after receiving Augusta's letter, rumours flew around the camp that a major battle was being waged near Ypres. Florrie's heart turned cold. Was Tim there? Was he in the thick of the fighting? Was he safe? And what of Gervase? She'd no idea where he was, though she knew he'd come to France. It was quite feasible that he was there too. The only thought that gave her hope was that James was still safely in England.

It seemed the trains bringing the wounded from the Belgian border would never stop. Soon the wards were bursting and time off was a thing of the past. Florrie's hours of duty were even longer and so heartbreaking that she could scarcely drag herself back to her tent, undress and wash, never mind writing letters. She'd never known such utter weariness or hopelessness – not even during her time in Holloway. To see a whole generation of fine young men mutilated and suffering made her rage inwardly. Where was the sense in it all? But she was too exhausted to do anything except get through each day and do the very best she could to help the wounded and dying.

Sister Warren was in charge of the operating theatres and organized the sisters and nurses to assist the surgeons. She assigned Sister Blackstock and her three nurses together and introduced them to the man for whom they'd be working.

'This is Dr Ernst Hartmann. You will work directly under his instruction, but of course you, Sister Blackstock, will be in charge of your nurses.'

Florrie's heart missed a beat. Ernst Hartmann was a handsome man. In his early thirties, he was tall and thin. Black hair smoothed back from a broad forehead, his face was lean with a strong jaw line set in grim determination. Straight nose and generous mouth, yet there was no smile of welcome. His bright-blue eyes swept over the four of them with disinterest. He merely gave a curt nod and in a deep voice that sounded more like a growl, muttered, 'More fine ladies come to smooth the wounded soldier's brow and write a last letter home for him.' He spoke in perfect English, but with a strong accent that sounded suspiciously German. Florrie glanced at Sister Warren.

'Dr Hartmann is Swiss.'

The man gave a wry laugh. 'Did you think for a moment that you had got behind enemy lines?'

It was Florrie who answered, even though it was not her place to do so. She grinned with a sudden spark of mischief and spoke in German. 'Not at all, Herr Doctor.'

Beside her Sister Warren gasped and Sister Blackstock looked thunderous. Dr Hartmann looked startled. Then he regarded her thoughtfully for a moment. 'Do you speak any other languages, Nurse?'

'French, sir,' she answered, still speaking in German. 'And English, of course.' Not for the first time did she have cause to thank her grandmother, who'd insisted that she have a good education, even though Edgar had always declared such learning was wasted on a girl.

'Of course,' Ernst Hartmann murmured.

'And I'm only a nursing VAD,' she said, now speaking in English. 'Not a pukka nurse.' She kept her face straight and looked directly at him, not glancing at her companions.

He frowned and turned to the others. 'But you three are *pukka* nurses, yes?'

'I'm a fully trained sister and these two are probationary nurses, but they have completed a full year's training, whereas Maltby—' Rosemary Blackstock tried to explain, but the doctor grunted again and turned away, saying over his shoulder, 'I need two at any time. Arrange it between yourselves and be ready to assist me in ten minutes.'

Already orderlies were bringing in a man whose leg had been blown off below the knee. They hoisted him up onto the table where he lay, biting his lip to stop himself crying out. Even so, a guttural groan escaped his lips now and again. The stump was covered with a filthy blood-soaked dressing and a dirty bandage was pulled tight around his thigh as a tourniquet. Without waiting to be told, Florrie whipped out the scissors she always carried in the pocket of her uniform and began to cut off the man's trousers.

Ernst Hartmann, readying himself to operate to staunch the flow of blood from the wound, paused, smiled grimly and turned towards Sister Blackstock. Raising his black eyebrows, he murmured, 'It seems we have a keen volunteer.' The note of sarcasm was not lost on Florrie, but she made no sign of having noticed and continued to get the patient ready.

'I will work with Maltby,' Rosemary Blackstock said, 'And you two can work together.' For a moment she and Sister Warren spoke together, organizing the shifts the four of them would work.

'It might not always be Dr Hartmann you'll be assisting,' Florrie heard Sister Warren say, 'but whenever he's on duty, two of you must be here.'

Florrie said nothing, but silently she determined that she would always be one of the two. Despite his gruff manner, the doctor had captivated her with his handsome dark looks and his capable, clever hands. Not normally given to sentimental outpourings, she would follow him to the ends of the earth to work alongside him.

Later Rosemary castigated Florrie. 'You'd no right to do that in such a forward manner. You should've waited for instruction.'

'The man was bleeding to death. The tourniquet wasn't working and, even if it had been, there was no knowing how long it'd been there,' Florrie defended herself. She'd no need to tell the sister what happened if a tourniquet was left in place too long without being released every so often.

'You still had no right to take action like that, *and* speaking in German to him—' She gave a tut of exasperation. 'Showing off. That's what that was.'

'I'm sorry – I didn't think.'

'Well, you should,' the sister reproved her. 'Nurses – *pukka* nurses – should always think what they're doing and saying.' Suddenly her mouth twitched and she lowered her voice. 'But I have to admit, Maltby, your spirit is just what we need here, but curb its waywardness a little, eh?'

'I'll try, Sister,' Florrie smiled.

To her surprise, Grace and Hetty thought it all a

huge joke. 'Trying to impress the handsome doc, that's what she was doing,' was Hetty's pronouncement.

'Well, she can have him. The dark, brooding type's not for me,' Grace said cheerfully. 'Give me ol' Doc Johnson any day of the week. I like a kind, caring man.'

Unbidden, Gervase's face was immediately in Florrie's mind. She smiled to herself. How Grace would love Gervase!

The days passed in a blur. Dr Hartmann seemed to need little rest. He worked from early in the morning until late at night, pausing only to eat because he needed to keep himself healthy.

'Enough!' Ernst declared late one evening. He threw down his instruments onto the metal tray with a clatter. There were still three patients needing urgent operations, but the doctor strode from the tent, leaving Sister Blackstock and Florrie staring at each other. They made the patient who'd just been operated on as comfortable as they could and called for the orderlies to take him back to a ward.

'Had we better find Dr Hartmann?' Florrie asked. 'See what's the matter? He might be ill.'

'Ill? Him?' The sister laughed grimly. 'Never!' She sighed. 'I think it's all just – just got to him.' She glanced around at the three men lying on the ground waiting patiently for their turn on the operating table. For the first time Rosemary was showing a hint of helplessness. 'Just look at them, Florrie,' she said softly. 'Look at these – these beautiful young men. Oh no, I know they don't look very beautiful at this moment. Caked with mud and blood, their unshaven faces twisted in agony. But they are – they are beautiful. And they're going to die – most of them. If not from their wounds, then from disease. Most of them will never see their home again. And if we do get the less seriously injured well again, what happens? Do they get sent back to their loved ones? Oh no! Back to the Front to be shot at again. And maybe killed next time.'

'But we have to try,' Florrie said. 'Don't we?'

'Of course we do. That's our job – our duty. But what are we really achieving? And I think that's what's got to Dr Hartmann. He's working round the clock nearly, and for what? Leave him, Florrie. Leave him to work it out for himself.' She turned away as she murmured, 'Like we all have to do.'

Sister Blackstock sent the three patients back to their wards, promising that they'd be first on the list in the morning. They made not even a murmur of complaint.

'Get to bed, Florrie,' she added wearily. 'At least we might get a few hours more sleep tonight.'

They parted outside and Florrie watched the sister disappear into the gloom of the chilly summer evening. Pulling her cloak around her, Florrie hurried in search of Dr Hartmann. She found him in the tent that served as a canteen, sitting alone at a table, his head in his hands, a cup of strong tea in front of him going cold. Her heart was in her mouth as she moved towards him and stood on the opposite side of the table until he became aware of her presence and looked up. She'd probably be told curtly to mind her own business and, if one of the sisters were to hear about it, she'd certainly be in trouble.

'Oh – it's you. Come to fetch me back to that – that butcher's bench, have you?'

Without waiting for an invitation or even permission, Florrie sat down. 'No,' she said gently. 'We've sent the patients back to their wards. The post-operative patient is fine and the other three – well – Sister told them they'd have to wait until morning.'

'Wait – wait – wait! That's all those poor devils do. And it's the waiting – the delay – that's killing them.'

'But you work as fast as you can. You and all the other surgeons. You—'

'It's not that, Nurse—' Despite the seriousness of their conversation, his use of the title that she didn't really deserve gave her a warm glow. 'It's the time they have to wait before they reach us here.'

Florrie stared at him, not quite understanding. He sighed, leaned back in the chair and explained. 'They're wounded. They get shot or blown up by a shell and injured by shrapnel. The ones that are so badly hurt they can't move for themselves have to lie wherever they are – out in the open, in a rat-infested shell-hole or a muddy dugout. They might be there for hours – days even – until their comrades or stretcher-bearers are able to find them. They're taken first to an RAP—'

Seeing Florrie's puzzled frown, he explained. 'That's a Regimental Aid Post – the first stop.' He began to tick off on his fingers the various stages the wounded had to go through. 'If they're still alive, they'd then be taken by stretcher-bearers or field ambulance to the advanced dressing station. Then they're moved again back to the main dressing station. If their wound is so serious that it cannot be dealt with there, they're then taken to the casualty clearing station by ambulance, lorries – any mode of transport available. And then – as the previous name implies – they're sent to a general hospital. That's us, but just look at how many times the seriously wounded have been lifted, carried and transported, their wounds not properly dressed or at least not often enough. Oh, I know there are medical staff aboard the trains bringing the wounded here, but do you suppose they can treat everyone properly on an overcrowded, rickety train?'

Florrie shook her head, unable to speak for the lump in her throat. She could see it all so clearly, feel it – and it broke her heart.

'The casualties we're getting now are from Ypres,' he went on.

Florrie felt a fresh jolt of fear as she thought again of Tim. But knowing nothing of the inner turmoil his words were causing her, Dr Hartmann went on, 'Ypres is about fifty miles away, but it's still a long way for men in need of urgent medical treatment to have to travel.'

Florrie said nothing. She was still having difficulty quelling her fears for Tim's safety and concentrating on what the doctor was saying.

'And now—' Ernst Hartmann's face was gaunt, his blue eyes dull with fatigue, his cheeks hollowed and his shoulders slumped in defeat. 'They're getting gassed, so that not only are their lungs damaged, but the wounds are infected by the gas too.'

'So that's that awful smell that still hangs about their clothes,' Florrie murmured. 'What is it?'

'Chlorine. It chokes them. If it doesn't kill them straight away, by the time they reach us they're suffering from acute bronchitis. And wounds become gangrenous. That's the awful smell. Gas-gangrene.'

'Is there anything they can do to protect themselves? Any sort of – sort of mask?'

Dr Hartmann shrugged. 'A cotton-wool pad wrapped

in some sort of loose woven material tied over their mouths would help.' He sighed. 'But how are we to get such supplies?'

Florrie thought of Augusta and Mrs Ponsonby and the ladies of Candlethorpe and Bixley frantically knitting socks. Perhaps they could make masks like that. It wouldn't be much amongst the thousands of men who needed them, but it would be a start. In this chaos, anything was better than nothing. She'd write tonight.

Then her mind turned to the other problem of the men having to wait so long before they received medical attention. 'But there must be hospitals nearer the Front than ours. I mean proper hospitals – not just dressing stations.'

'Oh, there are, but no doubt they're so overwhelmed they can't cope with every serious case. And by the time they reach us – it's too late. You've seen the terrible blood loss, the septicaemia, the gangrene . . .' He clenched his fist and thumped the table in frustration. 'If only I could be nearer. Treat them much earlier, I could do so much more. I know I could. I feel so wasted here.'

Florrie put her head on one side and regarded him steadily. 'Then why don't you?'

He stared back at her. 'Why don't I what?'

'Go to a hospital nearer the Front. Set up a field ambulance, if necessary. At least you'd feel you were doing your best.'

She held his gaze steadily. She could see his mind working. 'I'd need nurses,' he said at last. 'I can't ask young women to go so close to the danger. It wouldn't be—'

'I'd go with you.'

Now he gaped at her in astonishment. 'You would?

214

You'd really go that near the fighting? The shelling? The snipers? Do you know how dangerous it would be? You could be killed. A field hospital was hit recently and a colleague of mine killed outright.'

'I knew that was a possibility when I first volunteered. I've not changed my mind. In fact, having seen all that I have, my resolve has hardened, if anything. It's what I've worked for. That's if you think I'm good enough. After all, I've only a couple of certificates – no proper nursing qualifications.'

He laughed wryly. 'You're better than some *pukka* nurses – as you call them – that I've worked with.'

She felt a flush of pride and was about to say, coquettishly, 'Thank you, kind sir', but she could see that his mind had already moved on from her.

'I wonder if it's possible?' he mused. 'I'll talk to my colleagues. See what they think. If only we could get near to the Front, get to the wounded so much sooner, we could save so many more lives.'

'Speak to Dr Johnson. He said much the same thing back in London.'

He stood up, so invigorated by her suggestion that he would go this minute and talk to the other doctors. Wild and dangerous though the idea was, he wanted to do it. He turned back briefly and glanced down at her. 'Are you really sure you could stand it? The conditions we'd have to work in would be so much more primitive than here. You've seen some terrible sights already, I know, but there it would be even more ghastly. And the danger would be ever-present. I couldn't have you losing your nerve in the middle of an operation or showing fear or revulsion in front of the men.'

Despite the gravity of the moment, Florrie marvelled once more at his command of the English language. It far surpassed her knowledge of the German spoken by the Swiss, sufficient though that was.

She stood up slowly. 'Back home, before all this started, I was a suffragette. I was imprisoned for a while and suffered force-feeding. I don't give in easily, Dr Hartmann.'

'Ah! I have heard about that.' He smiled. For the first time he seemed to be seeing her as a real person, not just as a figure in a white apron to pass him instruments and do as he instructed her. The lines around his eyes deepened and there was a mischievous glint in the blue depths. 'So why are you not still waving banners and marching in protest?'

Florrie's chin rose defiantly. 'Because winning *this* war is even more important than the battle for Votes for Women. But believe me, once this is over – if I survive – I'll be back to the banner-waving and the window-smashing.'

His face sobered and he nodded slowly. 'I am so glad you said "if I survive". I hope you do – I truly hope you do – but the fact that you said it tells me that you understand how very dangerous our work will be.'

Florrie nodded and said softly, 'I do, Doctor. Indeed I do.'

Twenty-Six

Dear Gran— Florrie began her letter the moment she got back to the tent. Grace was asleep, snoring gently, and Hetty was snuggled beneath the covers.

Firstly, she explained about the masks that were urgently needed. *Perhaps you could get in touch with the authorities and see what is the best thing to do. Where you could send them, and so on. Lady Lee might be able to help.* Lady Lee, she knew, had contacts in the War Office. She would help. Florrie paused before writing the next bit. *It's likely I shall be going nearer the Front to help set up some sort of a field hospital so that the wounded can be treated more quickly. The doctor I work with most of the time is wonderful – so dedicated and clever. And he's very handsome!! Now you're not to worry about me, Gran, and please don't tell Mother. Let her think I'm still well away from the fighting . . .*

Florrie's idea, which Dr Hartmann had taken up so enthusiastically, was initiated with amazing speed. Supplies they'd need were requisitioned and promised for delivery in two weeks' time to a French village close to the border with Belgium and as near to the British front line as they could get, yet still be just out of reach of the enemy artillery.

'That's not close enough,' Ernst Hartmann fretted. 'We need to be as near as possible.'

'I think he wants us to set up in the trenches themselves,' Sister Blackstock muttered. As soon as she had heard about Dr Hartmann's plans she'd volunteered her services without even waiting for him to ask her. Grace and Hetty too had no intention of being left behind. 'We make such a good team,' they insisted to Sister Blackstock. 'You and us three nurses.'

Florrie smiled quietly. It seemed, at last, she was accepted.

'There are ten of us going initially,' Rosemary told them. 'Dr Hartmann and Dr Johnson, Sister Carey and myself and six nurses. The plan is that we find a suitable location as near to the Front as possible without actually being in the firing line and, if all goes well, we can then ask for further volunteers to join us. It has to be volunteers because it is likely to be extremely dangerous. You do all understand that, don't you?'

Of course they did. How could they not know?

'What about orderlies?' Florrie asked.

Sister Blackstock shrugged. 'We'll be sited somewhere near the rear lines, I expect. Dr Hartmann hopes some of the soldiers not actually at the Front will help out.'

By the time the supplies should be reaching their destination, the medical team was on its way north in three ambulance cars drawn from a motley variety of vehicles given by generous organizations in Britain. A fourth vehicle – a lorry – was packed with the doctors' own equipment and medical supplies that Sister Blackstock insisted on bringing, to say nothing of their own camp beds, folding canvas chairs and other personal belongings.

'I'd have thought we'd have gone by train,' Grace said as she, Hetty and Florrie squashed together in the back of one of the cars. Florrie chuckled. 'I think Dr Hartmann pulled a few strings.'

'He's a poppet, isn't he? Your Dr Hartmann.' One of the other girls travelling with them introduced herself. 'I'm Norah and I'm in Dr Johnson's team. He's a peach – but he's quite old. You're very lucky to be working for the dishy Ernst.' She leaned forward. 'But they say he's very demanding – strict, you know. Is it true?'

Florrie hesitated. She'd now seen another side to Ernst Hartmann: the deep concern he had for the wounded, and how he was almost frantic to give them a better chance of survival and recovery. 'He's very – dedicated,' she said slowly. 'He gives unstintingly of himself, and I suppose he expects the same of his nurses.'

Norah pulled a face. 'Then I think I'll stick with good old Dr Johnson. He laughs and jokes with his patients all the time. It keeps their spirits up – and ours.'

Florrie said nothing, but privately she thought: And I'll stick with my Dr Hartmann.

The journey was tortuous, made all the more heart-wrenching by the pitiful sight of the refugees: old men and women, pushing their belongings on hand-carts; young children, so tired they looked as if they couldn't take another step, trailing along beside the hand-carts or clinging to their mother's hand. Too tired even to cry or complain. Young women, weeping openly, all hope gone and replaced by a gnawing fear. But there were no young men amongst them – or even middle-aged ones. They were all gone to war.

A more heartening sight was a company of soldiers, marching along, their arms swinging in tune to someone playing a mouth organ. They waved and cheered and whistled as they saw the nurses' uniforms.

'Poor boys,' Sister Blackstock in the front seat of the car murmured. 'I wonder if they know what they're going into?'

The noise of the shelling grew louder as they drew closer to the battle zone. They passed battered houses and farmland laid waste. There was evidence of trenches, once occupied, but now deserted as the front line had gained a little ground and moved forward. They came to a hamlet where people were still living in some of the houses. But, like the folk they'd passed along the way, their faces were gaunt and their eyes hopeless.

The convoy halted and the doctors and nurses clambered out to stretch their legs and look about them. The two doctors talked together. Florrie watched them. They seemed to be arguing. Ernst Hartmann was waving his arms about and pointing towards the direction where the Front must be. The two men came towards Sister Blackstock. Florrie stepped closer to listen.

'We're still not as near as we'd like to be,' Ernst Hartmann said. 'But we feel this would be a *sensible* place to make camp.' His mouth twitched with wry humour, and Florrie knew that he'd lost his own personal battle to be even closer to the wounded and dying.

'We have to think of the safety of our nurses,' Dr Johnson said. The bluff, straight-talking, no-nonsense Yorkshireman laughed a lot and could be relied upon to raise the lowest of spirits and bring hope to those who'd given up. He would never accept that any patient of his was going to die until they actually breathed their last. And even then he'd been known to continue working on them, as if by the force of his considerable will he could bring them back to life. 'But,' his merry eyes twinkled at his colleague, 'we've agreed that Dr Hartmann should take a small party and see if he can find a suitable place even nearer than here. The earliest possible treatment is the key.' He glanced at his colleague and nodded. 'We're both agreed on that.'

'I need a couple of volunteers.' Ernst Hartmann glanced at the two sisters. 'Preferably one of you with a nurse.'

At once Sister Blackstock said, 'I'd be happy to go with you, Dr Hartmann.'

'And me.' Florrie stepped forward. 'That's if – if you think I'm good enough,' she added quickly, not wanting to push herself before the other, more qualified nurses.

She glanced at Grace, who shuddered and shook her head. 'This is quite close enough for me, thank you very much,' she said adamantly. The others smiled. They understood her feelings, though her bravery was not in question. To have come thus far proved that.

'You stay with me, Nurse Featherstone,' Dr Johnson boomed and put his arm around her shoulders. 'There'll be plenty to do here, when they send the wounded down the line to us.'

'How are we going to get them here?' Sister Blackstock asked. 'It's all very well establishing these first-aid posts – dressing stations or whatever they call them.'

'Ah, but what I want is something more than a first-aid post, Sister,' Dr Hartmann interrupted. 'I want the urgent cases to receive proper surgical treatment.'

'But we need to be able to move them on,' Sister Blackstock insisted. 'We can't keep them so near the front line. Besides, we'll be inundated with casualties.'

'There'll be the usual channels for bringing them out. But for our own purposes, we're being allowed to keep two of the vehicles that have brought us here. The lorry and one of the cars, but we can't keep the drivers.' He glanced around. 'Can any of you ladies drive?'

No one spoke until Florrie said hesitantly, 'I've driven a motor car, but only once or twice.'

Dr Hartmann nodded. 'That'll do. Get some instruction from the driver of the lorry before he leaves. And find out how we get in touch with the supplies depot behind the lines. It's all been set up for us to get anything we need from them. Somehow, we need to get in touch with a Sergeant Granger . . .'

The VAD drivers who'd brought them were volunteers who were too old for the army or who'd failed their medicals. When they'd unloaded all the equipment, Joe Hanson, the volunteer who'd driven the lorry, beckoned to Florrie. 'Right, miss, I'll give you a driving lesson and we'll see if we can find the supplies depot at the same time.'

The roads were rough, the gears difficult, but after a while Florrie mastered the controls. Above the noise of the engine, Joe shouted, 'You're a natural, miss.'

Tears sprang to her eyes as she remembered Gervase saying those very same words. Where was he now? Was he safe? She brushed aside melancholy thoughts and turned, with a wide grin, towards Joe. 'Thanks. Now we'd better try and find this Sergeant Granger.'

They drove around for a while longer until the sound of gunfire made them head back to the rest of their party. But, whilst they'd been away, Sergeant Granger had found the new arrivals.

He was a young man, not much older than she was, Florrie thought. He shook hands warmly with the two doctors and smiled and nodded at the nurses. 'We're so glad to see you,' he said. 'Our medical officers and stretcher-bearers do a magnificent job, but, to be honest with you, they're overwhelmed. This latest skirmish – they're calling it Hill 60, though in truth it's only a huge mound of earth from the building of the nearby railway – has been the very devil.' His face was bleak. 'We've lost a lot of men and there are so many wounded . . .' He lifted his shoulders helplessly and said no more. There was no need.

Dr Johnson clapped him on the back. 'Well, my boy, the cavalry's here, but we'll need your help.'

The young man nodded. 'We've received orders to help you in any way we can, sir. I believe medical supplies are on their way.'

'On their way!' Dr Hartmann exclaimed. 'Do you mean nothing's come for us already?'

Looking anxious, as if he felt he'd already failed them, the sergeant shook his head. 'I'm sorry, sir, but no. The supply train due yesterday hasn't arrived yet. A dispatch rider brought the message that the line'd been damaged and was being repaired.'

'I see,' Dr Hartmann said curtly. 'Have you any idea when it might arrive?'

Embarrassed, the young man shook his head. 'No, sir. I'm sorry.'

'Not your fault, my boy,' Dr Johnson put in. 'Just let us know when our stuff arrives.'

'Of course, sir. At once.'

'Now,' the doctor went on. 'There's something else we want you to help us with . . .' He went on to explain how Dr Hartmann and two nurses planned to get even nearer the Front. While he was speaking there was a whistling sound through the air, a loud 'crump' and the ground beneath their feet seemed to shake. Grace gave a little shriek and clung to Florrie, whilst the other women turned pale. Dr Johnson continued without even pausing, though the sergeant looked anxious. His concern, however, was not for himself, but for the new arrivals.

'Are you really sure three of you ought to be going any closer, sir? I mean—'

'We're here to do a job,' Dr Hartmann said firmly. 'To save lives, and the only way we can do that is to give treatment to the wounded as soon as we can. Then Nurse Maltby will drive them back here, where they will receive further treatment and care until they can be taken further by hospital train – when they're fit enough to travel,' he added with great emphasis.

Now the young sergeant gaped in horror at Florrie. 'You're going to drive an ambulance from – from there back here?'

She nodded. 'Well, this lorry. We'll have to kit it out as an ambulance.'

'But—' he began.

Dr Johnson laughed his loud, booming laugh and slapped the young man on the shoulder. 'Don't you worry about Nurse Maltby. She was a suffragette – a very active one, if you get my meaning.'

Florrie grinned. She hadn't been aware that Dr Johnson knew about her previous activities, but it seemed it was no surprise to anyone there apart from the sergeant, who was suddenly regarding her with fresh admiration. Another thought crossed the young man's mind and he frowned again. 'But she might encounter Germans. Odd ones do get separated from their company or – or desert.'

Dr Johnson guffawed loudly. 'Then I pity the poor chap who encounters her.'

'But she ought to carry a gun. Er, can you shoot, miss?'

Florrie thought of the times she'd gone out shooting with Gervase. How he'd taught her to hold the gun, to aim and to fire well enough so that by the time she was seventeen, she'd been good enough to join the shooting parties on the Bixley Estate. But never those held at Candlethorpe. Her father would never hear of her joining his shooting parties at home. 'A woman? Shooting? Ridiculous!' he'd said, and that had been an end of it. But now, thanks once more to Gervase, she was able to nod and say, 'A bit, yes.'

'I'll get you a revolver, miss,' Sergeant Granger promised.

'Oh, I haven't used one of those,' Florrie apologized. 'Only a shotgun.'

'Fancy – there's something she hasn't done!' Grace quipped, but it was said in good humour.

'Well, I'll give you a few lessons,' the sergeant promised. 'At least it's useful if you've used a gun of some sort, but the Webleys do kick a bit on firing. In fact—' He glanced around them. 'I suppose you all ought to have something.'

'We don't need them,' Dr Johnson said brusquely. 'We're here to save lives whatever their nationality, not take them. Though I do agree,' he acceded, 'that Nurse Maltby should carry one for her own safety, if she's to transport the wounded. Even with patients on board, they're unlikely to be of much use to her, and on the return journeys she'll be on her own.'

'We nurses are not *allowed* to carry weapons,' Sister Blackstock said firmly.

Dr Johnson put his hand on her shoulder. 'It's all right, Sister, I'll take the responsibility.'

Sister Blackstock still looked anxious, but said no more.

Sergeant Granger returned a short while later with a revolver and ammunition for Florrie. He also brought two young soldiers with him who, much to the annoyance of Sister Blackstock, winked and nodded cheekily at the nurses.

'I've set up some cans on a wall over there, Nurse,' the sergeant said, 'so whilst the lads get those tents up for you, let's see what you can do.'

Florrie followed the young man towards a derelict house that had fallen victim to the shelling. The roof had gone completely and some of the walls were badly damaged, yet there was still furniture amongst the ruins. Maybe the former inhabitants were amongst the refugees they'd passed on the road, Florrie thought sadly.

The sergeant had set ten empty tins on the wall. 'Right, let me show you how to load it.'

The sergeant was thorough. He made her load, unload and reload several times before he was happy she could do it properly. 'Now, aim at the first two cans on the left, miss.'

Florrie raised the revolver, took aim and fired twice. The two cans remained stubbornly where they were.

'Try the next two,' the sergeant encouraged. Florrie took aim again and this time both tins bounced in the air and fell off the wall.

Sergeant Granger grinned. 'That's very good, miss. Now, if you move back ten paces and fire at the next two, and so on.'

She did as he bade her, hitting all the cans except the first two and the last one.

'That's excellent, miss. Some of my men can't shoot

as well as that. You've got a good eye. Now, here's some ammunition. Keep it safe.'

They walked back to where the others were busily setting up camp. Florrie stowed the pistol and ammunition in the medical bag she would carry with her at all times.

As darkness fell, the shelling stopped, but the silence was eerie and, strangely, more unsettling than the sound of gunfire. Sleeping quarters were the smaller tents, whilst the larger ones had been set up as an operating theatre and recovery wards.

'Hardly ideal,' Ernst Hartmann murmured. Florrie, handing him a mug of tea, saw his glance turn towards where the sound of gunfire had come from. 'We need to get closer. At least as near as we can get to the support trenches. When they carry the injured out, we'd be right there.' He punched the air with his clenched fist. 'Right there!'

He took a sip of tea and then turned to her, his dark-blue eyes assessing her. His black hair was ruffled and she felt the foolish urge to smooth it from his brow.

'Let's take a look, Nurse Maltby,' he said softly. 'Are you game?'

She nodded, her heart lifting at the thought of being alone with him, even if only in such ridiculous circumstances.

Twenty-Seven

Through the soft light of evening, they walked in the direction Sergeant Granger and the two soldiers had taken. Grotesque shapes of shattered houses and outbuildings cast long, eerie shadows. There was no sign of life anywhere, not even cows or sheep in the fields. No birds flew overhead or roosted in the trees. Indeed, there were few trees left standing untouched by the shelling. Explosions and shrapnel had ripped away branches, leaving only bare stumps.

'These poor folk. They've lost everything,' Florrie murmured, more to herself than to the doctor, but Ernst said grimly, 'It's a tragedy.'

'We've had a lot of Belgian refugees come to Britain,' Florrie said. 'But how will they ever rebuild their homes, their farms, their lives when they come home?'

They walked on, but still there was no sign of any army personnel, of huts or tents or mounds of ammunition and other supplies. Just land laid waste.

'What are we actually looking for?' Florrie ventured.

'The guns. The long-range artillery. They're behind the system of trenches that lead to the front line. If we could set up a post there—'

'Near the guns?' Even Florrie was horrified now. 'But – but won't the enemy have their guns trained on that area?'

'Probably.' Ernst sounded nonchalant, completely regardless of his own safety – and consequently of the safety of anyone who was foolhardy enough to go with him!

'Oh.' Florrie was thoughtful for a moment, then she shrugged. Oh well. So be it.

He stopped and turned to face her. 'Still want to come with me?'

She stared at him through the twilight. His features were in shadow, but she could hear the passion in his tone, his determined dedication. There'd be fire in those bright-blue eyes, if only she could see them.

'Yes,' she breathed. 'Oh yes.'

Briefly, he touched her hand in gratitude. Then he turned and walked on, leaving her stroking the place on her hand where he'd touched her.

'It's further away than I thought.' His voice came back to her and she started forward to catch up with him. 'We must have walked a mile or more. We'd better go back.' He sounded annoyed that they'd not found the site he wanted.

They were about to turn around when a scuffling sounded in the ruins of a lone, abandoned house. A voice bellowed at them to halt. Against the night sky, they could see the shape of a soldier standing on top of a broken wall.

'We are doctors and nurses come to set up an emergency dressing station near to the trenches . . .' Ernst began, but Florrie saw the rifle against the soldier's shoulder and heard an ominous click. His wry laugh came out of the darkness. 'With that accent – I don't think so.'

'I'm Nurse Maltby and I'm English,' Florrie shouted. 'And Dr Hartmann is Swiss.'

'Swiss? Don't give me that. They're neutral. What would a Swiss doctor be doing out here?'

The sentry still wasn't convinced. He scrambled down from the wall and stepped closer, but all the time kept his gun pointing straight at them. 'You'd better see my sergeant. Come on.' He waved his gun, ordering them to move on. 'And put your hands up. I don't know who you are.'

'We've just told you,' Florrie began heatedly, but Ernst touched her arm and said gently, 'Do as he says. He's only doing his duty.'

They did as he bade them and stepped in front of him. 'Would that be Sergeant Granger?' Florrie asked.

Surprised, the young soldier said, 'Well, yes. 'Ow do you know 'im, then?'

Through the gloom, Florrie grinned at Dr Hartmann, who, still miffed at being thought an enemy, said with stiff sarcasm, 'He's been kind enough to help us set up our hospital tents and provide this young woman with a gun and ammunition for her personal safety. It seems she may well need it. And not only against the enemy!'

After another half a mile they neared the communication trenches, where another soldier repeated the challenge. 'It's me, Billy. I've got a couple here who reckon they're a doctor and a nurse. And they say they know Sergeant Granger. But one of 'em's a German.'

'Swiss,' Ernst muttered.

A soft chuckle came out of the darkness and the private stepped forward. 'S'all right, Walt. I know them. I've just helped put up their tents. Wouldn't 'alf mind sharing yours though, miss.'

'How dare you?' Ernst Hartmann began indignantly. 'I'll report you to your superior.'

Now it was Florrie who put her hand on his arm and said softly, 'It's all right, Doctor.' She raised her voice and said gaily, 'Well, you'd have a night of it, soldier. There's one of the sisters and two other nurses all sharing the same tent.'

'What? That sister I saw with a face like a horse? Ah, no thanks. Even I've got me pride.'

'Now, now, soldier.' Florrie stifled her laughter. Sister Blackstock had not exactly been at the front of the queue when the looks were given out, she thought. Nevertheless, she didn't deserve to be ridiculed. 'That's not nice,' she said sharply. 'She's a lovely woman and a *very* good nurse.'

The soldier called Billy guffawed. 'Well, I'll take your word for it, Nurse. Hope I never have need of her – er – services!'

Florrie tried hard to hide her smile. At her side Dr Hartmann gave a grunt of disapproval.

More seriously, Billy now said, 'Was there something you wanted, Doc? I can fetch the sarge if you like.'

'That won't be necessary,' Ernst Hartmann snapped. 'We just came to see if there was anywhere we could set up a treatment post as near to the lines as possible.' With an incredibly swift change of mood that surprised Florrie, he laughed suddenly and added, 'Trying to help you young rascals and your pals. That's all.'

'I'm real sorry, Doctor.' The soldier behind them now lowered his rifle and moved closer. Through the half-light, Florrie could see that he was no more than a young boy. He reminded her poignantly of James and her heart turned over. 'But if I'd let you come past and—'

'It's all right,' Florrie said. 'We do understand.'

'You'd best get back, Walt. Don't want you with your back to the post. I heard tell there's one in Poperinghe – all ready and waiting.'

'Oh God, no.' The young soldier sounded panicky for a moment, turned on his heel and ran back through the gloom.

'We'd better get back too, young man. Thank you for your help earlier. Perhaps you could tell Sergeant Granger that I will come and see him in the morning. I believe a supply train is due in tomorrow?'

'So I understand, sir. Goodnight to you both.'

As they retraced their steps, Florrie asked, 'What did that soldier – Billy – mean about the other one – Walt, was it – having his back to the post?'

'I think he was making a joke – a rather sick one – about the lads facing the firing squad. They're tied with their backs to a post.'

Florrie gasped. 'But – but why? He hadn't done anything wrong? Had he?'

'He was on sentry duty or lookout duty – whatever they call it out here – at that ruined house. He probably shouldn't have left his position.'

'And he'd be shot for something as – as trivial as that?'

'Oh yes.' Ernst was matter-of-fact, calmly accepting of what sounded to Florrie like a cruel atrocity.

They walked in silence for some way until Ernst said, 'I ought to report you to Sister Blackstock.'

Florrie stopped and turned to face him. He too paused whilst they stared at each other, but she couldn't read his expression in the darkness. 'Report me? Whatever for?'

'You were far too—' For once he had to seek the English word. 'Familiar, yes, that's it – familiar – with that soldier. And you allowed him to be discourteous towards Sister Blackstock.'

'No, I didn't. I slapped him down for that,' Florrie replied hotly. 'And as for being familiar, as you put it, don't you think that, if they're brought into our hospital, horribly wounded and bleeding to death, a friendly face and a cheery word helps?'

'Undoubtedly, but he's not wounded. He's a fit, healthy young male. You were flirting with him, Nurse. And it won't do. It won't do at all.'

'Oh, fiddlesticks! I can look after myself – at least against *that* sort of attack – gun or no gun.'

And as if to prove a point she marched off ahead of him into the darkness.

When she entered the tent she was to share with the three other women, she fully expected a further dressing down from Sister Blackstock for going off alone with the doctor. But every one of them, tired by the day's travelling, was fast asleep, and Rosemary was snoring gently. Florrie slipped into her bed quietly, but sleep was a long time in claiming her and when it did, her rest was disturbed by dreams of a pair of dark-blue eyes that changed with mercurial suddenness from laughter to anger.

Twenty-Eight

The following morning, Sergeant Granger came to their encampment.

'The train has arrived and your supplies are on it. I've arranged for everything to be brought to you here.'

'Thank you,' Ernst Hartmann said. 'Now we can get started, but there's something else you can do for us, Sergeant.'

'Anything, Doctor. Just name it.'

'We – that is, I and one of the nurses – walked towards the trenches last night to see if there is anywhere we could set up a treatment post, I suppose you might call it, even closer to the front line.'

'Oh yes, I heard about that. The lad on sentry duty reported it.' He was thoughtful for a moment before saying, 'Well, maybe I can help you. Have you time to come back with me now?'

'Yes, yes, certainly.' He turned to Florrie, who was hovering nearby and had overheard the conversation. 'Come along, Nurse Maltby. Since you've volunteered to be involved, then you should see what you're getting yourself into.'

'I'll just ask Sister Blackstock,' Florrie said, suddenly uncharacteristically circumspect. But the doctor waved his hand, 'No need, no need. I'm giving you an order. She has no authority to countermand it.'

Florrie followed the two men as they went towards

the mud-spattered, dilapidated vehicle the sergeant was driving. They bounced over the rough ground. As he drove, he shouted above the noise of the engine. 'That shell-damaged house you saw last night – where the soldier was on duty. It's uninhabited now, but it's a big place. The kitchen and a couple of the ground-floor rooms are still pretty much intact, and it's got cellars – a real warren of 'em. Is that the sort of place you're looking for?'

Excitement shone in Ernst Hartmann's eyes. 'Exactly.'

They drove back the way Florrie and Ernst had walked the previous evening.

'It's not far from our supply lines and rear-line billets, Doctor, but still well behind our artillery. Can't say you won't get a stray shell from the other side now and again, but the cellars are pretty solid. I think it's as near as you can get and yet still be comparatively safe.'

Florrie cast a sideways glance at Ernst. He made no comment and she was sure he was thinking: It's still not near enough.

Now, in the light of day, they could see the encampment behind the lines where soldiers took a respite from the Front, where the supplies of food and equipment and ammunition were delivered to be transported through the support trenches to those in the front line. They could see the tents and the hastily erected buildings that housed the reserve soldiers – men who would themselves soon have to go to the Front and give their fellow soldiers a welcome rest. Those who had not already been carried out wounded or dead, Florrie thought grimly.

She leaned forward from her seat in the back of the vehicle. 'How long do they stay in the very front line?'

'Usually two days. Then two days in the support trenches, another two in the reserve trenches and finally six days in the rear-line billets before they have to go up to the front line again. 'Course they can't sit on their backsides – 'scuse me, miss. When they're not at the front they have to repair trenches, bury the dead or carry supplies up to the Front. And all the time,' his voice wavered a bit, 'there's the bloody shelling.' This time he did not apologize.

'D'you get any proper leave? I mean, away from here altogether?'

'Oh yes, now and again we get a few days and go into the countryside.' He jerked his thumb over his shoulder towards the border with France. 'But none of us have been back to England yet. We're all hoping we'll get relieved soon and we can get right away for a while. Perhaps Paris, or maybe even right home this time.' There was longing in the young man's tone.

'I hope you do,' Florrie said.

'Thanks, miss.' He slowed the vehicle and drew to a halt. 'Here we are.'

They all looked up at the house. They could see now that it had once been a magnificent building and even though now it was battered and crumbling, it was still standing with proud defiance.

'It's not quite what the French would call a chateau, but it does remind me of the Manor House back home in our village,' Sergeant Granger said wistfully, reminding Florrie suddenly of Gervase and Isobel and of the beautiful Bixley Manor. Then the sergeant became practical once more as he added, 'There's still furniture in some of the rooms. You might be able to use it.'

'What about the owners?' Florrie asked. 'Where are they?'

The sergeant shrugged. 'No idea. But I'm sure they wouldn't mind us using it, if it's to help the men fighting to rid their country of the enemy.'

'Precisely,' Ernst Hartmann murmured. 'Let's take a look.'

They walked into the shell-scarred house, stepping over the rubble in the worst of the rooms.

'I don't think it'd be safe to use the upstairs and even one or two of the downstairs rooms – well, the ceilings look a little precarious to me,' Sergeant Granger said. He moved through to the rear of the house where the kitchen was situated. He opened several doors, most of which were cupboards or led outside to the back yard. But then he found the one he was looking for: steps leading down to cellars.

'Here it is,' he cried triumphantly. 'It's very dark. Do be careful if you're coming down.'

'We need a lamp or candles and matches.' Florrie looked about her. She glanced along the dusty shelves, but there was no lamp. Then she opened kitchen drawers. 'There's still cutlery here and table cloths and napkins,' she murmured. 'So much we could use. Ah . . . here we are!' Florrie lifted three candles from the drawer.

'And how do you propose to light them?' Ernst asked.

'I've got matches,' the sergeant offered and, after more searching, they managed to find candle-holders and lit the three candles. Taking one each, they went carefully down the stone steps.

The cellar was divided into several rooms, some still housing dusty bottles of wine in racks.

'This is perfect. It's dry and—'

'Doctor,' Sergeant Granger said worriedly, 'I must

impress upon you that the shelling can reach as far as this. You're very close to the trenches, you know.'

But Ernst Hartmann was nodding and smiling, pleased with what they'd found. He waved aside the sergeant's fears. 'This is exactly where I want to be – where I *need* to be.' He turned excitedly to Florrie. 'Nurse Maltby, I'm putting you in charge of getting these cellars ready to receive patients. They need cleaning from top to bottom, beds and linen moved in. An operating table in one of the smaller rooms and all the equipment and medical supplies we shall need.'

Florrie gasped. It was a mammoth task. She glanced helplessly at the sergeant. But he smiled and nodded. 'I'll detail some of our lads to come and help you, miss. We'll have it shipshape in no time.'

'Good, good,' Ernst Hartmann rubbed his hands gleefully. 'Now, we're really getting somewhere. If you'd be kind enough to drive us back, Sergeant? The sooner we can get things moving, the better.'

The next two days were a blur to Florrie. Dust filled her nostrils, clung to her hair and dirtied her uniform, but with the help of Billy and Walter and a couple of their pals, the cellars were cleaned thoroughly. Camp beds with pillows and blankets were moved in. Suddenly, the place started to look like a proper field hospital, and a comparatively safe one at that.

'Would you like the kitchen cleaned out too, miss?' Billy asked her. 'You could store a lot of dressings and bandages and stuff in them cupboards.'

'An' if we clean the range for you,' Walter put in, 'mebbe you could use it for cooking. I reckon we could get it working for you. It's an English one, would you believe, just like me ma's got at home.'

'And some of the lads will come and act as stretcher-bearers an' orderlies for you, if you want. Sergeant's cleared it with the major, so you've only got to ask. We'll organize it, miss, but we've been ordered to the Front tomorrow, so we'll have to get some of the lads that are coming back down the line to help you.'

'Thank you.' She glanced from one to the other and added huskily, 'Do – do take care of yourselves, won't you?'

'We'll do our best, miss.' Billy grinned.

'An' if we cop one, we'll be in good hands if we get brought here,' Walter chuckled.

Florrie smiled and promised, 'I'll look after you personally.'

She watched them go. Despite Dr Hartmann's reprimand, the two soldiers had been the epitome of propriety all the time they'd been helping Florrie clean out the cellars. Not once had either of them – or any of the four who'd helped – stepped out of line.

The next day, Sergeant Granger brought four different soldiers to help her, though the cellars were almost ready. There was only the kitchen left to clean now.

'Me name's George, and me mate Walt said I was to clean the range for you, miss, an' get it going.'

'That'd be wonderful.'

'Will it burn wood, miss? 'Cos there's not much else to use round here.'

'I expect so,' Florrie said, wishing she'd known more about the workings of the kitchen at Candlethorpe Hall. 'We can but try.'

As George bent to his task, she turned to greet the other three soldiers who'd come with him.

'Hello, Miss Florrie. Fancy seeing you here.'

Florrie's mouth dropped open in a gasp of surprise, her eyes wide.

'Ben! Oh, Ben!' She stretched her arms wide and gave him a bear hug – much to the amusement of the sergeant and the other three soldiers. She stood back and examined him from head to foot. 'Are you all right?' Physically, he looked well, but there was a haunted look in his eyes.

'I'm – fine, miss,' he said, with only the merest hesitation and a swift half-glance at his superior.

'It's – good to see you.' Her feelings were mixed. It *was* good to see the young boy, to see him still alive and well, but she wished it could have been anywhere but here. He was in the thick of the fighting now and anything could happen to him. But, at least for the next few days, he had a respite.

'Have you written home?'

'I'm not awfully good at the letter-writing, miss. Nor's me ma, but I've filled in a few of them postcards we get to send. She'll've got them. And I got a nice parcel t'other day from your grandmother.' He grinned suddenly. 'Some nice warm socks, miss.'

Florrie laughed. 'Just in time for summer, eh?'

But the boy shook his head. 'Weather's been bad, miss, even though it's May. I've been glad of 'em. Specially at night in the – the trenches. It gets really cold.'

'Right, lads, let's get cracking,' Sergeant Granger interrupted. 'What do you want them to do, miss?'

'The rest of the kitchen, please. Once that's done, we can move in all the equipment and supplies. And then we'll be ready.'

The four soldiers worked all day and by evening the room was clean. George had cleaned the range and now a fire was roaring in the grate.

'It's got a back boiler, miss,' Ben told her. 'Just like

our range at home. We've found you plenty of firewood in a shed out the back and we've filled it up with water from the pump in the yard. Luckily, it's still working. So you'll have plenty of water, an' now you can heat it an' all.'

'We'll be back tomorrow to bring more supplies, miss,' one of the other soldiers, whose name was Harry, put in. 'And help with whatever you want us to do.'

Florrie smiled. 'That's wonderful, I—'

'Look what I've found.' George came in from the yard, walking backwards and dragging something through the door.

Florrie clapped her hands. 'Oh, a tin bath!'

'It was in the shed. I've given it a good clean-out.' He stood up and turned to face her, grinning. 'So now you can have a nice bath in front of that fire. An' I'm first in line to scrub your back.'

'Watch it,' Ben said at once, frowning and stepping towards the other man. 'Miss Florrie's a lady, an' don't you forget it.'

'Whoa there, mate,' George said at once, his hands outstretched, palms outwards as if to fend Ben off. 'I was only having a larf. No offence meant, miss. Honest.'

Florrie laughed and put her hand on Ben's arm to calm him down. 'And none taken, George. Now, how about I make us all a nice cup of tea before you leave?'

They all sat down at the freshly scrubbed kitchen table on a motley selection of chairs that had been found in various parts of the house. Florrie set out cups and poured boiling water from the kettle on the hob into a cracked teapot. The lid was missing, but she improvised with a cracked saucer to cover the tea whilst it brewed.

They sat around drinking tea and swapping stories of their lives and loved ones back home. Florrie was able to reassure Ben that his family had been fit and well when she'd last seen them, and she promised that she'd write that very night to her grandmother with messages for the Atkinson family.

'So this is what you all get up to when my back's turned.' Sergeant Granger was standing in the doorway. At once the four soldiers scrambled to their feet and stood to attention, looking suddenly fearful.

'My fault entirely, Sergeant,' Florrie said cheerfully. 'They've all worked so hard they deserved a cuppa.' She lifted up the teapot. 'How about you? I think there's still enough in the pot.'

Sergeant Granger smiled, nodded to his men to relax and joined them at the table.

'Everything's done,' Florrie said as she fetched another cup for him. 'Thanks to you and your men. Just the medical supplies to come and we'll be ready.'

A little later the men left and Florrie was alone. It was growing dusk as she banked down the fire in the range and prepared to walk the mile and a half back to the camp. She eyed the tin bath sitting innocently on the hearth. There was plenty of hot water in the boiler. It was such a pity to waste it, she thought, and there was no one about now.

She found a tin jug, filled it from the tap at the side of the range and poured it into the bath. Six more jugfuls gave her a few inches to sit in. She rummaged through some clutter that the soldiers had heaped into one corner of the kitchen during their cleaning. They'd brought everything they could find from other parts of the house too. Anything and everything that might be useful: sheets, blankets, pillows, towels and even some clothing that had been left. They'd brought it all to the kitchen.

'So you don't go looking round the house, miss,' Ben had said. 'T'ain't safe in some parts.'

At last she found what she sought – a piece of soap. It was cracked and dried, but it was better than nothing. She lit two candles and, moments later, she was stepping naked into the bath and luxuriating in the warmth of the hot water. Every limb was aching with the fatigue of the last two days, but she'd completed the task. The cellars were ready and even the kitchen was usable. She couldn't wait to get back to the camp and tell Dr Hartmann. She chuckled as she soaped herself. She might even get a smile of thanks from him.

Florrie froze as she heard a scuffling noise outside. She glanced towards her clothes, strewn over a chair. Her gun was beneath them and she couldn't reach it from where she was sitting. She waited, holding her breath and hoping that whoever it was might go away. The footsteps came nearer, right to the kitchen door. It swung open, creaking on its hinges.

'Oh, thank goodness,' Florrie breathed as she saw Ernst standing in the doorway.

'Nurse Maltby – whatever are you doing?'

'What does it look like?' she replied with asperity, forgetting for a moment his senior position. 'I've done my bit these last two days – with a lot of help, mind you. But I'm hot and filthy and I deserve a bath, so, Dr Hartmann, if you wouldn't mind leaving whilst I get dried and dressed . . .'

But Ernst didn't leave. He came into the room and moved towards her, picking up the towel and stretching

243

it out so that she could step out of the bath and allow him to wrap it around her. She looked up at him, her heart beating a little faster.

He was even more handsome in the soft glow from the candlelight. His black hair shone and his blue eyes were dark with a sudden passion. Her body responded of its own volition. She was powerless against the huge tide of emotion and longing that swept through her. It was wrong – all so wrong – yet she wanted to be in his arms more than anything she'd ever wanted in her life . . .

He was still holding the towel stretched out for her. Slowly, she stood up. The candlelight glistened on her body. She stepped out of the water onto the flagged stone floor. He wrapped the towel around her and pulled her gently into his arms.

'Florence – my darling girl. From the moment I first saw you, I knew this was meant to be. It is Fate that has brought us together. Come . . .' He drew back and took her hand. Picking up one of the lighted candles, he led her towards the steps leading down to the cellar. They lay on one of the beds made ready for their first patients and there Florrie believed she'd found the love and passion she sought. She'd found a man she truly could love and be loved by. Willingly, she gave herself to him, body and soul.

Locked in their own private little world, they could have been a thousand miles away from the war.

Twenty-Nine

'So, tomorrow we begin,' Ernst said as they walked back through the twilight, holding hands until they came within sight of the encampment. 'No one must know about us, Florence. You do understand that, don't you?'

'Of course,' she said swiftly. 'Sister Blackstock would send me packing immediately. And I don't want to go – especially now.'

He chuckled. 'I don't think they would do that to me, but my reputation would not be so – how do you say – wholesome?'

She laughed softly. 'Oh, I don't know. You'd be forgiven. You're a man.' There was a tinge of irony in her tone. In Florrie's mind, it was another example of the inequality that existed between men and women. Whilst she would be sent home in disgrace, he would merely cause a nudge and a wink and be thought a bit of a 'jack the lad'. Even so, she didn't want to be parted from him.

'But how are we going to meet? Have some time alone together?'

'I'll think of something,' he murmured. He gave her hand a quick squeeze before releasing his hold. They walked back into the camp with a demure three feet between them.

The following morning, Ernst, Sister Blackstock and

Florrie set off to begin work in the ruined house. Rosemary Blackstock was full of praise for the work Florrie had done with the help of the soldiers. 'Dr Hartmann was right, wasn't he? We'll be able to do so much more, the nearer we are. And these cellars are comparatively safe.'

As if on cue they heard the thump of the guns begin again and it wasn't long before their first patients began to arrive.

Ernst insisted on seeing every one of them, though not all required his surgeon's knife. He picked out one here, another there that needed his skill and instructed Sister Blackstock to assist him in the small room set up as a crude operating theatre. Florrie was left to attend to all the other casualties carried down the steps and into the cellars. She felt a moment's pang of disappointment that it was Rosemary Blackstock at Ernst's side and not her. But her head, if not her heart, told her that the older woman was by far the more experienced at assisting him. And besides, Florrie told herself, they've trusted me enough to leave me in charge in the wards.

She bent over a man who'd been injured in the face. Gently Florrie syringed and washed the wound with peroxide to clean the blood and mud away. Carefully, she shaved his face and placed a dressing on the wound. It would need such treatment repeated frequently over the next three or four days. As she turned to leave him and go to her next patient, the man gripped her arm. He couldn't speak, but in the dim light of the cellar, lit only by lanterns and candles, the look in his eyes spoke his thanks.

She smiled and moved on. The next casualty had a badly smashed leg and was awaiting his turn in the operating room. He was in dreadful pain, but he was smiling through it all. 'This is a Blighty one, ain't it, Sister?'

Florrie grinned. 'Could be, soldier, but that's for the doctors to say. And by the way, I'm not a sister, I'm only a VAD – not even a proper nurse.'

The man winked at her. 'Well, you'll do for me, luv. Just get me patched up an' on that ship home.'

The three of them worked all day until at last the flow of casualties stopped, but already it seemed as if the cellars were full.

'First thing in the morning, Nurse Maltby,' Ernst said, 'you must ferry as many of these patients as can be moved back to our base camp.' He seemed to be avoiding looking directly at her and spoke now to the sister. 'We need more people here. Another doctor and more nurses.'

'We do, Dr Hartmann.' Rosemary spoke softly as she glanced around at the sleeping patients. 'You were right. Several – if not most – of these men would have been in a far worse state if they'd had to travel further before receiving attention.'

Ernst gave a grunt of satisfaction at hearing her admit it.

He moved away, towards the tiny room where he slept, without bidding them goodnight and – to Florrie's intense disappointment – without even glancing at her.

The days passed in a blur and there was no time for Florrie and Ernst to snatch a few precious moments together. The wounded poured into their field ambu-lance in the cellars, now nicknamed, with tongue-in-cheek wry humour, the Chateau. They were treated or operated on, nursed and moved back to what was referred to as Base Camp.

'Would you like to come with me, Grace?' Florrie asked. Grace had come to the Chateau to help out for a few days. 'There's a poor boy who's been gassed. He can hardly breathe, poor dear. If you could sit in the back of the lorry and—'

'Oh, Florrie, I'd love to – I know the one you mean. He's a lamb and so *young*! But I've got all these sheets to wash.' She leaned closer and lowered her voice. 'He's a fanatic about *everything* being washed.'

Florrie nodded, remembering the argument between Ernst and Sister Blackstock. Arms akimbo, Rosemary had faced him fearlessly. 'Doctor, if you want this amount of laundry doing – clean sheets for every new arrival – you must send for another VAD to do that and nothing else. I'd put Maltby on it, but she's too valuable driving the lorry, and besides, her nursing skills are—'

'Yes, yes, yes!' Ernst had put up his hands as if in surrender, but he was not about to give in. 'You must understand, Sister, how cleanliness is so important to prevent the spread of infection. We're getting all sorts of diseases coming in, not just gunshot and shrapnel wounds. Bronchitis, pneumonia and,' he paused deliberately for dramatic effect, 'tuberculosis.'

Rosemary Blackstock gaped at him. 'I'm sorry – I had no idea,' she said at once.

'I saw two cases at Camiers. We're almost bound to encounter it here sooner or later. Anyone who has a susceptibility to it is bound to develop it in the terrible conditions they're living in.' He shrugged. 'Besides, it's not pleasant for the wounded to be put into a bed to lie on another man's blood and pus – and worse.'

'No – no, you're right. I see you are. But how are we to cope?'

Florrie had seen Ernst's winning smile, his irresistible charm, turned fully on Rosemary. 'Ah, Sister, you will find a way, I'm sure.'

And so the laundry was done by anyone who could be spared – even the 'walking wounded' were coerced into standing at the white sink with their arms deep in soapsuds.

'Beats goin' over the top' was the opinion of men who'd likely never had to do any 'women's work' in the whole of their lives.

Dr Johnson greeted her as Florrie drew the ambulance to a halt outside the line of tents at Base Camp two weeks after their arrival here. She'd been driving the patients from the Chateau each morning, sometimes needing two or three journeys, but today there was something different about the original camp site.

'Oh,' she exclaimed as she jumped down from behind the wheel and shaded her eyes against the sun. 'You've got more tents. Lots more.'

'And more nurses and two doctors have arrived,' the big man beamed at her. 'They've begun to realize that the army medical officers in the field can't cope with the volume of casualties, not since this hellish battle began, and Hartmann's theories are proving effective. So we've been sent more help and, I think and hope, there's more to come. So, my dear girl,' he put his hand on her shoulder and squeezed it warmly, 'today you can take back Sister Carey and two nurses to help at the Chateau. And even,' he puffed out his chest, 'another doctor.'

'Oh, Dr Johnson . . .' Quite forgetting her place, Florrie flung her arms around him, stood on tiptoe and kissed him soundly on the cheek. Then, appalled at her temerity, she stood back. 'Oh, I'm sorry. I'm so sorry.'

But Dr Johnson's booming laugh echoed through the camp. 'Don't mention it, my dear.' He winked at her. 'But I shall expect that greeting every morning from now on.'

'Nurse Maltby,' Ernst Hartmann said when the last patient was carried away at the end of another gruelling day and there were just the two of them left in the operating room. 'You and I – we deserve a little holiday.'

Already it was the beginning of June and the worst of the fighting around the town of Ypres seemed to be over. Though the gunfire and shelling would never quite cease, they were less frequent. There would always be casualties, though thankfully not so many now. That dreadful, overwhelming tide of wounded and dying had ebbed a little.

Busy with the instruments, Florrie glanced up at him in surprise. 'A holiday?' Then she chuckled. 'I've almost forgotten what that is.'

'Then tomorrow we shall revive your memory. We shall take a little trip away from here to where it is safe. Just for a day we will have no more death and disease and the shedding of blood.'

Florrie bit her lip as her heart raced a little faster. 'But how?'

He smiled. 'I have it all worked out. When you drive your patients back to Base Camp tomorrow morning, I will come with you. There is an extremely sick patient who needs an operation that we cannot perform here. They have better equipment at the camp now, and Dr Johnson will be able to do a much better job. The soldier has a severe wound in his stomach and intestines and he will need care on the journey. It is the perfect excuse for me to come with you. And we need more equipment and supplies here. We can bring them back.'

Florrie laughed. 'It doesn't sound much of a holiday.'

He grimaced. 'Well, maybe only half a day and part of the evening. But we shall make a little detour. I have heard of a nice little cafe not too far away beyond Base Camp. It's in a small village that has not yet been affected by the shelling. And don't forget your identity certificate. We'll be going across the border.'

'But – but won't anyone guess? Sister Blackstock? And the others?'

'No, no, they will suspect nothing – if we are careful.'

Despite her excitement at the thought of the outing, and even more at the thought of being alone with him for a few precious hours, Florrie slept soundly, waking automatically at five thirty. By six o'clock, she was washed and dressed.

As they carefully loaded the injured man into the back of the ambulance, Florrie marvelled that he was still alive. She doubted he would withstand even the short journey or the operation ahead. The other three were 'walking wounded'. One climbed into the passenger's seat beside Florrie, whilst the other two sat in the back with the stretcher case and Dr Hartmann.

'Aren't you the lucky one?' Sister Blackstock teased as they were about to leave. 'Having the handsome Dr

Hartmann all to yourself on the journey back. But just you be careful, my girl. He's a devil with the women, you know.'

'Really?' Florrie laughed.

'Yes, really.' Now Rosemary Blackstock's tone was more serious. 'And being out with him alone – well, you've your reputation to think of.'

'My reputation? That was shot to pieces in Holloway – at least according to my father.'

Sister Blackstock pulled a face. 'Oh, don't tell me about fathers.'

'Strict, is he?'

Sister Blackstock smiled. 'Aren't they all?' She sighed. 'He was dead set against my making a career for myself in nursing. Said it would be a waste. I'd only get married. But, as you can see, I'm no beauty.' The statement was made in a matter-of-fact manner. She was not seeking compliments. She smiled impishly. 'Unlike you.'

Florrie opened her mouth to protest. In the cold and the mud and the horror she felt anything but 'beautiful', but Rosemary held up her hand. 'Don't deny it, my girl. I don't like false modesty.'

Quite truthfully Florrie said, 'Well, I don't feel it out here.'

'No,' Rosemary said soberly. 'I don't suppose you do, but your loveliness brings great comfort to the dying, my dear.'

Florrie stared at her and her lip trembled. 'But I don't want to be an ornament. I want to be *useful*.'

'Oh, you are, Florrie, you are. Never doubt that.' She chuckled. 'Believe me, pretty face or not, you wouldn't still be here alongside Dr Hartmann if you weren't useful and very capable. He always puts his work first. But he's a very charming man when he wants to be and that's why—'

What more the sister might have said, Florrie was never to know, for at that moment Ernst Hartmann came striding towards them.

'Ah, there you are. Everyone ready? Then let's be off.' Without even a glance at Florrie, the doctor climbed into the back of the canvas-covered lorry to sit beside his patient.

Rosemary Blackstock watched them go, her eyes clouded with anxiety. She sincerely hoped the young girl's head would not be turned by the attentions of the handsome, dark-eyed doctor.

Thirty

Florrie drove slowly, mindful of the terribly injured man in the back of the vehicle. The constant thud of the guns grew a little fainter and the soldier sitting in the passenger seat beside her began to relax.

'D'you reckon mine's a Blighty wound, miss?' he asked. It was the thought uppermost in every wounded soldier's mind. And if she'd a pound for every time she'd been asked that same question since coming here, Florrie thought, she'd be a wealthy woman. This soldier's arm, the bone smashed by flying shrapnel, was bandaged and in a sling. At the house they'd been able to clean the wound, but he too needed a more complicated operation than Ernst Hartmann could perform with the limited facilities in the cellars.

'Dr Johnson's marvellous with bones,' Florrie reassured him. 'But your arm will take a while to mend, so,' she grinned at him, 'you never know your luck.' She didn't add that she thought the arm would never mend properly and it was very likely he'd be invalided out of the army. It wasn't her place to guess the decision of the medical officers.

Despite the terrible pain he must be in, the soldier grinned back at her. 'Well, me luck's held out this far, miss. Not like a lot of me pals.' His face clouded again. 'At least I'm still alive.'

It wasn't long before they reached the camp. It

was a very different place now from when they'd first arrived. There were more tents and hastily erected wooden huts, with duckboards between to act as walkways. It was more like a real field hospital. Yet more doctors and nurses had arrived. Dr Hartmann had been proved right. Immediate treatment saved many a wound from becoming infected and consequently saved lives too. Most of the patients were still taken by train back to the larger hospitals on the coast, but many minor injuries were treated successfully and the soldiers returned more swiftly to their units. Whether the men themselves were happy about this was questionable. Perhaps they felt cheated of a longer trip away from the Front, even if it was only to the coast of France and not back home.

But the doctors were fair. They never sent a man back until he was fully fit. And if he showed signs of shell shock, they found a way to keep him a little longer or send him to the coast.

'If I send the poor bugger back in this state,' Florrie had once heard Dr Johnson mutter over a patient who was shaking and disorientated, even though the minor wound on his leg had healed, 'they'll have him shot at dawn for cowardice.'

Florrie climbed down from the driving seat and hurried round to the back to help the patients. The broad figure of Dr Johnson appeared from the largest tent, which was now an operating theatre. Blood spattered his white coat and his face was drawn with weariness. But he strode across the grass, his hand outstretched to greet his colleague.

'What brings you here, Hartmann?'

Swiftly, Ernst explained about the badly injured man and the need for further supplies. 'Sergeant Granger's been very good, but even he can't make the trains run on time. I'm hoping you might have what we need.'

'Some of our stocks are running low too. But we'll see what we can do.' Dr Johnson clapped him on the back. Two orderlies rushed forward to carry the stretcher case straight into the theatre tent. 'Come, I want more details about this patient.'

Ernst glanced at Florrie. 'Perhaps you'd see Sister Warren about the list of items.' He turned back to the other doctor. 'We can't stay long. We must get back, Johnson, as soon as we can. You understand?'

Florrie felt her heart sink. Perhaps Ernst had changed his mind about their outing. She sighed and went in search of Sister Warren.

The supplies were loaded and Florrie stood beside the vehicle waiting for Ernst. It seemed an age before he appeared from the tent with Dr Johnson, shook his hand and strode towards her.

'Right, Nurse Maltby,' he said, climbing into the passenger's seat without even glancing at her.

Florrie turned the lorry and headed back the way they'd come.

'When you get over the hill out of sight of the camp, turn left. We'll double-back.'

Florrie said nothing, but she smiled. Ernst had not changed his mind.

They drove through deserted countryside, but, further away from the Front, there were signs of life. Cattle grazed in the fields and farmers were scything the long grass and raking it up into mounds. On one farm they saw soldiers helping with the hay-making.

'Are they prisoners of war? Germans?'

'No, no, they're allies at rest.'

'I don't understand.'

'Do you remember Sergeant Granger telling us how our soldiers do so many days in the trenches and then so many in rear-line billets, but usually they remain where the supplies are, often acting as carriers?'

Florrie nodded. 'And he also said they come into the countryside when they've a few days off. How long do they get?'

'Oh, I've no idea. You'd have to ask an army chap. Varies probably, according to what's happening at the Front. But more than likely it's not long enough for them to go to Paris or the coast, so they just come as far as here to get away from the guns for a while.'

'Mm. But you can still hear them in the distance, can't you?' She glanced again at the young men, some stripped to the waist, working in the sunshine. Still they could all hear the thunder of guns and the explosions of bursting shells; they could never get right away from the constant reminders of the war. Several glanced up and saw the vehicle with its Red Cross emblem. One or two waved, but others looked away quickly as if it reminded them painfully of the war and all its horrors.

Florrie drove on and they came to a little village – no more than a hamlet – where children were still playing in the street.

Florrie gasped. 'I hadn't realized. It – it looks so normal. All those refugees we saw. I thought – I thought—'

Ernst smiled. 'You thought everyone had gone. Only from where the fighting is actually taking place.' He shrugged. 'But one day perhaps these poor folk will be forced to flee too, if our armies are driven back. It was the Kaiser's intention to march through Belgium and approach Paris from the west. Only he hasn't managed it.' Ominously, he added, 'Yet.' Trying to lighten their mood, Ernst went on, 'Now, let us see if Monsieur Gaston still has his little cafe open. Pull over to the right.'

The meal was surprisingly good. They dined leisurely, enjoying the luxury of being able to take their time and savour the wine. Across the table they touched hands briefly and gazed into each other's eyes. But they didn't talk much, they were just happy to be together.

'We are lucky,' the host told them in broken English, waiting on them himself. 'We still have local supplies.' He lifted his shoulders and spread his hands in a helpless gesture. 'But for how long?'

It was a question not one of them could answer.

But there was something that Florrie wanted to ask Ernst. She leaned across the table and touched his hand. 'Why are you here, Ernst? In a war that's nothing to do with your country?'

His expression was wary. He glanced away and didn't answer immediately.

'I'm sorry. I shouldn't pry. I was just curious, that's all. I never thought about it myself. It wasn't until that sentry said . . .' Her voice faded into silence.

With obvious reluctance, he said stiffly, 'My mother was French and I have cousins fighting with the French army. I couldn't just sit back and do nothing. Not when my skills could do so much good, even though . . .' He pressed his lips together as if to stop himself saying any more.

'Even though?' Florrie prompted gently, but Ernst shook his head. 'Oh, nothing.' His attitude made it quite clear he was not going to say anything more about his family or his life back in Switzerland.

They drove back as the light began to fade.

'The guns have never stopped,' Florrie murmured.

'Stop. Pull up here,' Ernst said suddenly.

'What? Why? What's the matter?' Alarmed, Florrie pulled to a halt.

'Switch the engine off.'

'Why? I don't understand—'

'Just do as I say. Now, get out and put one side of the bonnet up.'

'Whatever for?'

He turned and leaned towards her. Running his finger gently down her cheek, he whispered, 'You do want me to make love to you, don't you?'

Her heart thumped and her body tingled 'Yes, oh yes, but why do I have to put the bonnet up?'

'If anyone should come along, we'll hear them. You'll have to get out and play the "damsel in distress". Make out the engine's stopped and you can't restart it.'

Now Florrie giggled. 'You think of everything.'

'Naturally,' he said.

She did as he said and then they climbed into the back of the vehicle. They spread the blankets, which Florrie carried for her patients, on the floor of the lorry and lay down.

Slowly, Ernst unbuttoned the blouse of her uniform. He kissed her shoulders, her neck and, at last, her lips, his fingers struggling with the laces and buttons of her under-garments. They did not undress fully, not this time, for fear someone might come along the road. His hands explored her gently, arousing her to heights of longing. She groaned and writhed beneath him, willing him to enter her quickly, so urgent was her need of him.

She cried out in sheer joy, her fingers digging into his back as he buried his face in the softness of her breasts. He shuddered and groaned and lay still on top of her, panting. Florrie lay back, smiling and stroking his hair. She closed her eyes.

And all the time the pounding of the distant guns never ceased.

'Quick! Someone's coming. I hear marching feet and – and singing.'

Bleary-eyed, Florrie scrambled to find her clothes in the darkness.

'I'll stay here. Pretend I'm a patient,' Ernst suggested, pulling the blankets over him.

'I can't find my shoes. Ernst, you must help me.'

'Get out of the back. Be quick!'

She felt around in panic. 'Oh, fiddlesticks! I'll have to leave them.'

She stepped down into the road in her stockinged feet.

The squad of soldiers was only yards away, their voices filling the night air with the strains of 'Who were you with last night, out in the pale moonlight'. How appropriate, Florrie thought, suppressing a nervous giggle. Seeing her, the sergeant called a halt and came across to her.

'You in trouble, miss?'

'It – it just stopped. The engine and I – I don't know

how to start it again,' she finished lamely. She hated herself for sounding like a weak and ineffectual female, when in truth she'd probably learned far more about the internal workings of her vehicle during the last few weeks than any of these soldiers knew.

'No trouble, miss. We'll take a look for you.' He turned and yelled, 'Martindale – Robinson – at the double—'

'Please, not so loud. I have a patient in the back. I – I think he's sleeping.'

'We'll be as quiet as we can, miss.'

The soldiers he'd called out for stuck their heads under the bonnet.

'Can't see anything wrong, sir. We'll try an' start it up for you, miss.'

Seconds later the engine fired into life.

'Oh, how silly of me,' she said, finding it quite easy to feign embarrassment as she blushed furiously at her deception. 'I don't know how to thank you.'

'Think nothing of it, miss. It's us that should be thanking you nurses for being out here.' The two soldiers saluted her once again. As they turned and began to walk back to their comrades, Florrie distinctly heard one say, 'I wonder why she's got no shoes on?'

'Best not to ask, mate. Mebbe that patient in the back ain't as sick as he's mekin' out.'

Their laughter filled the air until the voice of their sergeant called them to order. But Florrie, left standing by the lorry, felt even more foolish.

She waited until they'd marched a good distance down the road before she whispered, 'They've gone. You can come out now.' And seeing Ernst emerging from the back of the lorry, half-undressed and with his

261

smooth hair decidedly ruffled, Florrie was overcome by a fit of the giggles she could no longer quell.

'The engine stalled and Nurse Maltby didn't know what was wrong,' Ernst explained smoothly to Sister Blackstock, who'd been watching out for them, her anxiety growing with every passing minute. 'But we were lucky. Some soldiers were marching,' he waved his hand airily, 'somewhere – and stopped to help. So, all is well. Goodnight, Nurse Maltby.' He didn't smile at her, didn't even glance at her as he strode away towards the house and his bed in the cellar.

Stiffly, Sister Blackstock said, 'You can see to the lorry in the morning. You'd better get to bed too.'

'Yes, Sister,' Florrie said meekly. 'Goodnight.'

Sister Blackstock watched her go, a worried expression in her eyes. There was something different about the girl. She couldn't quite put her finger on it, but there was definitely something.

She hoped it had nothing to do with the handsome Dr Hartmann. She didn't want to have to send this particular nurse home in disgrace.

Thirty-One

'There's someone asking for you, Nurse Maltby.'

Surprised, Florrie said, 'For me?'

'He was brought in half an hour ago,' Sister Black-stock said. 'He's very badly injured. I don't think he's going to make it.'

The colour drained from Florrie's face. Her eyes widened. If someone was asking for her by name, it must be someone she knew. Oh, Tim! Was it Tim? Knowing he was somewhere in the area, she'd dreaded seeing him brought in on a stretcher.

'Don't faint on me, Nurse,' Ernst snapped. 'Don't let go of that clamp or this boy will die. Get a hold of yourself.'

'I – I'm sorry.' Florrie swallowed and took a deep breath to calm her trembling hands. She struggled to concentrate on holding the instrument whilst Ernst stitched with expert fingers.

'He didn't say his name, but I think he's one of the boys who helped you clean out the cellar. He's insistent he wants to see you. So, Nurse, as soon as you can.'

A few moments later Ernst said tersely, 'You can go.'

'I—'

'Don't argue. I said you can go.'

Florrie took a last look at the patient. He was a good colour and seemed to be breathing normally. It was amazing after the trauma his young body had suffered.

But, thanks to Ernst's skill, he would live. Not to 'fight another day', but this soldier would certainly get home to Blighty and his family. Though, without his right arm, she doubted he would ever work again. She hoped he'd a loving family who'd care for him.

'Ben!' she whispered. 'Oh no!'

She knelt beside him and took his hand. The boy – for, despite everything, he was still no more than a boy doing a man's job – was white-faced and shaking with sobs.

'I can't see,' Ben struggled to say. 'It's got me eyes.'

His breath was a rasping, laboured sound. He sounded as if he was drowning and there was the stench of gas about him. But that was not all: his right leg was a bleeding, mangled mess and, though Sister Blackstock was doing her best to clean the horrific wound, she glanced at Florrie with wordless despair. Even Ernst Hartmann, with all his skill, would be able to do no more than chop it off above the knee.

'I want me mam, Miss Florrie. I want me mam.'

'I know, Ben, I know. I'll write to her for you. What do you want to say?'

'Tell 'er to come. I want 'er. I want to tell 'er I'm sorry. Sorry I went against her wishes and joined up. She were right. I should've listened. Tell 'er I'm sorry – sorry – Mam – oh, Mam . . .' He drifted off into blessed unconsciousness. Florrie sat beside him, holding his hand to her cheek. How was she ever going to write to tell Mrs Atkinson that her only son – her beloved boy – had been killed?

What an appalling waste this war was! There were no words to describe the ghastly carnage to those waiting back home. Though they read the casualty lists and mourned in their thousands, they still wouldn't be aware of the full horror of it all.

If she got home, Florrie vowed, she'd make sure they knew. She'd tell the world. A war like this must never again be allowed to happen.

Ben woke once more and seemed calmer. 'Miss Florrie?'

'I'm here, Ben. I'm here.' She'd remained sitting beside him into the early hours of the morning, knowing the boy did not have long. Ernst had been to examine him and shaken his head sadly at her. Then he'd left them alone.

'I've seen Master James, miss.'

'James!' Her heart contracted in fear. 'Here? Are you sure, Ben?'

'Oh yes, miss. Him and that other chap what married Miss Richards. He's a captain now, miss. Did you know?'

'No, Ben, I didn't.' She was about to ask more questions, but she saw that he'd drifted away again. He died at three in the morning without regaining consciousness. But all the while, Florrie sat holding his hand.

Ben was laid to rest at Poperinghe and, though they couldn't often attend the funerals of their patients – there wasn't time to spare – Ernst allowed Florrie to attend the burial of the young boy she'd known since childhood. She remembered walking across the fields to the Atkinsons' farm with her grandmother, taking a basket of goodies on the day that they'd heard Mrs Atkinson had given birth to her baby boy. Florrie had been four years old and had skipped alongside Augusta in the spring sunshine. And now she was standing beside his grave, with the rain pouring down and the incessant sound of pounding guns. Dead at just seventeen.

And all the while she couldn't help thinking: It could have been James.

Although she tried to make enquiries, she couldn't find out where James was. She began to think that perhaps Ben, in his delirium, had been mistaken. Perhaps he'd been dreaming of home and thought he'd seen him in reality.

But then came a letter from Augusta telling her the news she'd most feared to hear.

My dear girl, How dreadful for you to be with Ben when he died but, though the news has devastated the Atkinson family, the fact that you were at his side and were able to reassure Mrs Atkinson that he did not suffer, has been of great comfort to them. Though I wonder, privately of course, if you have not told us the whole truth. The number of telegrams that relatives are receiving saying 'He died instantly and did not suffer' seems incredible. I expect, for once, it is the War Office trying to be kind.

Florrie smiled sadly. Her grandmother was as shrewd as ever. But, as she read the next words, her smile faded.

I'm sorry to have to tell you, my dear, that James has been posted abroad. Where, we don't know, but if the action is where you are, then I fear that is where he might well be also. We have not heard from him since he went, so if you do have news, please, Florrie dear, let us know. Gervase has written – he sends his love. He says he's still moving about a lot. Your father is

*well, and your mother, poor dear, stays in bed most of
the day now . . .*

Florrie glanced at the top of the letter. The date in
Augusta's scrawling handwriting was already a month
old. She folded the letter slowly and tucked it away
amongst her belongings. So, she thought, James had
already been out here in France or Belgium for over a
month. Perhaps Ben had been right after all. Maybe
James was here somewhere quite close. And Gervase
and Tim? Where were they?

As she lay down to sleep, she prayed fervently that
she would not see any of them, for the only way that
might come about was if they were wounded.

No one seemed to guess about the love affair between
Florrie and the doctor. Their snatched moments of
privacy were few, but their lovemaking was passionate, heightened by the danger all around them. Ernst
couldn't even come to where she slept, for it was one
of the rooms in the cellar, with the patients sleeping on
the other side of the wall, and the room was shared
with any other nurse or sister not on night duty.

Late at night, when the orderlies had carried away
the last patient and the other nurses had stumbled
wearily to their beds, they made love in the operating
room, where earlier men had screamed in agony and
even died.

There was no time for sentiment or squeamishness,
no time for guilt or remorse. There was only this moment
of passion – for there might never be another. Every day
they lived with death: the death of those all around them
and the knowledge of their own fleeting mortality. There
was no thought for family or friends or loved ones.

Marooned in a world of carnage and horror, they hungered only for each other. They gave of themselves to others for many hours every day, so when they could snatch a few minutes, they were completely selfish and self-centred. For those few precious moments, nothing and no one else mattered. Not Tim. Not Gervase. Not even James.

By day they worked side by side the same as always, professional and efficient. Only when they'd done all they could for the wounded and dying did they fall into each other's arms and, for a brief moment of bliss, blot out the world around them.

They were blithely unaware that Sister Blackstock had her suspicions, but wisely she kept her counsel, though she worried for Florrie, for she'd become fond of the girl and admired her spirit.

'What's going to happen when this is all over?' Florrie asked Ernst.

They were in the dimly lit operating room, sharing a brief moment alone. They were both exhausted after a particularly harrowing day. But each drew comfort from the other's nearness. Ernst stroked her hand.

'Over?' There was incredulity in his tone as if he'd never even thought that one day it would be over – that it would *ever* be over. Now she was forcing him to think about it. He wrinkled his brow. 'It depends.'

'On what?'

'On who wins, for a start.'

'Oh, we'll win,' Florrie said promptly.

Ernst smiled, a little sadly. 'So much confidence,' he murmured and pressed her hand against his lips.

'What will you do? Go back to Switzerland?'

His eyes clouded and took on a far-away look. His home was in another world, another time.

When he didn't answer she pressed him. 'What d'you want to do with your life? What were you doing before the war started?'

Slowly, almost reluctantly, he murmured, 'I worked in a sanatorium in my home town. It was – is – what I always wanted to do. It's why I became a doctor.' He glanced at her and then looked away again quickly. 'Davos has become well known for the treatment of tuberculosis patients. There are many sanatoriums there and I wanted to make the study of the disease my life's work.'

'And you'll go back there when the war's over? Is there still a position for you at the sanatorium where you worked before?'

'Oh yes,' he said. There was a strange bitterness in his tone. 'There's a place waiting for me there.'

'I could come with you. I could help you.'

'We'll see, we'll see,' he said softly and kissed her hand again. Then he reached for her and pulled her down, holding her close and burying his face against her breast.

She said no more, asked no more, understanding that he could not envisage what the future would be. It seemed he did not have her faith.

Thirty-Two

Florrie had become adept at improvisation and soon everyone was calling on her for help.

'Maltby, there are no cradles left and I've got this casualty with a badly smashed leg.'

Florrie, just back from another run to Base Camp, went out into the yard. Looking about her, she saw a woodpile. She selected two pieces of plank roughly the same length and tied them tightly together at one end with a piece of string from the kitchen drawer. The other end she eased open just enough so that it stood up. She carried it inside. 'There you are, Grace, that should just hold the covers up enough.'

'Oh, ta, Florrie,' Grace said and hurried away with the makeshift 'cradle'.

At other times, she raided the kitchen cupboards for pie dishes to use to sterilize instruments and for saucepans to act as wash bowls.

'Ask Maltby' became the cry when they couldn't find something they needed. 'She'll know what to do.'

And through it all, she nursed the sick, the wounded and held the hands of the dying.

Then, at the very end of July, came a new horror for Ernst and his gallant band to cope with. Fierce fighting broke out near Hooge, only a mile or so from Ypres, and the enemy used a new weapon – liquid fire, spurting burning petrol from steel-nozzled hoses. The casualties were horribly burned, with blackened faces and scorched limbs. The Chateau was overwhelmed. Ernst and the nurses patched them up as best they could and Florrie drove them the agonizing mile or so to Base Camp. They were soon sent on by train to Camiers, where those that survived the trauma were treated in a special ward.

Florrie worked until she was exhausted and still she carried on, her pity for the scarred and screaming men driving her to the point of collapse. Grimly determined, she refused to give in. Work was the only thing that kept her from the dreadful fear that one day her patient might be Tim – or James.

Of Gervase, there was still no news.

In August, Florrie received a letter from Isobel telling her the wonderful news that she'd had a baby boy in July and that he was to be called Charles Timothy Smythe.

'*And we so want you to be his godmother, darling Florrie. Gervase, of course, will be one of the god-fathers . . .*'

Florrie smiled. Was Isobel trying to do a sly bit of matchmaking? She wrote back straight away saying she'd be thrilled and honoured to be the child's god-mother. '*But don't you dare have him christened until we're all home,*' she added. '*I so long to hold him for myself – not have someone stand proxy for me.*'

She chewed the end of her pen, not daring to ask the question uppermost in her mind. Had Tim got leave to go home to see his son? And what about Gervase? Where was he, and did he know he was now an uncle?

Instead she put, '*Do write again when you can and tell me all the news.*'

Florrie was weary and cross. She hadn't had a moment alone with Ernst for weeks. Her days and nights had become a blur and even Sister Blackstock was urging her to rest, but stubborn defiance drove her on.

The great surge of casualties they'd experienced during the first two weeks of August had lessened a little to a steady flow.

'We should be moving on now,' Ernst said one evening at the end of another long and tiring day in the operating room. 'It's quietening down here now and we should be where the battles are taking place. Nothing's happening here.'

'Really? You could have fooled me,' Florrie snapped tartly, for the moment forgetting that they were not alone. She was punished by a severe glare from Sister Blackstock, who snapped, 'Nurse, finish that dressing, then I'd like a word with you.'

She glanced up, but the sister was walking away. Ernst, too, was bent over another patient and ignoring her.

Florrie sighed.

'I hope you're not going to leave us, Nurse,' her patient, who'd been caught by a sniper's bullet in his left shoulder, whispered. 'All the lads say you're doing a marvellous job. Don't go, miss. Don't leave us.'

'I have to do as I'm ordered, soldier. Just like you. There,' she said, as she finished the dressing on his wound. 'You'll do, and I'll be taking you through to Base Camp tomorrow. You're fit enough to travel.'

The man grinned. ''Spect I won't get a Blighty ticket,

but a bit o' rest away from the trenches'll be welcome. By, what a summer we're having. Never know from one day to the next what the weather's going to be doing. Not like last year, eh? Blue skies all summer long.' His expression sobered. 'It'd've been a wonderful year if this bloody war hadn't started.'

Florrie chuckled. 'I had a letter from home yesterday and my grandmother tells me that people are saying it's the guns in France causing the changeable weather.' She found the idea amusing, but the soldier nodded seriously. 'Could be, miss. You never know. Them bombardments are the very devil.' His eyes took on the haunted look that Florrie had seen so often.

She patted his hand, 'Well, you're going to get away from them for a while now. See you in the morning. And now, I'd better go and find Sister. I think I could be in trouble.'

'Oh, I hope not, miss. You're too pretty for anyone to be angry with for long.' He grinned and she was pleased to see the agony fade from his eyes, even if only for a brief moment. 'But then, mebbe she's jealous. Not much of a looker, is she?'

'Now, now.' Florrie wagged her finger at him as she walked away.

'Really, Maltby, I expected better from you.'

Florrie knew Rosemary Blackstock was angry with her; it was the only time that she dropped the 'Nurse' title when addressing her.

'I know we've been thrown together in rather – intimate circumstances, but there's no need for standards to fall. You showed a distinct lack of respect to Dr Hartmann just now. I won't have it. Anyone would think—' She stopped abruptly and altered whatever she had been about to say. 'Well, it just won't do.'

'I'm very sorry, Sister,' Florrie said, anxious that the woman should not suspect the closer relationship that now existed between the doctor and the VAD. If she had the slightest inkling, Florrie thought, she'd send me packing back to Base Camp at least, if not back to Camiers, well out of harm's way, as she would see it.

Rosemary was watching her, trying to decide whether to express her fears openly. She had more than the 'inkling' that Florrie feared, but so far she had chosen to ignore it. But perhaps if Dr Hartmann were anxious to move on, their separation would come about naturally. The sister decided to hold her tongue a little while longer.

'Dr Hartmann.' Sister Blackstock faced him squarely with a determined expression. 'We're all exhausted. Nurse Newton has a dreadful cold. Nurse Featherstone is feeling constantly nauseous and Maltby – well, she's dead on her feet, though she'd never admit it. How that girl's kept going, I don't know. She'll fall asleep at the wheel one of these nights.'

Ernst regarded her thoughtfully. 'And what about you, Sister? Are you ready to go home?'

'We're not asking to go home, Doctor. None of us. We just need a break. Even the troops on the front line get rest periods – even if it's only a day or two.'

'Perhaps you're right,' he said slowly. 'Mm. I'll go back with Nurse Maltby to Base Camp tonight and arrange with Dr Johnson to send replacements for – let's see – shall we say four days?'

The sister nodded.

'And then we can all have a little holiday.'

Two days later, Sister Blackstock left for the coast, well away from the battlefields. Grace and Hetty set out together, seeking, they said, 'Bright lights, music and dancing and soldiers who don't need nursing!'

Ernst and Florrie took advantage of Rosemary's absence. They were able to arrange to spend three whole nights together away from the Chateau and Base Camp. Eyebrows might have been raised behind their backs, but no one dared to voice any questions. They went to stay in the little cafe in one of the attic bedrooms.

The host waited on them himself, bringing them breakfast in bed. Each day they rose late and wandered through the village and out into the countryside, watching the soldiers at rest helping the farmers with their harvest. Sitting at the edge of a field, their arms around each other, they saw a young, dark-haired girl in the distance carrying a basket. She approached the soldiers, who threw down their pitchforks and took the food she handed out. Across the stubble they heard the sound of merry laughter as the soldiers flirted and joked with the pretty girl.

'You'd never think there was a war only a few miles away,' Ernst mused.

'No,' Florrie said, her gaze still on the youngsters. How many of these fine young men, she was thinking, would be wounded or dead this time next week?

Even in the warm sunlight, with Ernst's arms around her and the sound of youthful gaiety, Florrie still could not forget the horror of it all.

At night, they lay together in the lumpy, old-fashioned bed, whispering loving words and sharing silly jokes.

'I adore you,' Ernst murmured as he made love to her. 'You are the love of my life.'

When they all returned to the Chateau four days later, Rosemary Blackstock brought someone with her.

'I believe you know this young man, Nurse. He was making enquiries about you at Base Camp.'

Florrie flung her arms wide to envelop him. 'James! Oh, James.' Then she stood back, holding him at arm's length. 'Let me look at you. Oh, how you've *grown*. And filled out. Goodness me – and all on army rations too. How've you managed that?'

James smiled, taking all her fussing over him with great good nature.

'Now, you can have a little time off, Nurse, but I can't allow you to go out anywhere – even though he is your brother. I'm sorry.' As ever, Rosemary was a stickler for the rules.

Florrie pulled a face at James and then grinned. At least they could spend a few hours together. They sat outside in the back yard behind the house, where freshly washed bed linen fluttered on the clothes lines.

'We have to do all this by hand in the sink in the kitchen,' Florrie laughed. 'Whatever would they say at home to see me up to my elbows in soapsuds?'

James laughed, but Florrie could see that same haunted look in his eyes that all the soldiers seemed to have.

'How long have you been out here?' she asked softly.

'We got here about the middle of May, just before things started to quieten down a bit. So, we saw a bit of action, but it's not been too bad since. We take our turn in the trenches and then go to billets in the country – just across the border into France. We help with the hay-making and the harvest.' He smiled wistfully. 'I could almost imagine I'm back home on the estate helping Mr Atkinson in the school holidays.'

She wondered if he'd been one of the young soldiers they'd seen working in the sunlit fields, laughing and flirting with the farmer's daughter.

'The – the local people have been very kind to us.' He glanced away and bit his lip. Florrie had the feeling that he would like to have said more. He suddenly had a dreamy, far-away look in his eyes. She touched his arm.

'What is it, James?'

'What?' She'd startled him out of his reverie. 'Oh – oh, nothing. Nothing at all.' But Florrie, who knew her little brother so well, was not convinced. However, she pressed him no further. No doubt it was what many a soldier was experiencing – a disillusionment with the war and a longing for home.

As he got up to go, he clung to her and buried his face against her shoulder. 'Take care of yourself, Florrie,' he said huskily.

'And you too. Keep out of trouble.'

James laughed wryly. 'That's a little difficult out here, but I'll try.'

They parted reluctantly, and as he walked away, Florrie called after him, 'Have you heard anything of Gervase? Do you know where he is?'

James shrugged and shook his head. 'Sorry, no, I haven't.' Then suddenly he grinned. 'But no doubt you'll see him on New Year's Eve.'

Florrie laughed too and, as she watched her brother

walk away, she remembered Gervase's words to her. 'Wherever you are, I'll find you.'

Towards the end of September, whilst the French armies attacked the German lines in Champagne, the British launched an offensive near Loos.

'That's less than twenty miles from here,' Ernst said excitedly. 'We must go there. We can still use the Base Camp. Nurse Maltby will just have a little further to drive, that's all.'

'Whatever for?' Sister Blackstock argued. 'There's still fighting going on here in the Ypres salient. We've got casualties coming in here every day.'

Ernst waved his arms dismissively. 'That's just the British High Command trying to draw the enemy away from Loos. But that's where the action is—' He smacked his fist into the palm of his hand. 'Dr Johnson will send one of his doctors and two nurses here to keep this going, but Loos is where *I* should be.'

'But where shall we be?' Sister Blackstock said worriedly. 'I mean – we mightn't find a house as suitable as this.'

'We'll take tents then. There's plenty at Base Camp now. They can spare a few.'

Base Camp had mushroomed over the months until it resembled a proper field hospital.

'No – oh no,' Rosemary shook her head decidedly. 'I'm not having my nurses under canvas in a dangerous position. I know you by now, Dr Hartmann. You'll want to get as near as you can to the battle front.'

'Of course I shall, woman,' he snapped back heatedly. 'That's the whole point.'

'Then I'll only agree to it if you can find somewhere

like this. A place with cellars. But tents? Oh dear me, no!'

Ernst Hartmann flung out his arm towards Florrie. 'Well, she'll come with me, won't you, Nurse?'

Nervously, Florrie bit her lip. His anger was making him careless. She met Sister Blackstock's frosty stare steadily. 'I can see both sides of the argument, Dr Hartmann, but I'm under Sister's command. I must do what she says.'

With a growl of frustration, he turned on his heel and stalked away.

Florrie watched him go, tears prickling behind her eyelids. She shivered, feeling suddenly cold. She hated it when he was so angry with her.

Thirty-Three

'I knew he'd win. Men like him always get their own way.'

Rosemary Blackstock was decidedly disgruntled to find that the other doctor now at the Chateau, and Dr Johnson and his colleagues at Base Camp, agreed with Ernst Hartmann. They'd seen for themselves the success of his theories and backed him wholeheartedly.

'Well,' she went on, 'he can do it without me this time. I'm going back to Base Camp, and you nurses,' she nodded at Grace, Hetty and Florrie, 'are coming with me.'

'Oh, but—' Florrie began, but the sister pointed her finger.

'Not another word. That's an order.' Secretly, she was trying to put distance between the pretty VAD and the handsome doctor. And not a moment too soon, she thought, if I'm not mistaken.

But even Sister Blackstock proved herself unable to withstand Ernst's considerable charm.

'This time we cannot find a house with cellars, Sister, but we have farm buildings – strong and sturdy – just outside the range of the enemy artillery. I promise you,' he murmured, raising her hand to his lips and fastening her with his blue gaze, 'I would not dream of endangering you or your nurses.'

So the sister relented enough to allow volunteers to

follow the doctor, though she remained resolutely at Base Camp this time. But, of course, one of the willing volunteers was Florrie. Rosemary Blackstock sighed, but could do no more.

They were in the very thick of the action again and Ernst was in his element. Florrie now drove the ambulance more than she actually nursed the soldiers, because of the greater distance to and from Base Camp. But whenever she could, she still stood at Ernst's side in the small barn where he carried out emergency operations.

'D'you know,' she told Sister Blackstock on one of her trips, 'the British are using gas now at Loos. Isn't that dreadful?'

But Rosemary was philosophical. 'What's sauce for the goose . . .' she murmured.

'Well, I think it's diabolical. It's not – it's not gentlemanly.'

Rosemary laughed wryly. 'Nothing about this war is, my dear.'

Angry and worried too, Florrie climbed back into her vehicle to go back to 'Poppy Camp' as they'd nicknamed their new first-aid post, after the blood-red poppies that grew in the fields of Flanders. It seemed a lot of nicknames were used. The soldiers even had names for the trenches, so she'd heard. As she drove, the sound of gunfire and shelling became louder and louder and, even from a distance, she detected the telltale smell of gas drifting on the wind.

And out there, somewhere, she knew, was James.

*

Eventually, the offensive ground to a halt and both sides settled down to a second winter in the trenches. Florrie breathed a sigh of relief. She'd been thankful not to see James brought into their post, and she'd not had word that he'd been wounded or worse. And there was no bad news, either, about Gervase or Tim. In fact, there was no news at all about any of them now.

Nightly she prayed that they were all safe.

Although there were still skirmishes, there were no major battles in their area. Now they treated chilblains, trench foot, bronchitis and pneumonia. Their main 'battle' was a never-ending one with the rats that invaded the farm buildings in search of food and warmth – more so since the onset of winter.

'You should see 'em in the trenches, Nurse,' one soldier told her as she threw her shoe at another unwelcome visitor. It scurried away and Florrie went in search of her missile. 'Big as cats, some of 'em, and they snuggle up to us at night to sleep. I woke up one morning to find one of the buggers nestled in me armpit.'

Lice were another perpetual problem when the mud-soaked, unwashed soldiers were brought in. Florrie could deal with those, but she hated the rats and feared the disease they might carry.

As Christmas approached, the team at the farm and those still at the Chateau went back to Base Camp.

27th November 1915, Dear Gran, Florrie wrote and then, with a wistful smile changed it to, *Dear Grandmother, Your welcome letter has arrived at last. It had taken three weeks to get here, and the one from Mother sent a week after yours was in the same batch. Mail is delivered spasmodically (sometimes I get three at once!) but, please, don't stop writing. You say that the redoubt-*

*able Mrs P and her group of ladies are still knitting for
the troops. Please thank her. It's getting very cold here
now. I'm sitting up in bed to write this by candlelight
and wearing my topcoat, socks and gloves! And talking
of socks – that is what is still badly needed. The boys
could have no better Christmas present . . .*

The next letter she received from Augusta told her
they'd heard from James that he was back near Ypres.

*So if you see him again, be sure to tell him how
proud we are of him. But tell him to take care . . .*

Over the next three weeks, Sister Blackstock put the
less seriously ill patients to work making decorations
for the wards for Christmas. 'It keeps them busy and
out of mischief,' she declared.

'Don't you think it reminds them too much of
home?' Florrie wondered.

'They'll already be thinking of home, Nurse. I don't
think making a few paper chains is going to make much
difference.'

'No, I suppose not.' Suddenly Florrie was overwhelmed with homesickness. It was the first time she'd
really felt it. She longed to be back at Candlethorpe
Hall, planning Christmas with her mother and Augusta.
How they'd always loved Christmas, and how lonely
the huge house would seem with only the three of them
there. No Florrie and no James. She wondered if Isobel
and her baby would join them, or if Tim might wangle
a few days' leave to get home and see his son and heir.
But then, even if he didn't, Isobel would probably go
down to Dorset to be with Lord and Lady Smythe.

Tears sprang to her eyes at the thought of them all.
She longed for news of James. She worried every minute
of every day for the safety of her young brother who,
in her eyes, was still only a boy.

'God keep him safe,' she whispered. 'And Gervase and the Hon. Tim too.'

Three days before Christmas, several large packages arrived by special delivery, all addressed to Nurse Florence Maltby.

'By heck, darlin', someone loves you,' the orderly who carried the parcels into the tent where Florrie slept teased her.

Florrie laughed. 'They're not for me. They're for the boys.' She tore open the brown paper of one of them and out tumbled pair after pair of thick, brown socks in different sizes. 'See.'

The man's mouth dropped open. 'You're going to be popular on Christmas morning, I can tell you.' He watched as she undid the rest of the parcels. There were gloves, soap, toothbrushes and powder, writing paper and envelopes. '*Very* popular.' He eyed the items longingly. Florrie smiled and picked up a small bar of chocolate from the parcel that had been addressed as 'personal'. 'Here, thank you so much for your help. And this is our secret, mind, until Christmas.'

'Oh, ta, miss,' he took the chocolate gratefully. 'And yeah, 'course it is. And if you want any help with the tree on Christmas Eve, miss, I'm your man.'

Now it was Florrie's turn to look surprised. 'A tree? We're getting a Christmas tree?'

'Oh yes.' The man was delighted to be telling her something she didn't know. 'Dr Hartmann has arranged it all. His family's sent one from Switzerland.'

Florrie was suddenly still. Ernst's family. She was shocked to realize that she knew so little about the man who had become so important in her life.

'Right, miss, if there's nothing else . . .' The orderly's voice interrupted her thoughts.

'No – no, nothing just now and – and thank you.' As he turned to leave she added, 'And I'll be very glad of your help with the tree.'

On Christmas Eve, the orderly, whose name she found out was Len Brewster, helped Florrie decorate the wards. Because she was not assigned to a particular ward here at Base Camp, she helped out anywhere she was needed. She was greeted with whistles and catcalls and Len fended off the cheekier remarks. 'Now then, lads, behave yerselves.'

Florrie glanced around and was gratified to see several of the men at whose operations she'd assisted Ernst at Poppy Camp. Some of them remembered her, but others could not. Most seemed to be recovering well and all were in good spirits. The parcels from home could not stretch to include all the patients, so Florrie decided to give her gifts to the men in the two surgical wards now run by Sister Blackstock.

On Boxing Day, with a brief hour to spare, Florrie wrote to her mother and enclosed a note for Mrs Ponsonby saying how much all the gifts had meant to the soldiers.

At dusk on Christmas Day, she told Clara, *the tree was lighted and several of the nurses who could be spared went around the wards singing carols. It seems strange to say it, but we all had a wonderful time and everyone tried to make the best of being away from their loved ones.*

'Another visitor for you, Nurse Maltby.'

Sister Blackstock beamed. She'd taken at once to the

tall, broad young man with fair curling hair and a small neat moustache. He'd arrived at Base Camp on New Year's Eve loaded with gifts for the sisters and nurses and had asked so politely if he might see Nurse Maltby.

Florrie gaped and her mouth dropped open. Then tears sprang to her eyes. She held out her arms to him. 'Gervase. How wonderful!'

His strong arms were around her and he was lifting her off her feet. For once, Sister Blackstock broke her own strict rules and crept out of the tent, leaving the young couple alone. She was mentally crossing her fingers that the arrival of this very pleasant young man would drive out any silly notions Florrie might have over a certain dark-haired doctor.

'Whatever are you doing here? And how are you? I've not heard anything from you. I was so worried.'

'Were you?' He looked down into her upturned face and held her even more closely. 'It's been very difficult to let anyone know, my dear. I've been travelling up and down the Western Front ever since I came to France. I don't seem to be in any one place for very long.' He smiled. 'And as for what I'm doing *here*. Well, it's New Year's Eve.'

Florrie threw back her head and laughed. 'James was right. He said you'd come.'

'James? You've seen James?'

'Oh yes . . .' Still holding his hands, she drew him to sit side by side on her camp bed while she told him everything that had been happening to her.

There was only one thing she did not tell him. She did not mention Ernst Hartmann.

Thirty-Four

'So, who was that who came to see you on New Year's Eve?' Ernst asked, his eyes dark and brooding, his manner terse. 'Another brother? A cousin? Or a *grateful* patient?'

Florrie stared at him, then she giggled. 'Oh, Ernst – I do believe you're jealous.' She moved towards him, stretching out her arms to embrace him, but he took a step backwards. 'You forget yourself, Nurse. We are working. We have a delicate operation to perform under ridiculous conditions. My patient will be brought here at any moment.'

She gaped at him, but he turned away and she was left staring, bewildered, at his back.

They worked with professional rapport as they always did, but in a tense, uncomfortable silence. As the patient was carried out, Florrie whispered, 'Ernst, it was an old family friend from home. I haven't seen or heard from him for almost a year.' It was the truth, even though she'd heard *of* him now and again.

Ernst stood very still, then he turned and smiled, his face creasing, his eyes bright with love and desire. He touched her cheek. 'That's all right then,' he murmured.

As the next patient was carried in, they turned back to their work, but now harmony was restored.

*

By the spring of 1916 the Western Front stretched from the Swiss border to the French coast. The British and their allies held the trenches from a point on the coast between Ostend and Dunkirk running inland to beyond Amiens, whilst the French were dug in as far as the Swiss border.

In February news came that the Germans were bombarding the French lines near Verdun. It went on for days, weeks and months. The enemy was, it seemed, determined to crush the resistance and bleed France into submission by overrunning an area of their country that had special significance for the French people.

'We must go there. We are needed,' Ernst insisted, but this time his colleagues disagreed.

'It's a French battle, Hartmann,' Dr Johnson said. 'If they ask for our help, we will go, of course, but until then we have our own soldiers to care for.'

Having lost his own personal battle, Ernst stamped away in frustration. Instead he divided his time between the house, Poppy Camp and Base Camp. And he insisted that more small first-aid posts in tents should be set up along the line of defence so that he could visit and give emergency treatment to the wounded.

'He'll upset the army medical officers if he's not careful,' Florrie heard Dr Johnson say to Sister Blackstock. 'He's making it look as if they can't cope.'

'Well,' Rosemary said rationally, 'they can just cope now, whilst things are quieter here, but I have to say, Doctor, that when we get a major battle, let's face it, they can't.'

The big man sighed. 'You're right, but I just wish the chap would calm down a bit and take a rest.' Then he added bitterly, 'We'll have another battle of our own before long, I've no doubt.'

As spring progressed into summer, the Ypres salient was becoming a rest area for troops from the battle zones or a place where new arrivals from Britain could be eased into life in the trenches. But there was enough gunfire, shelling and spasmodic trench raids to introduce the raw recruits to war before they were dispatched to more dangerous areas. Despite the steady flow of sick and injured men to care for, Ernst still chafed that their skills were not being fully used here.

To Florrie's disappointment, he did not ask her to go with him as he travelled up and down the line, visiting the dressing stations. Now she hardly saw him and they were never alone. He seemed to be ignoring her and she was hurt. After all they had been through together, after all they had shared . . .

Dr Johnson's prophecy came true on the 1st July when the British, in an attempt to relieve the pressure on the French at Verdun, launched a major offensive near the River Somme. It was the largest army the British had sent into battle and, though the French sent troops in support, they could not muster as many as they had promised. Their army had been drained by the continuing savagery at Verdun.

'Now we *must* go,' Ernst declared and, this time, no one argued. Everyone guessed it was going to be a long, weary and costly campaign.

James came to the Base Camp to say goodbye. His battalion had been ordered south. His young face was white and drawn. 'Fine way to be spending my eighteenth birthday next week, isn't it?' he said, trying to make light of it, although his voice was shaking. 'Oh,

Florrie,' he burst out, gripping her hands and clinging to her. 'I don't want to go. And I'm not just being a coward. There's a good reason why I should stay here – why I ought to stay here—'

'James, what is it? Tell me.'

'I—'

'Nurse,' Sister Blackstock's voice cut in. 'You're needed. Please say goodbye to your brother now.'

'James, come and see me later. Tonight,' she whispered urgently.

'I can't. We're moving out in an hour. I have to get back, but Florrie, please—'

'Nurse!'

He sighed and his shoulders sagged. 'You go,' he said flatly. 'I don't want to get you into trouble. I've done enough of that already.'

Florrie forced a laugh, 'Of course you haven't. It's just that we're so busy getting all the patients ready to go to a general hospital. We're all going as soon as we can – to – to the Somme.'

James tried to smile. 'See you there then.'

'I hope you don't, darling James.' She hugged him swiftly and then gave him a little push. Tears were very close and she didn't want him to see her cry. 'Go on – and take good care of yourself.'

'I'll – try,' were his last words as he turned and walked away.

'*Nurse!*'

'Coming, Sister.'

Two weeks later, they were still at Base Camp. There had never been any intention to close down the facilities there, or even the Chateau and Poppy Camp, but the promised replacement medical staff had not arrived.

Ernst fretted at the delay, but Dr Johnson was sanguine. 'We've no choice but to remain here until we're relieved,' he said, adopting the parlance of the army. 'And there's no point in just a few of us going.'

'There are thousands wounded and dying,' Ernst protested. 'Haven't you heard? They're lying out there on the battlefield for days until they're found. We're needed, Johnson, as we've never been needed before.'

The older, wiser and less impetuous man put his hand on Ernst's shoulder. 'I know, old boy, but there's no sense in rushing heedlessly down there without being properly prepared. I'm sorry to say it, but I don't think it'll end before we get there.'

For the next few days the team continued to treat the injured, nurse the sick and wait. It was not something Ernst Hartmann was good at.

Florrie drew her ambulance to a halt at the side of the Chateau least damaged by the shelling. She climbed down wearily. It had been a long day. She'd been up at five as usual, and now it was gone eight o'clock in the evening, the setting sun slanting its golden light across the fields. But it had been a good day. She'd been ferrying patients back to the Base Camp all day. Not one of them had died, and all were expected to recover well. And that counted as a good day. A very good day.

She leaned against the vehicle, shading her eyes and looking out over the fields towards where she knew the trenches were. There was no shelling here tonight, but now, in the stillness of the summer evening, she could hear the distant sound of artillery fire.

Could she really be hearing the guns on the Somme? She sighed. In a few days' time, they'd be there too, for surely their replacements must arrive soon. Then perhaps Ernst would come out of his black mood. When they were once more in the thick of battle and being useful, Ernst – perversely – would be happier.

A figure was striding towards her, silhouetted against the evening glow. Florrie gasped and new life flooded into her tired limbs. She stretched out her arms towards him and began to run. 'Gervase, oh, Gervase!'

He opened his arms and she ran into them. He held her close, his arms tightly around her as if he would never let her go. 'Florrie, oh, Florrie, my darling girl,' he murmured against her hair. At once she knew something was wrong. She pulled back and looked up into his face. 'What is it? What's happened? Oh! It's – it's not – James?'

He didn't answer immediately, but his solemn face and the anxiety in his eyes told her more than words could say.

'Oh no!' she breathed. 'He's – not—'

'No,' Gervase spoke swiftly. 'No, but he's in trouble. Serious trouble.'

Her eyes widened. 'Why? What d'you mean?'

'Is there somewhere we can go?'

'Well . . .' She hesitated, not thinking straight, the worry blotting out all sensible thought. 'The kitchen, I suppose, but the others might be there, having their meal. I – I've just got back. I – oh, Gervase, please tell me now.'

He took her hands and held them. 'My dear, James has been arrested for desertion. He's to be tried by court martial.'

'Court martial! Oh dear Lord, no!' Her face blanched and her whole body began to tremble. She'd been out here long enough to know exactly what that meant. If found guilty, her brother – her baby brother – could be shot. Her knees began to sag and she would have sunk to the ground if Gervase had not caught and held her. Her voice was a husky whisper as she asked, 'When is it to be?'

'The day after tomorrow. He's asked for me to stand as – as his "prisoner's friend".

This was something she hadn't heard about. 'What – what does that mean?'

Gervase sighed. The burden was resting heavily on his shoulders. 'Out here there's no such thing as a solicitor or a barrister to defend the – the accused, but they're allowed to have someone to speak for them, if they wish. Several don't even ask for that, but James has asked for me.'

Florrie looked up at him, tears streaming down her face. She clutched at his arms. 'Oh, Gervase, you must save him. You can't let him die. Not James. You can't.'

Gervase's face was haggard. 'Florrie dearest, you know I'll do everything I can.'

She gazed into his eyes and whispered, 'It – it sounds as if there's a "but".'

He sighed heavily and pressed his lips together before saying flatly, 'They're very heavy-handed about desertion or – or anything they see as cowardice. Some have been executed just for refusing to go over the top or for "throwing their arms away", as they phrase it. A top London lawyer would probably have argued a good case and got them off, but out here – it's rough justice.'

'Can we get someone to come out? If I send word home, maybe—'

'Florrie darling, I told you, the hearing's the day after tomorrow.'

'So soon? But when did this happen? How long's he been held?'

'He was arrested five days ago.'

'Five days! But that's ridiculous.' Now Florrie was angry. 'That's no time to gather evidence, to get witnesses.'

'They don't get witnesses,' Gervase explained sadly. 'The fact that he was found miles from his unit, without his weapons and trying to get here—'

'Here? Why was he coming here? Oh!' She clapped her hand to her mouth and her eyes widened. 'Was he trying to find me?'

'I don't know. He won't say. In fact, he won't say very much at all.' Gervase's face was bleak. 'If only he'd open up – tell me what happened – give me *something* to work on. But if he won't—' He said no more, but his meaning was clear.

Florrie covered her face with her hands and groaned. 'Last time I saw him, just before they all left to go to the Somme, he seemed upset about something. He said he didn't want to go, and I'm sure he wanted to tell me something, but we were so busy. Oh, Gervase,' she cried in anguish. 'I didn't listen to him. If only—'

He held her close again. 'You mustn't blame yourself, dearest girl. I'll talk to him – try to find out what was troubling him, and if that had any bearing on why he—' Again, he stopped, unable to put into words the bald truth. His beloved girl was already hurting enough. He glanced about him and, seeing the lorry, couldn't help asking, 'Have you been driving that?'

Florrie took a deep breath, trying to calm her inner turmoil. 'Yes. I drive it between here and the field hospital we set up about a mile away. It's well behind the danger zone.'

'But this isn't,' Gervase said bluntly. 'You shouldn't be so close to the trenches. How long have you been here?'

'Since the end of April last year.'

He looked at her in horror. 'When the battle of Ypres was going on?'

She nodded. 'That's why we came here. Ernst, I mean Dr Hartmann—' Swiftly, she explained Ernst's theory and how he'd been proved right. 'We've saved so many more lives, and the men's suffering.'

'I don't doubt it,' Gervase said grimly, 'but you've risked your own life.'

Quietly, Florrie said, 'Haven't we all?'

'Yes, but it's different, you're—'

'Don't say it, Gervase. Don't you dare say, "you're a woman".'

He looked into her eyes and said seriously, 'I was going to say, "you're the girl I love, and I can't bear to think of you in danger".'

'It's not so bad. We're using this house. We cleaned out all the cellars. That's where the patients are and where the doctors carry out emergency operations. Oh, Gervase, I wish you could see them at work. How clever they are. Especially Dr Hartmann. And we use the kitchen and a couple of the other ground-floor rooms when there's no shelling going on.'

Gervase's face was grim as he was reminded painfully of the reason he was here. 'Cellars, you say?'

'Yes, why?'

'I – we—'

'What is it?'

He swallowed painfully. 'I've come on ahead. I came

to find you – to warn you. James is being brought here for trial, to – to Poperinghe. And – and they're looking for somewhere to hold him.'

For a moment Florrie was confused. And then she understood the awful truth. His jailers would be looking for a suitable 'cell' in which to imprison him whilst he awaited his trial. 'I see,' she said quietly. 'And you think they'll want to use one of our cellars?'

Gervase nodded. Now he could think of nothing to say.

'So,' Florrie said bitterly, 'they want to use the very place where every day for more than a year we've tried to save lives to imprison a young boy they intend to execute without even a proper trial?' When he didn't answer, she asked, 'But why here? Why Poperinghe?'

Gervase's face was bleak. 'Because – because there's an execution post there.'

Florrie swayed. 'Oh, my dear Lord!'

He put his arms around her and held her close again and that was how Ernst Hartmann, coming out of the ruined house to see if Florrie had returned, saw them.

Thirty-Five

Ernst's face was thunderous as Florrie made the brief introductions. Her mind was in a whirl, she scarcely knew what she was saying or doing. Her heart was aching with fear and she felt as if every limb in her body was trembling. Even Gervase was tight-lipped. It seemed as if both men sensed at once that they were rivals. Unwillingly, they shook hands and eyed each other like a pair of fighting cocks.

'What are we to do?' Florrie whispered, her face in her hands and hardly aware of the unspoken antagonism passing between the two men. She turned to Ernst Hartmann and, haltingly, explained the terrible news that Gervase had brought her, ending by repeating the same unanswerable question. 'What *are* we to do?'

'Where is the boy now?' Ernst asked.

'Being brought here under escort.'

'They want a – a place to keep him in. They – they might want to use one of the rooms in our cellars.'

Ernst stared at her for a moment, then glanced at Gervase. 'That's quite impossible,' he said curtly. 'We need all the space for our patients.'

'I'm afraid the major might commandeer it,' Gervase said quietly, disliking the man before him intensely. Ever perceptive about anything concerning his beloved

Florrie, he sensed there was more between them than the mere professional closeness of doctor and nurse.

Ernst gave a grunt and turned away. 'We shall see.'

Major Grant was not a man to be trifled with. It was he who'd brought the charge against James and he who intended to see that what he believed to be justice should be done and seen to be done. He was already annoyed that it had not been possible to try the boy where his battalion was fighting. He wanted to use the case as an example to the men of what would happen to them if they were even to think of deserting. But circumstances prevented it and he'd been obliged to organize a Field General Court Martial near Ypres, where his men had previously been billeted.

The following day the major and an escort party arrived, marching James into the cellars. They took him to the far end of the warren of rooms, to a damp and crumbling small space that had not been thought fit to use for patients. Sister Blackstock, Grace, Hetty and Florrie watched in horror to see the young boy's gaunt, pale face. But he was marching straight-backed, looking neither to right nor left. There was a determined, defiant look – a look that Florrie had never seen before on her brother's face.

Sister Blackstock put a restraining hand on Florrie's arm. But Florrie had no intention of acting hysterically, even though the fear welled up inside her. She wanted to run to James, wrap him in her embrace and hold him safe from harm. But instead she stood dry-eyed, proud and erect. She must act sensibly and rationally if she were to be of any use to him. No one would take any notice of a hysterical woman. But as the three men guarding the prisoner drew closer, Florrie caught her breath and, at her side, she heard Sister Blackstock's gasp of surprise. One of the escorts was Sergeant Granger. Rosemary Blackstock's grip tightened. 'Leave it for now, Florrie,' she murmured as if already reading what was in the girl's mind.

They returned to their patients, where they all had to face a barrage of questions from the men, who'd heard rumours about the impending court martial and that the soldier on trial had been brought here. They'd seen him now, marched past them through the make-shift wards, to his dungeon.

'What's going on, Nurse?' 'What's happening?' 'What's 'ee done.' 'He don't look old enough to be out here in this lot. It's them officers that want shooting, nor that poor little bugger.' On and on the gossip and speculation wrangled until Florrie could stand it no longer. She fled from the cellars. Stepping into the kitchen, she stopped and stared at the three men sitting around the kitchen table. Two were strangers to her, but the one she knew turned his face towards her, the sorrow in his eyes plain to see. He stood up.

'Oh, miss,' Sergeant Granger said brokenly. 'I wish there was something I could do . . .' She saw the help-lessness she'd noticed in Gervase's eyes mirrored in the sergeant's. She moved slowly towards the table and sat down heavily. The sergeant sat down too. One of the other men rose, his chair making a scraping sound on the flagstones as he pushed it back. He went to the stove and poured a cup of tea. He placed it in front of Florrie. Automatically she murmured, 'Thank you.' Then he and the other soldier went outside, leaving Sergeant Granger and Florrie alone.

She raised stricken eyes to meet his gaze. 'I want to speak to the major.'

'I don't think—' he began.

'I must,' she cut in. 'I must try everything possible.'

He sighed and then nodded. 'I'll see what I can do. But the – the court martial is tomorrow.'

'I know and I'll be there.'

'Oh, miss, I don't think—' he said again, but she held up her hand to stop him.

'I'll be there.'

The man fell silent. He knew when he was beaten.

She stood up and, leaning her hands on the table, said, 'Please take me to the major.'

Now the sergeant didn't argue.

The major was a big, thickset man with a bristling moustache. Florrie guessed him to be in his late forties. His brown hair was thinning and his face was florid, his jowls flabby. His eyes, devoid of any feeling, bored into hers. 'And what can I do for you, Nurse?'

Florrie stood before him, thankful that she was not under his command and desperately sorry for those who were. She lifted her chin and faced him squarely. 'Private Maltby is my brother, and I would like to know what the charge is.'

'Ha-humph,' the man grunted, stroking his moustache. 'I'm sorry to hear that. I wouldn't have brought him here if I'd known he had a relative nearby.'

'I'm sure you wouldn't,' Florrie replied tartly. 'But since you have and I am here, would you have the courtesy to tell me with what he is charged?'

' "When on active service deserting His Majesty's Service",' the man quoted bluntly.

'And what grounds have you for that assertion?' She was speaking stiffly and correctly, drawing on every ounce of her upbringing and education to put this pompous major firmly in his place. But the man was a tough nut to crack.

'On the grounds – as you put it, miss – that he was found miles from his unit and thumbing a lift away from the battle zone. He'd deserted his post, thrown away his arms and was,' his lip curled disdainfully, 'running away.'

'And has he given any explanation as to the reason for this alleged "desertion"?'

'No. He refuses to say anything, other than to ask for Captain Richards to act as his "friend".'

'Are witnesses to be called?'

'There are none.'

She took a step towards him, gratified to see that the major actually blinked in surprise. He'd heard the phrase 'a formidable woman', but he'd never actually met one. He ruled his own wife and family with the proverbial rod of iron and not one of them dared stand up to him. But to his surprise, he now found himself facing a female who appeared unafraid of him. She had the air of a tigress protecting her young.

In a soft voice that was even more menacing – and certainly more effective – than hysterical sobbing or pleading would have been, Florrie enquired, 'And have you asked if there are any witnesses? Have you tried to find out why he was where he was? And what exactly do you mean by "he'd deserted his post"? Where should he have been?'

'He *should* have been on sentry duty in the support trenches.'

'And has he been questioned as to why he wasn't?'

'Not yet – but he will be tomorrow.'

'I see. So he was given no chance to explain before the charge was brought against him? By you, I presume?'

'That is correct.' The major answered her in the same formal manner.

'And has anyone talked to him since? Taken a statement? Or merely *listened* to him?'

'As I say, he will have ample time tomorrow at his court martial.'

'I see.' Florrie's eyes glittered with anger. 'In a proper court of law, Major, as you well know, the accused is allowed legal representation. His brief is given time to prepare a defence and—'

'There is no defence for a soldier who deserts his post and betrays his fellow men. I wish you good day, Miss Maltby.'

'So, you're telling me that the only person allowed to speak for him is Captain Richards?'

Two soldiers came to stand beside her, stamping their feet and coming to attention before the major.

Major Grant ignored her question and said curtly, 'Miss Maltby is leaving.'

And this time Florrie could do nothing but obey.

The following morning, Florrie stood outside the building in the town of Poperinghe where the court-martial hearing was to be held. At the door, two soldiers barred her way.

'Let me pass,' she muttered through gritted teeth.

'We have orders, miss, not to let anyone in other than those involved in the trial.'

'I am involved. I'm his *sister*.'

'The major was most firm, miss. No one.' The young soldier's manner was apologetic. His voice quavered a little and Florrie thought she saw tears in his eyes. But the fellow was only carrying out orders. He daren't do anything else!

She sighed and turned away. She crossed the rough road and sat on a low, crumbling wall to wait. However long it took, she would still be here when the verdict was announced.

It was hours before Gervase emerged into the sunlight. He was startled to see her sitting there. For a moment he hesitated before walking slowly towards her, his eyes downcast, his shoulders slumped.

Florrie stood up slowly, easing her cramped limbs. Her heart was pounding and her mouth was dry. Her whole being was trembling. The drawn, grim look on his face squeezed her heart. His eyes were full of a mixture of helpless rage and sorrow.

'Florrie, my dear – I'm so sorry. I've arranged for you to see him, but there's nothing more I can do.'

'You mean – you mean they found him *guilty*?'

He nodded.

'And his – his punishment?'

His face was bleak, his voice a strangled whisper. 'He's to be – to be shot. At dawn tomorrow.'

'So soon? No – *no*! Oh, Gervase, who can I see?'

'There's no one, Florrie.' He shook his head sadly. 'I've seen Major Grant and even his superior. I've,' his voice broke, 'tried everything. The major refused to make any kind of recommendation for leniency and it's likely that the brigadier-general will endorse the sentence of the court. I've done everything—'

'You can't have,' she screamed at him. 'You can't have tried hard enough. You can save him, Gervase, you *must* save him. Did James talk to you? Did he tell you why he was trying to get back here?'

'He wouldn't say anything. He offered up no defence.'

She gripped his arms fiercely, so hard that he winced. 'Take me to see the major – and the brigadier. Gervase, I'm begging you. I'll do anything you want. I swear it – I'll marry you – anything, but please – please help me save my brother.'

She was babbling hysterically. He gathered her to him and held her close, but there was nothing else he could say or do. She sobbed against him and when, at last, she was quieter, he said gently, 'Come, I'll go with you to see him.'

With a sudden violent movement she wrenched herself away. She squared her shoulders and, though her face was ravaged, she shed no more tears. Impatiently, she brushed away the traces of her weeping and looked him straight in the eye. Stonily, she said, 'That won't be necessary. I prefer to go alone.' She turned her back on him and walked away, her head held high.

Broken-hearted, Gervase watched her go.

Thirty-Six

They didn't bring him back to the cellars of the house, but kept him imprisoned in the building where the court martial had been held. The same two guards stood outside the door of the room that now acted as a cell.

A sergeant – not one she knew – met her at the door of the house.

'Your brother, is he, miss?'

'That's right,' she replied stiffly and there was blame in her tone.

Hearing it, the sergeant said, 'Don't think we're not sorry, miss, 'cos we are. But he shouldn't have done what he did.'

She paused and turned to face him. 'All I've been told is that he deserted his post. But no one seems to have bothered to find out why. Do you know?'

'He came back looking for his French bit o' stuff.'

'His *what*?'

The man had the grace to look ashamed. 'Sorry, miss. I mean – his girlfriend.'

'His *girlfriend*? What girlfriend?'

'When we was here before, miss, when it was all happening round Ypres and after—'

Florrie nodded.

'Well, there used to be this farm back across the border in France where we used to go when we was

305

on rest. And he met this French girl. Daughter of the farmer, she was. There was just her dad and her uncle and her. I reckon the mother must have died, 'cos there was only the three of 'em.'

Florrie felt a jolt. The pretty dark-haired girl, laughing and joking with the soldiers – had she been James's girlfriend?

'I didn't know soldiers were allowed to – to fraternize.'

He sniffed. 'They can't really stop it, miss, can they? They wanted us to help out on the farms, help with the work because so many of the workers are in the French army. And if there's women about—' He shrugged as if the answer was obvious.

'But James is only seventeen – no, eighteen now – he's a boy. He doesn't—' She stopped and felt the colour creeping up her neck.

'If he's out here in this lot, miss,' the sergeant said softly, 'he's a man.'

He said no more, but ushered her into the house. 'I'll be just outside,' he murmured as he nodded to the two soldiers on guard to allow her into the room where James was.

When her eyes became accustomed to the gloom, she saw him sitting on the floor against the wall, his knees drawn up, his head buried in his arms.

'James, oh, James,' she cried and rushed to him, falling on her knees and pulling him into her embrace.

He clung to her and began to cry hoarse, racking sobs. 'Florrie, I'm sorry. Tell Father I'm sorry. It's not like they're saying. I didn't desert my post. Someone was supposed to do my duty for me. I arranged it, but he let me down. He let me down and – and—'

She cupped his face in her hands and forced him to

look at her. 'Tell me. Tell me his name and I'll find him. I'll tell them it was him – I'll have him arrested and you'll be set free.'

Suddenly, it was as if time had tilted and they were back in the nursery and she was trying to get her little brother to do something he didn't want to. There was that same look of mutinous determination – it hadn't happened often, but when it had, there'd been no moving him, no persuading him. If only that stubbornness had come out against their father and his school's headmaster, maybe he wouldn't be here, maybe she wouldn't now be having to plead for his life . . .

'No.' His tone was adamant. 'No, I won't have someone lose his life in my place. It was my fault. I should never have tried to go to Colette. Florrie, find her for me. You must see that she's all right. I'm so worried about her. That's why I did what I did. I had to come back. Her family has disowned her. Thrown her out. I *had* to see her. I had to try to take care of her. I promised her—'

'Thrown her out? Just for – for consorting with an English soldier?'

He pursed his lips and shook his head as he whispered hoarsely. 'She – she's having my baby.'

'*What?*'

Florrie was still reeling. She couldn't take all this in. That her baby brother had been accused of deserting his post and was to be shot at dawn was hard enough, but to find that he had fathered a child by some unknown French girl . . . Florrie was in a living nightmare.

She shook him. 'James, what are you saying? Are you delirious?'

He was shaking, his head nodding and his hands

trembling. She'd seen this before amongst the patients in the field hospital. It was what Ernst called shell shock. 'The incessant pounding of the guns and the dreadful conditions they have to live in,' he'd explained to her. 'To say nothing of the constant fear that death is just around the corner, or "over the top" as they call it.'

Now she cradled James against her, stroked his hair and rocked him. 'I'll find her,' she promised him, even though she didn't believe a word of what he was saying.

'You'll take care of her and – and the baby? Promise me, Florrie.'

'Of course I will. Now, try to sleep and while you do,' she added grimly, 'I'm going to see Major Grant.'

'I don't want to sleep. I want to talk to you. I don't want to waste a minute. Please don't leave me. It's – it's so dark in here.'

Florrie closed her eyes at the poignancy of it all. When he'd been a little boy, he'd been afraid of the dark, and many a night he'd crept from his own bedroom to snuggle in beside her. How many times had she held him and soothed him – just like this?

'Besides,' James added bitterly, 'I'll have plenty of time to "sleep" after tomorrow morning.'

A shudder of dread ran through her and she held him more tightly than ever. She stroked his hair. 'I must go and find the major. But I'll come back – I promise.'

'They might not let you in again.'

'They'd better not try to stop me. Now, I want to know the name of the man who you swapped sentry duties with. Come on, James.'

'No, I won't, Florrie. It won't save me, and they might shoot him too.'

Florrie stood up. 'Then I'll go and ask the sergeant.'

'He doesn't know. It was just between me and Pete – me and him.'

'Pete,' Florrie pounced on his slip of the tongue. 'Was that his name?'

James groaned and dropped his head into his hands. 'Oh, Florrie, don't. Leave it. Please.'

She squatted down in front of him and tried to pull his hands away from his face. 'I won't leave it. I'm trying to save your *life*.'

She stood up and banged on the door for it to be opened. As she marched past the two soldiers, she warned them, 'I'm coming back, so don't you dare think you needn't let me in again. I've got to see your sergeant. Where is he?'

'In the house next door, miss.'

Three men were sitting in the kitchen, a bottle of whisky on the table in front of them. The major, the sergeant and – to her shocked surprise – Gervase. They looked up, startled, as she flung open the door. Gervase and the sergeant rose, but the major remained seated and merely muttered, 'Not you again.'

Florrie barely glanced at Gervase. She'd never forgive him for not having tried harder to save James. And now she was incensed to see them sitting there, drinking whisky just as if they were in the officers' mess, when, in only a few hours' time, a young man's life was going to be cruelly snuffed out in the cold light of morning.

She directed her angry gaze at the sergeant. 'There was another soldier – someone called Pete. James won't give me his full name in case you decide to shoot him too.' Her lip curled with bitter disdain to think that they could all have such a careless attitude towards life. She'd come out here, put herself in danger, to try to save lives, and these three – even Gervase, it seemed –

pandered to the belief that any soldier who broke the rules should be made an example of in the harshest of ways. 'Do you know who he means?'

'I – might do,' the sergeant said guardedly.

'James swapped sentry duty with him. He didn't desert his post. He arranged for it to be covered. But obviously, the man – this Pete – let him down.'

The sergeant and Gervase glanced at each other, but it was the major who said harshly, 'That alters nothing. The men can't just go altering their orders willy-nilly. Besides, he left the theatre of war without permission.'

'Sir, we were due to go into rest the following morning,' the sergeant put in. 'Perhaps—'

'Then he should have waited. Applied for proper leave of absence. Gone through the correct channels.'

'Would it have made any difference?' Florrie asked. 'Would he have been granted any leave, with things like they are at the Somme?'

The major had the grace to consider the question for a moment. 'Probably not. But that's what he should have done.'

Florrie turned towards the sergeant. She had the feeling that he was beginning to have some sympathy for James's plight. 'So, if you do know this Pete . . . Look, I'm not trying to get the poor man into trouble, but surely—?'

The sergeant was shaking his head. 'I'm so sorry, miss. But the only Pete whom James might have asked was Private Peter Shankley.'

'Then, please – will you ask him? Sergeant, I'm begging you—'

'If I could, miss, I would. Believe me. But Shankley was killed by a sniper on the evening of the day Maltby went absent without leave.'

Florrie clutched at the table for support as her knees threatened to give way. It was only Gervase's sudden movement towards her that made her call on her reserves of strength and straighten up. The look she gave him – as if to say 'Don't you dare touch me' – made him drop his hands to his side and turn away sadly. He went to stand looking out of the window with his back towards them all.

'Funny, that,' the sergeant was still saying. 'We couldn't understand how Shankley came to be where he was when he was killed. But if he was on his way to do Maltby's sentry duty for him, that would explain it.'

Florrie took a step forward, hope suddenly surging through her. 'So—?'

But the major forestalled any plea. He stood up, his chair scraping back. He thumped the table with his fist. 'The fact remains, he deserted. Even if he did try to cover his sentry duty, he still went AWOL. It's unforgivable. Young lady, the decision of the court stands.'

She could see that it was hopeless. She glanced around at the sergeant's anxious, now sympathetic face, at the major's belligerent, vengeful expression and lastly, at Gervase's rigid back. He was leaning his head on his arm against the window. He did not look round. Outside dusk was falling. The last twilight that her beloved brother would ever see.

Florrie turned and left the room.

Thirty-Seven

They talked through the night, reliving the whole of their lives until this moment, remembering the happy times and the sad. They spoke of everything – every event, every family celebration, everyone they knew and loved. And at last, James voiced the one name she'd been trying to keep out of the conversation. Yet it was impossible, for he had been so much a part of their lives.

'Gervase did his best, you know.' Florrie stiffened and James must have felt it, for he drew back and looked into her face, searching her expression in the light from the one candle they'd been allowed. 'What? What is it?'

'I begged him to help you. He *says* he's tried, but that there's nothing more he can do.' Her tone was stiff and full of censure. 'But I don't believe him.'

'Oh, Florrie, don't blame poor old Gervase. He *has* tried everything. He even put himself in danger of being court martialled for arguing with his superiors. For Heaven's sake, Florrie, he's only a captain, but he ranted and raved at the *brigadier*, would you believe, and at Major Grant too. They threatened to charge him and still he didn't stop. He did everything he could have done, and probably more than he *should* have. And in the court, believe me, he tried everything. I just hope he's not in trouble.'

'But did you tell him everything, James? He didn't

seem to know about this Pete person. Why didn't you tell him that?'

'I've told you – I can't have another man's life on my conscience. He could've been in trouble just for agreeing to it. You see, we didn't clear it with the sergeant.'

'I know. He said.'

'Oh, Florrie, what have you done? The sarge might guess who it is. I don't want old Pete to—'

'James, darling, the sergeant said he thought it was Peter Shankley.' Even in the half-light she saw the horror on his face.

'Oh, Lor'. I wish you hadn't said anything. Now they'll—'

She took hold of his hand as she said gently, 'No, they won't. He was killed by a sniper, probably on his way to do your duty.'

James closed his eyes and groaned. 'So that's how they came to find out I was missing. I wasn't at my post. And neither was Pete.'

Florrie shuddered at the word. Tomorrow morning he would be tied to a different kind of post.

They were silent for some time before Florrie murmured, 'I wish Gervase had told me just how hard he'd tried.' She was devastated and ashamed now to think how she'd treated him. She should've had more faith in his friendship for her brother, his love for her and his innate goodness.

'He's not the sort of chap to brag about what he's done,' James said. 'He's been mentioned in dispatches several times. You know he's up for a medal, don't you?'

Florrie shook her head.

'Mind you,' he added sadly, 'he might lose it now because of me.'

Florrie closed her eyes as she held James. Not only

was she to lose her beloved brother under circumstances she believed totally unjustified, but she had insulted both of her dearest friends. For what would Isobel say when she heard how Florrie had treated Gervase? Life really couldn't get much worse.

The morning came, pale and cold and terrifying. And with it came the padre accompanied by two officers.

James was white-faced, but dry-eyed and calm. He stood to attention when the padre entered the room. The man seemed surprised to see a woman there.

'This is my sister, sir. She's a nurse here.'

The man nodded. 'Now, my son,' he said gently. 'Have you written your last letters?'

James shook his head. 'No, sir. Florrie will – will tell them.'

'Then would you like us to pray together?'

The three of them knelt on the stone floor. Florrie bowed her head and bit down hard on her lip to stem the tears. She mustn't cry, she told herself, she must not cry. She must be brave for James's sake. If she allowed her tears to flow, then it might be the undoing of him and she knew he wanted to face his sentence with a courage his superiors did not believe he had.

They heard the footsteps coming, the door open and turned to face the grim-faced soldiers who'd come to march him to his death. They were only young themselves and looked even more terrified than James.

With Florrie and the padre at his side, James walked out to face the firing squad in the cold light of early morning, the sun just rising in the eastern sky. Florrie did not hold his hand or even touch him. She walked with her head held high, looking straight ahead.

As they walked, she whispered, 'I will fight for the rest of my life to clear your name. I'll see the King, if I have to.'

James actually smiled as he glanced at her. 'Chain yourself to Buckingham Palace railings, eh?'

Florrie nodded.

As they reached the place and saw the soldiers waiting, James paused and turned to her. Gripping her shoulders and kissing her briefly on both cheeks, he whispered, 'There's only one thing I want you to do for me, Florrie dearest. Go to the farm. You know where it is, don't you? Where you saw the soldiers hay-making? Find Colette and take care of her and – and the baby.'

'I will, James. I promise I'll find her.'

He was led away from her. He was positioned with his back to the post and his hands tied behind it. But when they came with the blindfold, he shook his head. His gaze found and held Florrie's as the soldiers shuffled to take their positions.

'You should leave now, miss.' It was Sergeant Granger in charge of the firing squad. He was white-faced and trembling. His eyes were pleading with her.

'I'm going nowhere, Sergeant. Do your worst and, when this war is over, I will do my best. Never again – in any future wars – will a soldier be shot for so-called cowardice if I can help it. I promise you that.'

The sergeant looked at her with a mixture of anxiety and admiration as he turned from her.

'Take aim.' The soldiers raised their rifles to their shoulders.

Through her tears, her gaze held James's and she smiled.

'May God bless you, my darling brother,' she murmured as the order was given and the shots rang out.

A shadow crossed the sun as James sank slowly to the ground, but even as he fell his gaze held hers. He lay perfectly still, his eyes wide open.

This time, he did not scramble up from the sand, wave gaily to her and then gallop towards the sea.

Sergeant Granger walked towards him and took out his pistol. Aiming it with a hand that shook, he delivered one shot to James's temple.

Florrie flinched as the echo reverberated round them. She glanced briefly towards the line of men who'd made up the murderous squad. Two were crying openly and one had passed out and was lying crumpled on the ground.

As the sergeant came back towards her, she could see that his face was drained of colour and his eyes dark with horror.

'When and where is he to be buried?' Florrie asked with a calmness she didn't feel inside. Two of the soldiers were already moving towards James, releasing his body from the post and carrying him away.

'In the cemetery here. Straight away.'

It was done with unseemly haste. The padre was on hand and James was placed in a plain wooden coffin, still in his uniform. A small bundle of his possessions was handed to Florrie as she stood beside the yawning hole after the brief and soulless service at the graveside.

Silently, she bade her baby brother goodbye, turned and marched away, speaking to no one and allowing no one to speak to her.

It was only then that she glimpsed Gervase standing silently in the shadow of a tree.

*

'Dr Hartmann,' Florrie began in her most professional manner. 'I must request a few days' leave.'

'Impossible. We'll be leaving for the Somme any day now. I can't do without you.' He smiled as he added softly, 'You know that. You're my right hand.'

But Florrie could not return his smile. 'I'm sorry,' she said stiffly. 'You know full well that there has been a tragic – event – in my family and I have to take some time off. I – can't do my work properly at the moment. I'd be no use to you anyway, feeling like this, and – and there's something I have to do.'

Ernst's face darkened. 'And how do you think the soldiers in the trenches feel? Don't you think they'd like to be able to say,' he mimicked a high-pitched female voice, ' "Sergeant, I'd like a few days off from the noise and the killing. I don't feel like going 'over the top' this morning." No,' he said harshly. 'You cannot have any more leave. You've just been absent for two days as it is. That I fully understand,' he added, mollifying a little. 'I'm sorry – deeply sorry – for what has happened to your brother. But work would be the best thing for you. It would help you forget. So why are you asking for more leave now?'

She fixed her gaze somewhere just above his head so that she did not have to meet his eyes. Help me forget, she thought. How would she ever – for the rest of her days – forget the last few hours? And she could hardly believe that the man who'd been so tender, had whispered such sweet words, could be so callous now. But even that seemed to be a thing of the past. He'd seemed distant lately and they'd not made love for weeks.

His tone softened. 'My dear, I do understand what you must be going through.'

He reached out for her, but she avoided his touch. Now she looked him straight in the eyes and said softly and sadly, 'Ernst, if you cannot believe that it's a very serious matter to make me ask for any more time off, then you don't know me at all.' She turned and began to walk away.

'But who is going to drive the lorry to take the patients to Base Camp?'

She glanced back over her shoulder. Always, always, his work came first. For a long moment they stared at each other, before she turned away again and this time she walked on without looking back.

Florrie drove the ambulance as far as the main camp, ferrying two patients. She'd told Sister Blackstock – not asked – that she was taking a few days' leave. There was something she had to do, she told Rosemary. Something that could not wait. Sister Blackstock was more sympathetic than Ernst had been.

'We're all so sorry, Florrie, for what's happened. I so wish there was something we could've done.'

Florrie smiled thinly. 'There was nothing anyone could do, Sister. They were determined to use him as an example.'

Gervase had tried his very best at least to get the sentence commuted, and all she'd done had been to castigate and blame him. In fact, he'd risked everything, even perhaps his own life, for he could have been charged with insubordination and disobedience. But she'd been so frantic to save James that she'd been blind and deaf.

Weary with sadness, she arrived back at the Base Camp. News had travelled and Sister Carey, who was now in charge there, greeted her with sympathy.

318

'Sister Blackstock has asked if you can send another nurse,' Florrie told her. 'And could you find someone to drive the lorry to and fro? I've brought it back. Perhaps Sergeant Granger could find you one of the soldiers to do it.'

'I'll ask him.' She eyed Florrie closely. 'But where are you going? Home?'

Florrie shook her head. 'No, no,' she said and added bitterly, 'I'm not deserting my post.'

When Sister Carey raised her eyebrows, Florrie said swiftly, 'I'm sorry. The last few days – well, it's all been a dreadful strain.'

'Of course. But—'

Florrie didn't want any more questions so she interrupted quickly, 'I'm sorry, I really can't explain any more. Not – not just now.'

She had to find Colette – had to establish the truth. And she didn't want to confide in anyone until she knew herself.

After a meal and a rest, Florrie set off to walk towards the village where Ernst had taken her to the little cafe. Tears burned her throat at the memory of the happy evenings they'd spent there with the genial, generous host. Despite the war and all its horrors, life had been wonderful then. Away – even for a few hours – from all the carnage and the suffering, they'd been cocooned in a little world of their own. But now, with the incessant sound of pounding guns still in her ears, she didn't think she'd ever again be able to get away from the thoughts of the war. She would never again be able to smile or laugh. She'd never felt so lonely or desperately miserable in her life.

When the news of James's death and the manner of it reached home, it would likely kill their poor mother. Augusta, though elderly, would cope, Florrie knew. Augusta always coped. But what about their father? Well, she knew what Edgar Maltby's reaction would be.

He would disown his son.

Thirty-Eight

The houses and buildings in the village were still intact. The shelling had not reached here, yet the place seemed deserted. Florrie knocked on several doors, but there was no sign of life. Even the little cafe was closed and shuttered.

Then, down the street, she saw an old man emerge from a low cottage to pile belongings onto a hand-cart outside the front door. She hurried towards him, calling out in French, 'Excuse me, monsieur – can you tell me where the Mussets' farm is?'

The man turned, surprised to see a young woman in a nurse's uniform, addressing him in passable French.

'Ah yes, Jacques Musset's farm. It's that way, but there's no one there now. He's gone.' He shrugged in a hopeless gesture. 'Everyone is gone, mademoiselle, or going. Like me. I go before the guns reach here. It cannot be long,' he added without hope.

'Did Monsieur Musset have a daughter? Colette?'

The watery old eyes regarded her solemnly. 'He had a daughter of that name – yes, but no more.'

He began to turn away, but she touched his arm. 'Do you mean she is dead?'

Again he shrugged. 'As good as.' He paused and then said firmly, 'I must go. I cannot help you any more. Bonjour, mademoiselle.' He gave a small bow and she knew herself politely dismissed. He'd no wish to say anything else, though she believed he knew more.

'Thank you, monsieur,' she called after him as he disappeared once more inside the cottage.

Florrie turned away, heartsore to witness the suffering that this dreadful war was inflicting on the innocent of all nations. She even spared a thought for the ordinary German families who, she believed, had not wanted this war any more than she had.

'Our politicians have a lot to answer for,' she muttered as she marched angrily along the dusty street. 'If only the world was ruled by women, there'd be none of this nonsense.'

Florrie left the village and retraced her steps. She glanced about her. She was sure this was where they'd seen the soldiers working in the fields, but the grass meadows had not been harvested this year. She shaded her eyes against the hot sun and, in the distance, saw the shape of a farmhouse and outbuildings. Crossing the nearest field, she waded through the long, neglected grass and approached the house.

The farmyard was deserted. There was no sign of life, either human or animal. She went to the house, where the back door stood half-open, and stepped inside. Like the old man had said, the farmer and his family were long gone. The place was inhabitable, yet only discarded, unwanted items of furniture remained: a broken chair, a worn-out rug and cracked pots and rusty pans in the kitchen. Florrie stood forlornly amidst the dust and cobwebs in the empty house. She didn't know where else to search for Colette.

She went to the doorway and stood looking out across the farmyard. She'd better check the outbuildings, but she didn't hold out much hope. She crossed the yard and peered into what had once been a pigsty, then the cowshed and lastly she came to the barn, where hay and straw littered the floor. A few bales were still stacked in one corner. She was about to turn away when she heard a soft moan.

'Oh, dear Lord,' she breathed and stepped inside. 'Colette?' she called. 'Colette, is that you?'

There was no reply, but she heard a movement in the far left-hand corner. She moved forward carefully and, as her eyes became accustomed to the gloom, she saw, in the light from a hole in the wooden wall, a heap of hay and a figure lying on it. She moved closer and looked down upon the pale, thin face of the young girl whom her brother had loved. The mound of the young girl's belly proved her identity.

Florrie dropped to her knees beside her and took hold of her limp hand. 'Colette, I'm James's sister,' she explained, speaking in French. 'I've come to help you.'

'James,' the girl croaked through parched lips. 'Where is he? I want James.'

Florrie bit her lip. The girl couldn't know what had happened to him, and she was in no state to be told such awful news. Florrie glanced around. There was no trace of food or water nearby and she guessed the girl was dehydrated and half-starving.

'Let me take you to your family. Where are they?'

The girl cried out at once. 'No, no. They've disowned me. They want nothing to do with me. I've brought shame upon them.' Tears streaked her grubby cheeks. 'But James promised to marry me. It was all arranged at the church in the village. We were to be married yesterday. The priest agreed to marry us – he was very kind and understanding – but James didn't come.' Her sobs grew louder, into a pathetic wail of desolation.

'We waited and waited at the church, but he didn't come. He didn't come.'

Poor James. Poor Colette. On the very day he should have been marrying this young girl, he'd faced the firing squad.

'Dear Colette,' Florrie fought back her own tears. 'He couldn't. He tried. He did try – I promise you – but . . .' How could she tell this poor girl that James had been arrested whilst trying to reach her, whilst trying to do the right thing by her and their child? And, because of it, he'd lost his life.

The girl cried out and this time, Florrie knew, it was in pain. She put her hand on the girl's hot forehead. Then she placed her hand over her stomach and felt the movement. 'Oh no!' she breathed. 'You're in labour. I must get help . . .'

She'd even begun to scramble to her feet before the awful realization hit her. There was no help to call for. They were alone amidst a barren, forsaken land. The village had seemed deserted, except for one old man, and there was no other dwelling in sight for miles. Even Base Camp was too far away for Florrie to fetch help from there. By the time they got back, the girl and her baby could have died. And this was James's child.

Florrie stood up.

'Don't go. Don't leave me,' the girl beseeched.

'I won't – I promise. But I must find some water.'

'The well,' Colette gasped. 'In the yard.'

Out in the yard, Florrie looked about her frantically. Then she saw the well and ran to it. There was a rope with a bucket still attached. Praying fervently that there was still water there, she lowered the bucket into the black hole. Lower and lower, until she closed her eyes with thankfulness as she heard it splash. Allowing it to fill, she hauled with all her strength, heaving and panting until it appeared over the edge of the well. Grasping the handle, she pulled it the rest of the way. As she carried it carefully back to the barn, she glanced about her once more, hoping to see someone – anyone. But there was no one. They were lost in a lonely world.

Strangely, even the distant guns were silent.

Tearing a strip of material from her own underskirt, Florrie knelt down beside the girl once more. She soaked the fabric in the water and squeezed it into the girl's mouth. Colette tried to suck at it, but was overcome by another pain. She writhed in agony and cried out, spreading her legs and grasping Florrie's hand with surprising strength for one so weak.

'It's coming, it's coming,' she cried, but sadly, although she was in great pain, the child was not going to enter the world without a great deal of struggling and agony.

Florrie did her best, but she'd no proper equipment and no one to help her. She had a vague idea what happened at a birthing, but the girl was so ill and undernourished, her strength quite spent. None of the horrific sights Florrie had witnessed over the past few months had prepared her to bring another life into the world. Yet she was poignantly aware that the life of her brother's child rested with her.

Through the night Florrie sat beside Colette, holding her hand, mopping her brow and wetting her lips. At last, the girl was grey with exhaustion and almost too weak to cry out when the spasms gripped her. She certainly had no strength left to help her baby.

But with the light of dawn on the following day, the child pushed its way into the world, crying even before the whole of its body emerged. It screamed lustily and waved its tiny limbs. It seemed to a bewildered Florrie that the child had sapped every ounce of its mother's strength, for the girl lay quite still, hardly breathing, once her ordeal was over. But now another battle was beginning. The battle for Colette's life, for Florrie could see it ebbing away.

She knew the afterbirth should come away, but it did not and the child was still attached to its mother. Taking a deep breath, Florrie scrabbled in her pocket for the scissors she always carried and cut through the umbilical cord, and then tied another strip of her petticoat tightly around the stump.

'Colette, you have a lovely baby boy. He's beautiful and so strong. You must try to rouse yourself. Please try.' The girl opened her eyes. They were sunk in deep, dark sockets. Her cheekbones seemed as if they would poke through her delicate skin.

'Call him Jacques,' she whispered. 'His name is Jacques. Tell James I love him and ask him to take care of our son. Tell James – I'm sorry.' She closed her eyes and her head fell to one side, her mouth gagging open. Florrie felt for a pulse, but sought in vain. Colette was dead, but all the while her son cried lustily.

The child was whimpering and, though it seemed heartless, Florrie squeezed a little fluid from the dead girl's breast and fed the droplets from her finger into the baby's mouth. It seemed that she did this for hours, feeling guilty as if she were desecrating the poor girl's body, yet she knew that any mother would give her life for her child and that Colette would understand. Somewhere from the deep recesses of a scant knowledge,

Florrie seemed to remember hearing that the first liquid from the mother's breast was important.

At last the baby fell asleep and Florrie removed her petticoat and wrapped him in it. With one last look at the still form of the girl her brother had loved so much that he'd risked his life to find her, Florrie turned away and left the barn. Holding the baby close to her breast for warmth and comfort – as much for herself as for the tiny infant – she began to walk back towards the village.

As Florrie approached the cluster of houses, her footsteps faltered. She had to find Colette's family and tell them what had happened. Surely, when they saw the baby – their grandchild – they would relent. After all, the child was all they had left of their daughter.

She went again to the cottage where she'd seen the old man, but this morning there was no sign of him either. Desperate now, she walked further along the street. In the centre she came to what had once been a shop, but now the door hung drunkenly off its hinges and, though bottles and tins still stood on the shelves, they were covered with dust. She stepped through the door, her heart beating rapidly. She passed into the living quarters and out into the back garden. Trees and bushes, loaded with ripening fruit, grew at the end of the unkempt lawn and flowers bloomed in the ordered beds, though weeds threatened to strangle them. Once this had been a loved and nurtured garden. Now it was growing wild. The owners of the shop and the house were gone too. Guiltily, feeling as if she were stealing, Florrie picked a few raspberries and ate them.

A well was set in the paved area near the back door and she moved to it eagerly. She was peering down into it when she heard a sound in the shop and her heart skipped a beat. Perhaps the owner had returned. She hurried inside and found herself staring into the barrel of a gun being pointed at her by a German soldier. How Florrie wished she'd had the foresight to bring the revolver that Sergeant Granger had given her. But when she'd left the Chateau, that had been the last thing on her mind. She'd never expected to find a German behind what, to him, was enemy lines.

Seeing she was dressed as a nurse with the child in her arms, he faltered and lowered the barrel, but then immediately raised it again, barking, 'Are you alone?'

'Yes,' Florrie replied in German. 'There's only me and the baby.'

He stared at her for a moment, taking in the uniform that he guessed was British. 'Who are you? What are you doing here?' he rapped out, but to Florrie's relief, he lowered the gun once more.

She took a deep breath. 'I was trying to find someone to help. There's a woman in the barn at the farm back there. She's – she's dead.'

'You killed her?'

'Heavens, no!' Florrie cried, but the soldier only shrugged as if he didn't care whether she had or not. 'Can you – can you get someone to see to her burial?'

'Me!' He gave a wry laugh. 'Oh no. I'm a deserter. I can't help you. I'm looking for food.' His hungry eyes scanned the shelves and he began to reach up, pulling down bottles and tins.

'There's fruit in the orchard at the bottom of the garden. Some of it's ready to eat. And vegetables too.'

He put the bottle he was holding down on the dusty counter and pushed past her.

'Wait!' she cried. 'There's something you can do for me – please. Draw me some water from the well.'

The soldier glanced at the child and for a brief moment his eyes softened. 'My wife has had a baby whilst I've been away,' he said sadly. 'A little girl. I haven't even seen her. Maybe I never will.'

'Is that why you – you've deserted? You're trying to get back to her?'

He nodded and then turned away, saying gruffly, 'Where's this well?'

Amazingly, the water was clean. With the soldier's help, Florrie washed out a container she found in the shop and filled it with water. She glanced along the shelves, but there was nothing there suitable for a newborn baby. She didn't know how long it might take for her to find the Mussets, and soon, she thought, the child would need to be fed.

'Do you know where there are people living? Another village?'

Fear crossed the German's face. 'You're going to report me?' He was reaching out again for his gun.

'No – no,' Florrie said hurriedly. 'Of course not. I just want to find someone who can help me get milk for the baby.'

'There's a village that way.' He pointed to the west. 'There's people still living in the houses there. I was near there last night.'

'Is it – is it behind the German lines?'

He shook his head and smiled bitterly. 'No. Even *I* don't want to be behind German lines.'

'Thank you.' She picked up the container of water. 'Good luck!'

He nodded. 'And good luck to you and your baby.'

As she walked away, Florrie marvelled that a deserter, desperate and afraid, had let her go. She smiled and dropped a tender kiss on the baby's head, amazed that the sight of the tiny being could melt even the hardest heart.

Thirty-Nine

As Florrie walked along the dusty road towards the next village, she smiled and held the baby closer. 'He thought you were mine, little one. But it's the next best thing – you're my nephew, aren't you? My darling James's little boy. I wish I could keep you, but I must find your grandparents – your French grandparents.' She carried on, talking to the child as she walked. Tears choked her throat as she added, 'Because your English grandparents wouldn't want to know you.'

After about two miles, she saw the village in the distance. 'Let's hope they're friendly towards the English,' she murmured, not knowing what sort of reception to expect from the poor folks whose country was being ravaged around them and their livelihoods wrecked.

Now she could see smoke curling from chimneys and one or two people moving about their gardens or walking down the street. There were cows in a nearby field and the hay had been cut. One or two houses looked empty, but there were certainly people living here. Her heart skipped a beat. There was a shop, with goods displayed outside the door – vegetables and fruit. As she stepped into the dim interior, an elderly man shuffled from behind a curtain.

'Do you have any food suitable for the baby?' she asked him in his native tongue. Once more Florrie was subjected to a curious stare. An English woman, dressed as a nurse, speaking French, walking into his shop only a few miles from the war zone with a baby in her arms and asking, quite calmly, for food for her child was not something that happened to him every day.

Why did she not feed the child herself? She could almost see the question written in his eyes. But the old man shrugged nonchalantly and, instead of answering her, turned back, pulled the curtain aside and called, 'Marie, come here.'

An elderly woman appeared. In rapid French that Florrie found a little difficult to follow, the man explained to his wife that there was a nurse in his shop asking for food for her baby.

The woman came round the counter and peered at the child wrapped in Florrie's petticoat. Marie gave a toothless smile. She looked up at Florrie and touched her own large breasts. 'You cannot feed the little one yourself?'

Florrie shook her head. Someone else who thought the child was hers.

'Ah! Come with me.' She beckoned Florrie to follow her beyond the curtain into the small living room behind the shop. Settling her in a chair by the fire, the old woman fetched milk and warmed it in a saucepan. 'I have no feeding bottle,' she said apologetically as she handed Florrie a cup of the warmed milk and a small spoon.

Florrie smiled her thanks and began to spoon the liquid into the tiny mouth. It seemed to take an age to encourage the child to swallow the milk, but at last he took just a little. It was enough.

'I will give you some milk to take with you. Where are you going?'

'I—' Florrie hesitated. But the only way to find

Colette's parents was to ask. She took a deep breath. 'The – the people who lived at the farm near the next village. The Mussets. Did you know them? Do you know where they are now?'

The woman's face brightened. 'Mais oui. They are living here. In this village. Jacques Musset has come to live with his brother, Pierre.' She shook her head. 'Ah, such a terrible time poor Jacques has had. First his wife died and then—' She lifted her shoulders in a helpless gesture and shook her head. 'Colette's trouble. Ah, this terrible war. It's to blame.'

'Can you tell me where the house is?'

Marie nodded. 'Come, I'll show you.'

Florrie rose, the baby still in her arms. She picked up the precious milk can and followed the woman back through the shop and out into the street. The old man watched them curiously, but said nothing.

'The fourth house on the right-hand side,' the woman said, pointing.

'Thank you. Thank you so much, madame, for your kindness and for the milk.'

'You're very welcome. *Bonne chance.*'

Florrie's heart was beating painfully as she approached the house and knocked on the door. A tall, thickset man dressed in black trousers, an open-necked shirt and stout boots opened it. His middle-aged face was deeply etched with lines of hardship and his expression was stern.

Florrie took a deep breath. 'Are you Monsieur Musset who used to live at the farm?'

The man shook his head. 'No, that is my brother.'

'Is he – is he here?'

The man nodded and, for the first time, his glance rested on the child in her arms. His frown deepened. 'What do you want with him?' he snapped harshly.

'I – I need to speak to him on a personal matter.'

'My brother has no secrets from me.'

When Florrie made no further attempt to explain, he sighed, stepped aside and gestured for her to enter. 'Jacques, there is someone to see you.' His tone was unwelcoming and he glared accusingly at Florrie and glanced at the child with an expression that she could not define.

As her eyes became accustomed to the gloom, she saw a man rise from a chair by the fire. He was very like his brother, with the same build and appearance. His face even had the same deep lines of weary defeat. And something else too . . .

Florrie swallowed hard, wishing there was a woman present. It might be easier if . . .

'What do you want?' Jacques Musset asked harshly, his gaze on the baby, who had begun to whimper.

'Monsieur Musset, have you a daughter, Colette?'

The man's face darkened and his eyes narrowed. 'I did have – once,' he said bitterly.

Florrie gasped. Did he know she was dead? But how could he, unless he had been to the farm and found her? Perhaps whilst Florrie had been in the back of the shop, but even then, there had scarcely been time . . .

'Then this is your grandson.' She held out the child, offering him to the man. 'His name is to be Jacques,' she added softly.

The man sat down again suddenly and stared up at her, whilst his brother moved to stand beside him as if giving support. 'Where is she?' It was the brother who spoke.

'She's at the farm. In – in the barn. I'm so sorry, but she died giving birth.' She paused a moment, allowing them time to take in the dreadful news. 'But she told me the boy is to be called Jacques. Please, may I sit down?' Suddenly, in the warmth of the stuffy room, she felt dizzy. She hadn't slept or eaten for hours and the traumas of the last few days suddenly overwhelmed her.

She sank into a chair, still holding the baby, whose cries were becoming more insistent now. 'I must give him some milk. Please could you . . . ?'

'No!' Jacques Musset roused himself and stood up again. 'Go! I want you to leave.'

'Of course I will, but the baby needs—'

'Take it with you. I want nothing to do with it. My daughter brought shame upon our family.'

To Florrie's surprise, his brother put his hand on Jacques's shoulder. 'The child is your grandson,' he reminded him softly.

'You heard me, Pierre. I want her to go. And she's to take the child with her.'

Roughly, he shook off his brother's hand, turned away and left the room. Stunned, Florrie and Pierre Musset were left staring at each other as they heard his heavy footsteps mounting the stairs. The slam of a bedroom door seemed final.

'Monsieur—' Florrie began as the man sat down heavily in the chair his brother had just left.

He shook his head slowly. 'It's no use, mademoiselle. You heard what he said – how he feels. Besides, there is no one to care for the child. No – no woman.'

'But his wife?'

'Jacques's wife died a while ago.'

'I'm sorry. And – and you have no wife?' She didn't like probing, but she had to.

'My wife died three years ago.'

'Is there no one else in the family?'

He shook his head. 'You heard him for yourself. He

disowned Colette for the shame she brought on the family, and now . . .' Pierre's voice faded away. Perhaps she could persuade this man, for he seemed not quite so adamant as his brother.

'Couldn't you find someone – a wet nurse – to look after the child?'

For a moment, Pierre seemed to hesitate. He looked up at her. 'Who are you? Just a nurse who happened to find her?'

'Er, no. I was looking for her. My – my brother was the child's father. He asked me to find Colette and help her.'

'I see,' he said, though she wasn't sure he did. He certainly didn't know everything. 'Then,' he added heavily, 'he'd better take care of his son.'

'He would if only he could,' she said bitterly, her voice breaking. 'But he's dead too.' She gave no further explanation, unwilling to tell this man how and why her brother had died.

Pierre Musset groaned and dropped his head into his hands. 'Then you'd better take it to an orphanage somewhere.'

'No,' Florrie cried swiftly, raising her voice above the child's cries. 'Never. I'll care for him. I'll take him back to England with me.'

Her mind was working quickly. Already, three people – the German soldier, the shopkeeper and his wife – had believed the child to be hers. So, she would make every-one believe he was. But first, she realized, if she was found out, she must have some sort of proof that the natural mother's family had given permission.

'Monsieur, I will care for him, I give you my word, but first there are three things I need you to do for me.'

'What?' he asked uncertainly.

'Firstly, I must give him some more milk, and can you find me a shawl or something to wrap him in? Secondly, I need you to provide me with a paper and pen so that I can write out a statement for your brother – and perhaps you too – to sign. And thirdly,' her voice softened to sadness, 'will you get someone to look after Colette and have her buried in a proper manner? I – I can't bear to think of her lying out there.'

His face was bleak, but he nodded and rose to do as she asked.

The baby was asleep, the precious paper signed by both brothers was safely in her pocket and Pierre had found her a shawl and some cloth for her to use as napkins. But it was growing dusk now and Florrie was almost dropping asleep herself. As she dragged herself to her feet, she swayed with exhaustion.

'You cannot go anywhere tonight, mademoiselle,' Pierre said with sudden, gruff kindness. 'You shall sleep in my bed and leave in the morning.'

Too weary to argue, Florrie followed him up the steep, narrow stairs and into a sparsely furnished bedroom. The man bent and, from a chest of drawers, pulled out the bottom drawer. He tipped the clothes out and then put a folded blanket in it. He set it beside the bed as a makeshift cradle.

'I'll bring you some bread, cheese, fruit and a drink. Then you must sleep.'

She hadn't expected such thoughtfulness from the formidable man who had first opened the door to her, but she accepted his kindness gratefully. She was awoken twice in the night by the baby's cries, but after a few spoonfuls of milk he slept again.

The following morning, Pierre Musset gave her fresh, warm milk from one of his cows for Florrie to take with her. He gave her a basket of food for herself and another warmer shawl for the child. 'I'd give you more,' he said, 'but if you've a distance to walk . . .'

'You've been very kind,' she said.

As he opened the door and walked outside with her, he went on, 'I'm sorry, mademoiselle, that we can't keep the child. For myself . . .' He shrugged, but said no more, no doubt not wanting to sound disloyal to his brother. There'd been no sign of Jacques Musset this morning and Florrie had the feeling that the man was keeping out of the way deliberately until she'd gone.

She sighed as she said, 'I suppose I can understand – it's often the same in England – but I think it's very sad. Goodbye, monsieur, and thank you.'

She turned from him and, as she did so, she glanced up at the bedroom window in time to see Jacques's face briefly. But he disappeared quickly.

Carrying the child, Florrie walked away.

There was nowhere else she could go. She had to return to the Base Camp, even though it was a totally unsuitable place to take a baby. Florrie walked for most of the morning, and the baby, though tiny, was heavy in her arms and she had to keep stopping for a rest. By midday she was nearing the field hospital, but what would happen when she got there? Would they all believe the child to be hers? And who would they think the father was? Most of all, what would Ernst say?

Of Gervase, she dared not even think.

As she approached the camp, she could see lorries and vehicles being loaded with equipment and personal belongings.

'Oh, goodness,' she murmured, 'they're leaving.' She hurried in search of Sister Blackstock, but found Sister Carey. There were several strange faces around the camp and Florrie guessed that the replacement medical team had arrived and that her own people were on the move to the Somme.

'Sister Carey . . .'

The woman looked up with a smile that froze on her face when she saw the baby in Florrie's arms.

'What on earth . . . ?' she began and then her expression hardened as she glanced first at the child and then back to Florrie's face. 'Of all people, Maltby, I would not have thought it of you.'

How easy it was, Florrie marvelled, a little dismayed to realize how ready the sister was to believe the worst of her. But she lifted her head defiantly. Wasn't this exactly what she wanted?

'What Sister Blackstock will say when she hears, I dread to think,' Sister Carey went on. 'She has always thought so highly of you. You'll be a sad disappointment to her.'

The words were so reminiscent of her father. This, and worse, would be what would happen at home.

'You must see a doctor at once,' the sister said, turning her mind to practicalities. 'You must both be checked.'

'Oh but—' Florrie's heart beat faster. She wanted baby Jacques to be attended to, but as for herself, well, the secret would be out at once if she allowed a doctor to examine her. There was only one person she could trust. 'I'll see Dr Hartmann. He'll see to him – to us,' she said firmly, turning away at once as if to find him. 'Where is he? Is he here?'

'He's back at the Chateau handing over to the new doctor. Sister Blackstock's there too.'

'Then I must go back there.'

Sister Carey gave her a strange look. 'Are you sure that's a good idea? Perhaps it would be better if Dr Johnson saw you—'

'I need to see Dr Hartmann,' Florrie said firmly.

Sister Carey sighed. 'Very well. You'll need to collect your belongings anyway, though I hardly think you'll be coming with us now. I expect you'll be sent home.' She glanced at the watch pinned to her left breast. 'I'll find someone to take you. In the meantime, get yourself something to eat and feed the child.' Beneath her breath the sister muttered, 'He's the innocent in all this.'

How true that was, Florrie thought bitterly.

Forty

She was driven back to the house. The soldier beside her, not knowing what to say, kept silent.

As she walked into the kitchen, carrying the child, Sister Blackstock's mouth dropped open. Florrie stood before her brazenly and offered no explanation. Let them think what they wanted. She wouldn't tell deliberate lies, but neither would she do anything to deny their assumptions.

'So, *that* was what was so very urgent, was it? I must say, you've kept it well hidden. Not one of us suspected you'd been foolish enough to get yourself pregnant.'

Florrie pressed her lips together to stop the truth bursting out. There was only one person in whom she was prepared to confide. She was sure she could trust him to allow her to take the child back to England. But she wasn't sure about the others. Sister Blackstock – rigid in her rule-keeping – might see it as her duty to report the matter to the French authorities. Perhaps, even though she had the precious piece of paper in her pocket giving her full parental rights, they would not allow the child to leave French soil.

'I must see Dr Hartmann.'

'I don't think that would be appropriate,' the sister glared at her reproachfully. 'Do you? We all know you've been – seeing each other. Oh, I know you think you've both been very careful, but there aren't any secrets round here. And by the look of it,' she nodded towards the child in Florrie's arms, 'you haven't been careful enough, in more ways than one.'

Florrie gasped, horrified that their love affair appeared to be common knowledge. The very thing that Ernst had been so concerned about: that his reputation would be tarnished. But even worse than that, if he were to be thought the father of her child . . .

Her daring plan seemed to be faltering at the first hurdle. She bit her lip. She must see Ernst and tell him everything. He would know what to do.

Florrie lifted her head and stared defiantly at the sister. 'Where is Dr Hartmann?'

'I've told you—'

'And I'm telling you, Sister Blackstock, I need to see him,' Florrie said with steely determination. 'Now.'

The sister shook her head in disbelief. 'You've got some nerve, Maltby, I'll grant you that.' She sighed. 'But then I suppose if you hadn't, you wouldn't be here in this hell-hole. Still, it's a pity it's turned out this way. You've been one of our best nurses – despite being only a VAD – and I'll be sorry to lose you.'

'Lose me? But – but why? I don't want to leave.'

Sister Blackstock laughed wryly. 'My dear girl, you can't stay here now. What would you do with your child? I'm sorry, you'll have to be sent home at once.'

'But I can come back. Once I've taken him home—'

'That's out of the question.'

Florrie swallowed her disappointment at having to abandon the job she loved, where she felt she was being of real service. And what of Ernst and their love for each other?

'Well, if you won't tell me, I'll find him myself.' Still

carrying the child, who was whimpering once more, she turned away.

'Wait!'

Florrie hesitated and looked back over her shoulder.

Sister Blackstock's expression softened as she held out her arms. It was miraculous, Florrie thought, what the sight of a tiny new being did to the hardest of hearts. Her disgust at Florrie did not extend to the innocent child. 'I suppose you *had* better see Dr Hartmann. I'm sure you have things to discuss.' She nodded meaningfully. 'Give the poor little mite to me. I'll try to pacify it until you get back to feed it.'

'I'm not feeding him myself. I – I can't. There's some milk in this container . . .'

'Not feeding him yourself?' The woman was scandalized. 'I expect you haven't tried hard enough. The little chap'll starve in this place. Oh, we'd better get you both to civilization as quickly as possible.'

Florrie was just about to place the child in the sister's arms, when Ernst walked in.

'What on earth is the noise?' he began irritably and then, as his glance took in the child, his agitation turned to horror. He stared at Florrie, who pushed the child into Sister Blackstock's arms and cried, 'Ernst, I can explain . . .'

But Ernst Hartmann turned on his heel and walked out again.

Sister Blackstock sighed heavily. 'Go after him, Florrie.'

Ernst hurried back down the steps to the cellars as if he wished to put as much distance as possible between them. Florrie picked up her skirts and followed him.

'Dr Hartmann, I can explain. Please – wait.'

But Ernst did not wait for her or look back.

She caught up with him in the room set aside for operations and the emergency treatment of the badly injured. He was leaning against the table where so many had bled their life away, his arms folded across his chest, his face a mask of anger.

'So that's why you've kept away from me just lately? Why we haven't made love? You were afraid I would feel the size of your belly and guess?'

'I haven't been keeping away from you. If only you knew how I've longed to be with you – but it's difficult here, with so many people about. You know it is. And – you've seemed so distant recently. You've never suggested me going with you when you've been doing the rounds of the first-aid posts. At least we could have been alone then.'

'I couldn't risk anyone suspecting. It would have looked too obvious. But how could you do this to me – how could you stay here? Why didn't you plead illness – think of some excuse – and go home? My reputation will be in shreds – my career ruined. Why didn't you tell me? I could have arranged for you to get rid of it.'

Florrie gaped at him in shock and disappointment. But still, she wanted him to hear her out. 'Please, listen to me, Ernst,' she pleaded. She wanted to tell him everything: about James and Colette, about the girl's death and Florrie's efforts to find her family. She'd even put her hand into her pocket to bring out the piece of paper to confirm her story, when a perverse stubbornness flooded through her.

His attitude appalled her. She couldn't believe that he was speaking to her so harshly, so cruelly. The truth was that he cared nothing for her or for the child that he believed was his. All Ernst Hartmann cared about was what this would do to his precious reputation. She couldn't believe the words that were issuing from his mouth. After all his words of love to her – all his promises – that he could talk like this to her shocked her to the core of her being. He believed the child to be his, and yet he was talking as if he would have arranged a termination for her. An abortion. An illegal act.

Well, let him keep his good name; hers was in tatters anyway. But she didn't care. All she cared about was her beloved brother's son. At his next words, Florrie froze.

'If this gets back to Switzerland, my fiancée will break off the engagement and I shall lose my position at the Schatzalp. *The sanatorium her father helped to build.*'

'Fiancée?' she breathed. 'You – you never told me you were engaged to be – to be married.'

He shrugged and glanced away. 'We live in dreadful danger – day after day. We live for the moment, because we don't know if there's ever going to be a tomorrow.'

'So—' She felt betrayed, used. 'You never intended that there should be a tomorrow for *us*?'

And now, suddenly, she knew what she had to do. Her resolve hardened, her course of action sealed by his callous words. She'd promised James she would care for Colette and their child. But Colette was gone and only their son remained. But now he would be hers. Hers completely. It would be as if she really had given birth to him.

She lifted her head and faced Ernst squarely. 'You can tell everyone he's not yours,' she said. The tremble in her voice had nothing to do with her bold resolve, but with the heartbreak she was suffering from seeing Ernst in his true light.

'And do you really think they're going to believe that?' Suddenly, his anger died. He groaned and closed his eyes. 'When Dr Johnson came here yesterday, he told me that there are rumours circulating about us. People are talking.'

'And that would never do, would it?' Her tone was laced with sarcasm.

He raised his shoulders. 'Well, now the gossip is confirmed, isn't it? They have the proof, haven't they?' There was a pause as they looked at each other, and she saw the love in his eyes once more. The sudden change in his manner startled her as much as his anger had a few moments earlier. Now he was holding out his arms to her. 'Forgive me,' he said gently. 'It was such a shock. It's my fault too. I'll help you. We'll think of something.'

'Something to keep your reputation intact, you mean,' she said bitterly.

'Please, Florence darling, I've said I'm sorry . . .'

Now her anger died too, yet the hurt he'd inflicted would not go away. She doubted it ever would. But for the sake of the love they'd shared, there was something she could do. She lifted her head with a new defiance. Already she felt as if little Jacques really was her child. She would defend the child, lie, cheat, even steal for him, just like any natural mother would do. She'd been on the point of confiding the truth in the man in front of her. The man she'd believed was the one true love of her life. But now, she couldn't trust him – not with this secret. To carry this deception through, she must tell no one. Not her parents – especially not her parents. If she did, she knew her father would never accept James's son. Not after the disgrace of her brother's execution. She wouldn't even be able to tell her grandmother or –

Gervase. But there was a chance – though perhaps it was a forlorn one – that she'd be allowed to stay at Candlethorpe Hall. Augusta, though disappointed in her, would never see her great-grandson turned away, Florrie was sure.

But she knew now that she could not confide in Ernst Hartmann. He'd have no compunction in telling the world in order to prove his own innocence. And she dare not risk anyone here learning the truth. They might take the child from her.

Florrie moved closer to him. 'Ernst,' she said on a sigh, 'I shall tell everyone that the child isn't yours. And you can do the same.'

'You – you'd do that? For me?'

For a moment, her resolution wavered. She felt mean and deceitful and that was not in her nature. But the revelation a few moments ago that he had a fiancée had hurt her beyond belief. She'd never forgive him for his deceit. Let him think that the child was his, she thought bitterly. Let him carry that burden for the rest of his life. That somewhere in the world he had a son that he'd disowned.

She smiled bitterly at his pathetic gratitude. He took her hands in his and kissed her on the mouth. 'Oh, Florence, you are a brave and wonderful girl,' he murmured. 'To lose your reputation to save mine. To do that for me. I do love you so, Florence, but . . .'

She stared at him and, suddenly, she could feel compassion for him. Reputation was everything to him – just as it was for her father. Even if she were to tell Ernst the truth, could he even begin to understand the power of her love for her disgraced brother? She would willingly have given her own life to save James, if it had been possible. And now she would sacrifice anything for his son. The loss of her good name was little or nothing to her in comparison to what she would be prepared to give for this tiny, helpless baby.

When she returned to find the child, Sister Blackstock was still holding him, pacing up and down and trying to still his cries.

'There's nothing I can do to quieten him,' she said, her face harassed and anxious. 'If you take my advice, Maltby, you'll try again to feed him yourself. Mother's milk is the best, you know.'

'Sister Blackstock, please, there's something I have to tell you, and I want you to believe me.' Florrie's cheeks burned with shame, but not for the reason that the sister would think. 'The baby is not Doctor Hartmann's.'

Sister Blackstock stared at her. 'You – you mean you've – you've . . . ?' The woman could say no more. She shook her head in disbelief. Then disgust came to the fore and her mouth curled. 'One of the soldiers helping us, I suppose. I should never have let you drive about the countryside on your own. Maltby, you're no better than a common – *whore*.' She thrust the howling baby at Florrie. 'Here, get out of my sight and take your little bastard with you.' She turned and hurried away.

Florrie cradled the child and laid her cheek against his head. 'There, there, little one.'

At once the cries died down to a whimper and then stopped. The baby slept. Florrie smiled as she looked down at him. 'We're going home,' she whispered. 'Home to England and to Candlethorpe Hall.'

But the thought merely brought new fears.

Forty-One

Back at Base Camp she braved the disapproving looks and sought out Dr Johnson.

'Now, my dear, what's all this?' His kind face was solemn, but compassion was still in his eyes.

'Would you examine the baby for me? Please? I think the umbilical cord needs attention and – and I want to make sure he's all right. We – we have a long way to travel.'

'Of course I will. But what about you, my dear? Has a doctor seen you?'

Florrie gave a wan smile. 'I'm fine, Doctor. Honestly.' To placate him, she added, 'I promise I'll see my own doctor when I get back to England.'

'Very well. I can't *make* you let me examine you, but I just hope you know what you're doing. Now, let's have a look at this little chap.'

He smiled down at the baby, who kicked and gurgled happily, blithely unaware of all the trouble his arrival was causing.

'Oh, Florrie,' Grace wept on her shoulder. 'You should have told us. Me and Hetty. We'd've stood by you.'

Florrie hugged the girl. Touched by her understanding, she was almost tempted to confide in Grace. But her resolution held. No one must know. Only the Mussets knew, and it was very unlikely they'd ever speak of it to anyone.

'We'll be fine, though I'm sorry to be leaving you all.'

Grace sobbed afresh. 'What'll happen to you? Will your family stand by you?'

Florrie's answering smile was a little uncertain now. 'I hope so.'

The journey home was not as arduous as she might have expected. Even the authorities let her pass unhindered. She travelled on a hospital ship and, despite a few strange looks at the child in her arms, the doctor and nurses on board were soon glad to make use of her nursing skills. Some less seriously injured soldiers cared for the baby, handing him round from one to another and acting like surrogate fathers. They didn't judge or condemn her, but took delight in the child. No doubt many of them had children of their own whom they hadn't seen for many months, and now they were counting the hours to a tender reunion with their families.

On her journey by train back to Lincolnshire, she encountered similar kindness and – accepted as the mother and possibly a war widow – no one censured or questioned her.

It was only as she drew nearer and nearer Candlethorpe that her resolve began to falter.

She'd known full well what her 'welcome' at the Hall would be, but she was unprepared for the vitriol spewing from her father's mouth as she stood before him in his study, the infant in her arms. Jacques was whimpering, almost as if he felt the tension in the room and was frightened by it.

'First James – and now this.' He flung out his arm towards her. 'Who's the father? Will he marry you?'

'No,' Florrie said, determined to tell the truth as much as possible. 'His father is dead.'

'And what *nationality* was he?' Edgar spat out the question.

Florrie chose her words carefully. 'The baby is half-French, Father.'

Edgar glared at her with fresh rage. 'Not – even – British?'

He turned and went to stand near the long window with his back to her, looking out over the slope of the lawn. An elderly man – Ben's replacement – was mowing the grass.

I must go and see Mrs Atkinson, Florrie thought, irrationally at such a moment. I must tell her about Ben, and how his last thoughts were for her. But I must remember to tell her that we kept him out of pain . . .

Edgar was silent for a long time. At last, he turned round and walked stiffly back to his desk. He pulled open a drawer and took out a piece of paper. He threw it down onto the desk in front of her. 'Here – you'd better read this.'

Holding the child in her left arm, Florrie picked up the paper. It was the notification from the records' office concerning James's death.

Sir, she read. *With deep regret I have to inform you that a report has been received that Private James Maltby was tried by Field General Court Martial at Poperinghe on the 20th day of July, 1916, on the charge of desertion whilst on active service and was sentenced by the Court to suffer death by being shot. The sentence was duly carried out at 5.30 a.m. on the 21st day of July 1916.*

'That,' Edgar said hollowly, 'has broken your mother's heart and has hardened mine. Never again will I allow his name to be spoken in this house. And now—' His voice was heavy with disappointment and defeat, but still he was unforgiving. 'You can pack your bags and leave. From this moment, I have no children.' He took the letter, pushed it back into the drawer and slammed it with a gesture of finality. He turned and went to stand by the window once more, with his back to her.

'But he's your grandson, Father. Your heir—' She hesitated, but she had to fight him even if it meant being cruel in return. 'Your *only* heir.'

She saw a shudder run through her father's frame, but still he did not turn round. Still he did not relent.

'I have no children,' he repeated. 'I have no – heir.'

He was implacable and now there was only one person to whom Florrie could turn.

Augusta.

Florrie stood in the centre of Augusta's sitting room, the child, now sleeping, in her arms. She returned her grandmother's steady gaze, lifting her chin resolutely, though she was chagrined to hear the quaver in her voice as she said, 'This is your great-grandson, Jacques Maltby.'

She waited for what seemed an age, staring at the old lady and trying to read the fate of herself and the child in the passive eyes and expressionless face. For her only hope now lay with Augusta. Her father had thrown her out and her mother would never dare stand up to him. But her grandmother . . .

The old lady held her granddaughter's gaze and at last, slowly, she stretched out her arms. Florrie laid the baby on Augusta's lap and watched as her grandmother bent over the little boy. With gnarled, but gentle, fingers, Augusta unwrapped the shawl and looked down upon her great-grandson.

Florrie sat down, but her gaze never left her grandmother's face. Still there was no indication of Augusta's thoughts. At last she raised her head and looked straight into Florrie's eyes. 'He's very like James.'

Florrie caught her breath. Had her perceptive grandmother guessed the truth? Augusta was staring hard at her and the young woman felt the colour rise in her face. Her voice was husky as she stammered, 'Well, I suppose that's – that's possible, isn't it?'

'Of course,' Augusta said smoothly. She looked down at the sleeping infant. Her expression softened and she began to smile. 'I suppose I don't need to ask you what your father has to say about all this?'

Florrie knew a moment's fear. Had she been wrong to risk everything? Would her father have been more lenient if he *had* known that the child was James's? No, she was sure she'd been right about that. He'd disowned James entirely – forbade the very mention of his name. In those circumstances, he'd hardly be likely to accept James's illegitimate son. No, she'd decided on her strategy and she would stick to it, whatever the cost. Even if – in the next few moments – she were to find herself cast out entirely.

'You've been a very silly girl, Florence.' The use of her full name spoke volumes of her grandmother's disapproval. There was a long silence and Florrie held her breath until Augusta said at last, 'But your child is – sadly – now the only male heir, albeit an illegitimate one.'

'Grandmother—' In a brief moment of weakness, Florrie was tempted to tell Augusta the truth. But she bit back the words. Instead, she said, 'I'm sorry.' The words were genuine for she was sorry – desperately sorry – for deceiving perhaps the only person who would have understood and accepted the truth. But she couldn't risk it. She couldn't put the burden of deceit on the old lady too. She alone must bear that.

Augusta held the baby close and bent to kiss the soft down on the infant's head. 'I will speak to your father,' she murmured. 'You have brought shame on the family, Florence, but I will not see my great-grandson turned away.'

She cradled him and held her wrinkled face close to the baby's soft cheek. Then she held him out to Florrie. 'Take him to the nursery. You can have Beth as his nursemaid.' She smiled fondly. 'She'll like that.'

Nothing else her grandmother could have said would have indicated more than those few simple words. That she was prepared to take them in, Florrie had never really doubted, deep down, but the giving up of her own maid to become the child's nursemaid was the gesture that told Florrie all she needed to know.

Augusta stood up and Florrie, with Jacques once more in her arms, rose too. She watched Augusta's face as the older woman reached out and tenderly touched the baby's head.

'Jacques is the French equivalent of James, isn't it?' she asked softly.

Not trusting herself to speak, Florrie nodded.

'Thank you, Florrie, for naming my great-grandson

after his—' There was the slightest of pauses in which their eyes met and held. 'After his uncle.'

Augusta turned away and Florrie, knowing herself forgiven, at least by her grandmother, watched her go. The elderly lady walked out of the room, determination in every step and ramrod resolution in the straightness of her back.

Edgar Maltby was about to have the fight of his life.

What passed behind the closed door of Edgar's study, no one ever knew. Not even the faithful Bowler, who knew everything there was to know about the family he'd served all his working life, had dared to stand in the hallway to eavesdrop. But Augusta emerged triumphant, with sparkling eyes and cheeks flushed with success.

No more was said about Florrie and the child leaving Candlethorpe Hall, though Edgar never spoke to his daughter. He ignored her if they passed on the stairs, he refused to engage in conversation with her at meal times and he was utterly implacable in not acknowledging the presence of the child in the house. Clara dithered between the two opposing wills that ruled Candlethorpe Hall. Alone with Florrie or in Augusta's presence, she cooed over the child, planned his future and cradled him lovingly. But under Edgar's glowering eyes, she froze into silence, her eyes downcast, her hands twisting nervously.

So it was Augusta who had the nursery redecorated and refurbished. It was Augusta who, still wearing her favourite hat with its purple feathers and green and white ribbons, walked proudly through the lanes pushing the unwieldy perambulator. And it was Augusta who arranged for the child to be christened in the local church by Mr Ponsonby, although Florrie shuddered at the incorrect entry in the baptismal register and determined that she would at least put right the legal side of the matter. She would see a solicitor – not the family's, for she feared he might feel it his duty to tell Edgar the truth – but she would have Jacques's birth certificate tell the truth and, when the boy was old enough, she would tell him too. She owed him that much.

'The child must have godparents,' Augusta decreed and Florrie's heart tilted in fear. She hung her head and murmured, 'But who can I ask? Will anyone we know agree?'

Augusta regarded her shrewdly. 'I think,' she said slowly, 'that Gervase will forgive you. Oh, he may not want to renew his proposal of marriage now, but I think he would do that for you. For the family, if you ask him.'

'I – I can't. The last time we met – we had harsh words.'

'Harsh words? You mean, he knows about the child?'

Florrie shook her head and tears spilled over. 'It – it was when James had been – had been charged. At James's request, Gervase acted as what they call the "prisoner's friend". He spoke up for him at the court martial. I – I accused him of not trying hard enough. It wasn't until I saw James afterwards – when I stayed that last night with him—'

Augusta gasped and put her hand to her throat. 'You – you were with James when – when—'

Tears filled Florrie's eyes as she nodded. 'I stayed with him till dawn – walked with him and stood watching when they – when they—'

'Oh, my dear, dear girl.' Augusta gripped her hands. 'My brave, wonderful girl.'

'I attended his burial too, Gran. I know where he is and one day, I'll go back.'

For a moment, there was silence between them until Florrie went on, 'James told me that Gervase had even risked his own – safety, I suppose – to try to help him.'

'What do you mean – his safety?'

'Gervase could have been court martialled for insubordination to his superiors. He ranted and raved at Major Grant, the man who'd had James arrested. He even dared to argue with a brigadier.'

Even amid the sadness, Augusta smiled. 'Good old Gervase. I always knew there was a lot more to him than being just the good-natured country squire.'

'He got a medal for bravery in the field. James told me.'

'Doesn't surprise me one bit.' There was a pause whilst Augusta regarded her granddaughter thoughtfully. 'Well, now I can understand why you're embarrassed to write to him – on several counts,' she added bluntly.

Florrie smiled thinly and bowed her head.

There was another silence until Augusta said, 'But I'll write to him.'

Florrie raised her head, 'Oh, Gran, would you?'

The old lady nodded. 'I've written to him several times whilst he's been away and now I have two special reasons. One, to thank him for his efforts on James's behalf and to reassure him that we know he did everything possible; and two, to tell him that—' She hesitated for a moment, searching for the wording she intended to use. 'And to tell him that you have returned home with a child.'

357

Florrie stared at her grandmother and wondered afresh, but her thoughts were interrupted as Augusta asked, 'Have you anyone else in mind for godparents? The boy needs two godfathers and one godmother.'

'I – I'd like to ask Isobel and the Hon. Tim, but I don't know . . .' Her voice trailed away in uncertainty.

'Then I'll write to them both too. Though you could go over and see Isobel yourself. And take the child with you. I'm sure Isobel will not turn her back on you.'

'Thank you, Grandmother,' Florrie said softly. She doubted any of them – even Gervase – would refuse the indomitable Augusta.

As she turned to leave the old lady's room, Augusta, with infinite sadness, said gently, 'And Florrie, when you feel able to talk about it, I want to hear all that James said that – that last night.'

Forty-Two

Florrie longed to see Isobel and when, a few days later, a letter arrived addressed to Augusta full of love and support and understanding for Florrie, she wrapped the baby warmly in a shawl and had Bowler drive her in the pony and trap to Bixley Manor.

Isobel greeted her with open arms, enfolding her in a bear hug and then turning her attention to the child.

'Oh, Florrie, he's beautiful. Oh, do let me hold him. Come, we'll take him up to the nursery. You must meet Charlie. *Your* godson.' She squeezed Florrie's hand. 'If only we could get Tim and Gervase home on leave, we could have both boys christened together.'

As they entered the room, a fair, curly-haired little boy came tottering towards them, beaming and holding out his chubby arms.

'Oh, Iso, he's *walking*.' She knelt and held out her arms and the little chap came to her and rested his head against her.

'Ah, that's right, give your Auntie Florrie a love,' Iso crooned. 'He's such a friendly little soul. He's been walking about four weeks. He's still a bit unsteady.'

Florrie played with Charlie whilst Isobel nursed Jacques.

'Well, I don't know who he takes after. I can't see a likeness to either you or Tim – apart from his fair hair, like yours.'

359

'I think he's a bit like Gervase, but then children often take after their uncles, don't they?'

'Yes,' Florrie murmured, feeling the colour rising in her neck. 'They do.'

They talked about anything and everything apart from what was really uppermost in their minds. Gervase, Tim and the war. Isobel told her what had been happening on the estate, but each topic seemed to bring them round to the very one they were trying to avoid.

'Of course, we didn't have a proper New Year's Eve celebration this last year. With – with all of you being away.'

'Have you heard how Lady Lee is?' Florrie changed the subject. She couldn't even bring herself to tell Isobel that Gervase had found her – as he'd always said he would – on New Year's Eve. Even that led back to thoughts of the war.

'She's fine and doing sterling work for the Red Cross. She's sure that the attitude towards the suffrage movement is going to change. So many women are doing men's work while – while they're away, and doing a grand job too. Lady Lee thinks that by the time it's all over, women will have *earned* their right to vote.'

Florrie smiled. 'She may well be right. So, there'll be nothing left for us to do.'

Isobel smiled. 'Well, I'm just looking forward to having the Hon. Tim back safe and sound and starting a proper family life.'

'Has he – has he ever got home on leave to see Charlie?'

'Oh yes, he came just after he was born. Two weeks we had together. It was wonderful.' Her face clouded as she added softly, 'But I don't know when he'll get home again. I take Charlie to the photographers in Lincoln once a month and send pictures of him out to Tim, so he doesn't miss seeing him grow up. I have to say, Florrie, I never saw myself as the maternal type, but I love being a mother and, with running the estate for Gervase too, well, I'm kept busy.'

There, his name had been mentioned at last.

'How – how is Gervase?' Florrie asked.

She felt Isobel's gaze on her, but she couldn't meet her friend's eyes. 'He's well,' Isobel said softly, 'but he's very sad about what happened to poor James. He – he blames himself and—'

Florrie's head snapped up. 'That's my fault,' she admitted in a rush. 'But I know now that it wasn't true. I'm so desperately sorry. But I was out of my mind and the thought of – of . . .'

Isobel touched her hand. 'I know, I know,' she whispered. 'It must have been the most dreadful time for you. Gervase will come to understand, I'm sure. Just give him time. Have you written to him?'

Florrie shook her head. 'I – I can't,' she said huskily. 'I wouldn't blame him if he never forgives me. And now that I've come home with – with Jacques, I don't know what he must be thinking.'

'Gervase is a very forgiving man. When all this is over and he comes home, I'm sure everything will be all right again between you.'

Florrie said nothing. She couldn't say to Isobel the thought that was uppermost in her mind.

If he comes home again.

Only a handful of people attended Jacques's baptism, for two of the godparents' promises had to be made by proxy. Gervase and the Hon. Tim were still in France and whilst Augusta had obtained their agreement by letter, their physical presence was impossible. Only Isobel was there in person and cradled the infant in her arms as she made her promises. Charlie was not to be christened until his father could be there too.

Augusta stood staunchly at Florrie's side at the font, defying the world and its biased opinions. Edgar, as expected, was not present and Clara had not dared to defy him to attend. But, to Florrie's surprise, Mrs Ponsonby asked to be allowed to make the promises on behalf of the absent godfathers. Beth stood in the background, ready to take the baby back home after the service whilst Florrie and her grandmother took tea at the vicarage.

'My dear girl,' Mrs Ponsonby linked her arm through Florrie's as they emerged from the church. 'These are difficult times we live in. I'm not prying, my dear, but just tell me this. Is the father of your child dead?'

Tears sprang to Florrie's eyes. 'Yes,' she said huskily. 'I'm afraid so.'

'Then I'm sorry – very sorry. But you know, my dear, there's always Captain Richards . . .'

Now Florrie didn't know whether to laugh or cry.

'Oh, Gran – Gran!'

Florrie flew up the stairs and burst into her grandmother's sitting room.

'Goodness me, child. Is the house on fire?'

One glance at the stricken look on Florrie's face and Augusta knew at once that the letter in the young woman's hand had brought terrible news.

She rose and held out her arms to her granddaughter. 'Oh, my dear girl, what is it?'

'It's – it's Tim. He's – he's been killed.' Florrie crumpled to the floor and Augusta knelt at her side and wrapped her arms around her, rocking her to and fro. She stroked Florrie's hair. 'There, there, my dear,' she soothed, but she could think of no words of comfort. There were none to give.

'Oh, poor Iso – and Lady Lee.' Florrie buried her head against Augusta's shoulder. 'Whatever are they going to do without him?'

'What everyone else who's lost sons and husbands – and,' she added quietly, 'brothers and grandsons – has to do. Carry on.'

'But Iso and he had so little time together. And poor Charlie – he'll never know his father.'

'Neither will – your child, Florrie,' Augusta said softly.

They were silent for a few moments before Florrie whispered, 'And he was Lady Lee's only son – her only child.'

'I know, my dear, I know. It's a cruel war. It's robbing us of a whole generation of young men.'

'Oh, Gran.' Florrie looked up at Augusta. 'What if Gervase doesn't come back and – and we parted the – the way we did? What if I never get the chance to tell him how sorry I am?'

Augusta took hold of her shoulders and shook her gently. 'Then write to him,' she said firmly. 'Write to him at once – before it's too late – and tell him how sorry you are for the things you said to him.'

'I will. I'll do it now.' Florrie kissed the wrinkled cheek. 'Thanks, Gran. I don't know what I'd do without you.'

'Oh, I don't know what this whole family would do without me,' Augusta remarked, half-joking.

As Florrie stood up, she was wholly serious as she said, 'No, Gran, and I don't either.'

As she turned to leave, Augusta said softly, 'And don't forget to tell him about poor Timothy. Word might not have reached him. And we should write to Lady Lee too. You'll be going to see Isobel, I suppose?'

Florrie nodded, unable to speak for the lump of sorrow in her throat.

Isobel was amazingly calm. Though her eyes were red from weeping and her mouth trembled when she spoke, she held her head proudly and forced a smile onto her lips.

'I'd half-expected it, Florrie, if I'm truthful. When he – when he came home after Charlie's birth, I could see the horror of it all in his eyes. He didn't talk about it – none of them do, so they say – but I could tell, he didn't expect to survive.'

She showed Florrie the letter she had received from the War Office. The usual, deceitful phrase was there. *Captain Smythe died instantly and suffered no pain.*

'Thank goodness he didn't suffer,' Isobel said. 'I couldn't have borne it if I thought he'd been badly injured and taken – taken a long time to die.' Her hand fluttered to her mouth as tears threatened again.

'Yes, it's a great comfort,' Florrie said, trying to make her tone sound sincere. She hoped that, for once, the statement had been the truth, but she doubted it.

Isobel drew in a calming breath and continued. 'Tim wrote me a last letter. He left it with Mr Ponsonby.' The vicar of Candlethorpe now covered the parish of

Bixley too, since the young incumbent there, who'd taken over from the elderly man who'd married Tim and Isobel, had gone to the war zone as a padre.

'It was a long letter, Florrie, full of love and his hopes for Charlie. How – how happy I'd made him and – and everything, but you see he was detailing a future in which he had no part. He knew, Florrie, he knew he wasn't coming back.' And now she broke down and wept in Florrie's arms. 'Oh, his poor mother,' she cried. 'I ought to go to her, but I can't leave Charlie. Not just now and – and . . .'

'Would you like me to go? I've been meaning to go to London ever since I came home. There's – there's something I have to do. I could go and see Lady Lee, if you'd like me to.'

Isobel raised her tear-stained face. 'But what about Jacques? You don't want to leave him yet, surely? He's so tiny.'

'Beth's lovely with him and very capable, and Grand-mother will keep an eye on them both. It's – it's not as if I've been able to feed him myself, is it?' She hated yet another lie to this dearest of friends.

'Well, it'd be wonderful if you could. I'm sure she'd appreciate it.'

'Then I'll go the day after tomorrow. Unless, of course . . .' Florrie hesitated. 'She won't want to see me. I'm – I'm a fallen woman, after all.'

Even amidst her tears, Isobel managed a smile. 'I don't think you need have any fears on that score, Florrie dear. Not with Lady Lee.'

Lady Lee greeted Florrie with the calm dignity that was to be expected of a woman in her position, but she couldn't prevent the grief of her loss showing in her haunted eyes.

'I – wasn't sure if I'd be welcome.'

'You'll always be welcome in my home, Florrie, my dear. Whatever made you think otherwise?'

Florrie stared at her. Was it possible that Lady Lee hadn't heard that she'd arrived home from the Front in disgrace, bringing an illegitimate child with her? As if reading her thoughts, Lady Lee smiled sadly and murmured, 'Oh that, yes, I know all about little Jacques. I grieve for you, my dear girl. You must have loved his father very much.'

'I did,' Florrie said quite simply. It was the truth, though Lady Lee was thinking something entirely different.

They sat a while talking and reminiscing until Florrie rose to take her leave. 'Lady Lee, I need the help and advice of a good solicitor and – and I don't want to use our family's. Could you recommend anyone?'

'Of course. We have used Jones and Parry for years. I'll write down the address for you.' She crossed the room to the desk standing in the window and wrote on a sheet of paper for several moments. Then she placed the brief letter in an envelope and wrote an address on the front.

'There,' she said. 'That'll suffice as a letter of introduction. I'm sure they'll help you in any way they can.'

'Thank you. I didn't expect you to do that, Lady Lee, especially not just now.'

Lady Lee sighed. 'Life has to go on, my dear. It's what Timothy would have wanted – expected – us all to do.'

*

366

She found the solicitors' offices quite easily and was ushered into the room of the senior partner, Mr Jones. He was an elderly man, grey-haired and stooping. He regarded her over the top of his steel-rimmed spectacles. He read Lady Lee's note and then leaned his arms on his desk. He smiled at her. 'How may I be of assistance to you, Miss Maltby?'

'It's a very delicate and complicated matter, Mr Jones.' Florrie bit her lip.

Sensing her hesitation, her uncertainty, Mr Jones said gently, 'Anything you tell me, my dear, will be in the strictest confidence. Even if you are still underage, as I suspect you might be, you need have no fear. I might have to *advise* you to tell your family whatever it is, but you are not obliged to do so and I wouldn't compel you or dream of breaking my word to you.'

'I'm twenty-two,' Florrie said, and hearing herself say it was a surprise. Where had all the years gone?

Seeing him nod, she relaxed a little. She took a deep breath and began her story, starting with her own love affair with a Swiss doctor, then about the circumstances of James's death and her shock at finding out about Colette and the baby. She told him everything and ended by producing the note signed by the Musset brothers.

Mr Jones was very thoughtful for a long time and Florrie grew agitated. 'All I want, Mr Jones, is for Jacques to have British citizenship – to be here legally. And that his birth certificate be truthful. I don't want him to have trouble when he's grown up.'

'Well, my dear, it *is* complicated and I shall have to take further advice . . .' He held up his hand as she opened her mouth to protest. 'It'll all be in the strictest confidence, I promise, but you've certainly set me a puzzler. However, I will do my best for you. How can I communicate with you?'

Florrie hadn't thought of that. She didn't want letters from a London solicitor arriving at Candlethorpe Hall where her father might demand to know what it was all about. He might even open her letters; she wouldn't put anything past him.

'If you write to me care of Bixley Manor – that would be best.' She knew that Isobel would respect her privacy and not ask questions.

Minutes later, Florrie stepped into the London street with a lighter step.

It took several months for the legalities to be sorted out, but at last, taking Mr Jones's advice, Florrie became Jacques Maltby's legal guardian. *It would be difficult to effect an adoption, since you are an unmarried lady*, the solicitor wrote. *But I have found a way for you to be the child's guardian in view of the fact that you are one of the boy's closest relatives and since his French grandfather has foregone any rights . . .*

So Jacques became legally Florrie's ward and, over the months and years, at times she almost forgot that she hadn't given birth to the little boy herself.

Forty-Three

Florrie's only news of the war now came from the papers or in letters from friends. Grace and Hetty wrote to her, but her only news from Gervase came via Isobel.

The battle on the Somme had been long and bloody, and both sides had lost thousands of men. It dragged on until November and, though the allies had gained some ground, it had been at tremendous cost. By March 1917 the enemy had withdrawn to a position that became known as the Hindenburg Line, a defensive stronghold with barbed wire and concrete pillboxes. The area they left behind was devastated, villages destroyed and the land laid waste.

In April, Florrie received a letter from Grace. *We're near Arras. The attack the allies launched has been a success, they say, but the number of dead and injured is terrible. We so wish you were still with us – we miss our courageous VAD.*

At home the newspapers rejoiced at America's entry into the war in April, but Grace's next letter brought mixed emotions to Florrie's heart. *You'll never believe this. We're back near Ypres – at Base Camp and the Chateau. But now the front line has gained ground. We're moving forward . . .*

For several weeks Florrie heard nothing from her colleagues. But Augusta's London newspapers told frightening tales of terrible summer rainstorms that turned the Flanders battleground into a quagmire.

Then came a letter from Hetty headed *Passchendaele, August 1917, Dear Florrie, I can hardly write this letter, we're all so heartbroken. Two of our team have perished. As you might guess we've moved nearer the Front yet again – on Dr Hartmann's orders, of course. We're existing – and that's the only word you can call it – in tents. With the rain and the mud and the appalling losses, we were already at our lowest ebb. Then, dear Florrie . . .*

Florrie felt a jolt. Oh, not Ernst, please don't say Ernst is dead. However much he had hurt her, there was a corner of her heart that loved him still. She didn't wish him harm. At Hetty's next words, she breathed again, yet now her heart was filled with an overwhelming sadness.

Poor Dr Johnson – that lovely man – was killed in a shell blast with two of the stretcher-bearers and the wounded man they were carrying. And then – oh, Florrie, I can hardly bear to tell you. Poor Grace is missing, and all we can think of is that she must have slipped from the duckboards whilst crossing the mud and been sucked down. What a terrible way for her to die, Florrie. We're devastated and the morale of the team is the lowest I've ever known it. We miss you – even Sister Blackstock said the other day, 'I wish Maltby was still here.'

Her words made Florrie restless. How she wished she could catch the next ship back to France, but her place was here now, caring for Jacques. Eyebrows would certainly be raised and questions asked if she left her 'son'.

The war dragged on. News of a massive British attack

Gervase had been injured and she hadn't known. He hadn't told her. Perhaps he hadn't told anyone, for Isobel had never mentioned it and she and Florrie were often together, watching over their boys and planning their future.

Florrie moved towards him, uncharacteristically nervous. Her heart was beating faster. Lines of weariness and disillusionment were etched deeply into his face. She was almost up to him before he noticed her and, in that brief moment before he recognized her, she saw the deep sadness in his eyes. She stood gazing at him, not moving towards him, unsure of her welcome.

And then he was holding out his arms and she was flying into them. 'Gervase, Gervase, oh, thank God you're safe.' She drew back and looked up into his face, tears flooding down her cheeks.

'Oh, my dear girl, don't cry. You never cry, Florrie. Whatever is it?'

'Can you ever forgive me for the dreadful things I said to you?'

He frowned and seemed genuinely puzzled. 'I don't understand—'

'When you came to help with – with James?'

For a moment his face was bleak as he relived that gruesome time. 'Oh yes, that.'

'Yes,' she said softly. 'That.'

He put his arm about her shoulders and they began to walk out of the station. 'You were under the most appalling strain, my dear. Please don't think any more about it.'

'But I do, Gervase, I do. I was most dreadfully unfair to you. James told me everything that you'd tried to do, that you put yourself in danger of being court-martialled too. But it shouldn't have taken him to tell me. I should have known for myself that you would have tried everything.'

He sighed heavily. 'I'm only sorry it didn't work.'

'Didn't you get my letter telling you how sorry I was and begging your forgiveness?'

He stopped and turned to face her. 'A letter? From you? You wrote to me?'

'Yes, yes, I did. Oh, don't say you didn't get it?'

Slowly he shook his head. 'I received one from your grandmother, but no, not from you.'

They walked in silence towards where the Richards' groom – now with the grand title of chauffeur – stood waiting by the car. Gervase's face brightened and he held out his hand. 'Good to see you, Bates.'

The man saluted and then took Gervase's hand. 'And you, sir. It's good to have you home safely.'

'How's the arm?' Gervase asked the man as he helped Florrie into the back of the car. Bates had served during the early part of the war, but had been invalided out of the army early in 1915.

The man grinned. 'Doesn't bend quite like it used to, sir, but it's good enough to drive your car.'

Gervase laughed and patted the man's shoulder. 'Glad to hear it.' Then he climbed in beside Florrie, his left leg stretched out stiffly. He turned to her and smiled. 'And now, young woman, I want to hear all about this son of yours.'

The two families settled back into a routine, but it could never be quite the same as before. James was gone, yet never spoken of. And though there was a young male in the Maltby family, Edgar refused to acknowledge Jacques as his heir.

Gervase, home just in time to celebrate the New Year of 1919, insisted on the revival of the old custom. Visiting Candlethorpe Hall, he said, 'I hope you'll all come to Bixley for New Year's Eve this year. I am right, aren't I, Mrs Maltby? I've lost count a bit where we are. It should be our turn, shouldn't it?'

'Yes,' Augusta said spiritedly. 'And it'll be nice to get back to doing normal things again. At least—' For a brief moment her old eyes clouded with sadness. 'We can try.'

Clara, sitting with them, gave a sob and hurried from the room.

Augusta cast her eyes to the ceiling. 'Oh dear, there I go again. I can't seem to say the right thing for two minutes put together.'

'Don't worry, Gran. She is getting a little better. Now Jacques is running everywhere and getting into mischief, it gives her something to do.'

They smiled at each other. The change in Clara had been gradual, but now, with the child's merry chatter echoing through Candlethorpe Hall, she had at last emerged from her room and begun to take an interest in life again. Whilst Edgar set his face resolutely against the boy and would not acknowledge his presence in the house, Clara had been captivated by the innocent child and, for the first time in her life, was ignoring her husband's dictates.

'I think you should know, Florence,' Edgar had told her when the armistice had been announced, 'that I intend to leave Candlethorpe Hall and the estate to Richards. Now that we know he is safe and will return, there is no better person to inherit. No doubt – after everything that's happened – the chap will come to his senses and find himself a *suitable* wife. He should have no difficulty in finding one. There'll be plenty of choice now.'

Florrie raised her head a little higher. 'And what of your grandson?'

Edgar glared at her, his eyes hard and cold. Slowly and deliberately he said, 'I have no son. I have no daughter. I have no grandson. The Candlethorpe Estate will be in good hands with Richards.'

'I have no doubt of that, Father,' Florrie replied. 'But what if he should choose not to marry?'

Her father stroked his moustache and his eyes narrowed as he delivered his final knife thrust. 'Then everything Gervase Richards owns will pass to his nephew – his *legitimate* heir.'

For a long moment, Florrie had stared at her father, then, giving a slight nod, she'd turned on her heel and left his study.

Now, as they sat together with Augusta in the morning room discussing arrangements for their lives to return to some kind of normality, Florrie wondered if Gervase knew what her father intended.

'So, you'll all come?' Gervase was insisting.

'Well, I can't speak for my son – or Clara,' Augusta answered. 'Her courage might fail her when it comes to the point, but we'll be there, won't we, Florrie?' Her level gaze met Gervase's as she added pointedly, 'With Jacques.'

Gervase smiled and said softly, 'I wouldn't have it any other way, Mrs Maltby.'

As she saw him out, accompanying him to his motor

car, Florrie asked, 'What, no Bates? Are you driving yourself?'

'Yes, it's much more fun than being driven. And besides, Bates's arm isn't quite what it should be. It causes him quite a lot of pain, and turning the steering wheel aggravates it.'

'But what about your leg?'

'Oh, it's not too bad. Driving doesn't seem to bother it.' He chuckled. 'But, of course, if I ever need a driver, I can always ask you.'

She linked her arm through his. 'It was thanks to you and your motor car that I was able to be useful in the war.'

Gervase's face sobered. 'It was very dangerous work. I worried about you all the time.'

'Did you? And I worried about you.' She hugged his arm to her. 'I couldn't have borne it if you – if you – hadn't come back.'

He turned to face her and took her hands in his. 'Florrie, I can't wait until New Year's Eve. I've missed two years already. Darling, will you marry me? And please, before you answer, think carefully. I'd look upon Jacques as my own – I promise you that. I'd adopt him, if you like. All that I have would be yours and, one day, would be his. He'd inherit everything . . .'

Tears ran down Florrie's face, but through them, she laughed. 'You make it sound like the wedding service.'

But Gervase was serious. 'The words of the wedding service have great meaning.'

'Yes,' she whispered, serious now. 'And should not be taken lightly. Dearest Gervase, you're a good man and – and deserve better than me.'

'Never say that, Florrie. Not to me.'

She was shaking her head slowly. 'I can't, Gervase. I can't do that to you.'

'There's someone else? You're still in love with Jacques's father?'

Florrie hesitated. How she longed to tell him the truth . . .

But Gervase misread her hesitation. Sadly, he raised her hands to his lips. 'I understand, my dear.'

Before she could utter another word, he'd turned away and the moment was lost.

Forty-Four

Florrie was restless. Whilst Jacques was the focus of her days, the growing child had Beth as his willing slave and Augusta, and even Clara, to dote on him. He didn't really need her, Florrie told herself, ignoring the fact that it was her he ran to every morning with arms stretched wide, her he cried for in the night or wanted close if he was ill.

The battle for women to be allowed to vote was almost won. At the end of December 1918 women over thirty cast their vote for the first time.

'Such ridiculous nonsense,' Edgar declared at the quiet dinner party held at Bixley Manor on New Year's Eve. They'd all been surprised that he'd come, especially as the two children – Charlie and Jacques – sat at the table as a special treat. But Florrie thought she knew the reason. Edgar didn't want to offend Gervase. 'They'll only vote as their husbands or fathers tell them to,' he went on. 'The whole notion is preposterous. What do women know of politics or running the country?'

Florrie opened her mouth to retort, but Augusta beat her to it. 'What arrogant nonsense, Edgar. You really do surpass yourself at times. I can assure you I cast my vote last week and I had no need to ask you for advice before I did so.'

Edgar's face grew red and he 'harrumphed', his usual reaction to his mother's censure. Then he looked puzzled, as the realization of what she'd just said sank in. 'But how come? You're not a landowner, Mother. Nor do you hold a degree.' It was a deliberate barb, a cruel reminder of her upbringing.

Augusta regarded him through narrowed eyes. 'Ah, but Edgar dear, have you forgotten? I own the Dower House on the edge of the Candlethorpe Estate. Nathaniel had the foresight to leave that to me. Just in case,' she added mildly as she glanced at Florrie, 'I should ever have need of it.'

'And I didn't ask my husband how I should vote,' Mrs Ponsonby put in. 'And as for Florrie – I know you're not quite old enough, my dear, and perhaps do not meet the other requirements yet, but when you do—' She turned her attention back to Edgar Maltby now. 'Surely her experiences in the war have given your daughter an insight into how the country should be run? She's an intelligent young women and it's in the hands of people like her – men *and* women – that our future lies.'

Edgar glared around the table and muttered, 'Then God help us all.'

But in the following December Lady Astor took her seat in the Commons and a new era was born.

As a new decade dawned – the Twenties – Florrie grew ever more restless.

'You need a cause,' Augusta said tartly. 'It seems that caring for your *son* isn't enough.' She paused and then eyed Florrie shrewdly. 'I thought you said you were going to start a campaign to obtain a pardon for all those unjustly shot at dawn?'

'I was – I am, but no one seems interested to help.

I've spoken to Mr Jervis. He was sympathetic, but suggested – very gently – that I should mind my own business and not meddle in matters that I don't understand.'

'It's too soon,' Augusta said sensibly. 'Emotions are still raw and the authorities daren't admit to being wrong. Not yet. It would cause an outrage.' She sighed sadly. 'It'll take years, my dear. I doubt I shall live long enough to see my poor grandson's name cleared, but you might. So just leave it a while, Florrie. Then you can begin the fight. Talk to other relatives, get their backing. But not now. It'll still be far too painful for them all.'

She watched her granddaughter move restlessly around the room.

'Oh, for Heaven's sake, go and stay with Isobel in London for a week or two,' Augusta said at last. 'Jacques will be fine with Beth, your mother and me. And he'll soon be starting lessons with the governess I've appointed. Though he'll miss you,' she added as a warning note that Florrie should not take this as a permit to stay away from her child for too long.

So Florrie cut her hair into a fashionable bob, shortened her skirts and took the train to London, where the young danced the night away and drank champagne into the early hours. Despite her love for Jacques, the child could not hold her at Candlethorpe Hall for more than a few weeks at a time. After the excitement of fighting the Cause and being needed as a nurse, Florrie found daily life in the countryside dull. And, even in the city, the endless round of parties, the flippant proposals from idle, rich young men, seemed empty in a meaningless existence that began to pall after a while.

Florrie was listless and unfulfilled. If only, she

thought, she could go to Switzerland. Perhaps if she saw Ernst again and told him the truth . . .? But no, she argued with herself, there was no way back. She'd made her decision and she would abide by it. For Jacques's sake if nothing else. But just sometimes, in the loneliness of the night, she longed to see Ernst again.

When Charlie turned eight years old in 1923, Isobel moved to the Richards' town house for the major part of the year, returning to Bixley only during the school holidays.

'I can't bear for Charlie to be a boarder. I'd miss him so, yet I know Lady Lee wants him to go to Tim's old school. And he would've wanted that too. But they've started taking day boys now, so we're going to live in London during term time.'

'And don't think, young lady, that you can do the same with Jacques next year when he's eight,' Augusta said when she heard of Isobel's plan and saw the devious light in Florrie's eyes. 'That boy stays here and it's where you should be too, Florrie. I fought your father long and hard that James should not be sent away to boarding school until he was at least ten, and I shall do the same for his—' She paused and glanced at Florrie with a strange look in her eyes. 'His nephew. And whilst we're on the subject, Florence.' At her use of her full name, Florrie held her breath. 'It's high time you spent a little less time plastering your lovely face with cosmetics and smoking cigarettes in those ridiculously long holders. And you're hiding your lovely figure – or at least you're trying to – by wearing this new style of shapeless dress. And another thing—'

'Gran!' Florrie was genuinely surprised. 'I never

thought you, of all people, would begrudge me a little fun.'

Augusta sighed and her manner softened. 'Oh, Florrie dear, I can quite understand why you young things have gone a little light-headed – a little mad. You're trying to forget the horrors of the war. All of you, I know that. And I indulged you at first because I thought – despite everything – you deserved a bit of fun.' Her mouth twitched with amusement. 'If I were your age, I'd be the first to try all these outrageous new fashions and hairstyles and the decadent dances from America that are all the rage. But, my dear,' she was utterly serious once more, 'you've a child to bring up. And,' she added simply, 'when you're away, he misses you.'

Florrie was torn. Her grandmother was quite right. She was trying to escape from her bitter memories. Not only the terrible sight of the wounded and dying that still haunted her nights, but also the face of a handsome Swiss doctor whom she'd loved and thought had loved her. If only she *could* forget. She'd tried hard enough. Tried to blot out everything with wild excesses, dropping exhausted into her bed in Isobel's London home with the dawn light. But the visions still invaded her alcohol-induced sleep.

The young men of the 'deb set' were feckless and shallow, the young women even more so. There was no substance to her life any more.

'Don't think I don't know what's the matter with you,' Augusta said. 'You've nothing to do any more. No cause to fight for. No banners to wave. No soldiers to nurse. You're bored, Florrie Maltby. That's all that's the matter with you.' She sighed. 'Seemingly, being a – a *mother* isn't enough for you, as it is for Isobel.'

Florrie glanced at her, but Augusta's expression was

blithely serene. Her face gave nothing away. But there were times when Florrie wondered.

'There's plenty of good works you could do around here. You don't need to go to the capital. There are still plenty of war veterans – even five years on – who can't find work and whose families are living on the breadline. Oh, Gervase is good and so, I have to admit, is your father, when it comes to seeing that all the wounded and maimed who live on our two estates are found something useful to do. But through the county there is still a lot of hardship. Why don't you take up their cause?'

She tried, but Florrie's heart wasn't in it. Involvement with the war veterans brought back too many painful memories. Even Mrs Ponsonby, who'd thrown herself wholeheartedly into trying to find employment for the wounded since the day of the armistice, couldn't persuade Florrie to join in her work. Instead, each season Florrie returned to London. She danced with earls and honourables, one of whom actually proposed, but was laughingly refused. 'You're drunk, Percy. And what would your father say to you taking up with a fallen woman?'

When he sobered up the next day the young man realized he'd had a lucky escape. He had nightmarish visions of his father 'cutting him off without a penny'.

But in the early months of 1926, there was a cause that ignited Florrie's enthusiasm once more.

Augusta had been reading the London newspapers avidly, no longer bothering to keep the fact secret from the rest of the family. Since she now proudly cast her vote, she deliberately turned the conversation to politics and the state of the nation at every meal time, watching Edgar's face with mischievous amusement.

'So, Edgar, do you think there's going to be a national strike?' she asked him over dinner one evening in April.

Edgar eyed Augusta. Secretly – though he would never admit it in a thousand years – he admired his mother. He always had done and, in his innermost heart, though he was loath to recognize it, Florrie was very like her. If only the girl hadn't disgraced herself by bringing home an illegitimate child, he could have forgiven her for having refused Richards' proposal. Maybe, Edgar ruminated, arranged marriages or marriages of convenience weren't the best idea. Not in this day and age. He glanced at Clara. His own marriage hadn't been a love-match and now – in his advancing years – he could see that they'd each lived out their separate existences. She'd not been a wife to him in the fullest sense of the word for several years. And now he rather envied the love-match that his own mother spoke of with such fond memories.

'It's the miners, isn't it?' Florrie was saying, bringing his thoughts back to the question. 'Who can blame them? They're being asked to take a reduction in their pay and an increase in their hours of work.'

The girl does know what she's talking about, Edgar had to admit. If only James had had half his sister's spirit . . . His mind shied away from thoughts of his son. He tried never to think of him. Tried to blot out all the memories, but with Jacques in the house it was hard not to be reminded of him; the boy was so like James had been at the same age. Edgar would never have thought that a child could resemble his uncle so closely.

He cleared his throat. 'It seems the miners are calling upon the TUC to back them.'

'And if they succeed?' Florrie regarded him with her clear gaze.

'If they do, we'll likely see a series of strikes right across the nation. The country could be brought to a standstill. Literally.'

'Well, I'm going to London tomorrow.' Florrie's eyes were alight with a fire that had been missing for years. 'That's where it'll all be happening. I want to be part of it. There are big changes in the air. I can almost feel it.'

Augusta eyed her thoughtfully. 'Well, mind you don't stay away too long. And talking of changes, I need to speak to you – and to you too, Edgar – about Jacques's education. It's high time—'

'Harrumph,' Edgar made his usual disapproving sound. He rose from his chair and threw down his napkin. 'Sort it out between you. I want nothing to do with it.'

Augusta thumped the table with a rare show of swift anger. 'Edgar, sit down. It's high time you took some interest in the boy. He's your *grandson*!'

Edgar glared at her for a long moment, whilst at the opposite end of the table Clara gave a little squeak of dismay, rose and scuttled from the room. Slowly, Edgar sank back into his chair, his mutinous gaze still locked in a silent battle with his mother's.

Florrie glanced from one to the other. What was her grandmother talking about? Jacques's education? The boy was perfectly happy with his governess. But Augusta, it seemed, had other ideas. As was her habit, she came straight to the point.

'It's high time that boy mixed with others of his own age. It's time he attended school.'

'I don't want him to go to boarding school,' Florrie put in quickly and, without thinking what she was saying, went on impetuously, 'James wouldn't—' She stopped, appalled. She'd been about to blurt out 'James wouldn't have wanted it', but just in time she caught herself. She glanced at her father. It was the first time she'd ever mentioned her brother's name in front of him since the tragic events of the war. Thankfully, it explained her hesitation and gave her time to alter her words. 'James wouldn't have recommended it. He hated boarding school.'

Edgar frowned, but still he said nothing.

'I wasn't thinking of boarding school.' Augusta's mouth twitched. '*My* family had no such privileges.'

Edgar's frown deepened.

'You mean he should go to the local school?' Florrie asked, but Augusta shook her head.

'No, I mean he should go to the same school as Charlie. He'll be ten when the new school year starts in September, and I'm sure Isobel would agree to you both living with them during term time. We could come to some acceptable financial arrangement, I'm sure.' She glanced at Florrie and added tartly, 'And Jacques might have the chance of seeing more of you.'

It was a reprimand and a well-deserved one, Florrie recognized. Staying away from him for weeks, even months, was not the action of a devoted mother. She blushed and bowed her head. 'Yes, Gran,' she murmured with surprising meekness.

'Good – so that's settled.' Augusta stood up. 'So, you have a few days in London, Florrie. And I *mean* a few days. And see if you can sort something out with Isobel.' With that, she swept regally from the room, leaving father and daughter staring at one another, wondering just how all that had happened.

Forty-Five

'Whatever are you doing here?'

'Catching the train,' Gervase smiled down at her. 'Like you, I imagine. I didn't know you were going to see Isobel.'

'I wasn't – I mean, it's a spur-of-the-moment thing.'

He eyed her with amusement. 'Going to do a bit of bus-driving in the capital, if this strike the TUC are calling for comes about?'

Florrie laughed. 'Certainly not! I'll be marching with the miners and the other strikers and carrying a banner.'

Gervase's laughter faded. 'Oh, Florrie dear, do be careful.' He sighed. 'I do wish you'd marry me and let me take care of you – of both of you.'

Florrie tapped his arm playfully. 'Now, now, Gervase. It's April the thirtieth, not New Year's Eve.'

He took her hand and tucked it through his arm and led her towards a first-class carriage. 'Well, just be warned – this year I shall press my case with even more vigour than ever before.'

'Oh dear,' Florrie gave an exaggerated sigh. After the war, with the two families partying each year's end once again, Gervase had resumed his annual proposal. It was always light-hearted, but Florrie was never in any doubt that it was nevertheless earnest.

*

'Darlings, how lovely!' Isobel threw her arms out wide, trying to embrace them both at once. 'I didn't know you were coming with Gervase, Florrie dear.'

'Neither did I.' Florrie smiled. 'And forgive me for arriving unexpectedly. I hope it's all right?'

'Of course, of course – you're *always* welcome.'

There was a shout from the landing above and Charlie pounded down the stairs and skidded to a halt in front of them. 'Where's Jacques? Hasn't he come too?'

Florrie hugged her godson. 'Not this time.' The boy's face fell and he pouted.

Gervase laughed and ruffled his hair. 'Next time, old chap. But it was just as well he didn't come. If this strike goes ahead we could be trapped here for weeks.'

The boy's eyes shone. 'That'd be top-hole.'

The three adults laughed and Isobel explained, 'That's his latest word. Everything is "top-hole" or "topping". Come along, get yourselves settled into your rooms and we'll have a sherry before dinner. And you, young man,' she hugged her son to her side, 'as a special treat, can join us.'

'Oh, topping!'

When Charlie, eyes drooping, had gone to bed, the three adults lingered over coffee and liqueurs.

'This strike business could get very serious, you know. And ugly,' Gervase said. 'What's the latest news, Iso?'

'The TUC have called for a general strike to start at midnight on the third.'

'That's only two days. Doesn't give us much time.'

'Time? To do what?' Florrie asked.

'To get organized so that the strike disrupts things as little as possible.'

Florrie stared at first one and then the other. 'What d'you mean? That's what the strike's for. To disrupt everyone's lives so that they listen to the miners' case.'

'We've every sympathy with the miners' cause, but—'

'No, you haven't, if you're trying to undermine what they're hoping to achieve.'

'We can't let the whole country grind to a standstill. Think about food supplies and other essentials. How is this going to affect the sick and the elderly, Florrie, to say nothing of babies and infants? We can't stand by and see people starving.'

'Oh, it won't come to that.'

'It might very well,' Gervase said grimly.

Florrie's face was mutinous. 'Well, I'm still on the side of the strikers.' She stood up. 'So, if you'd rather I didn't stay under your roof, Iso—'

'Don't be silly, Florrie. This has nothing to do with our friendship. We just disagree for once. It's not often we do.'

Florrie sank back into her seat. She looked at Gervase. 'What – what do you intend to do?'

'I'm not sure yet. I'm going to wait and see what happens. It might be settled at the eleventh hour.'

There was silence amongst them, his choice of words reminding them poignantly of the armistice signed at the eleventh hour of the eleventh day of the eleventh month.

'Lady Lee is organizing helpers,' Isobel said, trying to bring their maudlin thoughts back to the present. 'They intend to help out at London's General Post

Office if the workers go on strike there. And I hear some of the society ladies are planning to open up soup kitchens.'

Florrie shook her head. 'I don't believe this. Lady Lee! So she's a traitor too, is she?'

'Oh, Florrie, that's a bit harsh.' Isobel was hurt.

'But we all fought for our rights. We believed in the same things. What's happened to you?'

'It's a bit different—'

'No, it isn't.' Florrie was adamant. 'We all sit in our grand houses with roaring coal fires in every room, and we never give a thought to the men who hew it with their bare hands in dark and dangerous conditions. It's one of the worst jobs in the world.' She shuddered. 'And you're begrudging them a fair day's pay.'

'Militant action isn't the way to go about it,' Gervase began.

'You never agreed with the things we did as suffragettes,' Florrie rounded on him. 'So I'm not surprised at you. But Lady Lee – and you, Iso. I still can't believe what I'm hearing. The miners haven't been treated fairly since the end of the war. You know that. We've had strikes before. Remember the one that lasted three months in 'twenty-one? Talking does no good.' She glanced at Isobel again. 'We both know that.'

Florrie stood her ground. She refused to be swayed and the following morning – Saturday – she went out into the streets. There was a feeling of unrest and agitation in the air. Florrie felt herself swept along in the pent-up excitement. There were groups of people marching in an orderly fashion, some holding banners declaring *Support the Miners* and the slogan the miners' leader had thought up: *Not a minute on the day, not a penny off the pay.*

'Where's everyone going?' Florrie asked a woman marching along with the men.

'Hyde Park. There's to be a demonstration.'

Florrie's eyes shone as she fell into step beside her. 'Where are you from?'

'A party of us have come from up north. We're peaceful, like. We aren't looking for mekin' trouble, but ya know what they've tried to do the miners, dun't ya? Well, our men aren't goin' to stand for it no more. An' now workers all over the country are prepared to come out on strike wi' us. The printers here in London are refusing to bring out a newspaper that's got an article in it criticizing the trade union. And now dockers, railwaymen – all sorts of transport workers – and others are prepared to come out an' all.' She grinned. 'There'll be urgent talks in Downing Street, you mark my words, but it won't mek no diff'rence. We're solid this time and we're going to bring London to a halt.'

Florrie walked beside her, feeling the old thrill of being involved in something worthwhile. Once again, she was fighting for the right for the voice of ordinary people to be heard.

As the marchers reached Hyde Park, Florrie exclaimed, 'My goodness, there must be thousands of people here.'

'I told you, didn't I? This time they'll have to listen to us.'

For the rest of the day Florrie listened to impassioned speeches by the miners' leaders and officials of other unions. They stayed in the park until it began to grow dusk. Tired, but exhilarated, Florrie walked home.

The moment she stepped into the house, Charlie came rushing down the stairs, calling out, 'Mother! She's home.' He danced about in front of her. 'Where've you been, Auntie Flo? There have been such ructions here. Mother's been in such a state and Uncle Gervase is out looking for you. Even Grannie Lee's been here.'

Isobel appeared from the morning room. 'Oh, thank goodness you're safe. We've been worried sick. Gervase has been beside himself. We heard there were demonstrations taking place and—'

'Oh, Iso, I'm sorry you've been worried, but I've had the most marvellous day.' She linked her arm through Isobel's and held out her hand to Charlie. 'Come – I'll tell you all about it.' She laughed. 'There've been *ructions* out there too.'

Whilst Meredith poured them a glass of sherry and a drink of cordial for Charlie, Florrie stood in front of the fireplace, her eyes shining and feeling more alive than she had for the last ten years.

'Thank you, Meredith. Oh, Iso – I *wish* you'd been with me. It was like the old days again. There was a demonstration in Hyde Park, just like our suffragette meetings. There was this man from Durham who got up and spoke to the crowds – there were *thousands* there and—'

At that moment, they heard Meredith open the front door and voices in the hall. Then the door to the morning room was flung open and Gervase came striding in. His face was like thunder as he moved straight to Florrie, took her by the shoulders and shook her, making her spill her sherry. Florrie gasped, more with shock at such a reaction from the normally gentle, placid man than from physical pain.

'Where have you been? We've been worried out of our minds. I've had the police out looking for you.'

Florrie faced him squarely, glaring back at him. 'I don't need your permission to go out,' she said through gritted teeth. Out of the corner of her eyes she saw Isobel's anxious face, but Charlie was grinning from ear to ear and bouncing up and down on the sofa. It seemed the young rascal quite enjoyed a 'ruction'.

'Tell him where you've been, Auntie Flo.' But before she could open her mouth to say a word, Charlie went on excitedly, 'She's been to a demonstration about the miners' strike in Hyde Park. She was just going to tell us all about it when you came in. Oh, do tell us, Auntie Flo.'

Gervase seemed not to hear him. 'You're a guest in this house,' he went on as if Charlie had not interrupted. 'It was discourteous to Isobel, if nothing else. And I don't suppose you care a jot about how I feel. How terrified I've been for your safety.' He released her and stepped back. His temper cooling swiftly, his shoulders drooped as he added with infinite sadness, 'But then, you never have, have you?' Then he turned on his heel and left the room, leaving Florrie staring after him. Seeing his genuine distress upset her far more than his anger could ever do.

There was a moment's silence before Charlie piped up again, 'Come on, Auntie Flo, do tell us.'

But Florrie's bubble of excitement had burst. 'Oh, Iso, I'm so sorry. I didn't realize – I never thought you'd both worry about me.' Her gaze was still on the door as she shook her head slowly and added, 'Not like that.'

Isobel smiled. Though she'd been worried too by Florrie's absence all day long, her anxiety had mainly been fuelled by Gervase's fear. 'Darling, he loves you,' she said simply. 'That's why.'

Charlie – to whom all this was new – beamed again. 'Are you going to marry him, Auntie? Oh, do say you are, and then Jacques and I will be – will be—' He turned to Isobel. 'What will we be, Mother?'

'Cousins, darling.'

'Yes, that's it. We'll be cousins. And that'd be absolutely topping!'

Forty-Six

By the end of the following day, it was clear that the talks had failed and a general strike was to begin at midnight on the 3rd May.

Florrie went out each day to join in the throngs of strikers milling about the streets, intent on disrupting any attempt at a normal day.

She returned home the next evening to find that Isobel had joined the ladies manning the food kitchens in Hyde Park and Gervase was planning to present himself at the nearest police station to sign on as a Special Constable.

Now he and Florrie – and Isobel too – were really on opposite sides.

By the time the strike was a few days old, a veritable army of city workers – barristers, stockbrokers and undergraduates amongst them – were driving trains, buses and lorries and keeping the essential supplies moving. Food coming in from abroad was escorted from the docks into the city by the army and the police. Gervase was on duty as a Special Constable.

'Oh, we can't have the Prime Minister missing his tot of whisky every night, now can we?'

'Does he drink whisky?' Isobel asked innocently.

'I don't know,' Florrie snapped. 'I was just being sarcastic.'

Isobel regarded her thoughtfully. 'That's not like you, Florrie. This is really getting to you, isn't it?'

'I—' she began and then groaned. She hated being at loggerheads with either Isobel or Gervase. She still felt guilty for the time she'd blamed him for failing to save James's life. It hadn't been his fault. The regulations of army life were so harsh and rigid; there'd been nothing more he could have done. She saw that now.

Isobel's voice interrupted her thoughts and brought her back to the present.

'Florrie, dear—'

'I just want a fairer society for everyone. I thought that's why we fought for the vote. I thought we might make a difference.'

'It'll take time,' Isobel said gently. 'And this strike – it's all bound up with politics and economics, and I can't profess to understand it all. Maybe Gervase does, but I don't. I just think that hurting the innocent is not the way to go about it. Whatever we did, Florrie, for the Cause, we never hurt people.'

'I'm sorry, Iso,' Florrie said, with genuine contrition, 'but I just can't agree with you. This is about people's livelihoods.'

Isobel laughed. 'Then we'll agree to go our separate ways. You to march with the strikers, me to dole out soup.'

Each morning they parted company – in more ways than one – outside the front door.

The streets were thronged with people: men in cloth caps and trilbys, some in their workaday clothes, others obviously dressed in their Sunday best, hoping no doubt, Florrie thought, to make a good impression – to prove that they were not just a rowdy mob out to cause trouble. Florrie glanced about her. She could see no other women at all. The milling crowd was all men.

For the most part they were orderly and well behaved, but when an armoured car drove down the street, it seemed to incense them. They surged forward to surround a tramcar manned by volunteers. The driver, fearful of causing injury to someone, brought it to a halt. The crowd cheered and jeered and thumped the air in victory with clenched fists, whilst the driver looked terrified and his passengers shook angry fists at the mob.

'You ought not to be out 'ere, miss,' someone said close by. 'You'll get trampled to death in this lot.'

Florrie grinned back at him. 'Thanks, but I came to march with you. To show support, but—'

Whatever she had been going to say to the young man was drowned by a howl from the crowd surrounding the tram. They were surging forward, trying to grab hold of a man in uniform who was attempting to climb onto the tram. Florrie caught her breath as she recognized the figure.

'Gervase, oh, Gervase.' She pushed and shoved her way through.

''Ere, mind what you're doin', miss. They mean business,' the young man tried to warn her. But her fury gave her strength. How dare they manhandle Gervase? After he'd fought in the war for them, after he'd won medals.

She kicked and pushed and shoved. Behind her the young man laughed and joined in. 'Let the lady through.'

At last she came to where Gervase was now lying on the ground and some of the strikers were holding him down. One aimed a vicious kick at his ribs, to be rewarded by the well-aimed toe of her sturdy boot on his shins.

She bent down and hauled Gervase to his feet. He was bleeding from a cut on his forehead. She turned on the rebels. She shook her fist in their faces. 'I'm on your side, damn you,' she shrieked. 'At least I was – but not if this is the sort of thing you're going to do. He's a war hero. He won medals. He fought for you lot to win the freedom for you to make peaceful protests. But not like this. Not injuring folk—'

'He's not on our side now,' someone shouted. 'He's helping to break the strike.'

'No, he's trying to keep order. Trying to stop folks getting hurt. That's all he's doing.'

'Florrie—'

'Shut up, Gervase, and let me handle this.'

Those near enough to hear her laughed and some of their anger eased.

'Eh, that's put you in your place, feller.' 'Hiding behind her petticoats, a' yer?' 'She ought to've been one o' them suffragettes—'

Florrie rounded on him, but grinned. 'I was. I marched with banners and broke windows. I went to prison for my beliefs, so you lot don't frighten me one bit. Now,' she looked about her again. The crowd was calmer now, no longer baying for blood like a pack of hounds at a hunt. 'If you'll let us pass, this constable needs his head attending to.'

'Needs it testing, if you ask me.'

'I agree with you there, but he doesn't deserve to have it knocked off.' She smiled again, knowing she'd won them over. 'At least if he does, I'll be the one to do it.'

The young man who'd helped her push her way to Gervase's side now parted the crowd for them to walk through to safety.

'By heck, feller, you've got a cracker there,' someone called out. 'Wish she was my missus.'

'So do I,' Florrie heard Gervase mutter as she hustled him away, pausing only to thank the stranger who'd helped them.

The young man doffed his cap and watched them go. My, he thought, she was a beauty and no mistake. And a fiery piece an' all. He echoed the sentiments of the wag in the crowd. I wish she were mine.

'Oh, whatever's happened? You're bleeding.'

'It's nothing, Iso. Don't fuss.'

But his sister sat Gervase down and fussed over him like a mother hen. Whilst Isobel dressed the wound on his forehead, Florrie paced up and down angrily. 'I was wrong and you were right – again!' She paused and glared at Gervase as if it was all his fault. 'They were like a pack of – a pack of – oh, I can't think. They were an unruly mob, surrounding that poor tram driver and all the passengers on it. I bet they were all terrified.'

'They didn't look it,' Gervase remarked mildly. 'And the "poor" driver was an off-duty policeman.'

Florrie rounded on him. 'How do you know that?'

'Because I met him when I was signing on for special duties. He's a regular.'

Florrie was silent for a moment and resumed her pacing. Then she said, 'But that doesn't alter the way the crowd behaved.'

Gervase, now sporting a white dressing on his right temple, grinned up at her. 'Some of your suffragette meetings got just as unruly, if you remember.'

She stared at him for a moment and then suddenly burst out laughing. She sank to the chair beside him. 'You're right. You *are* right. It's – it's different when you're passionately involved and part of it all. But when you stand back and watch others – well, it is a little—' She chuckled again. 'Unseemly, as Father would say.'

Isobel stood with her hands on her hips, regarding the two of them. 'So, what are you going to do now?'

'Go back on duty,' Gervase said.

'Try to find a *peaceful* protest,' Florrie smiled.

But, on the 12th May, the TUC called off the strike.

'Thank goodness for that,' Isobel said with a heartfelt sigh. 'Now perhaps we can get back to normal and you two can stop arguing.'

'I do feel for the miners, though,' Florrie commented. 'They've been deserted.'

'They're going to carry on their fight, but the general strike was undermined.' Gervase shrugged. 'The city didn't go short of supplies.'

'Thanks to you and your cronies,' Florrie said, but the accusation was without heat now. She'd been shocked that the crowd's militant action had not stopped at the injuring of persons. At least the suffragettes had always said that only property, never people, should be their target.

Gervase was watching her face. 'You could still help the miners. Get involved.'

Florrie wriggled her shoulders. 'I don't know enough about it. Besides,' her eyes narrowed, 'there's something else I should do.'

'What?' Both Gervase and Isobel chorused.

Florrie smiled and tapped the side of her nose. 'Never you mind.'

'Oh, Florrie dear, do be careful,' Isobel pleaded.

She would say no more, but becoming involved in the general strike had reminded Florrie just how much she needed to be busy. As Augusta had said, she needed a cause. And perhaps now the time was right to carry out the promise she'd given to her beloved brother.

The cause of fighting to clear the names of all those – not just James – who'd been shot at dawn. It wouldn't bring them back, but it would mean so much to their families, who lived daily with the shame and horror of how their loved ones died. But whilst there were still people around like her father, she realized it might take years. Perhaps more than her lifetime. It would be up to the next generation to bring it about. When Jacques grew older she would instil in him the need to carry on the fight to clear his father's name.

It would be a long, hard road, but she could – and would – make a start.

Forty-Seven

In the September of 1926, when Jacques had just passed his tenth birthday, Florrie enrolled him in the same London school that Isobel's son had been attending for the past three years. Charlie was a kindly boy, merry-faced and cheeky, but good at heart, and he took the younger boy under his protective wing, shielding him from the bullying that new boys sometimes had to endure. But Jacques, a quiet, introverted child, did not take to the city or to the rough and tumble of school life. After months in the city he grew thin and pale, and caught colds and influenza during the winter months with disturbing regularity. Florrie, who'd hardly known a day's illness in her life, was impatient.

'I think he makes the most of it,' she told Augusta during the long summer holidays when the boy returned to Candlethorpe Hall. 'He doesn't like London, or school, and I think it's all a ploy to be sent back home. Look at him – cycling over to Bixley to play tennis with Charlie, row on the lake or go hiking. He's hardly sickly now, is he?'

'Well, he's better now it's summer again, I have to admit, but his cough never seems to quite go away, though,' Augusta said worriedly. 'You should get him checked. Take him to one of the Harley Street doctors. I'm sure Isobel or Gervase will recommend one.'

'Oh, fiddlesticks! There's nothing wrong with him.

You watch – come September again, when he gets back to school, he'll have a cold or a sore throat or a headache. Anything to try to get sent home again. I don't know why he makes such a fuss. He's got Charlie there. And it's not as if he's even a boarder, for Heaven's sake. He comes home every night.'

'But the beginning of term, when the pupils all come together again, is the time when they catch things from each other.' Augusta paused a moment and then added with deceptive mildness, 'James was just the same.'

Florrie stared at her. 'James was? I don't remember him being ill. At least – not like this.'

'Oh, he was. The school used to write to us, but your father would never allow him to be brought home. Don't you remember, your mother getting in such a tizzy – always thinking he was ill?'

'Well, yes. But I always thought that was just – just—'

'Just your mother. Some of the time, maybe. But not always.'

Florrie was thoughtful for a moment, then she smiled and kissed her grandmother's cheek. 'Well, Jacques seems fine just now and will be for the next five weeks, I've no doubt. So I'm going back to London. There's rather a good party that Lady Lee is organizing and I understand the Home Secretary's going to attend. I want to bend his ear.'

'The Home Secretary? Florrie, what are you up to now?'

'Never you mind, Gran.'

'Well, whatever it is, just be careful.'

But to that Florrie made no answer.

*

By the time Jacques was fifteen, he was tall and thin and stooped a little. He had a hacking cough that never seemed to leave him, not even during the summer months now. On New Year's Eve 1931, which was being celebrated at Candlethorpe, Gervase drew Florrie aside.

'Florrie darling, forgive me for what I'm about to say,' he began, his forehead creased with anxiety.

She smiled up at him. 'Forgive you, Gervase? I've forgiven you for the last – how many years is it now?'

He stared at her for a moment, as if he didn't know what she was talking about. Then his expression lightened, just a little. 'Oh, that. Well, yes, of course, there's that too. But this is something more serious.'

'More serious than a proposal of marriage? Oh, Gervase, don't tell me that all these years you've not been serious.'

'Of course I have, Florrie dear, but – but this is something, well, delicate and you might think I – we're interfering.'

'Go on.'

'It's Jacques. Iso and I are really worried about him. He's not well. We – we both think you should take him to see a specialist. One who knows about chest complaints. We know a very good one in London.'

'Gervase, it's growing pains, just like Dr Miles said. He must be sick of seeing us, the times we've trooped into his surgery just recently. And it's Christmas. He's always ill at Christmas. He just doesn't want to go back to school after the holidays. That's all.'

Gervase shook his head. 'No, Florrie, it isn't all. He hardly ate his Christmas dinner. I was watching him. And he looked to be running a fever.'

'Nonsense. Why, he came over to Bixley yesterday to play football with Charlie.'

'Yes, he did and he couldn't run around the lawn for more than a couple of minutes before he collapsed wheezing and coughing. Florrie, you should seek advice. You're neglecting—'

'Neglecting him! How dare you say such a thing? No boy has ever had more than he's been given. Or has been more loved.' She choked back the words. Jacques was growing more and more like James with every day that passed. So much so that it hurt Florrie to look at him sometimes.

'I don't doubt you love him, Florrie. You see he has everything he needs. He wants for nothing. I know that.'

'I'm *always* with him. We live with Isobel in the term times and we're here in the holidays.'

Gervase smiled sadly. '*He* is. You aren't – not always. If there's something more – more interesting in London, you're gone. And even when you are there together, you're out most nights. Iso says—'

'Oh, been telling tales of me, has she?'

'She's worried about Jacques,' Gervase insisted. 'That's all.'

'Just because I don't smother him, like she—' She broke off, realizing how petty she was being. Gervase chose to ignore what she'd obviously been going to say about his sister. 'He's well cared for,' she said instead. 'Gran—'

'He needs his *mother*. Florrie, if he were fit and well and busy – robust would be the word – with a young boy's activities, it would be different. Like, I have to say it, like Charlie. But he's not. He's sickly. He needs to be seen by a doctor and he needs you with him.'

For a long moment, Florrie stared at him. Guilt flooded through her. She'd been so wrapped up in her effort to start a campaign to clear her dead brother's name – and all those she felt had been executed without a fair trial or just cause – that she had forgotten the living.

Gervase was right. She had neglected James's son.

Florrie took Jacques first to their local, family doctor. When he'd examined the boy and then sent him out of the consulting room, he turned a sober face to Florrie. Before he could say anything, Florrie took a deep breath and said, 'I want a second opinion, Dr Miles. No offence – you're a wonderful doctor – but—'

To her surprise the doctor was nodding agreement. 'No offence taken, my dear. In fact, I was about to suggest that Jacques see a colleague of mine. One who specializes in chest complaints. This is more serious than a recurrence of the common cold or even attacks of bronchitis.'

Florrie felt a stab of fear. If Jacques had a serious illness, she would never forgive herself for her absences from his life. She should have kept a better watch over him.

'Now,' Dr Miles pulled a pad of paper towards him and began to write. 'This is a note of introduction. I would recommend a Dr Harris in Harley Street. He's a consultant physician.'

Florrie gasped. 'Why, that's the name that Gervase – I mean, Mr Richards – mentioned. How strange.'

Dr Miles looked up and smiled. 'Not so strange at all, Florence.' Knowing her from her childhood – indeed, he had attended her birth – the doctor had earned the right to use her Christian name. 'Dr Harris is a well-known specialist in his field, respected by all his colleagues. I've been privileged to know him for a number of years. There—' He folded the piece of paper, placed it in an envelope, sealed it and handed it to her. 'This is a note for you to take to him, but I will contact him myself and arrange an appointment for you and the boy. You will have somewhere to stay in London, I presume?'

Florrie nodded. Her hand trembled as she took the letter.

'And whatever Dr Harris says, my advice to you would be to keep him here at home at least for the spring school term. The damp city, with its smoke and fumes, is not the best place for him just now.'

Florrie contacted the school and told them that, due to ill health, Jacques would not be returning to school for the new term.

I will, of course, she wrote, *continue to pay the fees and I would like you to keep his place open for him. I am very hopeful that he will be able to return for the summer term. In the meantime, perhaps his tutors could let me know what work he should be doing so that he does not fall behind in his studies.*

In the middle of January 1932 they travelled to London to stay with Isobel and Charlie and to see the specialist.

'They all miss you at school,' Charlie told him. 'All the chaps in your form keep asking after you and when you'll be going back.' The older boy's merry eyes were unusually anxious, his manner less boisterous.

Jacques smiled thinly and glanced at him as if he didn't really believe him. Isobel and Florrie looked at each other but said nothing, watching as Charlie tried to involve Jacques in a game of chess. But he soon lost interest, pleaded tiredness and went to his room.

'Is he really ill, Auntie Flo?' Tall and broad for his age, Charlie looked older than his sixteen years. He'd soon be seventeen, Florrie realized with a shock. Old enough to fight for his country. She shuddered, praying that his generation of young men would not get caught up in a dreadful war.

The following morning, Florrie and Jacques took a cab to Harley Street. Dr Harris was a jovial elderly man, who nevertheless regarded his patient with shrewd eyes. After a long consultation and several tests he called both of them back into his consulting room. For a long moment he watched Jacques coughing wheezily into his handkerchief before saying, quietly, 'I don't hold with the practice of keeping the diagnosis from the patient himself or herself. I trust I am right in thinking you are a sensible young man?'

Jacques glanced at Florrie, before saying quietly and with such adult dignity that Florrie's heart twisted, 'Yes, I'd like you to tell me what the matter is. I've been feeling ill for so long now, I am quite – prepared.'

'I fear you may have consumption, my boy. Tuberculosis of the lungs.'

Jacques accepted the terrible news calmly – it was Florrie who cried out in agony. 'Oh no. No!'

She wanted to scream and rage against an unfair world, but she did none of those things. The image of James, standing with his back to the post, came into her mind. She remembered his courageous demeanour, his composed acceptance.

It was that same serenity she was seeing now in the face and bearing of his son. Her heart overflowed with love and pride, just as it had on that fateful day.

'There are several things I can suggest you do,' the doctor went on, still speaking to the patient, yet involving Florrie with a glance in her direction every so often. 'You could go to a sanatorium – there are several very good ones throughout the country. I would recommend one in a mountainous region, as high as you can get. Or you could stay at home and be nursed by a private nurse, though in this case you must have no contact with the rest of your family, not even,' again he glanced at Florrie, 'with your mother.'

'We have a large house. We could live in one wing, well away from everyone, but a nurse, no. I – I've done a little nursing. With your and Dr Miles's help, I'll look after him.' When Dr Harris seemed about to argue, Florrie added in a tone that brooked no argument, 'No one else.'

The doctor spread his hands and smiled helplessly at Jacques. 'You have a formidable mother, my boy.'

'She was a suffragette,' he said and Florrie heard the note of pride in his voice. 'And a VAD nurse in the war. She went right near the front line.'

'My goodness me,' Dr Harris was suitably impressed. He turned to Florrie. 'Then you must have encountered the disease before?'

She nodded. 'Yes, there were a few from the trenches who'd contracted it. They – they were sent home, of course.'

They exchanged a look, and the doctor was fully aware that perhaps those poor boys never made it home before the disease – or a sniper's bullet – ended their lives anyway.

'Well, I'm sure you're well qualified then, my dear. Between us, we'll have this young fellow here well in no time. Plenty of rest, fresh air and good food, and we'll see how you are in a few weeks' time.'

Isobel and Charlie were devastated.

'I must telephone Gervase at once. He'll meet you at the station tomorrow. Oh, Florrie dear, is there anything else we can do?'

Florrie shook her head. 'I just want to take him home to the Hall and get him started on the treatment Dr Harris has set out. He's sending a letter to Dr Miles too, and I'll be able to call on him at any time for help.'

For once poor Charlie didn't know what to say. He was always merry and bright. He revelled in excitement and activities, sports and games. Being fit and healthy himself, he didn't know how to react to illness – especially a sickness as serious as tuberculosis.

He hugged Florrie and, ignoring her warnings, put his arm around Jacques's shoulders. 'You'll soon be all right, old chap. Chin up.'

But Jacques sought her gaze and held it – just as James, under sentence of death too, had done all those years ago.

Forty-Eight

A grey-faced Gervase met them at the station. He enfolded Florrie in his arms and held her close whilst she rested her face against his chest. Then he turned to Jacques and, as his own nephew had done, he put his arm around his shoulders.

'Uncle Gervase, you're not supposed to come near me. You might catch it.'

Gervase smiled at him. 'As your mother would say, "Fiddlesticks". Come on, let's get you home. At least, if that is where you want to go.' He looked across at Florrie. 'You're very welcome to come to Bixley, you know. For as long as you like.'

'I know,' she said softly, 'but Candlethorpe Hall is where he should be and – for once – I shan't leave this particular battle to my grandmother. *I'll* see Father.'

She stood before him in his study later that evening. On the way home, Jacques and she had agreed that nothing be said to anyone else until she'd had time to talk to Edgar. 'We'll make the excuse that you're tired from the journey and need to go straight to bed. I'll bring you something to eat, and then I'll face your grandfather. After that, we'll make proper arrangements.'

Jacques didn't argue – he hadn't the strength – and

412

all Gervase said about the plan was, 'If you need me, send word and I'll come at once. I meant what I said.'

'Father, I understand your feelings about me and about Jacques,' Florrie began. 'Truly, I do. But we need your help. Jacques is very ill—'

Edgar, sitting at his desk, looked up quickly.

'We've been to London,' Florrie went on, 'to see a specialist in chest complaints.' She licked her lips nervously, though whether her agitation was caused by her dreadful anxiety over Jacques or because she was facing her father, even she didn't know. She took a deep breath, but could not prevent her voice trembling as she said, 'This specialist thinks Jacques might have consumption.'

Edgar continued to stare at her and for several moments neither of them moved or spoke. At last, he said stiffly, 'I'm very sorry to hear that, Florence. What can we do?'

Florrie explained all that the doctor had recommended and the choices he'd given them, ending by saying, 'But we're both agreed that he should remain at home – at least to begin with. He'll need to be kept well away from everyone. I shall nurse him myself and I'll restrict my contact with the rest of the family and the servants too. So, I'm here to ask your permission to use the south wing of the house.'

'Of course,' Edgar said at once and his voice was strangely hoarse as he added, 'And anything you need – special food, anything at all – just say the word.'

It was more than she'd hoped for. Her father was not a man to change overnight or ever to display his affections, but his words and his manner told her that he did, after all, have some feelings for his grandson.

'Thank you, Father. There is just one thing. The

south end of the house is ideal because one of the rooms has a balcony, and part of the treatment is that he must lie outside in the fresh air. He'll need a day-bed.'

'Of course. Order whatever you need.' As she turned to go, he said, 'I thought the hills were the best – treatment.' She noticed the hesitation and his choice of the word 'treatment' rather than 'cure'. 'High up in the mountains. Lincolnshire's hardly the best place, is it?'

'When I told the doctor where we lived, near the coast, he was happy that the bracing air from the North Sea would be as good.'

Edgar nodded and Florrie went out of the room, leaving him sitting motionless at his desk, lost in thought.

The following morning, she told Augusta and together they broke the news to Clara.

'You mean – you mean I can't see him?' she wailed.

'It's best not, Mother dear,' Florrie said. 'Not for a while anyway.'

'You should have left Edgar to me, Florrie,' Augusta said.

'There was no need, Gran. Not this time. He seems genuinely sorry about Jacques's illness. And he's given his blessing to do whatever we need.'

'Oh dear, we'll need more servants if those rooms are to be opened up,' Clara fretted.

'Don't worry, Mother. Beth and I can clean the rooms, and the menservants – under Bowler's instruction – can move the furniture.' She stood up. 'And now I must take Jacques some breakfast. He should be awake by now. He's to eat as much as he can to build up his strength, and the sooner we get started, the better.'

'I'll see Cook. We'll sort out some nourishing meals.

I'll go now,' Clara said, getting up and bustling out of the room with a vigour that they hadn't seen for years.

Augusta and Florrie exchanged a glance. 'Well, well, well,' Augusta murmured softly. 'Who'd've thought it. It might give her something else to think about other than her own ailments. Shame it has to be something like this to do it.'

'I didn't see it for myself, of course, but didn't you tell me in one of your letters that she was an active member of Mrs Ponsonby's little group in the war?'

Augusta nodded. 'That's right. She was. I'd forgotten that. But of course when we had the dreadful news about James, and then you coming home with – with Jacques, she slipped back into her old ways.' She was thoughtful for a moment. 'Couldn't blame her, I suppose. It was a dreadful time.'

A fresh stab of guilt – something she hadn't felt for a long time – struck at Florrie's heart. She so hated being deceitful, but now was not the best time to reveal the long-held secret. Maybe when Jacques was better . . . ?

'Now,' Augusta said, getting up, 'I'll go up and see Jacques.'

'Oh, Gran, I don't think—'

Augusta turned and looked down at her. 'My dear Florence, if you think you are going to keep *me* away from the boy, you are sadly mistaken. The rest of the household, yes, it's the right thing to do, but I'm an old woman and what better way to use my declining years than to help care for my great-grandson.'

Without even waiting for a reply, she marched purposefully out of the room with the vigour of someone half her age. Florrie smiled as she watched her go.

*

Everything that could be done was done. They followed the advice of the doctors to the letter. Augusta spent many hours wrapped in blankets sitting on the balcony with Jacques, quietly reading whilst he slept, or playing cards or board games when he felt up to it. Florrie helped him with his lessons, but some days the boy felt so ill, he could not concentrate.

When word filtered out amongst the estate workers and into the villages, even as far as Bixley, the family was overwhelmed by the outpourings of affection and concern for the young boy. A stream of well-wishers bearing cards and small gifts arrived at the back door of the big house.

'Who'd have thought it,' Florrie joked to Gervase in private, 'and all for the illegitimate son of a fallen woman?' Tears shimmered in her eyes. She was deeply touched by everyone's kindness.

'That's not how they see Jacques,' he said quietly. 'Or you.'

Dr Miles visited weekly, and each time Edgar would be hovering in the hall to take the doctor into his study for a progress report.

'It's not good, I'm afraid, Edgar.' The two men had been friends for years and were on first-name terms. 'I'm not happy about him. Not happy at all. We've tried this treatment for four months now. I thought that perhaps once spring came and the better weather, he might pick up, but I'm sorry to say there's no real sign of improvement.'

'Should we get a trained nurse in?'

'Good Heavens no, man. There's no need for that. Florrie's as good as any professional nurse I've seen. No, but I do think the boy should see Harris again in London.'

'I presume it would be best if he didn't travel by train?'

Dr Miles nodded. 'Best not. For his own sake as well as the other passengers.'

'I'll arrange for him to be driven there by motor car.'

'I'll contact Harris tonight. As soon as I have a date, I'll let you know.'

'Florence drove vehicles in the war, perhaps we could hire one that she could drive.'

Dr Miles eyed him. 'Why don't you ask Richards? I'm sure he'd be willing to take the boy.'

Gervase was more than happy to, and he and Isobel insisted they should stay at their town house as usual.

'We shouldn't. Think of Charlie.'

'We'll just have to tell him to steer clear, but Iso won't hear of you going anywhere else,' Gervase said firmly. 'And neither will I.'

But Charlie had other ideas and showed a stubbornness they hadn't seen in him before. He refused to stay away from Jacques. 'He's my cousin – well, nearly.' He grinned and winked saucily at his uncle, who had to turn away to hide his smile.

'I suppose it's in the blood, when you think about it,' Isobel laughed, 'having me as a mother and Lady Lee as a grandmother.'

'But I don't want him to get it,' Florrie said anxiously.

'Don't worry about Charlie. He's fit and healthy.'

'That's not the point, Iso. He could still contract it from Jacques.'

Isobel shrugged, surprisingly calm. 'He's his own man, Florrie,' she said softly, watching her son helping the weaker boy up the stairs. 'And that's the way I like

it. He's not one to desert a friend when they're in need.
None of us are.'

Florrie hugged her gratefully. 'I don't know what
we'd do without you.'

'Switzerland,' Dr Harris said. 'That's where he should
go.'

Florrie gasped and stared at him whilst her heart
seemed to be doing somersaults. But the doctor, unaware of her inner turmoil, carried on blithely. 'Davos.
That's the place. They're doing wonderful things there.
It's become a centre for the treatment of tuberculosis.
There are some very clever doctors at the sanatoriums
there—'

I don't need to be told that, Florrie thought, but she
kept silent.

'I'll draw up a list of names and send it to you.'

'There's no need, thank you, Dr Harris.'

He looked at her sharply as if he thought she was
about to reject his suggestion. But he relaxed and smiled
as she added, 'I already know of one. The Schatzalp.
We'll go there.'

'Very well. I'll write to the director and see when he
can take you. It may be a few weeks before they have a
vacancy.'

Florrie shuddered. Did that mean they had to wait
for someone to die?

'Jacques may be there for weeks, even months,' Dr
Harris went on. 'You do realize that, don't you? And
the cost for the individual patient varies according to the
standard of the accommodation, the food, the treatments
they may require, X-rays, even perhaps operations. Your
family can afford it, I presume?'

'That's not a problem,' she murmured, remembering her father's words just before they'd left. 'Whatever they recommend, Florence, you are to agree. Cost is of no importance. You hear me?'

'Thank you, Father,' she'd said and, impulsively, she'd stepped forward and kissed his cheek.

He'd looked startled for a moment, then patted her shoulder before turning away abruptly, but not before she'd seen tears glistening in his eyes.

Dr Harris's voice pulled her back to the present. 'I'll find out the name of the director there and—'

'I think you'll find,' Florrie said, 'that the doctor in charge is a Dr Ernst Hartmann.' Even after all these years, she was sure he'd still be there.

Dr Harris glanced at her, his voice tight as he asked, 'Have you been making your own enquiries?'

Florrie smiled and reassured him. 'No, but I met Dr Hartmann during the war. I worked with him. That was the name of the sanatorium where he'd worked, and where—' The heartache was still there, though not so sharp, when she remembered his words. 'Where he planned to return.'

Dr Harris's voice relaxed and he smiled again. 'Then you must have great faith in his abilities.'

Oh yes, she thought, I have. The only problem is: will he see us? Will he be willing to treat the boy he still thinks is his own son?

Forty-Nine

Florrie took a deep breath as she faced Emmi Bergamin. So, after all this time, she was being forced into doing what she should have done years ago. She was going to have to tell the truth.

She leaned forward and lowered her voice. 'Jacques does not know the truth about his birth. I – I know I should have told him before, but – well, I've been very cowardly. Does he need to know now? I really don't think this is a good time.'

The woman stared at her, a small, puzzled frown drawing her fine eyebrows together. The nurse was a pretty young woman and Florrie couldn't help feeling a flash of jealousy. Emmi Bergamin worked with Ernst every day. It was this young woman who was now his 'right hand'.

Slowly, the nurse shook her head. 'No. These papers are confidential. Only Dr Hartmann and his colleagues will see them, I promise.'

So, at last, Ernst would have to know the truth too. She would face his anger, she knew, but she was sure that he would not punish her by refusing to help her, by refusing to treat the boy who – at the moment – he believed to be his.

Florrie let out her breath and glanced towards the balcony. Jacques's head was lolling to one side. He appeared to be asleep. 'I will tell him,' she murmured. 'He has a right to know. But – not now. Not until . . .' She couldn't complete the sentence. She didn't want to face the fact that she might be forced to tell a dying boy a truth that he might not want to hear.

'I – am not – Jacques's natural mother,' she began in halting German, struggling now and then to find the right words. It had been sixteen years since she'd used the language, but as she explained she found that the words – and the explanation – came more readily. She could only hope and pray that when she had to tell Jacques, it would be as easy. But she doubted it.

Florrie went on, telling the sympathetic nurse about how her young brother had volunteered underage. How he'd fallen in love with a French girl and how, when he'd heard she was carrying his child, he'd tried to reach her.

'He arranged for a pal to do his sentry duty, but the man was killed and James was accused of desertion and – and court-martialled.'

Emmi's eyes widened.

Florrie went on, relating the rest of the tragic tale and how, eventually, she'd taken Jacques to England. The only thing she omitted to tell the girl was about her own love affair with Ernst Hartmann, though she did reveal that she'd worked alongside him during the war.

'So,' she said at last, 'there you have it. It was all done legally. Somewhere in a solicitor's vault in London there are the papers to prove it – and to prove what a coward I've been.'

Emmi finished writing her brief notes, looked up and

smiled. 'I don't think you've been cowardly at all. I think what you did was wonderful. What sort of life would the boy have had if you'd left him? He would never have survived – or if he had, he would have had a miserable existence.' She leaned forward a little and touched Florrie's hand. 'You saved his life and secured your family name. He is a Maltby, after all.'

Florrie nodded, tears of gratitude in her eyes for this young woman's understanding. But perhaps she was used to hearing all sorts of tales as she took down patients' family histories.

'And, I promise you, Jacques will not learn any of this until you are ready to tell him yourself.'

'Thank you.' Florrie's words were heartfelt.

'And now,' Emmi said briskly, standing up. 'I should take you to meet Dr Hartmann.' She smiled. 'He will be so pleased to see you again after all this time.'

Will he? Florrie was suddenly unsure and unusually nervous. For sixteen years she'd longed to see him again and, now that she was about to do so, her courage almost failed her. She was hoping for so much and didn't know if she could face disappointment.

Emmi went out onto the balcony and touched Jacques's shoulder gently. 'I'm so sorry to wake you, but we must go to see the doctor now.'

As he pulled himself up, he began to cough and scrabbled in his pocket for his handkerchief. The spasm over, Emmi led them from the room and along the corridor. This time they used the lift to travel back down to the ground floor. She led them through the hall and into the lounge area.

'This is where the patients can enjoy a relaxing time,' she explained, waving her hand to encompass the empty room. 'But of course, everyone is outside now enjoying the sunshine. And that,' she indicated an area in the corner of the large room, 'is the games room. Perhaps you play chess, yes?'

Jacques, still holding his handkerchief to his mouth, nodded.

Florrie glanced at him, knowing that he, like her, was thinking of the many games he'd played with Gervase. How sad that it had never been his grandfather who'd played the game with him. How much they'd both missed. She thought briefly of how Edgar's attitude had begun to change towards the boy since he'd learned of his illness. She shuddered. But would that tenuous bond be severed irrevocably when Edgar Maltby learned the truth?

They climbed a few steps and came to a door. Here, Emmi paused. 'This is the X-ray room, but it is also where Dr Hartmann has his office.' She knocked and, for the first time in sixteen years, Florrie heard his deep voice say, 'Come in.'

Emmi opened the door and went in, but then she stepped to one side, holding the door for Florrie and Jacques to enter. He looked up as they walked the length of the room towards him and then came round his desk, holding out both his hands.

'My dear Florence, how wonderful to see you again.' She put her hands into his and the old thrill surged through her at his touch. He raised her hands and gently brushed her fingers with his lips. 'As beautiful as ever,' he murmured. As he released her and turned his attention to Jacques, Florrie felt foolishly bereft, yet she managed to say quite steadily, 'This is Jacques.'

Of course he hadn't seen the sister's notes. She watched Ernst shake the boy's limp, slightly clammy

423

hand and say, 'Come and sit down – both of you – and I will explain what we are going to do.' She couldn't help wondering what Ernst must be thinking and feeling as he met for the first time the boy he believed to be his son.

Florrie scarcely took in the details of the room: the heavy desk and chairs, the glass panels on the walls, which lit up to enable the doctors to study the patients' X-rays. There were two switched on now, lighting up the negatives, the dark shadows of both lungs denoting a very sick patient. Florrie shuddered, praying she would not see such a picture of Jacques's thin body.

'Now, my boy,' Ernst's whole attention was on his patient. After his first warm greeting, it was as if Florrie were not even in the room. She gazed at him, drinking in the sight of him and hardly hearing what he was saying.

He'd aged over the years. The dark hair was still thick and smoothed back, but now it was liberally flecked with white. He was no longer clean-shaven, but had a small goatee beard and was wearing glasses. Deep lines of worry were etched into his face and his eyes had lost some of their brightness. That sparkling joy of living that she'd seen, even amidst the horror of the front-line hospital, was no longer there. He'd not put on any weight that she could see beneath the long white coat he wore. The longing to be held in his arms again flooded through her and she was sure he must hear her heart pounding. He was turning to her now and she almost put out her arms in expectation of his embrace.

'You'll be allowed to visit every afternoon if you wish, but not to enter the building again. You must meet Jacques outside on the veranda or on the sun terraces. After this first visit, we do not allow families to come into the building. It is for their own good.'

Florrie frowned. 'But – but how will I see you? I mean—' she added swiftly, conscious of the listening nurse. 'How will I know how he is? About his treatments and—?'

'Oh, I will see you. I will come to where you are staying.'

Her heart lifted and it was only with a supreme effort that she stopped herself from reaching for his hand and clasping it to her breast. She realized, with sudden startling clarity, that this was the reason for her restless behaviour. She'd been living in limbo, waiting only for a word, a sign from him, and she would have come running. But they'd parted in such bitterness and deceit.

And always there'd been the spectre of the fiancée waiting innocently back home in Switzerland.

But now, for her at least, it was as if they'd never been apart. As if all the intervening years had never happened. She could not hide her love for him from showing in her eyes. And she knew he could see it. He *must* see it. For a long moment he stared at her, then he turned his head away, cleared his throat and shuffled his papers.

'And, Jacques, you will not be permitted to mix with the other patients until I have had a chance to reach a proper diagnosis of your condition. You will have your meals in your room for the time being.'

Florrie could not prevent a little gasp of surprise and disappointment from escaping her lips. Ernst was like a stranger. He was speaking as if they'd only just met, as if they'd never shared the dangers and horror of the front-line hospital, as if they had never lain in each other's arms . . . Then she shook herself mentally. He was being professional. In front of Jacques and his nurse, he could be nothing else.

'Now,' he was saying briskly, yet not unkindly, 'say your "goodbyes" – no,' he added swiftly, as Florrie held out her arms to embrace the boy. 'No more hugs. I'm sorry, but until we know . . .'

Florrie and Jacques smiled a little uncertainly at each other as she tried to joke, 'We must do as we're told now, darling.'

'Go with the sister now, Jacques, and I'll see you in the morning.'

When the door had closed behind them, Florrie turned to Ernst and held out her hands. 'It's wonderful to see you again. How are you? How have you been all this time?'

After a moment's hesitation that Florrie couldn't miss, he took her hands in his. 'My dear, it's good to see you again, though I could wish it were in happier circumstances.'

'Yes,' she whispered, her eyes drinking in the sight of him. She touched a scar on his forehead, just above his left eyebrow, with the tip of her finger. 'When did that happen?'

'When Dr Johnson and Grace were killed. One or two of us were injured too.'

'I didn't know. It must have been deep to still be so visible.'

'There are some scars that will never fade.'

Hoarsely, she whispered, 'Broken hearts, for example?'

He shook his head sadly and, with a deep sigh, pulled her to him. 'Oh, my dear, I'm so sorry. I blame myself. I should never have—'

She put her finger on his lips to silence him. 'Shh,' she whispered. 'I was a big girl. I knew the score. None of us knew if there was ever going to be a tomorrow. We took our brief happiness where we could.' She put her arms around his neck and rested her cheek against his. 'But I've missed you so.'

Fifty

As she took the funicular back down the mountainside, she could still feel Ernst's arms around her, his breath on her neck. Reaching the exit, she walked a short distance along the road and found the pension easily.

'You must be Frau Maltby? I am Frau Schwarz-Hemmi.' The woman was welcoming and friendly and spoke only in Swiss German. She was plump and plainly dressed in a black skirt that reached her ankles and a white blouse. 'You are very welcome. I will show you to your room.' As she led the way up the stairs, she said over her shoulder, 'Most of our visitors are people with a relative in one of the sanatoriums.'

'You don't mind then?' Florrie asked. 'I mean – I thought perhaps you might be worried about infection.'

Frau Schwarz shrugged and waved her hand. 'Ah, some are, that's true. But I don't take the sick themselves. I have no facilities, you see, but I don't mind the relatives. They need somewhere to stay.' She paused and then asked kindly, 'Who is it you have brought?'

Florrie hesitated fractionally. Soon it would be time to tell the truth, but not now. There was no need for this woman to know. But, as she always had, she avoided calling him her son. Instead she said, 'My boy, Jacques. He's sixteen.'

The woman's face was sympathetic but she said no

more as she opened the bedroom door and stood aside for Florrie to enter.

The room was light and airy with light-blue painted panels on the walls, pictures, a patterned rug near the bed and white-painted furniture.

'We have running water in all the bedrooms,' Frau Schwarz said proudly, indicating the large washbasin in the corner of the room with a mirror above it.

'It's lovely,' Florrie said in German.

'I hope you will be comfortable,' Frau Schwarz said as she left. 'Dinner will be at seven o'clock.'

She found the dining room just before seven. There were four long windows giving plenty of light, carpet on the floor and a bracket clock on the wall. Each table was covered with a white cloth, in the centre of which stood a vase of flowers. The small tables were set for one or two, but were positioned close enough if the diners wished to converse. However, it would be easy, Florrie thought, to nod politely to the other guests, then avoid eye contact if one wished to sit quietly. As she entered the room, two other guests were already seated at separate tables.

'I'm Mrs Milner from Kent, England.' The woman spoke loudly, enunciating every word.

Florrie smiled and held out her hand. 'I'm English too. How do you do?'

The woman beamed. 'And this is Mr Petrov,' she said flapping her hand towards the gentleman sitting at a nearby table. She leaned forward as if confiding in Florrie, but did not lower her voice to say, 'He's Russian and can't speak a word of English, and I can't speak German or Russian, so we just smile and nod to each other.'

To demonstrate, she smiled coyly at the man and inclined her head. He was a tall man with broad shoulders and a thick beard and moustache that seemed to cover more than half his face. His mouth was invisible beneath the whiskers and only his eyes gave away any expression. As he rose from his seat and bowed his head towards Florrie in polite greeting, she noticed that his grey eyes were sad. It was an expression she was likely to see in many of the visitors to Davos, and she thought it a shame that such a beautiful setting should be the gathering place for such anguish. And yet, by coming here, surely some of them had hope for their loved ones. Just as she had for Jacques. Ernst would help him – she believed that with all her heart.

She held out her hand. 'I'm sorry I don't speak any Russian,' she said slowly in German. 'Only German and French.'

She heard Mrs Milner give a girlish cry of delight and the woman actually clapped her hands. 'Oh, how clever you are, you can speak to him.' Though she hadn't understood a word of what Florrie had said, she could see that the man had done so. He replied in German. 'And I too speak German, a little French and even less English, I regret to say. But your German is very good, madam. Come, let us sit down and partake of Frau Schwarz's excellent dinner.'

Florrie sat down at a separate table, but close enough not to appear stand-offish. Mrs Milner talked continuously, even between mouthfuls, whilst the other two listened politely. Most of her chatter sailed over the Russian's head, though Florrie was not so lucky!

'It's my husband who's ill,' she began. 'He's in the sanatorium just down the road from here, so I'm nice and close. And Mrs Schwarz,' she pronounced the name

'Short', 'is such a good, kind woman. But, oh my dear, there are so many sick here, aren't there? But do you know,' she leaned across the table and touched Florrie's hand, 'there are a lot of skiers too. That's a strange mixture, don't you think? The very sick and the very fit all coming to the same place? Of course, a lot of the pensions and the hotels won't take even the relatives of the sick. Don't you think that's unfair?'

'It must be very difficult for them,' Florrie murmured. 'I suppose they're worried that they might contract the disease.'

Mrs Milner gave an exaggerated sigh. 'I suppose you're right, dear. But we really have to be near our loved ones, don't we?'

'Of course,' Florrie nodded.

'And this gentleman, Mr Petrov, can you ask him why he's here?' She smiled brightly at the Russian. 'I don't think he's a sportsman, do you?' she added, assessing the middle-aged, round-shouldered, bulky figure of their dinner companion.

Florrie hid her smile. Phrasing her question politely, she said, 'Mrs Milner is asking if you are here for the sport, or if you have someone in one of the sanatoriums?'

For a brief moment there was a spark in the dull eyes, as he exchanged an amused glance with Florrie, but it was gone in an instant as he said in a voice that was heavy with sadness and halting as he fought to find the right words, 'It is my daughter who is ill. She has been here a year and I cannot visit often. It is too far and I have to work long hours to pay for her treatment.'

'I'm so sorry,' Florrie said huskily.

'What's he say?' Mrs Milner tapped her arm impatiently.

'His daughter is here for treatment.'

'How old is she?' the woman demanded.

Florrie repeated the question.

'Nineteen.' He shook his head sadly. 'So young and she is all I have. Her mother died when she was born.'

'What's he say?'

Now the questions and answers continued throughout the remainder of the meal, though Florrie edited some of the man's answers. She'd quickly recognized Mrs Milner as a gossip. Good-natured and good-hearted though she undoubtedly was, the woman would prattle to anyone and everyone.

As soon as she could, Florrie excused herself on the grounds of tiredness after the long journey and went to her room. Closing the door behind her, she leaned against it for a moment and breathed a sigh of relief.

The following morning, Florrie breakfasted early before either of the other two guests in the pension made an appearance. The day was bright and sunny and, whilst she knew she couldn't visit the sanatorium until afternoon, she wasn't going to sit indoors all day when such marvellous scenery awaited her. Dressed in hat, coat, gloves and sensible walking shoes, she left the pension and walked along the main street. Davos was set in a valley, with mountains rising on either side.

She set off along the road, taking a path into the trees just behind the pension and walked towards Davos Dorf, following the winding trail and smiling as she heard the distant sound of cowbells. It was cool and shady beneath the trees and she tracked down the sound of rushing water, coming upon a stream bubbling over boulders and rushing on down the stony bed into the valley. She dabbled her fingers in the water, revelling in its clear, clean freshness.

Florrie sat a while beside the stream. It was so tranquil, the only sounds around her the babbling water and the clanging cowbells. She felt herself relax a little, but the anxiety over Jacques's health could never leave her, and now there was the growing fear that had been present ever since she'd decided to bring him to Davos.

What was Ernst's reaction going to be when he learned the truth?

Despite the invigorating walk in the clear, pure air, Florrie was anxious to return to the sanatorium. She wanted to know how Jacques was. It was the first time since his illness had been diagnosed by the consultant physician in London that she'd been separated from him, and she hated not knowing how he was every minute of the day – and the night too, if truth be told. And she could not deny that she wanted to see Ernst again.

After a light lunch at the pension, she took the funicular up the mountain and walked the few yards to the gracious building. The communal veranda at ground level was crowded with day-beds, most of them occupied by patients. A few walked slowly up and down on the two levels of grass sun terraces. Florrie scanned the faces, but Jacques was not amongst them, so she climbed the steps towards the main entrance. As she was about to step into the hallway, she heard someone calling her name.

'Frau Maltby, you cannot go in.' She turned to see Hans Meyer hurrying towards her across the terrace.

'Ah, yes. I remember now. How foolish of me.'

He looked at her with sympathetic kindness. 'It is only natural you want to see your son.'

'You're with your wife? She's out here on the terrace?'

'Sadly, no. She – she is in her room.' His voice dropped and shook a little. 'She is very ill. She suffered a very bad haemorrhage last night. They want me to take her home – but she is too sick to travel now. She – she will die here.'

'Oh, Herr Meyer, I'm so sorry.' Impulsively, Florrie touched his arm. 'Is there no hope?'

He shook his head, unable to speak for a moment.

'And they won't let you see her?' She was appalled to think that this nice man was being kept away from his dying wife.

'Oh yes, but I have just come out for a breath of this fine air. It is very – how do you say – harrowing to sit there. And she is sleeping just now.' He pulled in a deep breath and tried to smile, despite the terrible sadness that was weighing him down. 'But you – we must get someone to help you find your son.' He waved behind him towards the open-air terrace. 'There is a nurse down there. Come with me. She will help you.'

Florrie turned and followed him back down the steps.

As they approached the nurse who was attending to one of the patients lying on a bed chair in the sunlight, Hans Meyer said, 'Excuse me, Nurse, Frau Maltby has come to see her son. Is that possible?'

As the woman straightened up, Florrie saw that it was Sister Bergamin. She smiled as she greeted Florrie. 'Good afternoon, Frau Maltby. Jacques is with the doctor now. Dr Hartmann is carrying out all the usual tests for a new arrival and arranging X-rays and so on. I'm afraid it won't be possible for you to see your boy today. It is best that we don't interrupt the tests.'

Though disappointment flooded through her at not being able to see not only Jacques but Ernst also, Florrie nodded. 'How is he?'

'A little better this morning. He slept well last night after the journey and he has been out on the balcony of his room all morning.' She waved her arm to encompass the glorious scenery all around them. 'I'm sure our wonderful air will soon begin to work its magic.'

'So – like me, you have the rest of the day to fill, yes?' Hans Meyer said.

'So it seems,' Florrie murmured.

'Then will you permit me to take you to a little cafe I know for afternoon tea?'

Florrie forced a smile. 'That would be very nice.'

He gave an old-fashioned courtly bow and held out his arm. She took it and together they walked back towards the funicular, but not before she'd glanced towards the windows of the X-ray room. Jacques was in there with Ernst and how she longed to be with them both.

Fifty-One

As they began to descend in the cabin, Florrie sighed. 'It really is a beautiful place.'

'It is, and it seems so sad that there is so much sickness here.'

'I know what you mean – it's a sort of cruel irony, isn't it?'

'Yes, yes – that is what I mean.'

'But it's becoming a centre for sports too, so a woman at the pension where I'm staying was telling me.'

Hans Meyer smiled, though the sadness never left his eyes. 'Yes, it is good to see the young ones enjoying themselves, but, like you say, it is a strange mix.'

He took her to a restaurant in one of the smart hotels and ordered afternoon tea. 'Like you have in England, yes?' he teased her gently.

Florrie laughed. 'Almost.'

They chatted, though now and again they fell into silence, but the long pauses were companionable. There was no compulsion to speak if they didn't feel like it. There was a mutual understanding of the personal anxiety that was never very far away.

As they rose to leave, Hans said, 'Tomorrow morning, will you walk with me? May I suggest we take a carriage to Davoser See and walk around the lake? We saw it from the train.'

He touched her arm. 'We will visit the sanatorium in the afternoon. By then, they may have some news about your son. And perhaps you will be able to see him.'

Florrie smiled weakly and nodded. 'Perhaps,' she whispered, not daring to hope too much.

The morning was bright and clear, but cooler.

'Wrap up well, my dear,' Frau Schwarz said as she saw Florrie's sturdy shoes and the walking stick.

'I will, Frau Schwarz-Hemmi.'

The woman smiled. ' "Frau Schwarz" will do,' she said. ' "Hemmi" was my maiden name. It is the tradition in Switzerland that when a woman marries she adds her maiden name to her husband's. My husband was "Schwarz".' Her face fell. 'He died two years ago.'

'I'm sorry.' There was a slight pause before Florrie asked. 'Have you any family? Children?'

The woman's face lit up again. 'Oh yes. Two sons. They live in Geneva. They're doing very well,' she added with a note of pride in her tone.

'So – they're called Schwarz-Hemmi?'

'Oh no. What a mouthful that would become if their wives then added on their birth names. It could go on forever.' Frau Schwarz laughed aloud at the thought. 'No, no, the children of a marriage just take their father's surname, though the father can be known by the double name. My husband could have been Schwarz-Hemmi if he'd wished, but he preferred to keep it short, so I always say my name is just Frau Schwarz. Do you see now?'

Florrie laughed. 'I think so. The custom must be very helpful for anyone tracing their family history.'

'Yes, yes, it must be. I'd never thought of it before, but I see what you mean.'

There was a knock at the door and Frau Schwarz opened it to see Hans Meyer standing there.

'Enjoy your walk,' she said cheerfully as the two set out.

They took a carriage to beyond Davos Dorf and alighted near the lake. The sharp air stung Florrie's cheeks as she tucked her hand through Hans Meyer's arm and matched her stride to his. The water of the lake was a smooth grey-blue and the path around its edge was covered with a sprinkling of snow.

Florrie closed her eyes and breathed in deeply. 'How fresh and clear the air is and how magnificent the autumn colours.'

'In a week or two it will be even more picturesque, with gold and browns and yet still with the dark green of the firs.'

They walked and talked, telling each other of their homes, their lives, but the shadow of their sick loved ones was always with them. They returned to their separate lodgings for lunch, but met again to ride up the funicular. They were quiet now, their pleasure in the morning gone as the weight of their shared anxiety descended once more.

As they approached the entrance, Sister Bergamin was standing on the top of the steps. It seemed she was waiting for them.

'Herr Meyer,' she said softly as they drew near. 'If you would like to come with me, I'll take you to your wife's room.'

Hans stood very still for a long moment. Florrie touched his arm gently, but couldn't find the words to express her feelings for him. They both knew instantly why the sister had been waiting for them. Eva was close to death. For a brief moment Hans grasped Florrie's hand, but he couldn't look at her. He moved away, his shoulders hunched and his footsteps leaden. With a heavy heart, Florrie watched him go.

When he was out of earshot, the sister said, 'You will find Jacques on the lower sun terrace this afternoon. His temperature is down this morning and Dr Hartmann wants him to get as much fresh air as possible. He is not to mix with the other patients yet and still takes his meals in his room. But he is on the terrace so that you can visit him.'

'May I see Dr Hartmann?' The words were out before she sought to check them. 'I mean – I want to ask him the results of the tests.'

'Of course. I will tell him you are here. Meanwhile,' she gestured towards the lower sun terrace and added firmly, 'Jacques is waiting for you.'

'Hello, darling.' Florrie forced a cheerful greeting. 'How are you feeling?'

He was lying on a bed chair, wearing his topcoat, a woolly hat and gloves, with warm blankets tucked tightly around him.

'D'you know, Mother, we have to sit outside all day? The whole day. And even if it rains we have to sit under the covered part or on our own balconies.' There was belligerence in his tone; he was feeling better this morning.

She was delighted to hear it, yet it amused her too. No one could ever deny he was a Maltby! She sat down on a chair beside him. 'It's for your own good, darling—'

' "For your own good" – that's all I ever seem to hear these days,' he muttered morosely. 'How long am I going to be here? I hate this place. And I hate *him*.'

'Who?' Florrie asked, but she knew the answer already and her heart began to thump painfully. That was the very last thing she wanted.

'Dr Hartmann.'

'How can you say that, Jacques? You hardly know him. And he's the one who's going to get you well again.'

'Really?' His tone was laced with sarcasm. He pulled his arm out from under his blanket and gestured towards the other patients lying nearby. 'Look at them all. He hasn't cured them, has he?'

'It takes a long time, but this sanatorium has a very good record here. That's why I – I chose it.' She bit her lip at the partial lie.

'Oh, I'm sure it has, but do you know why?'

'Because they cure people.'

'Some – yes. I'm sure they do. But the reason they don't record a lot of deaths here is because they send them home to die.'

Florrie stared at him. She was thinking of what Hans Meyer had said. As if reading her mind, Jacques said, 'They wanted to send Frau Meyer home, but she got too sick to travel, so she's going to die here. But if they can still travel, they ship them out. It's common sense, if you think about it. It would be harmful for their reputation to have a catalogue of deaths, wouldn't it?'

Florrie stared at him. 'Oh, Jacques, I'm sure you're wrong. Ernst – I mean, Dr Hartmann – wouldn't do such a thing.'

So intent on his theory was he that Jacques didn't seem to notice her slip of the tongue. She would have to be more careful, Florrie reminded herself. She plunged on, babbling to hide her mistake. 'It'll be because – if they can do no more for them – the patients will want to be with their own families when – when—'

'Well, you can think what you like, but that's what the other patients say. I can still talk to them, you know, out here in the open air.' He laughed wryly. 'Trouble is, if we're being sent home, we're not going to be sure if it's because we're cured or because there's no hope for us.'

Florrie sighed. How sad it was to see such bitterness and fear in the young boy. And worse still, she could think of nothing to contradict him. Ernst, she remembered bitterly, would do anything to safeguard his reputation. She gazed at the mountains across the valley, but today their beauty had turned sour.

Fifty-Two

'May I see Dr Hartmann?' Florrie asked the sister again as the afternoon of sitting out on the sun terrace came to an end.

'He has asked me to tell you that he will come to the pension this evening to tell you of his findings.' She turned to the boy. 'Now, Jacques, you must return to your room.'

'Can't I go into the dining room with all the others?'

'Not until Dr Hartmann says so.'

'Dr Hartmann – Dr Hartmann,' he muttered. 'I seem to hear nothing but that name.'

But Emmi Bergamin only smiled. 'Now, say "goodbye" to your mother. No physical contact,' she said sharply, as Florrie held out her arms to embrace Jacques. 'I'm sorry,' she added, softening. 'I know how hard it must be.'

As they were about to part at the foot of the entrance steps, Florrie asked, 'How is Frau Meyer?'

The sister stared at her for a moment and then shrugged and grimaced. 'Not good, I'm afraid. It's only a matter of time.'

'And – and Herr Meyer?'

'He will stay with her now.' She didn't add 'until the end', but Florrie knew that was what she meant.

As she went down the mountain in the cabin, she missed Hans Meyer's quiet companionship, and only the thought of facing Mrs Milner's inane chatter over the dinner table made her relish these moments of quiet solitude.

After dinner she watched the road from the window of the sitting room, waiting for the first sight of him. Her heart was beating foolishly like a young girl's. And then she saw him, striding along, purpose in every step as he came towards the place where she was waiting for him. For a fleeting moment, all her anxieties left her: the anguish of their parting, the loneliness of the years that had followed – even her fear for Jacques – all were swallowed by her joy at seeing Ernst and knowing that he was coming to see her and her alone.

She was trembling as she opened the door herself and led him into the sitting room. Mercifully, they could be alone.

She turned to face him and held out her hands to him. After a moment's hesitation, he took them. The warmth of his touch sent a thrill coursing through her. The years between had not lessened her desire for him. They sat down side by side, staring at each other.

'You haven't changed at all,' he murmured. 'You're still just as beautiful.'

'Why did you never write? Not once?' she whispered.

He sighed and shook his head, avoiding her direct gaze. 'It – wouldn't have been right.'

'Because of your wife, you mean? I take it you married your fiancée?'

'Yes,' he said hoarsely.

'And?'

'And – what?' He met her gaze once more, but now his eyes were wary.

Florrie lifted her shoulders. 'Have you any children?'

He hesitated before being forced to reply. 'Yes. Three. Two boys and a girl.'

It felt like a betrayal. It was one thing to make a suitable marriage – wasn't that exactly what her own father had wanted her to do? But to have children, to raise a family with another woman, after everything he'd said to her, was something else. So that was why he'd never written to her, had never contacted her, had never wanted to carry on their love affair, even though he'd felt obliged to honour his promise to another woman. Hadn't he realized that he'd only had to call and she'd have come running? She would willingly have become his mistress. She'd have been content to live nearby quietly and unobtrusively. She was finding now that there were many English people living in Davos. They were like a community within a community. They even had their own church, St Luke's. No one need ever have known about their secret life. But it was not what he'd wanted. That was becoming obvious.

'So – until I contacted you about – about Jacques – you'd forgotten all about me.'

He squeezed her hands. 'I have never forgotten you. There has never been a day that has gone by that I haven't thought about you. But it was not meant to be. Our love grew out of a terrible time, a time when we never knew if there was to be a tomorrow for us. We lived with danger and death all around us. We – we snatched at our happiness. But the real world – *our* real world – awaited us back home. If we survived. And we did.'

'You regret everything that happened between us?'

He held her hands tighter. 'No, never. I should, but I don't.'

'And your wife? She – she knows about me?'

'Monika? Of course not. No one knows.'

He'd called Florrie 'the love of his life' and yet he'd never spoken of her – to anyone. No doubt he'd tried to forget her, along with the horror of the trenches. She didn't believe that there was any regret.

She swallowed, suddenly feeling very foolish. Somewhere, deep down, she'd hoped this visit would rekindle their love; a love so strong that even the years in between, his wife and family, would all fade into nothingness before the strength of their passion. But it was not to be.

'You want to know about Jacques?' He was bringing her back to the present, back to painful reality.

'Of course,' she whispered hoarsely.

'I'm afraid today there is nothing much I can tell you. I still have more tests to do and I must observe him for several days before I know.'

'Can't you tell me *anything*? Can't you give me some hope?'

Ernst smiled – that funny, lopsided smile that twisted her heart. 'There's always hope. Especially here in Davos.'

Briefly, Hans Meyer's face came into her mind. There was no hope for him, not now. But she remained silent. Ernst had unshakeable faith in his vocation. He'd given his life to it – and hers. He'd sacrificed their love for his career, for his reputation and to honour his promise to the girl he'd left behind.

Slowly she withdrew her hands from his grasp.

'Thank you for coming to see me,' she said stiffly. 'I realize how busy you are.'

Ernst shrugged, and it seemed the lines on his face deepened. 'Not so busy as we used to be. The economic

situation has meant we don't get so many patients now.'
He smiled wryly. 'People are still sick, but they cannot
afford to come here. Even the rich are feeling the – how
do you say – the pinch? And besides, I prefer to visit
the relatives where they are staying. Too many prying
eyes and listening ears at the sanatorium. The patients
seem to find out everything that goes on. But as for
Jacques, we have already put him on a strict daily
regime. Plenty of fresh air, a little exercise – there are
some beautiful walks in the mountains – good food,
especially milk. Lots of milk. There's every reason to be
hopeful, my dear.'

Fervently she prayed there was hope for Jacques, for
now she knew there was none for her.

It wasn't until he'd left that she realized he'd never
mentioned reading the notes that the sister had made.
The notes that would tell him the truth about Jacques.

Standing on the upper sun terrace at the sanatorium the
following afternoon, Florrie glanced up at the first-floor
windows.

'Jacques, do you know which is Frau Meyer's room?'

'Who? Oh, the wife of the man we met on the train?
No – but it doesn't matter now. I think she died last
night.'

Florrie looked down at her son. 'Who told you?'

'No one. They don't broadcast any deaths, Mother.'

'So how—'

'I was awake in the night and I heard a lot of scuffling. I peeped out of my door and saw them carrying
a coffin out of a room at the far end of the corridor.
They took it down in the lift. I expect it was being taken

to the cellars. They have a tunnel to the funicular, you know.'

Florrie shook her head. 'No, I didn't know.'

'That's how they take the dead out, and at night so no one knows.'

'Have you seen Herr Meyer?'

Jacques shook his head. He leaned back and closed his eyes. He wanted to rest, so Florrie tiptoed away. She went in search of Sister Bergamin, but knew she mustn't go into the building. She paused near the steps leading up to the covered communal balcony.

'You look a little lost,' one of the patients lying on his day-bed near the steps spoke to her in German.

'I was just wondering if you had seen Herr Meyer this morning.'

'Ah, the man whose wife died last night?'

So, Florrie thought, the patients were not supposed to know when there had been a death, but they all did. She remembered Ernst's words the previous evening.

'No, I haven't seen him this morning,' the man went on. 'But I believe he stayed here the remainder of the night after she – well, afterwards. He'll no doubt be making arrangements. It's a sad thing for our relatives to have to do.' He lapsed into silence.

Gently, Florrie said, 'How long have you been here?'

The man wrinkled his forehead. 'A year, I think.'

'No, you haven't,' the patient lying next to him said. 'You were here when I got here and I've been here fourteen months.'

'Oh yes. I forget,' the first man smiled. 'One loses track of time here.'

The front door opened and Florrie looked up to see Herr Meyer emerge. His face was grey with fatigue, his shoulders hunched with sorrow. He came down the steps towards her, but he didn't appear to notice her until she touched his arm.

'Herr Meyer, I'm so very sorry.'

He blinked and looked round at her. 'Ah, Frau Maltby. Thank you. It has been a difficult time, but Eva is at peace now.'

Tactfully, Florrie drew him out of earshot of the other patients. 'You – you're taking her home?'

He nodded. 'Yes, all arrangements have been made. It will be very expensive, but she would like to be buried at home, amongst her family. If – if I don't take her home, she will be cremated here. I don't want her burned. I – I know it's the sensible thing, but I can't bear to think of it.' Tears filled his eyes and ran down his cheeks. Feeling helpless, Florrie patted his arm. 'You must do whatever you feel best – for both of you.'

Fear clutched at her heart. What if she had to make the same dreadful decision over Jacques?

'What makes it worse, dear Frau Maltby, is that I have just been presented with a bill for the cost of burning all her possessions, all the bed linen – even the mattress she died on – and for fumigating the room before another patient can occupy it.'

'Oh, how dreadful!' Florrie was appalled. It seemed heartless and yet she could understand it. There were cases of mis-diagnosis. It would be dreadful if a patient who hadn't actually got the disease already were to contract it by occupying a room where someone had died of it. But she couldn't say all this to the poor man. It was the hope she was still clinging to – that perhaps Jacques hadn't really got tuberculosis. That was why she was prepared to see him kept apart from the other patients – and even from meeting her, other than in the open air – until Ernst had carried out all the tests.

She put her arm through Herr Meyer's. 'Come, I'll go back to your lodgings with you. Is there anything I can do to help you?'

He covered her hand with his own. 'Dear lady, how kind you are. But I fear there is nothing anyone can do. Not now.'

Florrie awoke the following morning to find that snow had fallen during the night. She was filled with a mixture of apprehension and delight. Fear because she might not be able to travel up the funicular, and joy because the scenery that had been beautiful before was now breathtaking.

But she found that a light covering of snow did not bring life to a halt in a land where the residents were used to it. She travelled up the funicular, half-expecting that she'd not be allowed to see Jacques until the afternoon. No doubt he'd be on his balcony and out of bounds to her. But she found him on the covered veranda on the ground floor, sitting a little apart from the other patients, but still near enough to engage in conversation.

'They're changing the beds, Mother,' he greeted her with a smile. 'They do it every day. *Every* day! Can you imagine the work that would cause Beth and the others if we did that at home?'

Florrie, heartened to see him more cheerful today, laughed, thinking of the clouds of steam, red hands and sweating faces that 'wash day' caused their servants. And then she remembered the laundering of bedding that Ernst had insisted be done in the field ambulance, even when the guns pounded and shells burst nearby. No doubt it was here at the sanatorium as a young doctor that he'd learned the value of strict hygiene.

There were few other visitors, but Florrie braved the cold to sit for an hour or so with Jacques. Snowflakes danced on the breeze and settled on the blankets covering the patients.

The man sitting a few feet away from Jacques called to her, 'Good morning, Mrs Maltby. I'm Philip Henderson from Yorkshire. I wish I could shake your hand, but it's not allowed.'

Florrie smiled at him, pleased to hear another English voice. Though Jacques could speak both French and German, it would be less taxing for him, she felt, to be able to chat in his native tongue.

'I'm pleased to meet you, Mr Henderson.' She hesitated to ask questions, not knowing how ill the man was or what his prospects were. He didn't look too sick – not like some of the others. Further along the veranda two women sat side by side and one, Florrie thought, looked dreadfully ill. Her thin face was flushed as if she was feverish and her cheekbones were sharp beneath the paper-thin skin. Her hands, when she took them out briefly from beneath the covers, looked skeletal. But Philip Henderson, a man of fifty or so, Florrie guessed, had a lightly tanned skin. His grey eyes did not yet have the hopeless, defeated look. He was tall and thin, but not unhealthily so. His next words explained. 'Like your son, Mrs Maltby, I'm a recent arrival and still awaiting a diagnosis. That's why me an' Jacques here can't sit with the rest of 'em.' He winked saucily at her. 'Still, I don't mind if it gives me a chance to talk to a pretty lady.' He laughed, but the joyful sound turned into a cough that was altogether different – a juicy splutter that had him reaching for his handkerchief to hold to his mouth. When the spasm had passed, he lay back for a moment and closed his eyes as if exhausted. She could hear his rasping, painful breathing and she shuddered inwardly, fearing that the poor man was sicker than she'd thought. The sound reminded her of the gas victims she'd nursed. And there'd been little hope for most of them.

A few moments later, he raised his head again. 'By 'eck, it's a bugger – this!'

Florrie pretended she hadn't heard his muttered oath, but silently she agreed with him wholeheartedly.

She turned her attention back to Jacques but, with a glance, she included Philip Henderson in her question. 'What did you have for breakfast?'

'It was huge,' Jacques said. 'I couldn't eat it all. Oatmeal, yoghurt, scrambled eggs and cold meats, cheese and fruits and then coffee or tea.'

'And dinner last night was seven courses, would you believe?' Philip, feeling better, put in. 'Wonderful food, mind you, even better than my missis cooks. But don't tell 'er I said so.'

'Is she here with you?'

The man's eyes clouded. 'No, we couldn't afford for 'er to be here an' all.' He lapsed into silence again, while Jacques returned to the subject of food.

'We had soup, Mother, then—' he hesitated. 'What was next, Mr Henderson?'

'Do call me Philip, young feller, and you too, luv. We're all in the same boat out here. Might as well be friendly.' He wrinkled his forehead, trying to recall the previous evening's fare. 'Stuffed tomatoes, wasn't it?'

'Yes – yes, that's right. Then roast beef with loads of vegetables.'

'No Yorkshire pudding, though,' Philip added indignantly. 'How can you have roast beef and no Yorkshires?'

Florrie smiled. 'Then what?'

'Roast goose—'

'*Two* roast dishes?' Florrie exclaimed.

'Then apple pie followed by cheese and biscuits.'

'That's only six,' Florrie said as she counted the courses.

'Well, there was fruit and coffee after that, so I suppose that counts as the seventh.'

'And chocolate. Don't forget the chocolate,' Philip teased. 'Made a right pig of 'imself, so I heard. Don't know where he put it all after that huge meal.'

Florrie laughed. 'Jacques can always make room for chocolate.'

There was a moment's pause before Jacques said more seriously, 'I had an examination with the doctor today. He taps you – well, almost thumps you at times – all over your back and then your chest. Then he listens with his stethoscope and you have to take deep breaths and cough every so often.'

'Did he – say anything?' Florrie had to ask, even though she was fearful of the answer.

Jacques shrugged. 'Not to me. He said things to Sister Bergamin and she wrote it down, but it was all medical jargon. I couldn't understand a word. Then I had to have X-rays. I'm to have more in a week's time.'

'For comparison?' Florrie asked, but Jacques only shrugged. 'Dunno. But Sister Bergamin's taught me how to take my own temperature several times a day and keep a note of it.'

A movement in the doorway caught Florrie's eye and she glanced up to see Ernst Hartmann come out onto the veranda. He was wearing his white surgical coat this morning and moved amongst the patients, talking to each one of them in turn, unhurried and as dedicated as she remembered. He made each patient feel that they were his only concern. It was a gift, she mused, as she watched him.

He came towards them and though he nodded briefly to her, Florrie could see that his attention was still focused on his patients. When he'd spoken to Philip, he came to stand near Jacques. 'How are you feeling today?'

'A little better, thank you, Dr Hartmann. My breathing feels easier.'

Ernst nodded. 'That's a very good sign, especially as you have only been here a matter of days.'

At last, he turned to Florrie. 'Mrs Maltby, it is almost lunchtime and Jacques will have to return to his room. It's also time he took his temperature again.' He gave a curt little bow that included both Jacques and Philip Henderson, and then turned and walked back along the veranda.

'I think,' Florrie murmured, 'I've been dismissed.'

'Shouldn't let it worry you, luv,' Philip said cheerfully, heaving himself to his feet. 'He's a moody bloke. Clever, mark you – I'll not deny that. But you never know how you have him from one day to the next.'

Florrie's gaze still followed Ernst's retreating figure.

Oh, how true that was and didn't she know it! But she was sure too that he still hadn't fully read the sister's notes. She rather feared his mood would be all too easy to read then.

Fifty-Three

Since Herr Meyer's departure, Florrie had felt very much alone. She avoided Mrs Milner as much as possible. The Russian had left, so there were only the two of them in the pension for the moment.

'How is your husband?' Florrie felt impelled to ask out of politeness.

'A little better today,' Mrs Milner answered. 'His doctor is very pleased with him.' She leaned towards Florrie. 'I heard that your son's doctor came to visit you here. That was very kind. Does he do that for all his patients?'

'I – I don't know. Perhaps. He's a very dedicated doctor.'

'They all are.' Mrs Milner was still eyeing her with something like suspicion. 'But not all of them visit the relatives where they're staying.'

Though she longed to give the woman some explanation, Florrie was silent. Mrs Milner was a gossip and not to be trusted. Whatever she told her, the woman would likely make more of it. Even so, Florrie couldn't help hoping that Ernst would visit her again – and not just to tell her about Jacques. She was angry with herself. Why, when he had made it so obvious, did she still hanker after a kind word from him, the touch of his hand?

You're pathetic, she told herself. Though she'd

always been rebellious and strong-minded, where Ernst was concerned she was weak. She despised herself for it, yet still she yearned to be near him.

After dinner, the two women sat together in the lounge, Florrie in the window seat, watching the road. But Ernst didn't come. By ten o'clock, when she could stand Mrs Milner's inane chatter no longer, Florrie excused herself and retired to her room. But she spent a restless night and awoke the following morning heavy-eyed and with a slight headache.

She would go for yet another lonely walk, she told herself. At least the sharp, clean air would clear her head.

To her surprise, as she was finishing breakfast alone – Mrs Milner did not rise until after nine o'clock – Frau Schwarz showed Ernst into the room. Florrie glanced up, her heart thumping when she saw the serious – almost angry – expression on his face.

She half-rose. 'What is it? Is it Jacques?'

'Yes – and no.'

'What – what do you mean?'

'Come, we will go out. I have a morning off. I will take you up the new Parsenn that has opened recently.' He smiled, but it did not reach his eyes. He was still angry. Florrie was afraid. Was this how he looked when he had to tell a relative that there was nothing he could do for the patient? Is that what he had to tell her now? She was trembling as she put on her hat and coat.

As they walked side by side, Ernst said nothing. She longed to question him. The suspense was unbearable, but they needed to be somewhere secluded, somewhere quiet, where he could take her hands and gently tell her the worst . . . A lump rose in her throat. Oh, Jacques, darling Jacques, surely she wasn't to lose him too?

He took her to Davos Dorf to the Parsenn cable railway.

'We'll only be going up in the car as far as what's known as Mittelstation,' he explained. 'The upper section is almost complete, but it isn't due to be opened until December. If you're still here,' his black mood lifted for a moment and he actually smiled, 'I'll bring you to travel right to the Weissfluhjoch station at the very top.'

Still the same Ernst, Florrie thought, with his unpredictable temperament: sunshine one minute and thunder clouds the next.

The red railcar glided smoothly upwards and in ten minutes they were stepping out into the stone-built station and then onto the mountainside.

Ernst swept his arm in a wide arc. 'Is it not beautiful, this homeland of mine?'

'Yes – yes, Ernst, it is,' Florrie said flatly, but this morning she could take no joy in the magnificent panorama before her. Tears blurred her vision. Why didn't he tell her? She could hardly bear the suspense.

'We can climb to the top, if you like,' he offered, 'though the path is rough and stony and there are still workmen up there. It may be dangerous – but then you were never one to shy away from danger, were you?'

Her nerves were in shreds. She couldn't stand it any longer. 'Ernst, what is it you want to say to me?'

He didn't answer at once, but led the way along a narrow pathway for a short distance until they came to a rock. They sat down, side by side, looking out over the valley below them. She could see the lake where she'd walked with Hans Meyer and then beyond it, the darkness of the forests climbing halfway up the mountainside giving way to green swathes, then bare rock and finally the snow-capped summits, sharp against the blue sky.

'Tell me,' she whispered.

He turned to face her, but there was no sympathy in his eyes, no gentle touch.

'How could you do that to me, Florence? After all that we had meant to each other? How could you let me go on thinking – all these years – that I had a son by you?'

She lifted her chin higher and defiance flashed in her eyes. 'And how could you make love to me, make all those sweet promises, when you had a fiancée waiting for you at home?'

He had the grace to look ashamed and glanced away. There was a long silence between them before he said heavily, 'So, it was revenge, was it? A game of – how do you say it – tit for tat?'

'No, it wasn't – at least—' It was time for honesty, an end to all the lies and deceit. 'At first it wasn't. I was going to tell you everything, but when you wouldn't give me a chance, when you blurted out that you were to be married after the war, well, then . . .'

She bowed her head. Even if she'd allowed him to believe it at first, there was no excuse for having let bitterness and disappointment keep her silent all these years.

'I see,' he said flatly, his tone giving nothing away. Then he sighed heavily. 'I was wrong. I'm sorry. You were only young and I should not have taken advantage of you.'

'You didn't.' Florrie sought his hand and held it. He

did not pull away. Huskily, she said, 'I wanted it as much as you did. More, probably. I thought at last I had found true love. I thought you were the love of my life. I believed you when you said you loved me.'

He squeezed her hand and groaned. 'Oh, Florence. I did – I still do. I meant every word I said. And sometimes, I believed that perhaps – when the war was over – I could come back home, explain everything to Monika, she would release me, and we – you and I – could have been together. But it was only a foolish dream of something that could never be. When you came back to the field hospital with the child in your arms, I – I panicked. I knew I would be in disgrace. I realized just how much I had to lose. Not only the humiliation of being sent home from the Front, where I felt – no, I knew – I was doing so much good, but also the thought that they would get to know at home. Monika and her father would hear and my future would be in ruins.'

Florrie frowned. 'Why? Oh, I realize he would have made her break the engagement, but surely you'd still have had a career?'

'Maybe, but not the one I wanted. Not here in Davos. Monika's father was a leading figure in the town. He'd invested money in the building of the sanatorium along with my own father. They were partners, but he would not have hesitated to have had me dismissed from my post, and without any kind of reference. I would have been hard pressed to have found a position anywhere in Switzerland.'

They sat side by side, still holding hands, but in silence now. There was nothing left to say to each other. They'd both been at fault.

Florrie sighed and suddenly, amidst the splendour of

458

the mountains, it was as if a great weight had been lifted from her heart. She was free from the bitterness and resentment she'd carried for years. And strangely, from the hope too. She squared her shoulders. It was time to start afresh. She'd tell Jacques everything, and all the family too, when she got back home. Since hearing of Jacques's illness, there'd been a noticeable change in her father's attitude towards the boy. Perhaps, faced with the thought that he might lose him, Edgar had been forced to examine his true feelings for his grandson. She was sure that now was the time that he would accept the truth. As for Augusta, Florrie had always wondered if she guessed more than she ever divulged

For a moment, her mind was wandering, but it was brought back sharply to the present by Ernst's voice. 'I did love you, Florence. Please believe me. I still do and I always will, but it was a passion born amidst horror and tragedy and we grasped at whatever happiness we could. Just as your brother did. But he paid the ultimate price.'

Florrie nodded, unable to speak. Now she just felt a deep sadness for a love that was lost, for what might have been, but never could be. And she had to face it now with as much fortitude and bravery as she'd faced everything else in her life. It was a love that was never meant to be.

'And Monika,' she asked softly at last. 'Do you love her?'

'Yes, I do. But in a very different way. It's a gentle kind of love. Because of her, I have the life I always wanted. The life I still want. And – she's the mother of my children.'

She turned to look at him, searching his face. He smiled – a little sadly – as his gaze met hers. 'You thought I was too,' she reminded him softly.

'That's true,' he admitted. 'But I could never have acknowledged an illegitimate child.'

So, now she had the whole truth. His career, his standing in the community of his home town, meant more to him than anything else. More to him than his love for her. She realized now, with sorrow, that he was not the man she'd thought he was.

Unbidden, Gervase's face came into her mind. The man who'd risked his reputation to rescue her from prison and his life to try and save her brother, and who'd selflessly offered to marry her to give a name to the child he thought to be hers. Tears came to her eyes, but they were not now for the man beside her, but for the wonderful, caring, loving man she'd taken so much for granted all their lives.

She leaned forward and gently kissed Ernst's cheek. It was a kiss of goodbye, tinged with regret for what might have been, but, in a way, she was released at last from the heartache. She too would always love him – in a way. But it was not the way she wanted to love and be loved now. Their time together had been heady and exciting. Fraught with the danger of discovery and the closeness of death, it was a passion that had burned itself out, a love that could not stand the test of ordinary, everyday life. A brief affair that had no future.

'I'm sorry,' she whispered, 'that I didn't tell you the truth about Jacques sooner. I'm glad you know now, but I'm ashamed that it took his illness to bring me here.'

Ernst nodded.

There was a long silence between them before she

asked tentatively. 'About Jacques? Have you – any news for me?'

He squeezed her hand. 'I don't want to say too much yet. I don't want to give you false hope.'

'You mean – you mean you can cure him?'

Despite his warning, hope leapt in her heart.

'It might – and I repeat *might* – not even be tuberculosis.'

'Might not—? But he's so ill. That dreadful cough. He's had it for months. And – and the doctor in England was so sure.'

Ernst lifted his shoulders. 'It is sometimes difficult to diagnose,' he said diplomatically. 'Particularly if you are not a specialist in the disease.'

Now tears flowed down her face. He drew her into his arms and she buried her face against his chest. He'd never seen this brave, passionate, wonderful girl weep before, but now – with only a glimmer of hope – she could not stem the flood. He stroked her hair and sighed as he gazed out across the valley to the mountains beyond and wondered silently, for the first time, if he'd been right to follow the path he'd chosen. He had all that he thought he'd ever wanted. But at what cost? Just what had he sacrificed to get it? He would never know.

As she became calmer, he drew her to her feet. He smoothed back the hair from her face and gently touched the faint scar she still bore. Then he kissed her gently on the mouth. His, too, was a farewell kiss. There was no turning back the years.

'Like I say, Florence, I am hopeful – very hopeful – but I must be certain. And that may take days, possibly weeks. But, please, not a word to Jacques – or to anyone – until I am sure. You promise?'

She nodded and whispered, 'I promise.'

Fifty-Four

Time hung heavily for Florrie. She took a walk each morning, towards Dorf or in the opposite direction, walking by the river. Sometimes she climbed the hills and found a seat to rest on and look out over the valley. But she was lonely and anxious. There was still no word from Ernst about Jacques's condition. Since that day on the Parsenn when he'd given her a tiny glimmer of hope, he'd said nothing and already it was the end of October and they'd been here over six weeks. She'd scarcely seen him since that day.

She wrote home every week, trying to keep her letters cheerful and hopeful, but it was increasingly difficult. And answering Gervase's concerned and caring letters was almost impossible. She knew her replies were stilted and formal. He'd even offered to come out to stay with her to keep her company, but she'd written back at once to refuse.

The last person she wanted out here was Gervase.

And yet she began to think of his kind, craggy face with longing. She badly needed a friend at this moment and he – more than anyone except perhaps Isobel – had always been her friend.

On Sunday evenings she walked to St Luke's, the English church, to attend the five o'clock service. She found comfort in the friendliness of the other English residents and visitors there. One evening in early November, as she returned for her evening meal, she was surprised to see Ernst waiting for her outside the pension.

Her heart leapt in fear, but as she approached him she could see through the gloom of the winter's evening that he was smiling. He held out his hands to her. 'I have good news for you, my dear,' he said at once.

'Oh, come in – come inside. I'm sure Frau Schwarz won't mind . . .' She led him to the communal sitting room, removing her gloves and coat. They sat down as she looked at him expectantly.

'We have monitored his temperature, his pulse and his weight carefully during the weeks he has been here. I have listened to his lungs almost every day. There is evidence of a severe lung infection—'

Florrie gasped and her eyes widened. He'd said 'good news'.

'But I have also analysed his blood and made a microscopic analysis of his sputum and he's had a series of X-rays. My dear Florence, there is no sign of tuberculosis.'

'Oh, Ernst—' She clasped her hands together, tears running down her face. 'Thank you, thank you.'

He held her for a few moments whilst she wept tears of joy and relief. She eased herself from his comforting arms and accepted the white handkerchief that he offered.

'So, this lung infection? What is it?'

'I think it is a congestion that he has not been able to shake off, and he is suffering from asthma because of it. But don't blame your doctors in England, I beg you. Mis-diagnosis of consumption is quite common. They may not have the benefit of all the equipment and knowledge that we have here. I – and my father before me – have made a lifelong study of the disease,' he added, as if it explained everything.

Florrie stared at him and it all seemed to fall into place. The path he'd chosen – to devote his whole life to the medical profession and the study of tuberculosis, its causes, its treatment and cure – had all been for an altruistic purpose. He'd been prepared to sacrifice anything else that might have diverted him from that course.

Even love.

She'd seen the people to whom he brought hope and often a cure, and now she knew how that felt. Where others had failed, because of all his learning, his dedication and his knowledge he'd been able to tell her that her beloved Jacques did not have the frightful illness. For that, she could forgive him anything, and everything.

Now, it was she who took hold of his hands – those clever, devoted hands – and pressed them to her lips. 'Thank you,' she whispered again. 'And thank you for being so – forgiving. You could have turned us away.'

Ernst shook his head. 'I would never do that – whoever he had been.' He sighed. 'And I must ask your forgiveness too. I treated you badly. I don't blame you for – for taking revenge.'

'I shouldn't have done. I could have done you great harm, if the belief that you'd fathered my child had become common knowledge amongst the medical team out there. It – it didn't, did it?'

He was silent for a moment, glancing away in what seemed to be embarrassment. 'No.' His voice was hoarse. 'Oh, Florence, it is I who should be on my knees begging your forgiveness.'

'I don't understand.'

'After you left, Sister Blackstock spread the rumour

that your baby was that of a dead soldier. Without actually saying so, she squashed any idea that the child could be mine. And I – coward that I was,' his voice trembled with shame, 'did nothing to stop her.'

'Good,' Florrie said promptly, and Ernst stared at her until she explained. She squeezed his hands again and said softly, 'It's what I asked her to do.' Her mouth twitched with amusement as she remembered Rosemary's shocked face. 'I promised you I would say the child wasn't yours – and I did. All Sister Blackstock did,' she ended simply, 'was to repeat what I'd told her, just as I hoped and expected she would.'

'But your reputation?' This was something Ernst would never grasp.

Florrie laughed and shrugged. 'I never cared about my reputation. That's why—' She paused as realization came slowly. 'That's why I couldn't understand you.' She sighed. 'But now I do. You had – still have – a cause you believed in and I, of all people, should have understood.'

They sat a while longer together, remembering the passion and reliving the pain. But now there was mutual forgiveness and understanding. At last, Ernst broke the silence. 'I would like Jacques to stay another few weeks to build up his strength before,' he smiled, 'you have to take him back to face your English winter. But you will be home in time for Christmas with your family. And you will have so much to celebrate at the New Year.'

New Year, Florrie thought. Oh yes, this New Year there would indeed be cause for rejoicing.

'And now,' he added, 'will you let me take you tobogganing tomorrow night?'

'I – I'd love to. But why at night?'

'It's more – breathtaking – at night. You will see. And now I must go. Come tomorrow afternoon to see Jacques. Have dinner with me and then we will go tobogganing.'

As he took his leave at the front door, she asked, 'Have you told Jacques the good news?'

'Oh yes. I told him at once. He's a young man now and had a right to be told first. Goodnight, my dear.' He raised his hat and she watched him walk away into the darkness.

When Florrie arrived at the sanatorium the next afternoon, she couldn't hide her joy. She saw Jacques at the far end of the veranda, still sitting a little apart from the others. She rushed towards him and flung her arms around him, laughing and crying at the same time.

'Shh, Mother,' he said, trying to push her off, but he was grinning as he said it, like her, delirious with relief. 'It's not fair on the others.'

But Philip, sitting close by, asked, 'What's to do, lad?'

Florrie turned, her mouth already forming the words, but they remained unspoken. As her glance took in the line of sick patients, some of them so weak and ill she doubted they could ever really hope for a full recovery, she bit back the words.

'Well, I can see summat's up. Come on, lass, out wi' it.'

Softly, so that only he could hear, she said, 'He's all right. He's not got consumption. It – it was a misdiagnosis back home.'

Philip stared at her and then his face broke into a wide grin. He raised his voice, 'Hear that, folks?'

'Oh no,' Florrie began, but Philip was determined to spread the good news.

'The lad's all right. He's—' He hesitated a brief moment and then, with a huge wink at Florrie and Jacques, he added, 'He's cured.'

There was silence and then clapping and cheering broke out. The sound carried and some of the patients on their balconies leaned over and shouted down to know what all the noise was about.

Philip stood up, his blanket dropping to the floor unheeded. 'He's cured. He's going to be all right. He's going home.'

The cheering filled the air, carrying up and up from balcony to balcony, even, it seemed, echoing across the valley and into the mountains.

Philip turned and said quietly, 'See? It gives them hope. Forgive the little white lie, eh?'

Florrie nodded, a lump in her throat. 'Of course.'

As a junior nurse brought out the tray with their afternoon drink, Philip snatched up a glass. 'Here's a toast to you, lad, in milk! Good health and a long life!'

Later, when Ernst came to collect her from the veranda, he asked, 'What was all the noise about?'

'They were celebrating Jacques's – cure.'

'Cure? But—'

She held up her hand. 'It was Mr Henderson who – well, shall we say – rephrased it a little. We don't mind. It gave them all such hope and,' she added mischievously, 'did your reputation no harm at all.'

He had the grace to laugh a little sheepishly as he led her into the building. Although, as they passed Emmi

Bergamin, the sister raised her eyebrows, Ernst took Florrie's elbow and led her through the X-ray room and beyond it to a small room set out as a comfortable sitting room. Behind a curtain in one corner was a single bed.

'I often have to stay the night when we have a very sick patient. When the funicular no longer runs, it is a long way down the mountain after a hard day. Please, sit down. I will ring for some dinner to be served.'

They dined together in the little room and later they stepped out of the front door and walked towards where the toboggan run began. They sat on a sledge, Ernst in front and Florrie behind him, her arms around his waist, her body pressed close to his back. And then they were speeding down the deep, icy channel, emerging suddenly from beneath the trees. The sharp night air snatched her breath away as the sledge rocketed down the run. She gasped at the sight below them: a thousand twinkling lights from the windows of Davos, and then they were beneath the trees once more. She screamed once, though whether with terror or sheer joy, even Florrie herself didn't know.

Breathless, yet exhilarated, they slowed down and stopped. Ernst stood up and held out his hand to her.

'That was wonderful,' she said, slipping her arm through his as he escorted her back towards her lodgings.

They paused outside the front door of the pension and, in the shadows, Ernst took her face between his hands and kissed her gently on the mouth. 'This is goodbye, Florence. Jacques will be well enough to travel in a week or so.'

She knew she would not see Ernst again. Tenderly, she returned his kiss. 'Goodbye, Ernst.'

One last kiss and he turned away from her and was swallowed up in the darkness.

This time Florrie did not watch him go. Instead, she opened the door, stepped inside and closed it firmly behind her.

Fifty-Five

They were sitting once more on the train from Davos to Landquart, but how very different this journey felt to their arrival. The dark cloud that had hung over them both for several months was lifted. Jacques looked so much better. With all the food he'd eaten, he'd put on weight. His skin was healthy and his cough almost cured.

And best of all, he'd been cleared of the dreaded disease.

Florrie had sent a telegram to Candlethorpe Hall, and to Gervase and Isobel too, telling them all the good news.

Not TB. Coming home.

And she'd followed it up with a long letter to her grandmother. There was no need to hurry back – they'd still be home in time for Christmas, but first there was something she had to do.

'Jacques, are you feeling quite well?'

The boy grinned at her. What a miraculous change in him since he'd sat huddled in the corner of the compartment, feeling ill and frightened.

She'd so much to thank the Schatzalp sanatorium for – and Ernst Hartmann. And she was glad that, at last, they'd parted friends. She doubted she'd ever see him again. Strangely, the thought no longer troubled her.

She was finally over him. Her love for him had been

real once, but, unforgiving of his deceit, she'd exacted a revenge that had been unfair.

'I've never felt better, Mother,' Jacques was saying.

'Then there's something I'd like to do before we go back to England. If you're sure you feel up to it, I'd like us to make a little detour into Belgium.'

Jacques's eyes clouded. 'That's – that's where Uncle James was – was killed, wasn't it? D'you want to visit his grave? Is that it?'

Florrie nodded and touched his hand. 'We're going to Ypres.'

'That's where a lot of the fighting was. Is that where he was killed?'

'Yes, but – oh, Jacques, there are things I have to tell you. So much you don't know.'

'What – things?'

'Not here, Jacques. Not where we can be overheard.'

'But there's no one else in the compartment, Mother.'

'Please, Jacques, not now. We'll find a nice little hotel and then tonight, I – I promise I'll tell you everything.'

It was the second most difficult thing she'd ever had to do. The first had been to stand and see her brother shot for desertion. Haltingly, she began to explain. 'Jacques, you're probably going to be very angry with me for not having told you all this before, but there've been reasons. Good reasons. But I should have told you.' She took a deep breath. 'You know your grandfather is a hard man. For years he's ignored your presence in the house. It's really only because of your great-gran that we're both still there.'

'Because I'm illegitimate, you mean? I'd guessed that,

Mother. Or rather, some of the chaps at school taunted me about it. Calling me "the little bastard". Saying my sort shouldn't be allowed in a school like ours.' He smiled ruefully. 'Charlie was great. He always stood up for me. Told them my father had been killed in the war. He got into a fight about it once and got a bloody nose.'

Florrie gasped. 'I remember that. Isobel was beside herself because he stubbornly refused to say who he'd been fighting with and what it'd been about.'

'It was about me.'

'Well, Charlie was right about one thing. Your – your father was killed in the war. You see, your father was James.'

He stared at her horrified. 'Your – your *brother*?'

She nodded.

There was a look of utter disgust on his face and he shrank away from her. 'You mean, you mean – you and he . . .'

Florrie's mouth dropped open, her eyes widened and she flushed furiously. 'Oh no, no, Jacques. Not that. I'm not your mother – not your natural mother.' She ran her hand across her forehead. 'Oh dear, I am explaining this so badly. Listen, please just listen to me.'

She told him it all, just as she'd explained it to Emmi Bergamin, who, in turn, had told Ernst.

'Shot? For trying to get back to – to my mother? Didn't he tell them?'

Florrie lifted her shoulders helplessly. 'No – and he wouldn't let me. He didn't want to bring further trouble on Colette Musset. Her family had already disowned her. That was why he was trying to get to her. They were going to be married – your mother told me.'

'So – so how do I come to be with you?'

She was relieved to hear there was no anger in his tone, no blame; he just wanted to understand everything. When she'd finished he sat for a while, gazing out of the window, yet seeing none of the wonderful scenery. His young mind was trying to take in everything she'd said. Florrie, though she longed for him to say something – anything – made herself sit quietly.

'So, you could have left me. Put me in an orphanage. You didn't have to ruin your own reputation for me.'

'Yes, I did. There was no other way. If I'd taken you home – back to England and told everyone the truth, that you were James's son – then there's no knowing what my father would have done. He'd disowned James and had forbidden his name to be mentioned in the house. Though he was incredibly angry with me and didn't speak to me – or you – for years, at least he couldn't turn us out. Not while Grandmother is still alive, anyway.'

Jacques smiled at the thought of Augusta.

'I haven't always been the mother I should have been,' Florrie went on. 'The mother I vowed I would be.' She rarely shed tears, but they glimmered in her eyes now.

Jacques glanced at her and shrugged. 'Weren't you? You were away a lot, I suppose, but I always had Grannie and Great-Gran. When you came home it was such fun, because you spoilt me rotten.'

'Guilt,' Florrie said promptly, not sparing herself.

Jacques grinned impishly. Florrie's heart turned over. How good it was to see the mischief back in his face. Then he sobered. 'So, we're going to visit my father's grave?'

She nodded, her throat full of tears.

'And my mother's?'

'I – suppose we could try. We could go to the village near the farm. See if your grandfather or great-uncle is still there.'

Jacques shook his head. 'No. Let's not disturb them. The past must be painful enough for them. Maybe we could just take a look at the farm – where I was born – if it's still there.'

'Of course.'

They found the military cemetery near Poperinghe easily, but James's grave took them some time to locate.

'I should remember exactly where it is,' Florrie muttered, angry with herself. 'I shouldn't have forgotten. But it all looks so different now.'

Jacques said nothing, but squeezed her hand sympathetically. He couldn't begin to imagine what she must have gone through on that awful day.

'Here it is.'

A simple white marble cross marked the spot with James's name and rank, date of birth and date of death and a simple inscription, which read: *Not forgotten by those who loved him best*. They stood in front of it, their arms linked together.

'Who put that up?' Jacques asked.

'I arranged for it to be done through the solicitor in London who organized all the legalities over you.'

'It's – nice,' he said and sighed. 'How sad, though, to end like that.'

'Jacques, I've started a campaign to try to get a pardon for all those shot at dawn. But I'm not having much success yet. I think it's too soon. Attitudes haven't changed. But they will – in the future – I'm sure they will. But it may take years and years.' She bit her lip, hesitating. It was a huge burden to place on a young boy's shoulders.

Slowly he turned to face her. 'Of course I will.'

She stared at him. 'What?'

'Carry on the fight. That's what you were going to ask me, wasn't it?'

She laughed. 'Yes, yes – it was. It *is*.'

Jacques looked back at his father's headstone, reached out and traced his fingertip over the name. ''Bye for now, Dad. We'll come again. Some day, we'll come again.'

As they walked away he said, 'There's just one thing, Mother. You do realize you've set yourself a bit of a job now, don't you?'

She pulled a face. 'It's not going to be easy. There'll be a lot of opposition to it at first.'

'Oh, I don't mean that.'

'So, what *do* you mean?'

'I want to know everything about my father. Every little detail you can remember. I may never get to know much about my mother, so you're just going to have to make up for it.'

Florrie laughed. 'It'll be a pleasure. You don't know how I've longed to talk about him all these years and never been able to, for fear of either angering my father or upsetting my mother and grandmother. But now,' she hugged his arm to her side, 'I've a good excuse.'

The farm was still derelict and more dilapidated than Florrie remembered it. The yard was overgrown with weeds, the house crumbling. The barn had all but fallen down completely.

'The farmland round it looks used. Look, there are cattle and sheep grazing. It's just the house and buildings that are deserted.'

'Maybe someone else bought the land, but didn't want the house.'

'Are you sure you don't want us to try to find the Mussets?'

'Quite sure,' Jacques said firmly. 'Let's leave them in peace.'

Fifty-Six

Florrie and Jacques arrived home the day before Christmas Eve to a rapturous welcome. Clara wept on Florrie's shoulder and then clasped an embarrassed Jacques to her. Augusta beamed from ear to ear, and even Edgar patted the boy on the back and submitted to Florrie's kiss. He looked down into her upturned face and nodded. Then he cleared his throat. 'Er, welcome home, my dear. Both of you.'

It was all Florrie needed to hear.

They were swept at once into Augusta's Christmas preparations. 'Did you have a chance to do any shopping?'

Florrie nodded. 'We stopped overnight in London and went shopping this morning.' She laughed and glanced at the boy. 'Jacques hated it.'

He grinned and shrugged his shoulders. 'It was just so crowded. We couldn't move. It – it was just – so different to – to—'

Augusta linked her arm with his. 'Now, now, you must try to forget all about that. We're all so thankful that you haven't got that terrible disease. But if you hadn't gone,' she added with asperity, for she knew they were all thinking, deep down, that perhaps the trip had been a complete waste of time and money, 'you'd only have got steadily worse in our unpredictable weather. As it is, the wonderful Swiss air has quite

477

cured you and you're well and strong. And spring is just around the corner. Now, come along.' She gave him a gentle push. 'Upstairs you go and change and then, after dinner, I need your help with the tree. We waited until you were home.'

For the first time Florrie noticed the huge tree standing in its traditional space at the side of the staircase. It was so tall that it almost reached to the landing above. But it still awaited its decorations.

She smiled. Now she knew they were really home.

'Grandmother?'

For the first time Florrie could ever remember, she felt nervous and unsure when seeking out her grandmother. But it had to be done. She'd promised herself. She'd promised Jacques. And she had to do it now, before New Year's Eve. Christmas was over, celebrated with just the family and with quiet thankfulness for Jacques's return to health. But Florrie could no longer avoid telling them the truth.

Augusta was sitting up in bed with her breakfast tray. It was the only concession she made to her eighty-eight years – breakfast in bed each morning. In every other way she was still remarkably sprightly. She raised her eyebrows in surprise as Florrie hovered uncertainly in the doorway. 'Come in, dear.' She held out her hand.

Closing the door quietly, Florrie moved across the room and sat down beside the bed. Her fingers twisted nervously.

Augusta was smiling gently. 'You've something to tell me?'

Florrie swallowed and nodded. But still, she couldn't speak.

'About – Jacques?'

Again, she nodded, running her tongue nervously round her lips. 'I haven't been entirely honest with you.'

Augusta's old eyes twinkled with merriment. She'd intended to tease Florrie, watch her drag out the halting explanation, but suddenly she took pity on her granddaughter. She leaned forward and touched her hand. 'I know,' she said, 'that Jacques is not your son. He's – James's, isn't he?'

Florrie's eyes widened. 'You knew?'

'Oh yes,' Augusta said softly. 'I suspected as much from the first moment. But then, when he got a little older and you started gadding off to London – leaving him for weeks on end – then I was certain.'

Florrie felt herself redden as Augusta regarded her severely. 'You've been a loving, devoted *aunt*, I'll not deny. But you haven't really acted like a *mother*.' Her old eyes were suddenly sad. 'I expect you felt you had to deceive us because of your father. But you could have told me, Florrie dear. Really you could.'

'I'm sorry, Gran,' she said huskily, clutching at the wrinkled hand. 'I – didn't want to put you in an awkward position by involving you in the – in the lie.'

'As far as I know, my dear, you've never actually lied. You've never called him your son, have you? You've just said he's Edgar's grandson and my great-grandson – which he is. You've told the truth, but not the whole truth.'

They were silent a moment before Augusta asked gently, 'Does Jacques know?'

'Yes, we – we took a detour on our way home and went to – to Ypres. We saw James's grave and I told him everything.'

Augusta nodded, satisfied. Again, a pause before she said softly, 'And now you have to tell your father?'

Florrie swallowed. 'Yes,' she said hoarsely.

'Want me to come with you?'

Florrie shook her head. 'No, Gran. This is something I have to do myself.'

If she had been nervous facing her grandmother, she was terrified as she knocked on the door of her father's study.

Hearing his gruff 'Come in', she opened the door, stepped inside and closed it behind her, leaning against it for a moment to steel her nerve.

He eyed her over the top of his spectacles as she approached his desk.

'Father, I need to talk to you. May I sit down?'

Wordlessly, he indicated a leather chair at the side of his desk and leaned back, waiting for her to begin.

'I want to tell you about – about Jacques.'

'I thought you said he's well now? That it was a mis-diagnosis?'

'Yes – yes it was. He's fine and actually looking forward to going back to school in January.' She hesitated.

'Go on,' Edgar said, but his tone was not encouraging.

'I – haven't been entirely truthful about – about Jacques.'

Edgar's perpetual frown deepened.

'He – he is your grandson and he is half-French, but – but I'm not his mother. Not his natural mother. Jacques is – is James's son.'

Edgar stiffened and stared at her. At last, almost against his will, he muttered, 'Explain yourself.'

So she did. She began by telling him all about James and his arrest and the unfair charge brought against him. The farcical court martial and how Gervase had tried in vain to save James's life. She spared him nothing now, telling him – in every heartbreaking detail – of the last night she'd spent with her brother, of his execution and unceremonious burial. And then she told him about how she'd found Colette, the birth of the baby boy, the girl's death and how she had tracked down the child's French grandfather, who'd turned them away.

'I got them to sign a paper and when I got back home I had a solicitor in London arrange everything legally. I am Jacques's aunt, his legal guardian but – I'm not his mother.'

Edgar was silent for a long time and Florrie couldn't read his expression. It was stern – angry almost – but then it always was.

'I'm sorry I deceived you, Father, but I thought that if I told you he was James's son, you – you wouldn't have let him stay.'

Edgar allowed himself a wry smile. 'You're right. I wouldn't.' He paused, whilst Florrie's heart plummeted, but then he added slowly, 'Not then.'

There was another long silence. Florrie said nothing, biting her lip to stop herself pleading with him. It wouldn't do any good. Even Augusta would not be able to sway him if . . .

He looked up, regarding her steadily. 'I'm glad you've told me, Florence, even though it's sixteen years late. But—' He paused, glanced away and fiddled with a pen lying on his desk. 'I can – understand,' the word, not one that Edgar Maltby used very often, came haltingly, 'why you didn't tell me at first.'

'So, may we stay?'

Slowly, he nodded. 'Yes.'

He gave no explanation, made no comment about having become fond of the boy. That would have been totally out of character and Florrie didn't expect it. But the fact that he hadn't lost his temper and thrown them out onto the street told her all she needed to know.

She rose, went to stand beside his chair and bent to kiss his cheek. 'Thank you, Father.' Then she hurried from the room without looking back at him.

If she had, she'd have seen him staring after her, a pensive expression in his eyes. And she'd have been shocked if she'd heard the softly spoken words to the empty room.

'I must see my solicitor. Change my will. It seems, after all, I have an heir from the male line. Someone who truly bears the name of Maltby.'

The illegitimate bit, Edgar decided, he would ignore.

'Of course, we should be at Bixley for New Year, but under the circumstances, we're having it here,' Augusta told them. 'We've such a lot to celebrate.'

'I can't wait,' Florrie murmured and meant it, for this year her answer to Gervase's question would be different. She hugged the secret to herself, revelling in the anticipated pleasure it would bring everyone. Even poor Iso, who'd had so much tragedy to bear, would be delighted. They'd always felt like sisters and now they really would be. Well, the next best thing: sisters-in-law.

Gervase, Isobel and Charlie arrived in Gervase's

latest motor car, coming to a shuddering halt outside the front door. Florrie ran out, her arms open wide. 'My dears, how wonderful to see you – and looking so well.' She kissed them all and ushered them inside, chattering nervously. But neither Isobel nor Gervase seemed to notice; they took her gaiety for the heady relief that Jacques did not, after all, have tuberculosis.

Isobel linked her arm through Florrie's. 'My dear, we're all so glad to hear the wonderful news. I've written to Lady Lee and she sends you both her love.'

'How kind of her,' Florrie said. 'Now, come along in. Grandmother is holding court in the drawing room.'

'And your mother?' Gervase enquired gently.

'Much better,' Florrie said. 'She was so busy organizing meals and such when we were nursing Jacques here. It gave her something to focus on other than herself. And Gran says she's been all right whilst we've been away. Worried, of course, but she didn't take to her bed.'

Gervase touched her arm. 'I'm glad.'

There was an extra merriment to the evening and it was not only amongst the two families. Word of Jacques's return to health had spread amongst the estate workers and, taking it for granted that he was Edgar Maltby's heir who'd one day be their young master, they rejoiced.

'Illegitimate he might be,' they whispered, 'but there's no one else, now is there?'

Whilst refreshments for the household staff and estate workers were in the barn, the family dined together and then gathered in the hall. As the grandfather clock struck midnight, they raised their glasses. And this year the toast of 'Good health' had an extra meaning. They trooped back into the drawing room to watch the customary fireworks in the field beyond the lawn from the long windows, for the night was cold, a biting east wind whipping in from the sea.

Florrie stood beside Gervase, glancing up at him every now and then. Excitement churned in her stomach. She could hardly wait until he drew her aside, took her hands in his, looked into her bright eyes and posed the question that he always asked on New Year's Eve.

With a jolt, she realized that the moment had passed. Already it was the 1st January 1933 and he hadn't asked her. He'd never left it so late before. He'd always made sure that he proposed before midnight, just in case she said yes and the toast could be 'the happy couple'.

But this year – of all years – he hadn't asked her!

They were preparing to go. Isobel had called for her wrap. Gervase slipped his arms into the warm coat Bowler held ready for him, then pulled on his driving gloves, wrapped the long scarf around his neck and perched his cap on his head. And still he said nothing.

'Gervase?' Florrie put her hand on his arm. She looked up at him, her eyes wide and questioning. 'Haven't you – forgotten something?' she whispered.

He smiled down at her, his eyes twinkling. He glanced at his hands. 'Gloves?' He clapped his hand to his head. 'Cap? Coat? Scarf? No, all in place. I don't think so, my dear.'

'You know very well what I mean,' she snapped, her agitation, held in check all evening, now bubbling up. She pulled him to the side of the hall, away from the others bidding each other 'Goodnight' and 'Happy New Year'. 'Do you really mean to tell me that this year, of all years, you're not going to ask me?'

He began to laugh. 'My darling girl, every year for twenty years – well, apart from a couple of years I missed during the war – I've asked you to marry me, and every year it's been the same answer. Now why—?' Suddenly, he stopped and looked down at her, his laughter subsiding as he realized what she'd just said. Softly, he asked, 'What – what d'you mean by "this year of all years"?'

She put her head on one side and the delighted chuckle began deep inside her and gurgled up, until she was clutching at him to stop herself collapsing with laughter. 'Because,' she spluttered, 'because this year it was going to be different.' She wiped away the tears of laughter at the astounded look on his face. Aware now that the sound of her mirth had caught the attention of the rest, she took his hand in hers and dropped to one knee.

'Gervase Richards, will you marry me?' Her voice echoed round the vast hall, surprising and delighting them all. They were all holding their breath. She could feel it.

But there was no joy in Gervase's face. His eyes clouded and his mouth tightened. 'Don't tease me, Florrie,' he said softly, so that no one but her could hear him. 'Not about that.'

She rose and stepped close to him, her gaze holding his. 'I'm not teasing you. I mean it.' She laughed nervously, suddenly unsure. 'The very year I mean to say "yes", you don't ask me. So – I'm asking you.'

'But – but why? Why – now?'

Dimly, she heard Augusta say, 'I think we'd all better

go back into the drawing room for a little while. Come along, my dears. Let's leave them to sort it out. Bowler, bring some cocoa will you? We could be some time.'

There was a murmuring, a door closed and they were alone.

'What's changed, Florrie?' he persisted. Now there was no one else to overhear them, he added, 'Was it – was it when you went abroad? Did – did you see Jacques's father?'

Tears started in her eyes and she shook her head. Huskily, she said, 'No – no, I'll never see Jacques's father again. He – he is dead, Gervase. Like I told you, but – but there are other things—'

Now he drew her to him and kissed her gently, silencing her mouth. 'Nothing matters now – if you really mean it. Do you, Florrie? Will you *really* marry me?'

She looked up into his dear, kind face and wondered why on earth it had taken her so long to realize that she loved him. Loved him wholeheartedly in every way there was.

'Yes,' she whispered. 'But first, there's something I must tell you . . .'

She was not afraid, for she knew that even when she explained everything – even about Ernst – Gervase would still love her as he always had.

ACKNOWLEDGEMENTS

I met the author and poet, Gervase Phinn, at a Hull and East Yorkshire Literary Luncheon. Seated at the same table, we chatted about what we were working on. He suggested I should call this book *Lust in the Trenches*! Now, that doesn't quite fit my profile as an author of regional sagas, but I promised I would call one of the characters after him. So his name is the inspiration for Gervase Richards in this novel. Gervase Phinn is, of course, the author of wonderful books, including *The Other Side of the Dale*, *Over Hill and Dale*, *The Heart of the Dales*, and others, based on his work as a teacher and school inspector in Yorkshire. He is also a fantastic speaker. If you ever get a chance to go to one of his events, you will ache with laughter and be quite unable to resist buying his latest book – signed, of course!

Readers often ask me where I find the inspiration for my stories and if I'm ever 'off duty'. The answer is 'Anywhere and everywhere' and, no, I'm never off duty. In 2004 I went abroad for the first time to Davos in Switzerland. Finding that it was once a centre for the treatment of tuberculosis, I made a beeline for the local library, where there were bound copies of old local newspapers in German, French and English! I took notes and, as the idea for a novel grew, I returned to Davos in 2007 to do more research. That year I visited the magnificent Schatzalp Hotel, which was once a sanatorium. Joining a conducted tour round the luxurious building, I learned that much has remained the same as when it was built in 1900. I am very grateful to the Schatzalp for allowing me to use the name. The characters and story are, of course, entirely fictitious.

My grateful thanks to Timothy Nelson and Liselotte Dürr of the Dokumentationsbibliothek Davos for their help, advice and information.

A great many sources have been used for research, most notably: *The Suffragette Movement* by E. Sylvia Pankhurst (Longman, Green, 1932), *A V.A.D. in France* by Olive Dent (Grant Richards, 1917), *The Roses of No Man's Land* by Lyn Macdonald (Penguin Books, 1993), *Shot at Dawn* by Julian Putkowski and Julian Sykes (Leo Cooper, 1998), *The Great War Magazine*, which has been published bi-monthly by Great Northern Publishing, Scarborough, since 2001, and *The Magic Mountain* by Thomas Mann, Everyman Edition (Alfred A. Knopf, 2005).

Special thanks to my great-niece, Nicola Hill, for translating passages from *Davos – Profil eines Phänomens* – Ernst Halter (HG.) (Offizin, 1994) and to my brother, David Dickinson, who not only read the draft typescript but also helped enormously with my research in Switzerland.

Last, but never least, my love and thanks to my family and friends who read and comment on the typescript, to my agent, Darley Anderson, and his wonderful 'angels' and to Imogen Taylor, Trisha Jackson and Liz Cowen and everyone at Macmillan.

extracts reading groups
competitions books new
books discounts extracts extracts
competitions events
books new
extracts discounts
events books reading groups
new extracts
new titles reading groups
interviews
reading groups events extracts extracts
books discounts events books
new books events interviews
events new events
discounts extracts discounts new books
www.panmacmillan.com
extracts events reading groups
competitions books extracts new books